MW00991021

NORTH

SCALE

ONE DAY'S
JOURNEY

RASHINASTI
FOREST

Avie Lake

Avie

PALAMORE
FOREST

To
Xanaga-
Mor and
Marglamesh

Lord
Mazzul's
Keep

Maylan

Abengroth River

Torvin

Rorenth

ASKYINOTH

Keratost

Lake Keratost

MOUNTAINS

Map by
DARLENE
2016

The
First Fable

"THIEF!"

KRBourgoine

The
First Fable

K.R. Bourgoine

Map by Darlene.

Cover illustration by Jian Guo.

All other interior illustrations by K. R. Bourgoine.

ISBN: 1540724573
ISBN-13: 9781540724571

10 9 8 7 6 5 2 3 2 1

For Lucien and Julien

PRELUDE

V ictory was near. Orgog, the Troll King of Marglamesh, lumbered angrily through the rough limestone passageways deep beneath his mountainous castle. He forced his bulk through a crumbling archway and turned impatiently down another dank, winding corridor. The passages were so small that some of the large, bony spikes protruding from his spine grated against the low stone ceiling; nonetheless he marched on, ignoring the smell of must and mold in the air.

Although he was nearly thirteen feet tall, Orgog's massive build seemed too wide for his height. His head and shoulders naturally craned forward, as if the weight of his reptilian head was too much for his neck to bear. His sickly green skin was covered with innumerable grotesque lumps. His eyes, squinting in the darkness of the deep tunnels, were a startling icy blue—like those of no other troll.

He seethed as he strode along the dim corridor. He hadn't been king for long, but up until now the war had gone perfectly. He had already pushed beyond his borders and expanded back into Xanga-Mor, taking back custody of the land the humans had claimed from the trolls in their last war. For some of his advisors, that triumph was enough, but with all Orgog had achieved, he still wanted more. Much more.

He wanted the humans' homeland. Nothing would please him more than to move beyond Xanga-Mor and into Elronia, to trample it underfoot and claim all three kingdoms as his own. With three kingdoms he would no longer answer to "king," but to a much more glorious and deserving title. *Emperor.* Nothing sounded more pleasing to the Ruler of Trolls.

Orgog planned to carry the war deep into human lands and then end it with such force that there would be no chance for retaliation. This was the war that would finally end the conflict between the two realms.

He mused his plan again. It was simple. He would simply subjugate every human in Elronia, and, failing that, eradicate the abysmal race.

He strode on, continuing to chafe at the narrowness of the passages. How had the old kings stood for this? He made a note to have some prisoners expand the corridors to a more suitable height and breadth. *Not all trolls were spawned small,* he thought in frustration.

With the new title of Emperor, there would obviously come deeper vaults of gold.

"For gold and glory," he chanted the ancient troll dogma. *"For gold and glory."*

Those four short words epitomized Orgog's philosophy of life. Every decision he had ever made had been based upon them.

There will be much of both, he reflected. When the final battle against Elronia came, he would ride out himself and slay their weak king with his own hand, crushing his delicate golden crown underfoot before adding it to his hoard.

Ducking through another archway, he envisioned putting a new mint immediately to work in the conquered land, replacing the human king's likeness with his own on every coin, so all would know who their new master was. The first golden coins from the mint would be struck from the remains of the human king's bent and trampled crown.

This pleasing daydream faded as he remembered an unpleasant reality. Even though he had enjoyed great success so far in his campaign, there was now a chance that the tide of the war might turn against him. Somehow the humans had gained an inexcusable wartime advantage—an advantage that could potentially cost Orgog everything he had earned. As he thought about it rage rose and churned inside him like a hungry beast.

Tonight's news had better be good, he thought, *or this man will suffer for summoning me.* He hadn't killed the last two kings for nothing. He also hadn't become king to waste away upon a soft throne or to lose his lands—or spend his time squeezing through these damned cramped corridors.

He pressed on, eventually reaching a gloomy but cavernous chamber that had been hewn from the damp earth in some long forgotten age. To his relief, it was large enough for him to stand in his full, intimidating height. As he entered, he heard a crisp voice speak from across the chamber.

"I offer greetings to the lord of the land." The speaker was shrouded in the shadows. Although King Orgog could barely make out the shape in the dimness, he could see it had a hand resting on the pommel of its sword.

"Why have you called upon me, wretch? I have no patience for traitors today," growled Orgog.

The shadow seemed undeterred by the insult. "I have come to tell you that soon I will have recovered your war plans from Elronia. It's just a matter of time."

The king showed no outward pleasure at this grand news. He knew it was a tactical mistake to celebrate success before success was actually accomplished. Instead, with great quick strides he crossed the chamber, his spiked tail lashing behind him.

He closed the distance so fast that the smaller figure was taken by surprise. Towering over the creature, he reached down, seized its neck and lifted it off the ground. Tiny in his hands, the creature squirmed and coughed, clutching at the Troll King's thick, scaly wrists. Orgog slammed it against the uneven wall with jarring force, causing a stale cloud of dust and dirt to fly from the rocky surface.

"Do so, and I will dig deep into my coffers to reward you," the king grated through his pointed yellow teeth.

"That's all I need to know," the messenger managed to cough. "Consider the blow struck."

The Troll King leaned close, his rank breath enveloping his captive. "If you fail me, I shall wipe you and all who share your name from this world. I will see that you are all cast into Narekisis, and it will be as if you and your line had never been." He leaned closer still. "The only hope the humans have, the only way of stopping me, lies in those bewitched plans."

His grip on the creature's neck tightened in frustration, his wrist shaking with the urge to do violence to the whelp. "Their importance to me is incalculable. Their magic tells the humans my every move! Get them back for me!"

With those words the king released his hostage, who dropped back to the floor. Instantly the shadowy creature withdrew into the darkness and disappeared from sight.

Orgog retraced his steps to the upper recesses of Castle Darkmoor, a fortress carved from an enormous floating mountain. As he went he mulled over the prospect of regaining his lost battle plans. Once the plans were back in his possession, the Kingdom of Men would no longer be able to foresee the movement of his troops, and the advantage would undoubtedly return to the Troll Kingdom's far superior warriors. The Marglamesh forces would be able to march upon Elronia with such brutal strength that the only possible outcome would be total victory.

Against his morose nature, the mighty war king allowed himself a brief smile as one thought filled his savage mind.

The humans of Elronia will fall.

CHAPTER 1

Kneeling in the garden, Macal Teel stabbed the earth again with his rusty spade. His scrawny arms ached as he wrested another stubborn weed from the dry dirt and tossed it into the battered basket beside him. He had spent most of the day out here under the warm summer sun.

The boy finally stood and stretched his aching back, and kicked the loose soil from his worn sandals. He was twelve, but his thin frame was smaller than other boys his age. Earth stained his worn tunic and breeches from many long days in this field. His shaggy brown hair curled slightly at the ends, and his bright green eyes held a look impressively thoughtful for a boy so young.

Macal looked around his uncle's little farm, set serenely into the surrounding hilly landscape. To the far North, just beyond the lush meadows and green pastures he could see the edge of the great woods of Rotelen. A part of him wanted to drop the dull spade in the basket and forget about the farm work for a while—to run off into the woods and play, or go for a swim down by Minstrel's Stream. But he had already snuck off once today, to have lunch under the shade of the large, full maples that grew on the hill to the west.

Looking back at the rundown stone cottage, the boy let out a defeated sigh. There was still so much left to do today. Macal helped his uncle as much as he could with farm chores. Uncle Melkes was the only family he had really ever lived with; his mother had died when he was born and his father was a soldier, away, as always, at war. He would have felt guilty leaving all the work to his uncle alone.

There were no schools in Hormul, so Macal had never learned to read or write; everything he knew he had learned from his uncle—or his father, on those rare occasions when he was around. They had taught him how to

4

farm, how to plow and till the soil, when to harvest the different crops, how to care for the animals, fix fences and mend the leaking thatch roof. He knew how to cut down trees and cook meager meals, where to take the pigs to eat in the Rotelen Woods to fatten them up, how to thresh the corn from the stalks; everything he needed to know to run the farm someday, when it was his.

Macal liked the idea of one day owning the farm. It had been his home all his life and he hoped it would remain so all his days. He liked it here. He liked Hormul. It was small and quaint. What he liked most about it was that not much happened here, which he thought was perfect.

There were days when he could think of nothing better than lying in one of the high fields of tall grass and thistle, watching the billowing clouds float by while butterflies danced on the soft wind and the smell of sweet alyssum, marigolds, and poppies gently tickled his nose. He liked to lie and enjoy the quiet afternoon sun as the flowers swayed gently around him. Later in the day he would walk among the gloomy willows, under the aching oak trees, and spend hours down at the river's edge fishing or just watching the frogs jump among the lily pads.

Although it was sometimes lonely, he considered those days to be his happiest and he looked forward to a lifetime of them.

"Macal!" A gentle voice called his name as he was about to start on another row of weeds that were doing their best to crowd out the leafy rhubarb, just as they had the beets, yellow squash, and chard. He looked up and saw his uncle leaning on the garden fence, watching him.

His uncle was thin, bent, and aged. He was starting to lose his graying hair, but his beard and mustache remained thick and neatly groomed, a habit he retained from his time in the King's Army many years ago. His blue eyes were the kindest and most caring Macal had ever seen, with heavy ridges of sagging skin under them and high brows arching above.

"You almost done out there?" asked his uncle.

"Soon. I hope," the boy replied in his usual meek tone. "I just have three more rows to do."

Uncle Melkes rested one of his booted feet on the lowest rail of the wooden fence. "Well, it looks to me like you've done enough for today. How about we go down to the Waywitch for a few rounds of Devils and Kings? What do you think about that?"

A rare smile brightened Macal's face faster than a dragon could sack a village. It was only a small smile, but Uncle Melkes couldn't suppress one of his own. He had learned not to expect much more from the forlorn boy. Macal was a lonely child; he had no brothers or sisters, nor did he seem to have any friends. So, whenever he had the chance, Uncle Melkes tried to do what he could to cheer the boy up. Tonight he was going to do that by taking him into the village.

"I'll take that as a yes. Come on, then. Put away the tools and clean yourself up a bit; you look worse than a goblin coming out of a coal mine. Then we'll head down to town. I think Doshemel will be with us tonight."

With haste Macal collected the basket, rusty hoe, bent spade, and other tools to return them to the barn not far from the cottage. "I just have to feed Germ before we go."

Germ was the mule they used to pull their small cart of produce from town to town. Uncle Melkes had used him for an errand earlier today, and Macal guessed the animal was hungry and waiting for something to eat.

Uncle Melkes had acquired Germ free because the poor beast was frequently sick and his previous owner didn't want to be burdened with taking care of him anymore. Uncle Melkes couldn't let the mule be put down merely because he was sickly, so he had offered to take him off the other farmer's hands. To Uncle Melkes, this wasn't a burden, it was just the right thing to do.

After he brought the mule home Uncle Melkes had asked Macal to name him, and without much thought he had decided the name Germ fit perfectly. Since the day Germ came home to them, regardless of how ill the creature became, or how often, Macal cared for him without complaint.

As he headed toward the barn, encumbered by his awkward burden of tools, Macal found himself filled with excitement. He was happy to stop working for the day and elated to get off the farm for a while. It wasn't often that Uncle Melkes let him stay up after sundown. The constant list of necessary chores—tending the animals, tilling the soil, or delivering the taxes to Lord Antis—kept Macal busy. But every now and then, Uncle Melkes would, to his delight, take him down to the Waywitch Tavern for the evening.

The boy had deduced that these rare times only came when Uncle Melkes had done a good day's trade from his produce cart.

Macal loved watching the games of Devils and Kings. It was a card and dice gambling game of great renown; no game was more popular in all the lands of Aerinth. He knew his uncle was lucky at cards, so there was a good chance that by playing Devils and Kings, Uncle Melkes would head home with more coins than he had brought.

Just as Macal was putting away the last of the tools, through the open barn door he noticed a mounted soldier riding up the hill from town. The rider rode on a tired looking black mare. Over his worn suit of chain mail he wore a red tabard with a gold border displaying a black dragon's head: the crest of their kingdom, Elronia.

One gauntleted hand held the reins of the weary steed, the other a long lance bearing a standard with an amber dragon on it. Macal immediately recognized the symbol of the Amber Dragoons. It was his father's company!

The rider galloped up to his uncle near the fence, and came to an abrupt halt, his horse's iron-shod hooves kicking up a billow of dust.

Anxiety flooded Macal.

What did the man want with my uncle? Macal wondered. *Has something happened to my father?* He couldn't imagine any other reason for the rider's presence. Not many soldiers passed this way, especially heading away from the war front of the troll lands to the west. Macal dropped the remaining tools with a clatter and ran toward the two men.

"Yes, that's right," the soldier was saying as Macal ran up to them. "The Amber Dragoons are returning tonight. General Gazel Akelris has ordered a few weeks' leave on our way through this region before we continue the campaign as the pinnacle force along the trolls' borders."

The soldier looked sturdy even though his frame was thin. He had sharp features and sunken dark eyes that contrasted with his fair hair.

"*What?*" Macal burst out in excited disbelief. His eyes went wide with joy as worry fled. He could barely contain himself. He lived for the moments when his father returned.

"The Amber Dragoons are coming home? My father's coming home? Are you *sure?*" he asked, almost afraid to trust the news.

"I'm quite sure, boy," the standard-bearer replied brusquely. "If I am here, you can be sure the rest of us are not far behind. If your father's one of us, you shall be feasting with him tonight."

"Well, Corporal, we thank you for the good news," said Uncle Melkes. His years of military service were far in the past, but they had equipped him to recognize the soldier's rank.

"It's my pleasure. Now I must be off if I'm to inform Bronel of the company's return by nightfall." With that, the Corporal kicked his horse into motion, enveloping them in dust as he rode east toward the next village. "May the Crown stay strong!" he called back over his shoulder.

"May the Crown stay strong," Uncle Melkes echoed absently as he turned to look back at the thunderstruck Macal. He could see the boy's thoughts were racing.

How long had it been since he had last seen his father? thought Macal. *A year and a half, maybe even longer.* He couldn't believe it. He didn't think he could put into words how much he missed his father. How much he wanted just a few hours, even a few minutes with him, just to tell him everything he had done, how much he missed him, and how much he loved him.

It didn't seem real. For so many months, it had seemed that this would never happen. Yet tonight, finally, *his father was coming home!*

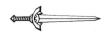

"We have to hurry!" urged Macal impatiently as he walked with his uncle down the gentle, tree-lined hill toward town. "Come on!"

"Don't worry. I'm sure we'll be there long before your father arrives." Uncle Melkes' response was as calm as his customary ambling gait. Behind them the setting sun filled the sky with a wondrous display of warm oranges and yellows.

"I know, but I want to wait in the plaza for the Dragoons to arrive."

"You will likely have plenty of time to wait. If the standard bearer only just passed through, they probably won't arrive until well after nightfall. Remember that most of the other soldiers have to walk. I'm pretty sure you'll even have time to come into the Waywitch for a bit and watch me play."

Macal looked up with a twinge of annoyance. He had always thought his uncle was the most patient person he had ever met; now he was sure. Uncle Melkes exhibited barely a hint of excitement at the prospect of his brother-in-law's return, but Macal knew the truth of it. He knew his uncle felt exactly like he did, but was holding it in.

"I know what you are thinking," said his uncle casually, without looking at him, as they followed a gradual twist in the well-worn road at the base of the hill.

Macal peered at his uncle trying to see what he was getting at, but Uncle Melkes' face was as passive as a dove. Looking away again, the boy missed the humorous little smirk growing at the corner of his uncle's mouth.

After a pause Macal asked, "What do you mean?"

"You were wondering why I'm not bursting at the seams with anticipation like you. You were wondering how I can remain so calm and contain myself when we have been blessed with such fair news. Am I right?"

"Um, yeah," Macal said slowly. *How did his uncle always know what he was thinking?*

"You don't have to be shy. It's a good and fair question, and you should never be shy about wanting to understand something. The more you learn, the more you can understand. Anyway, did I ever tell you the story of Greykus and the White Horse?" asked his uncle as they continued down the road. Small quaint stone cottages with fenced gardens and livestock were starting to become more frequent, set closer together, as they neared the town center.

Macal shook his head. He was used to his uncle telling stories all the time, but he had not heard this one.

Uncle Melkes maintained his slow and steady stride. "No? Good, then I'll tell you now. How about that?"

Macal had long ago decided that storytelling was his uncle's defining trait. Whether Macal had fallen and scraped his knee, caught a rabbit jumping through the hawthorn, or won a game of Devils and Kings, his uncle always had a story to tell him. Afterwards, and usually to Macal's disappointment, the story had a *meaning*. At the end of the telling, his uncle would look expectantly at his nephew to see if he had understood.

Macal had to admit that usually he didn't understand. Full of dragons and gods and sometimes even goblins and princesses, the stories enraptured him. He became too distracted by the characters and their terrifying, heroic adventures to seek for meaning. With his endless patience, Uncle Melkes never seemed to mind. Macal's enjoyment alone was meaning enough—*At least for now,* as his uncle always said.

"You see, once long ago in the Age of Fallen Legends," began Uncle Melkes, "there was a great and valiant knight named Greykus. He was a vassal of the King of Brinizarn, a great wooded kingdom on the Eastern shores. For a steed, Greykus the knight had a beautiful white horse. Some say it was the most elegant creature in the entire kingdom. It had been a gift from the King and Queen themselves for his service in saving their lives from marauders from Saramel, a land of savage ogres.

"Greykus was the noblest of knights and a man of great valor, but nearly a year had passed since he had saved the royal family from gruesome slaughter, and he had not yet found a new quest on which to embark. He was a knight of the kingdom, a man of adventure, a man who needed danger to feel alive—"

"He is more than welcome to my share of danger," Macal interrupted. "I never want any of that. Staying here in Hormul is fine by me."

"And I am sure he would take your generous offer if he could," replied his uncle with a fond look, as they stepped to the side of the road to avoid two trotting horses pulling a large squeaky wagon. "But as I was saying, he was a hero. He needed to be out in the world, doing all the stuff heroes of legend do. Sitting around the castle for almost a year was nearly unbearable for him."

"So what did he do?"

"What do you think he did?"

"I don't know. Left the castle to chase a dragon who had stolen a princess of another realm?" Macal offered hopefully.

"Well, close. He did leave the castle. But first he paid a visit to one of the realm's Great Seers of Eight Limbs. He begged to learn what his next quest was, and to his surprise and joy the Great Seer told him simply to wait for the following dawn. As the sun rose over the world, the gods would speak to him and reveal the nature of his next quest."

Macal's curiosity was too much for him. "What was it?"

"I'm trying to tell you, but you can't have the end of the story without the beginning and middle, correct? As I was saying, the knight Greykus was so elated by the prospect of a new quest, a new sense of purpose, that he couldn't restrain himself. He needed to know what the quest was as soon as he could. He didn't want to wait until the following morning, even if it was only a day away.

"He had an idea. If he rode toward the horizon he would see the dawn sooner than if he waited in the castle for it to come. He rushed to the royal stables, mounted his wondrous horse, and rode east as fast as he could.

"All day and through the dark night, he rode far and fast across rough terrain to meet the approaching dawn. Exhausted as he was, he pushed on and never once stopped to rest. He desperately needed to know the nature of his new quest. But as night waned, his splendid white horse began to slow and then to falter. Eventually it stopped of its own accord and fell to its knees, its skin slick and its chest heaving.

"Then slowly before Greykus's eyes, his beautiful horse died. The strain of the grueling journey without rest or water had been too much even for such a fine creature.

"The knight stood brooding, knowing he had caused the death of the most beautiful horse Brinizarn had ever seen.

"Filled with guilt and despair, Greykus looked east and saw the first rays of the sun shine upon the world. As the Seer had promised, the gods spoke to him. He received his new quest and walked in silence back to the castle," Uncle Melkes said, ending the story.

"That's it?" Macal was surprised and disappointed. "I expected more."

"Well, unfortunately, that's all this tale has to offer. Don't worry, though; there are plenty of other stories for you to hear. Anyway, the point of the story is…" Uncle Melkes asked, leaving the sentence unfinished, as he often did when telling a tale to Macal.

"*The point is* that no matter how much you want something to happen now, it is going to happen in its own time anyway, so there is no point in trying to force it to happen sooner."

"Exactly! Very good, if I hadn't already known you were such a smart boy, I would be very impressed. Had Greykus just stayed in the castle, the dawn would have come anyway. He didn't need to do anything at all but wait patiently." Uncle Melkes glanced sideways at his nephew. "And what you were saying before, about me not being excited? This *is* me excited."

"No, it's not. You are acting exactly the same way you always do."

"Am I? I'm sorry you don't see the change, subtle as it is. How's this?" Uncle Melkes broke into an enormous grin that took over his wrinkled face. His lips curled high, showing all his teeth, and his eyes twinkled in the dusk as a rush of blood reddened his pale cheeks. He could only hold the monstrous smile a moment before the two of them burst into laughter.

"Another smile from you—so many in one day! Surely the world must be amiss!" exclaimed Uncle Melkes.

Macal couldn't stop smiling. He loved his uncle. He had never seen him angry or heard him raise his voice. He always had the stillness of a pond and the gentleness of a baby lamb, and Macal guiltily suspected that he might love Uncle Melkes even more than he loved his father.

He knew he should love his father most, but his father was always away. Macal rarely saw him; he had never really had the chance to know his father at all, not the way he knew Uncle Melkes. He could tell with a glance what his uncle was thinking or implying by the way his eyes crinkled, or his bushy eyebrows raised, by the curl of his lip or the redness of his cheeks.

Macal could only guess that love was something that came with time, and time was the main thing he lacked with his father. But tonight that would change.

He wouldn't waste a moment with his father. He would make the time amount to something. He would get to know his father, and his father would get to know him. They could go fishing together, wander through the woods in the afternoon, and sit together for a long dinner while his father told of his travels and the strange and far lands he had seen. Macal wanted to know every detail. He wanted to know his father.

Yes, tonight things would finally be different. He would tell his father everything he had ever wanted to say to him. The prospect filled Macal with overwhelming excitement; despite the story Uncle Melkes just told, he felt he couldn't wait for his father to arrive home.

As they eventually entered the village, he turned to his uncle. "So what did the gods tell Greykus his new quest was, anyway?"

"Ah, I thought you might have forgotten about that. Do you have any idea what it was?"

"Maybe. A few. Like he had to go to Leximore, the ancient empire of men, elves, and goblins, and defeat the sorcerous emperor? Or he had to return his grandfather's spirit to Malkvloria, the island of the dead—or, or he had to go to Gelegius and extinguish the eternal flame of the City of Fire?"

"Well, no, not quite, though I'm sure he would have enjoyed those journeys very much. Did you know that when you get excited, you become very creative?" Uncle Melkes seemed impressed. "Greykus's quest was actually much more simple."

"What was it?"

"To find a new horse."

Macal rolled his eyes. "I should have guessed. And I'm pretty sure there's some other meaning in that I'm supposed to understand."

"Perhaps," replied his uncle enigmatically. "Perhaps."

By now they had reached the small circular plaza at the heart of the village, which was lined with shops that were closed for the evening. There was a copper smith, a general goods merchant, a blacksmith, a scrivener, an apothecary, a wine merchant, and more, about dozen shops in all. The two hundred or so residents of Hormul could find almost everything they needed here.

The only other large road in Hormul ran north and south across the plaza, bisecting the one on which Macal and Uncle Melkes had arrived. The crossroads divided the town into four quarters, each of which was woven together by numerous small paths and roadways.

In the center of the plaza stood an aged statue of Merculess Hormul, the man who founded the village in a long forgotten time. In its left hand the statue held aloft a large sword, pointing to the north. Macal was sure there was some meaning behind the gesture, but he had never found out what it was.

The Waywitch Tavern was located at the southeast corner of the dirt plaza, not far from where they had entered. Usually the tavern wasn't busy until well after the sun went down and the work in the fields, shops, and smithies was complete. Uncle Melkes was always reminding Macal that daylight was not a commodity to waste. Tonight, however, things seemed different.

As they approached the two-story tavern, they were surprised to find it already very much alive. Macal could only guess it must be due to the news of the Legion's return. Everybody from the village must have gravitated to the tavern to await the soldiers' arrival.

The Waywitch was a large timber and oak building with a thatched roof. On warmer nights like this one, its double doors stood open, light and smoke spilling out onto the plaza along with shouts of mirth and the shadows of the revelers.

As Macal and his uncle approached the stairs, a man strode angrily out the front doors. They recognized Lalliard, a bitter wizard who seemed to care little for anything or anyone. He had a well-founded reputation for being difficult, rude, and excessively irritable. The blue-gray pallor of his skin gave the wizard an almost inhuman look. He was just under six feet in height, with a gaunt, stooping frame. He walked with harsh quick steps and tonight he radiated even more intensity than usual.

Even though Macal knew the wizard couldn't be more than thirty, he looked far older. Lalliard's short hair had already turned from brown to white, matching his furrowed eyebrows. His piercing blue eyes looked coldly at everything around him.

Nonetheless, he was the most intelligent man Macal had ever met. Lalliard could read and write, something most of those in town couldn't do, and he read more books than anybody Macal had ever seen—even Quul the Elf, Hormul's local scrivener.

Macal tried to start a conversation with the moody wizard as he stomped down the stairs. "Hello, Lalliard. Having a good night?"

"*No!*" the tall man said sharply as he stormed past them, shoving them out of his way with his walking stick as he went. His dirty slate-blue robe billowed in his wake as he limped angrily across the plaza. "I never have a good night."

"Don't worry about him, Macal," Uncle Melkes said as they watched Lalliard disappear into the new fallen darkness. "He's always like that. Probably lost the last of his drinking money in a game of Devils and Kings."

"I know. I like him anyway," confessed Macal. "He acts mean, but I think he likes it when I try to talk to him."

"I'm sure he does." Uncle Melkes smiled uncertainly and patted Macal's shoulder, saddened that his nephew was so desperate for friends that he would attempt to befriend even the brooding wizard. "I'm sure he does. Now come on, let's see what fun's to be had tonight."

CHAPTER 2

The Waywitch was surprisingly busy this evening. Many of the tables were full, and the long stretch of bar along the right wall was lined with assorted customers sporting half-emptied tankards, horns, and bumpers.

Although not the largest of villages, Hormul had its share of diversity, evidenced by the tavern's patrons. Among those out for a festive evening were elves, a couple of orcs, a few goblins, some halflings, flying sprites, gnomes, and many humans.

The hubbub of conversation and smack of empty goblets on wooden tables was loud; several tables were already covered in cards and dice, deep in games of Devils and Kings. A hearth with a sputtering fire lit the far end of the taproom. On either side of the bar, staircases led to a catwalk that ran directly over the bar and gave access to the guest rooms in the back of the building. There was a prevalent smell of pipe smoke and the creaking floor was covered in a thin layer of wood shavings and sawdust, which helped absorb the spill of ales and ciders.

As Uncle Melkes and Macal entered from the cooling night into the warmth and comfort of the main room, they recognized many of the other customers. Among them were Methalin, a halfling and pewter smith; Antis, the Lord of Hormul and several of the surrounding lands; Oliven, the town's most prominent merchant; Captain Gazabel of the watch; the foul old woman Matris Norle and her equally nasty dog, Hex.

Grunc, barkeep and proprietor of the Waywitch, tended the bar area while Allana, a tall, pretty half-elven girl, worked the floor, carrying around an oak tray crowded with foaming flagons of the local brew.

Grunc was a dwarf, and he was a dwarf to most other dwarfs, far shorter than average even for his small race. With this in mind, he had commissioned the bar with a raised floor behind it, almost flush with the bar top itself. This enabled Grunc to tend to his customers, which he did well. His stature was matched by an equally short temper, always ready to flare when mayhem broke out in the tavern.

Not surprisingly, Grunc was the only dwarf in Hormul. Dwarves were not welcome in most towns, because of their race's reputation for nastiness and savagery, but Grunc had long ago proved to the people of Hormul and most importantly to Captain Gazabel of the watch and Lord Antis, who ran the hamlet, that he harbored no insidious intentions. Over time, the Waywitch had become a popular and respectable place to go.

Moving through the thick crowd, Macal and Uncle Melkes were lucky to find a couple of free spaces along the bar, where they leaned and waited for Grunc to make his way over to them. The brown-bearded dwarf had already noticed his new patrons and waddled over to them on his short legs, eager for their coin.

"Evenin'," offered the dwarf, his voice deep and gruff. "Glad you could make it tonight. Looks like we have a full house. Too bad every night's not like this."

Like all dwarves, Grunc loved gold more than anything else in the world. An evening like this, with the village celebrating the return of the army long into the night, was what he lived for. He ran the Waywitch with a strict policy of profit. It was simple and straightforward: nothing at all would be done in the establishment unless it added to his personal trove of gold.

Melkes glanced around at the crowded tavern. "Yes, you could finally go off and retire."

"What? *Me*, retire? Never! No honorable dwarf retires. If there's money to be made, I'll be right here in the thick of it all, collecting the coin until my heart stops beating and tells me it's time to go. And even then, I might hang about for a bit to make sure the last patrons pay before they leave! What can I get for you tonight? You boys look impressively thirsty...." Grunc's voice trailed off as he looked uncertainly at the two. Knowing them as he did most of his patrons, he was quite aware that they rarely had extra shillings to spend on drinks. He scrutinized them as only a dwarf could, sizing them up to see how much he might profit off of them. "You *did* bring money, right? I'm just mentioning this now, because as you may know, there are no free rounds in this establishment."

Uncle Melkes' warm smile never flickered. "Some might think that a rude question." Macal, realizing what Grunc was implying by his question, started to turn red with embarrassment. He really wanted to say something sarcastic to put the dwarf in his place, but he just remained quiet.

"Nothing rude intended. Business is business," explained the dwarf flatly.

"Well, to ease your overly troubled and greedy mind, you can be assured that *my* business is doing just fine and that I can pay our way," Uncle Melkes said. "You have anything on special tonight?"

Grunc scowled at the minor insult, but quickly shrugged it off. He wasn't here to make friends, and to be truthful he knew Melkes was right. He *was* greedy.

"Special? Nah. That's for those taverns that like to lose money. How 'bout a bumper of my new dark ale for you? I just tapped a fresh keg. And for the boy, let's say a small measure of our new cherry cider, imported all the way from the elves in Taloria. Came in on a wagon just a few days ago. All the kids really like it."

"That sounds good. So…what was Lalliard in a huff about?" inquired Uncle Melkes.

"Oh, you know—the usual." The dwarf began to pour some beer into a flagon for Uncle Melkes. "The dice were not working for him tonight. He got beaten in several games."

"That's surprising," commented Uncle Melkes thoughtfully. "He rarely loses."

"I know, and it's not a pretty sight when he does." Grunc handed the foaming ale to Uncle Melkes and began to pour the cherry cider. "I'm pretty sure it was his tax money he gambled away, too. Our jolly Lord Antis was near collapsing in frustration with the wizard, demanding he pay his taxes *before* he played any games. But you know Lalliard. Not much stands between him and whatever he wants to do."

"Well, I hope my luck's better than his tonight."

"It will be," Macal confidently assured his uncle. "Lalliard probably took all the bad luck with him."

Uncle Melkes smiled at the boy. "Let's hope so."

"What? You're gonna play a few games?" Grunc couldn't hide his surprise. Melkes must have done very well in trade recently, he thought, if they had enough money to buy drinks *and* play Devils and Kings. That was an extremely rare occurrence, as rare as Lalliard losing. "You know, if you're going to waste your money, you might as well waste it on drinks. That's just my *unbiased* opinion. I'm sure you'll find a full belly of ale much more satisfying."

"Thank you, but no. And if I didn't I plan to play, why else would I be here?" responded the old man.

"Maybe for my fine company?" interjected a surly and unfriendly voice from behind them. "Why else would you be here? We all know you can't afford a fine place like this."

All three of them turned to see Venk Warnege, a retired mercenary who had done very well for himself on a few campaigns in the southern lands. He was a stocky, well-muscled man of average size with dark sunned skin.

His bushy brown beard was matched by the thick, raging locks on his head.

"Hello, Venk," said Uncle Melkes politely, too nice to show his distaste for the man, but Macal knew the rude and arrogant man did not get along well with his uncle or anybody else. The boy wished he could be more like his uncle when he didn't like somebody. Instead he tried very hard to stay clear of such people, like he would the plague.

Standing with Venk was his son, Menk. He was a cruel boy the same age as Macal. There was nothing Menk enjoyed more than inflicting misery and anguish upon Macal. There were times when Macal actually believed that tormenting him was all Menk thought about. He was also by far the dumbest boy Macal had ever met. He hated and feared Menk. As they stood there, the bigger, stronger boy fixed him with an evil glare and a stupid smile, mouthing words Macal knew far too well. *The pain is coming.*

"If you're interested in a game," challenged Venk through his yellow teeth. "I'm looking for another to play against."

"Really?" Uncle Melkes said lightly. "Sounds like a delightful time."

Unable to contain himself, Grunc snickered. Like everybody else in town, he knew just how far from delightful Venk and his kin really were.

Meanwhile Macal could see Menk balling his fingers into a big fist. Involuntarily he stepped behind his uncle.

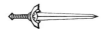

"Well, better get back to the rest of my customers. You gents have a good game." Grunc walked away from the men chuckling. "Just make sure both of you save enough coins to buy more drinks after the game."

"Don't you worry, Grunc. There is no risk of me going broke," gloated Venk, tapping the thick pouch of coins that hung heavily at his waste. "Let's get to it then. It'll be nice to take whatever money you've got."

Venk turned and walked over to the table he had already claimed. The three others followed.

"It'll be far easier beatin' you than Lalliard," said the mercenary snidely, hoping to rattle his new opponent.

"You're the one who beat Lalliard?" asked Macal in surprise. He couldn't figure out how that was possible. How could this dimwitted oaf beat Lalliard?

"Look who's turning into a chicken now!" spat Menk, who was even stupider than his father, though no less cruel. Refusing to respond to this inept sneer, Macal stayed behind his uncle and tried to avoid eye contact with Menk.

Laughter jostled Menk's thick body. "See, he's a chicken! Can't even stand up for himself. I seen maggots with more spine then you!"

"I think that's enough," said Uncle Melkes, cutting off Menk.

"He started it," lied Menk. "He made a face at me. You better watch the faces you make, if you want to keep yours intact!"

Macal instinctively took a step back, causing both son and father to burst out laughing.

"Good one, boy!" Menk's father patted him roughly on the back as he sat down in his chair.

Uncle Melkes put a soothing hand on Macal's shoulder, guiding him to a place on his left at the table. His conspiratorial glance said it all: *Don't worry. They're about to get what they deserve.*

That was all the comfort Macal needed. He was going to enjoy this. He hoped beyond hope that his uncle was right and that he could put these two oafs back in line.

"Shall we begin?" inquired Uncle Melkes.

"Let's get to it. The sooner the better, because let's be honest—I really don't like to be seen with you. Maybe it would be better to just give me your money right now and be on your way. It would save you some time and humiliation."

"As nice as that sounds, Venk," began Uncle Melkes serenely, as if he hadn't heard the insult, "I think I will just play it out and see what happens."

Macal saw there was already a Devils and Kings board laid out, probably the one Lalliard has just been beaten on. The deck was also there, the fifty-four troll-skin cards already removed from their chipped maple box and placed in a neat stack in the center of the table. The regenerating green skin, a natural property of some trolls, made it impossible to cheat by marking such cards, as they always returned to their original form.

The two bone dice had been taken out of their linen pouch. Each die had six sides and was fashioned from medusa knucklebones, which resisted enchantment and thereby nullified any magic cheating attempted by either party. Next to several tankards Venk had emptied was the playing board itself, called the Life Board. It was a long thin board, divided into twenty-three spaces set in a row across its surface.

Although Macal had witnessed many Devils and Kings games, he rarely ever got to play. Not many people would actually play unless it was for money, and money was something he always lacked. Even if he had possessed any coins, he wasn't sure he would risk losing them on a game. Not when there were so many far better uses for his money.

He knew play would start with either Venk or Uncle Melkes dealing three cards to each man. The player not dealing would get to go first.

After looking at their cards each player then had the option to trade in one card for a new one. This happened often if the player thought his hand could be improved by a new card. The only cards that could not be traded in were the Devil cards, of which there were two in the deck. The other fifty-two cards were numbered one to thirteen in four different suits, while the two Devil cards were numbered zero.

On each player's turn, he chose two cards from his hand, turned them face up on the table and added them together. He then rolled both dice and added their sum to the single card left in his hand.

Macal liked how quickly the game progressed. All that was required was for each player to compare the sum of two cards face up on the table with the sum of the card in his hand and the dice, and note the difference. That number determined the movement of the player's token on the Life Board.

Macal glanced at the Life Board. He wished he had one of his own, although most people just used the ones supplied by Grunc. On each space was a number from one to ten, starting in the middle and numbering outward towards the edges. There were three symbols on the Life Board as well.

Đ – 10 – 9 – 8 – 7 – 6 – 5 – 4 – 3 – 2 – 1 – Ҏ – 1 – 2 – 3 – 4 – 5 – 6 – 7 – 8 – 9 – 10 – Қ

On the space farthest to the right was a symbol of a crown. This was the King Position. Farthest to the left was a devil's trident, indicating the Devil Position. In the center was a small painted picture of a peasant: the Peasant Position, where play would begin. Each player started by placing his token in the Peasant Position.

For each point of difference between the two sums—that of the two cards on the table, and that of the dice and the card remaining in the player's hand—his token moved one space. If the former was higher, he moved toward the King Position; if the latter was higher the token moved toward the Devil Position.

Any player who moved onto the Devil or King Positions would be eliminated from the game, an automatic loss. The player nearest the Peasant Position after ten rounds won the game.

Venk flamboyantly reached into the pocket of his jerkin and pulled out a small piece of silver sculpted into a coiled snake with a burst of flame rising from the center of its coil. The piece was intricate and quite impressive, but everybody in the tavern was familiar with it; this was the token Venk always used when he played Devils and Kings.

Sitting next to his father, Menk grinned in pleasure at his father's showmanship and the glorious extravagance of the trinket. Along with being the biggest boy of his age in village, he was also one of the wealthiest. As a mercenary in the Drakenmoor conquests on the southern islands, his father had amassed a significant fortune. While he wasn't rich, he was still very well off.

Uncle Melkes watched Venk place the flaming snake on the Peasant

Position on the Life Board. Then, without much show, he reached down and picked up a large wood shaving from the floor, and placed it likewise on the Peasant Position.

"Always were a fancy one, weren't you?" mocked Venk.

"The game is not about the token," Uncle Melkes reminded him. "It's about skill, and whatever blessings Devera sees fit to offer."

Venk grumbled a curse. "We'll see about that. What're the stakes?"

"A silver crown?

"A *silver crown?*" Venk seemed startled. That was a large sum. "You can afford that? If so, I'd think you'd dress your boy a bit better."

This verbal thrust got a raucous laugh from Menk, and another from the table to their left, who had overheard the exchange.

"He is not my *boy*, and my *nephew* is dressed just fine," Uncle Melkes remarked, while Macal again turned red with embarrassment. He was starting to think it was time to leave all of them to their game.

"If you say so," retorted Venk with a malicious laugh. "Fine. Fine. A silver crown it is. But you don't mind if I ask to see it first, do you? 'Cause you know, I'm a bit surprised you have that kind of money to be wasting on a game. I gotta ask, where you getting coin like that?"

"You see, that's the thing. I don't have to explain myself to you. But in the spirit of competition," Uncle Melkes said, reaching into the leather pouch at his waist, "I'll show you the coin."

Venk greedily eyed the shiny coin Uncle Melkes placed on the table. "Good. Good." He placed his own matching coin on top of it.

Macal stared at the coins. He seldom got so close to so much money, and he was surprised to see his uncle set the stakes so high. It wasn't as if his uncle and he were totally poor, it was just that his father could only bring the money he made to them when he came home—and that wasn't often. The money his father did occasionally bring home always ran out eventually anyway, and they had to make do with what they could make from the farm.

Emblazoned on the glittering coins was the visage of King Stormlion, the head of the Troll King in his left hand, and in his right a mighty sword. Macal liked the design. He guessed the coins had been minted after the war began, to remind all the people that a war with the trolls was in full swing.

As he stood there watching his uncle prepare for the game, Macal intercepted Menk's smug, hostile glare. *I'm gonna enjoy watching my father take your money.*

Macal looked away and instantly despised himself for doing so. He wished he wasn't so afraid. He wished he was tough like Menk, or Venk, or even his father, but he wasn't and he knew he never would be. He hated that about himself. He didn't want to be afraid anymore. Macal didn't see it, but as he turned away in fear, Menk smiled with pleasure.

As the game began, Macal reminded himself that the first few rounds weren't particularly important. Those rounds were merely about staying on the board. He just had to hope that his uncle's luck held out. If it didn't, and he careened off to either the Devil or the King space, the game would be over and the silver crown lost. Worse still, Macal would have to hear Menk and his father gloat about their victory.

The first few rounds went by in a bland, but skillful fashion, with both players managing to stay near the Peasant Position at the center. Neither man played any daring hands; the pace was safe and steady. It wasn't until later in the game that they would likely tighten their play style to try to land on the peasant position by the end of round ten.

By the end of the third round, Venk was on the King's side of the board at a respectable position on the fourth square. Uncle Melkes was just behind him on the fifth square.

"Feel that Devera luck now, do you?" Venk didn't waste the opportunity to lord his marginally better standing over his opponent.

Uncle Melkes looked at Venk calmly. "It's still very early."

"Yeah, plenty of time for you to fall even farther behind me!" chuckled his opponent. "Come on then, it's your go again."

Uncle Melkes picked up the cold dice, running his thumb over them for luck as they rested in his palm. When he dropped them on the table, they clattered for a second before coming to a stop. Instantly his face was all smiles.

Adding the total to the card he kept in his hand, he compared the result with the total of the cards on the table. He was under by five. That meant he was back on the Peasant Position—the best position in the game!

"Well, isn't that interesting?" he murmured, placing his dirty wood shaving on the Peasant square.

"Fine," snapped Venk, yanking on a tangle in his mangy beard. "Just let me have my go! You just got lucky, is all."

"And that's all I need."

By the end of the fifth round Macal was starting to get excited. Venk was in the eighth position near the Devil, and Uncle Melkes was once again in the fifth position toward the King. Venk was in a bit of danger if the cards and dice turned against him. He could be tossed off the board and out of the game.

Macal offered a small prayer to Devera, the Goddess of Fate, for that to come true, because if that didn't happen Venk still had plenty of time to put himself back in a position to win the game.

Venk was becoming frustrated by his bout of bad luck. Since the third round, Melkes had kept a better position, and if things continued like this, he would surely lose the game. Sometimes, if a game attracted a large crowd, there would be betting among the spectators on who would win the most rounds. Venk felt pressured and irritated by this prospect; his pride was offended by the idea of other people losing money through his lack of skill at the game. Fortunately for him, none of the other patrons seemed particularly interested in the game.

Noticing Venk glancing around the room, Uncle Melkes could see that his rude foe didn't want an audience. With a guilty little smile, Uncle Melkes leaned over to the next table where Nomesh, an orc mercenary, and a friend of Venk's, was sitting with a few strangers.

"We got a good game going on over here," he announced loudly enough for other nearby patrons to overhear. "I'm feeling pretty confident. Care to have a side wager on it? I'll bet you my last silver coin that I can beat your friend here."

"*What?* That's illegal!" protested Venk.

"What? Making a bet on a gambling game is illegal? Surely not," countered Uncle Melkes. "What does it matter to you what I do with my money?" He turned back to Nomesh. "Well? Care for a wager?"

Macal was stunned to learn that his uncle had another silver coin. He could never have imagined his uncle having such a great day in trade, although it had been quite a while since Melkes had gone to the markets in Bronel. Maybe that explained the sudden surge in income.

The squat, orange-skinned orc looked uncertainly at Uncle Melkes, then shifted his black oily gaze to Venk.

"You better win!" he said to his friend as he stood up to get a better look at the game.

The exchange had the exact effect Uncle Melkes wanted. As he clasped wrists with Nomesh to seal the bet on their honor, he noticed that others in the bar had overheard the conversation and, intrigued by the high stakes, had become interested in the game.

Venk looked uncomfortable and angry as a ring of people formed around their table, all eager to watch the game play itself out. It was his turn to deal. Dismally he picked up the deck of cards, but as he began to shuffle, his nervous and distracted hands dropped a few of the cards onto the floor causing laughter to erupt among the crowd.

"I hope you play better than you deal!" a heckler called.

"Me too! I just bet a copper shilling on you!" The voice from the crowd sounded regretful.

Menk and a few others retrieved the dropped cards as Venk pulled ferociously on his beard, a few strands coming off in his hands.

"Give them to me!" Venk angrily tore the fallen cards from his son's hands as he tried to hand them back to him.

"*I was!*" snapped Menk before he could stop himself.

His father gave him a glare that implied a beating was in Menk's future, and the boy cringed. Watching their interaction along with the rest of the crowd, Macal couldn't help his pleasure at the sight of Menk looking afraid. Never before had he seen Menk shrink away from anything. This was a moment Macal was going to store away for future reminiscence.

The game continued. By the end of the seventh round, it seemed Devera had truly blessed Uncle Melkes. He maintained a couple of points' lead in position over Venk.

In the crowd around them, numerous side bets were being won and lost as the game progressed. At this point it seemed favorable to bet on Uncle Melkes; the cards Venk was being dealt were of little use to him.

It was then that Macal felt a firm hand grasp his shoulder and glanced back to see that Menk's two goon companions had come up behind him. They were just as cruel and violent as their leader. The hand on his shoulder belonged to Nesty, a skinny boy who was still taller and bigger than Macal. He had short-cropped blond hair and a long stretched face. His arms were also unusually long, like an ape's, and some mixed blood in his heritage had given him the slightly pointed ears of an elf.

Nesty's hand clenched painfully on Macal's slender shoulder, his grimy nails bit through his tunic into his skin. It took all Macal's willpower not to cry out in pain. He didn't want these boys to make him cry. Not again. Not in front of all these people. Next to him, his uncle hadn't noticed what was happening, distracted as he was by the game.

"Your uncle better lose, or your face will pay," a voice whispered in Macal's ear. "Much worse than last time."

Macal knew the voice without looking. It was Gornod, Menk's other goon, a stout boy with dark eyes and hair, and an even darker desire to inflict pain on anything he could. He had the largest nose Macal had ever seen on anyone, man or boy. Macal had often thought that even a giant would be embarrassed by such a nose. Gornod also had a malformed hand, which he always kept tucked in his pants pocket, embarrassed by the deformity. The hand was just larger than the palm of the other, with stubby bent fingers dangling off it at crooked angles. Macal had seen it once, when he had gone to the river to swim and Menk and his companions were already there. He had watched them for a few minutes, hidden behind a bush.

Now, to his relief, Nesty's hand left his shoulder. He saw Menk staring at him from across the table, pleased to see that his message had been properly delivered. His goons then made their way back to him.

Macal didn't want to be here anymore. Although he wanted to see the end of the game, he didn't want to be near Menk and his stupid brutes. He rose from the table and pushed in his chair. The movement finally caught Uncle Melkes attention; he gave Macal an inquiring glance.

"I'm just going to stand over by the window, to watch for the legion's arrival." It wasn't really a lie, not totally, he consoled himself. He just didn't want to admit the main reason he was leaving, especially with an audience watching.

Uncle Melkes smiled at him. "Let me know when you see them."

"I will." As Macal walked away from the table, heading toward the open windows that faced the plaza, he could feel Menk's scowl locked onto his back. He considered going outside to sit on the base of the statue in the plaza's center, like he normally did when waiting for his father to return, but decided to stay in the tavern to see if his uncle won or lost the game.

Everyone knew that the eighth round in Devils and Kings was where strategy and skill came into play. At this point both players were trying their best to move their tokens back toward the Peasant Position.

Back at the table both of the players took their turns and to the surprise of the spectators Venk took the lead from Melkes, moving to the King's fifth position with a lucky roll of the dice. Meanwhile, Uncle Melkes slid unluckily to the Devil's seventh position. He seemed only mildly concerned. He was behind now by two slots, but he had two more rounds to catch up.

Round nine, however, proved no better. The crowd muttered as Uncle Melkes moved unluckily even farther away from the Peasant Position to the Devil's ninth slot. Venk, to his glee, had another good round that moved him up two more spots, placing him now at the King's third position and leaving him in an excellent position for the final round.

Now that the tide of luck seemed to be turning against him, Uncle Melkes began to doubt the wisdom of having wagered so much money. Although he was trying to remain calm, he had to admit that he was a mortal man, and Venk's insults to Macal had been too much. He didn't believe in violence as a means to any end, but he did hope to get back at Venk by taking coins from his pouch.

Sitting by the window, Macal couldn't actually see the thronged table, but it was clear from the crowd's reaction what was happening. Everyone was loud and anxious, shouting out comments for favorable luck and jeering at those who bet against them.

"This is it, then," said Venk as Uncle Melkes shuffled the cards for the final hand. "This is where I become a silver richer."

Uncle Melkes seemed as calm and composed as always. "Or perhaps, this is where you get what you deserve."

"Yeah, we'll see about that. Just hand me my cards," retorted Venk with a pompous laugh.

Each player quickly gathered his cards from the table and glanced at them. Venk seemed pleased. Without hesitation, he placed two of his cards face up on the table: a ten and an eight. He held the last card close to his chest to keep Uncle Melkes and those in the crowd who couldn't see it in suspense.

Then without a word he picked up the dice and tossed them roughly onto the table. The crowd held its breath for the result. A great many bets were riding on this game. The dice came up a six and a three, for a total of nine.

"Whoa, the gods have blessed me!" exclaimed Venk with a grin. "With eighteen showing on the table cards, compared to the nine on the dice, plus —" he paused for dramatic effect, enjoying his own theatrics, "the nine on the card in my hand—" dropping the card on the table for all to see, "makes for a stasis! I don't move at all! Beat a three position from way out there, Melkes, *if* you can."

Uncle Melkes let the competitive banter slide off him. He had to focus. Annoying as Venk's chatter was, Melkes knew that the mercenary was right. It was going to be a tough play, and he would need a lot of luck.

First, he traded in a card, since the cards he held were not that impressive and he needed some help getting them to work for him. He discarded a nine that was replaced by a seven, which was not much better. He knew he needed a low card if he was going to roll a higher number than the cards he would play on the table. It was the only way he could win.

Dismally he placed the two sevens in his hand on the table and kept the ten. At the moment it was the best play he could think of. In his head, he calculated he needed to roll an eleven or a twelve to win. He also knew that the odds were greatly against him; he had learned long ago through playing these games that the average roll on two six-sided dice was a seven.

It was becoming evident to Melkes that very likely all was lost. Everything—the two silver, all the earnings from the farm as of late— would be gone. Not to mention the ridicule he would have to endure from Venk and the others. A twinge of guilt came over him. He had planned to use some of that money to buy Macal new shoes to replace the ones that were little more than old pieces of frayed leather tied to his feet. He had felt it was time for his nephew to have a proper pair of shoes, or perhaps boots. He hoped that with Bertran, Macal's father, finally coming home with money, he might still be able to do that.

"Come on now, it's your go," urged Venk, anxious to win the game. "Let's get this over with, so I can buy my next round with your money. I might as well, since I bought the last round with Lalliard's!"

"Yeah, that's a good idea, the lot of you!" shouted Grunc from the bar.

"This is a tavern *and bar*. Stop watching the game for a minute and buy a few more drinks. Charity don't keep this place open, you vagrants!"

Much to Grunc's frustration the crowd ignored him. It was obvious they wanted to see the game's end.

This was it. Having no other choice Uncle Melkes picked up the dice, shook them for a moment, looked back through the crowd, caught Macal's eye, gave a faint smile, and then let fate take over as he dropped the dice onto the table.

The crowd watched with such baited breath that Macal could hear the clatter of the dice from the far side of the room. The end of the game, for better or worse. The crowd was silent as the dice bounced about, spinning as they went. Praying his uncle's luck had returned, Macal heard the crowd burst into astonished cheers as the dice came to a halt. Everyone was jumping up and down, shouting and calling for their winnings to be paid. At first he didn't know if the news was good or bad.

Most of the people were obviously pleased, but perhaps they had bet against his uncle in the end and were now happy he had lost. Or maybe they had bet on his uncle, and by some great fortune Uncle Melkes had prevailed.

Macal was gathering the courage to go back to the table to see what happened when a traveler he hadn't seen before, clad in a dark green sooty cloak over a suit of black mail, turned to him and said, "He rolled an eleven! He won!"

"Who won?" Macal didn't know what the final plays had been, so he didn't know *who* needed an eleven to win.

"The man you were sitting with. He won! He ended in the two position!" The man grinned. "And he just made me a tidy little profit, so please let him know I'm much obliged."

As the traveler turned back to his companions, Macal smiled to himself, his anxiety giving way to relief. His uncle, surrounded by congratulations, was collecting his winnings, talking to several village acquaintances. The general feeling in the tavern was one of approval that the haughty Venk had met defeat, and Macal couldn't agree more.

Happily he turned back to look out the window. He would let his uncle enjoy the few moments of glory and accolades the victory gave him.

Outside in the silent night, the dim plaza was nearly deserted; most of the village was inside the tavern. Then a rider appeared, coming down the western road. Macal's heart leapt. *Was it the army? Was it finally his father come home to see him?*

In just a few seconds this hope was dashed. The rider was clearly not a soldier. He was dressed gaily, like a well-off merchant, with a heavy beryl cloak and tailored clothing. Macal saw that his horse was injured, walking with a heavy limp. Yet the heavyset merchant seemed indifferent to the beast's sufferings, repeatedly kicking it into a faster gait as he crossed the plaza toward the stable adjoining the tavern. The empty plaza echoed with his frustrated oaths, unheard except by Macal and the horse.

Finally, the animal came to a halt, its injured leg unable to carry the overweight rider any farther. With more curses, the merchant clumsily dismounted, nearly ending up in a crumpled heap of fine silks and bulging fat on the ground. Pulling harshly on the reins, he yanked the beast forward.

The black horse took a few painful steps and stopped again. Macal could see it just wanted to lie down right where it was, but the merchant spun around and began lashing it with his riding crop, as if beating dust out of a rug. At last, he stopped and dragged on the reins again, pulling the horse into the stable.

Anger filled Macal as he watched. He couldn't imagine treating Germ with such cruelty, and he couldn't fathom how anyone could do that to an animal. No longer caring about what was happening in the tavern Macal ran out the door. Wanting to check on the horse but afraid to confront the brutal merchant, he decided it would be better to make sure the man had left the stable before he ventured inside. Ducking behind a bush outside the stable door, he saw the gluttonous man strike the horse once more with his crop.

Macal clenched his fists, wanting to go in there and beat the man, show him what it felt like. But, as always, his uncontrollable fear overtook him and he couldn't force himself out of the shadows. How could he stand up to such a man? What if the merchant came at *him* with the crop? Instead he waited until the fat man, cursing aloud, finally bustled off toward the tavern.

His attention on the horse, Macal didn't see the three infuriated boys leave the tavern as the merchant entered.

CHAPTER 3

H urrying in to see to the horse, Macal breathed in the stale odor of the place. Although it could comfortably accommodate a dozen mounts, at the moment the stable held only four. The merchant hadn't bothered to wait for the stable-hand, but had left his mount tied to one of the railings. The animal's black coat was covered in sweat and marked with blood where the crop had struck. As Macal approached, it shied away from him.

"It's okay." The boy's voice was soothing. "I'm not going to hurt you, I promise."

The horse tried to pull away, but the length of the reins kept it from going far. Slowly and patiently, Macal approached. In the flickering lamplight, he could see that the horse's flank was swollen and bruised from the rider's kicks.

Hatred for the merchant swelled up inside him. The horse had an obviously injured ankle, yet its owner, probably late for whatever he was doing, had used his crop to relieve his frustration with the creature's slow gait.

Finally, Macal was close enough to place a kind hand affectionately on the horse's neck. "It's okay. I just want to help you."

To his surprise, the horse stood calmly, seeming to understand his words. Uncle Melkes had often told him that he had a way with animals, an empathy they could sense. It was a useful ability in handling the animals on the farm, and especially useful with the stubborn Germ.

"I wonder what your name is," said Macal softly as he gently stroked the horse's neck. "You don't need to be afraid anymore. How about some oats?"

He found a feedbag and offered it to the horse, which began to eat hungrily. Macal could understand the creature's fear; there were so many things he himself was afraid of. He had never been more frightened than when he had encountered some scavenger Orcs from Gromula. The raiding party had swarmed down from the northwest mountains to attack a caravan that he and Uncle Melkes had joined on their way to Bronel.

By some great blessing Macal and his uncle were spared from the initial attack because their battered wagon was in the center of the procession. The first attacks had come on the rear and front of the caravan in an attempt to box them all in.

Fortunately, some of Elronia's cavalry and footmen were making use of the same road on their way to a borderlands fort, and they had arrived in time to make quick work of the orc party.

Even so, seeing the foul creatures using their two-headed wolves to attack, watching the joy on their faces as their roughly-wrought blades spilled blood, Macal had fled into the back of the wagon and hidden under a blanket between two empty crates.

After that, he had refused to leave Hormul again. He had no desire to set foot outside the little community where he lived. In his mind this was his home, and outside its perimeter there was only war and violence. He was happy to stay here in this little hamlet, far from the dark threats of the world beyond.

Somehow, Macal was sure the horse felt the same way about the cruel merchant. He was sure it wanted nothing more to do with the man. If its leg hadn't been injured, Macal would have toyed with idea of letting the horse go free to find a new home and a master, one who would care for it properly.

Setting the feedbag on a sill near the horse, the boy bent down to investigate its hurt ankle. There probably wasn't much he could do to help, not possessing his uncle's knowledge in these matters, but he saw no harm in trying.

"Look who I finally found." A dull voice spoke unexpectedly behind him. Macal knew that voice. Quickly he spun around to see Menk standing in the stable door.

"I been looking for you. It took me a minute to find you. I knew you would run. You always do." The bully had his usual tormenting tone. "But I figured you would have run home crying, but I'm glad you didn't."

"L-le-leave me alone," Macal stammered as he backed up into the horse, trying to put as much distance between him and Menk as possible.

"That's not gonna happen." Menk's smile was vicious. "You know it's not."

To Macal's growing horror, Gornod stepped out from behind Menk.

"I found him, boys," Menk boasted. Evident in his eyes was eager anticipation of what was to come.

29

"Good," said Nesty as he stepped into the barn from the rear door, his droning voice gave the impression that the act of speaking exhausted him. "'Cause we didn't."

"Of course you didn't, ya idiot! How could you find him if I did?"

Macal stared from one to the other of the three boys, realizing he was trapped. He didn't know what to do. He could only think how much he hated Menk and his friends. He knew very well what happened every time he encountered them, and he didn't think this time was going to be any different.

As Macal took a step back, the three boys moved toward him with clenched fists.

As the bullies closed in, Macal decided to run. He could slip past Nesty and out the back entrance of the stables. But he had forgotten about the horse. Spinning around, he slammed into it, prompting a burst of laughter from his attackers.

Startled and frightened by the commotion, the horse jerked its reins free and hobbled out the back door of the stable, leaving Macal all alone. He tried to follow it, but Menk was too close now. The bully shoved Macal roughly from behind, sending him sprawling on the ground. The impact with the hard-packed dirt knocked the wind out of him.

Nesty and Gornod cackled in delight as they flexed their muscles, ready to put them to use.

"Where you running to, maggot? You got no friends who can save you," mocked Gornod.

Macal knew it was true. He didn't have any friends. For the most part he was always alone. It wasn't even his fault. He hadn't wanted to win the riding contest for youngsters at the King's Fair last year. He had only been lucky, but Menk hadn't seen it that way when he had come in second. That was when Menk had turned all the other kids against him. Now anybody who tried to befriend Macal risked the bully's wrath, and nobody wanted that. Macal was an outcast.

"I told ya you was gonna pay, didn't I?" Gornod taunted.

"Please just leave me alone," begged Macal as he tried to crawl away.

"Look, now he's a worm in the dirt," Nesty sneered, looming above him.

"That's your problem, Macal. You whine too much. And the thing is, I'm really gonna enjoy this." Menk cocked back his leg and kicked Macal in the ribs. The impact spun the smaller boy over in the dirt. He let out a yelp of pain as the three bullies laughed in enjoyment.

"Please." Tears welled up in Macal's eyes. He started to crawl away again.

"Stand up for yourself, runt," said Nesty.

"Yeah, come on. Stand up for yourself!" jeered Gornod.

Macal knew he would never get away by lying on the ground, but he knew he had no chance of standing up to the three boys either. Through a blur of tears he could see them laughing in pleasure at his plight.

He scrambled to his feet, still hoping to escape out the back door, but Nesty was waiting for him. His bony fist struck Macal savagely in the mouth. The punch spun Macal around; blood spilled from his broken lip as he collapsed to the floor again, curled up into a ball in the dirt, and cried.

He fell into a kind of trance as the boys kicked him relentlessly. He had never felt so alone. Through the haze of pain, all he could think about was that Menk had everything he didn't have. He was big and strong, he had friends, and he had a father.

The boys continued their assault, kicking him until his body convulsed.

"This is what you get for your uncle winning!" said Menk.

"Yeah," said Nesty.

"You should tell him to stop his cheating," Gornod advised.

Macal didn't know how long he lay there, taking their blows, before a commotion outside caught the bullies' attention and distracted them.

"What's that?" asked Gornod.

"What do you think it is, ya idiot? It's the stupid soldier boys coming back," Menk told him.

"Come on," said Nesty. "Let's go see who didn't make the return trip."

"Yeah," agreed Gornod excitedly. "I bet ya the Crawlems' kid ain't gonna be there."

"And I bet Macal's loser father didn't make it back either," Menk added. Nesty and Gornod joined their leader in laughter.

"Ain't that the truth. Not if he fights anything like his son," Gornod sneered.

Afraid and in pain, Macal didn't say anything, didn't stand up for himself, didn't stand up for his father. Instead he lay there in tears.

"Let's go." Menk cast a look of disgust at their victim. "He bores me. He's such a loser he don't even fight back."

"How about once more before we go?" asked Gornod hopefully. "I never get bored of this."

"Go ahead, you can have him. He's too easy." Menk turned and walked away.

"I'm not done yet either," said Nesty.

The two boys each gave Macal one last mighty kick in the ribs, then one to the head. As he received the final assaults Macal abruptly floated off into a hazy black abyss somewhere deep in his mind, where there were no dreams and, to his great relief, there was no pain.

Was it true? The question hovered in Macal's mind as he slowly returned to consciousness. *Was it true the soldiers had returned?*

He had heard what the other boys had said. He had heard them talking about his father, but they were wrong. His father was a great warrior. His father had seen many battles and fought many wars to keep the kingdom safe. He wasn't some lowlife mercenary like Menk's father. No, his father was a hero.

Sometimes many months passed between his father's visits; once it had been almost a year. That time, Macal had begun to think the worst. Never had his father been away so long, and never had he missed him so much. But this time was the worst of all: never had he been gone longer. Even as he lay in the dirt aching in pain, Macal couldn't help thinking fondly of the times he had seen his father walking slowly toward him down the dusty road or mounted high on a tired steed, clad in the uniform of Elronia.

When the soldiers marched into town, there were cheers and prayers of thanks for their safe return. The last time his father had come home was during the final battles against the Wolf-King of Regnorex. Elronia had won, defeating the Wolf Lord. *Just like they will win against the trolls,* he thought. And his father had come home, just as he was coming home tonight.

The cheers he remembered were sounding outside in the plaza right now, penetrating his stirring consciousness. Menk had been right. The soldiers were here. The army had returned at long last.

Macal knew some of the soldiers would stay in Hormul and others would continue down the road, heading for their own hamlets or villages even farther away from the theatre of battle.

By Elronian law, all men must serve in the army for at least two years. His father had done the initial two years and continued his service. Fortunately, for Macal, his uncle had left the army. There were times when the boy wondered what would have become of him if his uncle had remained a soldier as well.

There were days when his heart ached so intensely for his parents that he couldn't speak. But that was over now; he knew it. Now that the soldiers had finally returned, he would see his father again. The thought gave him the strength to force himself up to his knees in spite of the pain. His entire body ached, but he had to get up. He had to see his father. He wiped the tears from his face with one sleeve and used the other for the blood.

Grasping one of the stable doors, he pulled himself to his feet. He wanted to walk out of the stable and see his father walking towards him with his arms stretched wide for a hug. Right now Macal wanted that hug more than anything else in the world.

He wondered what his father looked like now. Sometimes he had a short beard, sometimes a long one, or he might be clean-shaven. Macal knew he would be in military garb, his favored silver sword hanging from his hip. Etched upon the sword were ancient legends that nobody could read, not even the learned wizard Lalliard.

As his strength returned, Macal slowly made his way out of the stable. He wasn't sure how long he had been unconscious, but it couldn't have been long; through bleary eyes he could see the tavern was emptying its patrons out into the plaza, Captain Gazabel among them. The square was crowded with soldiers clad in red tunics bearing the black head of a dragon. On their shoulders was stitched a small amber dragon—the insignia of the Amber Dragoons. Ignoring his aching ribs and throbbing head, Macal hastened to join the procession.

His eyes darted around the crowd. There were joyous cries of relief from mothers and fathers, brothers and sisters, wives and children as they found the men they had sent off to war. Beneath the din of celebration, Macal could hear a small, anguished undercurrent as some families broke down in tears at the news that their kinsman was not coming home.

Lonesome and desolate not long before, the plaza was now a sea of activity and energy. Macal continued to search for his father, but couldn't see him anywhere, nor could he find his uncle. Already some families were leaving, heading back to their homes or into the Waywitch to continue their celebration.

Macal continued his search, forcing himself to hurry regardless of how much it hurt, intently searching every soldier's face for the one he needed to see.

He had already gone around once. As he started a second circuit he became frantic, tugging on random soldiers' garments to get their attention so he could see their faces.

The crowd was thinning now. Macal's heart began to sink, weighed down by the greatest fear he had ever known. Standing alone in the plaza, he stared down the western road, willing his father to appear.

A gentle hand touched his shoulder and he looked up to see Uncle Melkes.

"Where is he?" cried Macal. "Where is he? He has to be here! *He has to be?*"

Uncle Melkes' face was compassionate. "He's probably just a little behind," he said in a comforting tone. Looking around at the empty plaza, Macal wasn't sure he believed his uncle.

"Let's go home and wait for him there," suggested Uncle Melkes softly. An hour or so had passed since the last Dragoon arrived. Uncle and nephew now sat on the base of Hormul's statue, their eyes on the quiet western road.

"I don't want to! I want to wait for him here!" Macal was adamant, rooted in his spot.

"Macal," urged his uncle gently, "you're hurt. Let's go home, so I can minister to these cuts and mend you up."

"No, I'm fine. I'll be all right. Please let me stay here, *please* let me wait."

"What happened to you?" Uncle Melkes already had a pretty good idea. It wasn't the first time he had seen Macal like this.

"You know what happened. The same thing that always happens. I hate them. I hate them so much!" The boy was stammering, close to tears again. His whole body ached; he could barely see out of his left eye. Several of his fingers were swollen and blue with bruises where Menk been kind enough to stand on them. That didn't matter, though. None of it did. All he wanted was to see his father, and he would wait here until that happened.

"Hating somebody isn't a good thing," Uncle Melkes remarked, turning Macal's head left and right to get a better look at his injuries. "But I can definitely see they gave you good reason. Come, let's go home. Your father can find us. He knows where we live."

Uncle Melkes hoped to get a smile from Macal, but the boy was resolute in his decision. Battered or not, he wasn't going to leave the plaza without his father.

"All right, then." Uncle Melkes gave in. "Mind if I wait with you?"

"No," Macal whispered. His lip had begun to bleed again.

It was then they heard somebody approaching from behind. Turning, they saw a soldier who had obviously come out of the Waywitch—a man of average height with greasy, short-cropped black hair, walking with an arrogant stride. Beneath his heavy black cloak, the links of byrnie chinked with every step he took.

"Hello, Lieutenant." Recognizing the lean, angular soldier, Uncle Melkes stood up to greet him. As was traditional, he added, "For the glory of the kingdom."

"For the glory of the kingdom," offered Macal quietly, turning away to watch the road again.

"For the glory of the kingdom," responded the soldier, adding with a self-satisfied smile, "And it's no longer Lieutenant. It's Captain."

Uncle Melkes' mouth fell open and Macal's head snapped back to stare at the man. Sure enough, the soldier's insignia revealed his rank with three crowns. He was a captain.

"Captain?" Macal said. "You can't be the captain. My *father* is the captain."

"Perhaps." The captain's deep black eyes had noted the boy's battered condition. "We should talk in private, Melkes, once you've seen to your boy here. What happened to you, lad? Fall under a moving wagon or something?"

"No." Macal offered no further explanation. He had never liked Jengus. It was obvious to anybody who met him that he was jealous of Macal's father. He had a slithering, snaky way about him. Macal had the feeling he would do whatever was needed to work his way up the chain of command.

There's something about him tonight, the boy thought. Jengus seemed too pleased, almost anxious to talk to Uncle Melkes. It was as if he had always wanted to be in charge, and now his dream had finally come true.

"He's just had a bad night," Uncle Melkes said. "Let's talk at our cottage. Will you walk with us?"

"Of course," agreed the captain.

Together the three of them left the plaza. Macal lagged behind, the pain of his injuries overshadowed by his yearning to wait for his father. Gently his uncle herded him toward the cottage. "Come along, Macal." He turned to the captain.

"It's not a long walk."

"Yes, I recall," the man answered as they headed down the eastern road.

The journey was made mostly in silence. Macal was lost in his own thoughts. He wanted to know what the captain had to say, and he wanted to know why he was not allowed to hear it. He could only guess from the spring in the captain's step that the news would not be welcome. Glancing at his uncle's solemn face, Macal wondered what he was thinking.

Did he know what the captain was going to say?

Dozens of terrible possibilities tore through the boy's mind. What could be the news? Why wasn't his father here? Why was this horrible man now the captain? And most important, when would his father be home?

Everything that Macal could imagine the captain saying was dark and bleak.

Soon they could see their cottage at the top of the hill. The moon hung high above it in the sky, nearly full, casting a gloomy light down upon the landscape. It looked lonely, with no stars about to befriend it. Macal imagined the moon, scared and alone just as he was, praying for nothing more than the company of the stars.

Reaching the cottage, they passed up the walkway and mounted the porch strewn with the empty crates Uncle Melkes used to transport their goods to market. Macal could hear Germ braying in the barn around back as Uncle Melkes opened the door. The interior of the cottage was simple: a fireplace flanked by shuttered windows, stone walls lined with shelves loaded with crocks, vials, jars, and flasks containing stored vegetables, herbs, balms, and unrecognizable solutions. In the center of the room stood a small worn table with three chairs. To the left of the door was Macal's cot, its straw mattress so thin it had almost ceased to exist.

A low doorway to the right led to another small, shabbily furnished room where Uncle Melkes slept. There was a night table, a small bed that was not much better than Macal's, and a small storage area on the north wall where he kept his old soldiering gear and supplies.

Uncle Melkes lit a squat piece of tallow and placed it on the center table. "Please have a seat, Jengus."

"Thank you. It's much appreciated after a long walk. You never realize how much you can miss sitting until all you're doing is walking."

Macal sat on his cot, easily pushing through the thin mattress. The supporting strings were loose; he had been meaning to tighten them, but normally by the end of the night, he had been too tired to bother.

Absently he fingered the blanket that sat on the edge of his cot. He had been told his mother used to weave the thickest woolen cloth his father and uncle had ever seen. This blanket was one of her last creations. It was all Macal had of her: the blanket she had made while waiting for him to be born. It was his most treasured possession, a thing of comfort, and right now he needed comfort more than anything.

"Would you like something to drink?" offered Uncle Melkes. "I'm afraid though, all I can offer you is water."

"No, thank you, I'll not be here long."

"So, whatever news you have to tell me is brief?" said Uncle Melkes.

The captain glanced at Macal. "Again, I will say it's best to hear this news yourself."

"Ah, yes," said Uncle Melkes. "I will assume you are right, since I don't know what you plan to say. Macal, let's tend to your cuts before I hear what the captain here has to say. Then you can go outside for a bit."

"I'm fine," the boy said. "I can clean myself up later. I want to hear what he has to say."

"All right then, if you say you can wait, you can wait. How about running to the well to fetch me some water? I'm a bit thirsty after all the walking we just did."

Macal didn't want to go. He wanted to stay here. He wanted to hear what the captain had to say. He wanted to know where his father was. He stood looking at his uncle, his feelings evident in his face.

"Please, Macal. I promise to tell you everything later," assured his uncle.

"Fine." Reluctant as the boy felt, he knew his uncle wouldn't lie to him. If Uncle Melkes said he would tell him, he would. Macal also realized that the sooner he left, the sooner the news would be told. He grabbed the pail near the fire pit and went back out the front door.

Uncle Melkes got up and closed the door behind him, then turned back to his guest with an inquiring look. As Melkes sat down, the captain began his tale.

Outside, Macal didn't go to the well. Instead he slipped around behind the house. He didn't want to wait. He needed to hear the news as his uncle heard it, to be sure he got the whole story. He knew his uncle wouldn't lie to him, but there was a chance he might omit part of the narrative. Macal crept across the grass as quietly as he could, toward the candlelight flickering in the open window. Crawling up under the sill, he could easily hear the voices of the men inside.

"As you can imagine," the captain was saying, "it bodes ill for the Teel family. No longer does that name hold any honor."

"What do you mean?" Macal had never heard such a sharp tone from Uncle Melkes.

"Your brother Bertran left the Dragoons some time ago," informed the captain.

"What do you mean, left? He wouldn't just *leave*. And if he had, he would have come home."

Jengus's response was icy. "We have reason to believe that Bertran Teel is betraying the army and the Kingdom of Elronia."

Uncle Melkes stared into the black eyes of the man before him, stunned by what he had just heard. "That's absurd. Bertran would never do such a thing! He would never be a traitor!"

"Wouldn't he?" asked the captain relentlessly. "Is he here now? No. Important battle plans, stolen by our spies from the enemy forces, have disappeared. These plans mark the location of the Troll King's forces. They gave us a great advantage over the trolls, and Bertran has taken them."

"How do you know this," asked Uncle Melkes in disbelief. He knew his brother-in-law well; they had even served together in the legion. He knew Bertran would sooner give his life than betray his kingdom.

"Because the same night the plans disappeared, so did Bertran. The plans were somehow dweomered, probably by the Troll King's witches, to change continually, always showing the current location of his troops. With that knowledge, we would have been unstoppable. These documents were essential to our strategy, our ability to win the war."

"Why did he take them? Why would he do that?" Melkes' head was spinning.

"Why do *you* think? There is only one reason. He means to trade the plans back to the trolls. For what gain I can only imagine, but I'm sure it will be a reward that many kings would envy."

"Again I'll say it," Uncle Melkes insisted. "Bertran would never do such a thing. He loves this kingdom and its people. How many battles has he fought on its behalf? How many wounds has he suffered in its name? He would never betray us!"

Jengus shrugged. "The facts say otherwise, don't they? He's not here. He has the plans. He left no explanation for their disappearance, or his for that matter. No, I think it's pretty clear. He grew tired of everything you just said, tired of fighting wars he didn't start. He wanted a new life, and he found the means to make a fantastic new one. It has not yet been officially declared that he is a traitor, but General Gazel Akelris, Son of Aoemeth, Lord of Heraldry and the King's Army, is soon to be informed of what has transpired. I'm sure he will see matters as I do. I just thought you should know before everyone else does.

"The name Teel will no longer stand for honor and bravery. Instead it will bear the brand of coward, thief, and traitor."

Uncle Melkes stood up suddenly. Outside beneath the window, Macal heard the stool clatter to the floor. He had never heard his uncle shout, but right now he seemed on the brink of explosion. Melkes struggled to control himself and finally succeeded.

"Just get out," he said flatly, his tone said there was no need for further talk.

"As you wish." The captain seemed satisfied by the shock and misery his news had caused. "I just hope I find him before the king's huntsmen and assassins do. I might show more mercy to him before he is justly put to the sword."

Macal felt his heart stop. *His father a traitor? Put to death?*

He couldn't believe it. Not his father. A soldier, but still a gentle man with a caring heart. These accusations could not be true. Macal didn't believe it. He refused to believe it. His father would never be a traitor!

Once the captain had left, the boy forced himself to stand on shaky legs and look through the window. He saw Uncle Melkes pick up his stool and slowly sit down. On his uncle's face was a look of sadness and desperation, as if he had just been told his whole reality was a lie. The look told Macal a great deal. Suddenly Macal was even more worried, even more afraid.

If his uncle believed what the captain had said, how could he refute it? Uncle Melkes looked like a man in despair, the walls of his life and his family collapsing around him.

Macal wasn't sure, but as he stood there he thought he heard his uncle give a muffled sob.

I don't believe it, Macal thought. *It's a lie.* But what could he, a mere boy, do about it?

He didn't know, but he had to do something. Anything. His world was falling apart. He turned and ran. Without a clear idea of where he was going, he ran as fast as his aching legs would carry him. In a few moments he found himself back on the road heading toward town.

He couldn't stay home, not right now. There were too many things happening in his head. Too much had gone on today. He was used to slow, quiet days when almost nothing happened to disrupt the routine of farm work—but today, *today* had turned into the worst day of his life. He couldn't fathom how it could get any worse.

Resolve rose up in his heart as he ran down the hill. He would find his father and prove the captain wrong. He had to. He would prove his father innocent if nobody else would.

Panting and out of breath, he burst across the plaza, heading down the western road, dust flying from beneath his sandals. He ignored the sting of the sharp rocks that occasionally bit into his feet. He had to keep going. The captain had to be wrong. His legs were burning and his chest heaved. He didn't think he had ever sprinted so fast and so far.

By the time he had reached the far edge of Hormul he couldn't run anymore. Slowly he came to a halt and hunched over with his arms on his thighs, trying to catch his breath. The road stretched ahead of him, leading far from the safety of Hormul to the world beyond. He stared at it blearily, his heart longing to continue his journey, his wobbly legs unable to take another step.

His brain supplied a host of arguments to combat the yearning in his heart. There was so much out there. So many new things to be afraid of. So many new things to hurt him. He remembered the stories his uncle told him of far and wondrous places, of scary monsters, dark castles, and vile men. Memories of hungry, rampaging orcs filled his mind, making him shiver as he had when they had attacked the caravan.

He couldn't move his feet forward. He couldn't go on. He couldn't leave Hormul. He was too afraid of the dangers out there. There was a war on; orcs could be behind every tree and every rock, trolls around every bend, ageless dragons circling hungrily in the sky.

Where would he begin the search for his father, anyway? The royal army had already failed to find him. Did he really think he could do better?

Remembering his uncle's face just now back in the cottage, Macal knew he couldn't leave him here all alone. Uncle Melkes would have nobody left. He would have been abandoned by everybody he loved: his sister, his brother-in-law, and now his nephew.

What could a small weak boy, one who couldn't even take on a hamlet's bully, hope to accomplish in a world teeming with savage creatures, danger, and war?

Standing in the stark moonlight, his world swirling in chaos about him, he saw a tall figure limping up the rough road ahead of him, making for a rundown cottage off to the side.

Macal recognized Lalliard right away. He had been to the wizard's house before. It was the last house on this side of the village, the farthest from the center of Hormul. Lalliard had once bluntly explained to him that he preferred to live as far as possible from the annoying people in town.

Looking down the endless road, Macal knew he couldn't leave Hormul. It was just one more failure on his long list. He couldn't even help his father, the man who had given him so much. He began to hate himself—for his weakness, for his small size, for his lack of courage, for everything.

At last he forced himself to move, not down the road, but toward the wizard's cottage. He needed to talk to somebody. Not his uncle; he would be kind and consoling, and right now the boy felt he didn't deserve kindness. He wanted harsh words. He wanted to be seen as he truly was. A part of him even wanted to find Menk again, to receive another beating that might dull the pain in his heart.

Hope had always seemed out of Macal's reach. Life hadn't offered him much, and he saw no reason why things should improve. Was that why he liked Lalliard so much? The old wizard didn't pretend the world was a happy place. He didn't utter lies about how wonderful everything was going be, and how it was all going to work out. The wizard had no qualms about saying exactly what he thought, with no concern for anyone's feelings or need for comfort.

Tonight Macal found a perverse comfort in that prospect. If he needed to know something, Lalliard would be as blunt and accurate as it was possible to be.

Macal ran toward the wizard's cottage, catching up with Lalliard just as he was about to enter his door. Distracted by his own thoughts, the gaunt, unshaven man seemed not to notice the boy until the last minute.

"Oh, it's you," Lalliard snapped. He seemed startled by the boy appearing out of the darkness beside him. Leaning heavily on his staff, favoring his right leg, he glared down at Macal. "What do you want? I don't have time for children. As a matter of fact, I hate children. Men. Women. The world. Ducks. Especially ducks. I hate it all. Leave me alone."

"Sire, it's about my father," Macal mumbled.

"I hate him too. And what did you call me?" The wizard spun to face the boy, icy blue eyes freezing Macal where he stood. "What have I told you about calling me that? Or master, or sir, or any of that pretentious dribble?"

"You said not to. Sorry."

"I doubt you really are," retorted the wizard without much conviction. "Isn't it a bit late for you to be wandering about? Aerinth is not as safe as it once was."

"Was it ever safe?" asked Macal in all seriousness.

The wizard considered the question for a moment. "Actually, probably not."

"My father has gone missing," said the boy at last, as if that explained everything.

"So what? I never even had a father. Things could be worse for you."

"The new captain of the Amber Dragoons says he's a traitor!" Macal burst out. "He says my father stole plans from the military to sell them to the trolls!"

"Well, the new captain is an idiot. Now go home. I have to feed my cats."

Macal took in his surroundings for the first time. There were cats everywhere. Dozens of them, lying on the steps of the house, curled on the sill of the open window, rustling in the bushes. He even saw one high up on the slanted thatched roof. From inside the house came the sound of claws being sharpened on the door.

"You like cats?" The boy was amazed. He had never seen so many cats, nor had he ever seen any at Lalliard's house before. He reached down to pet a calico that rubbed against his legs.

"Of course I do. That's a stupid question. Why else would they all be here? Unless they were pests like you, who just wouldn't go away. But to ease your startled mind, I *am* allowed to like some things," said the wizard haughtily as he opened his door. Candlelight spilled out into the night, softening the evening's dreary shadows. Several cats sauntered out to rub themselves against the hem of the wizard's robe. "What are you doing out this way, anyway? Plan on running after your father? Prove his innocence? You're better off going back home, then to sleep. Forget all about it. It will sort itself out."

"I can't!" shouted Macal, his voice raw with pain.

"Yes, you can." Lalliard turned on his threshold, fixing the boy with his chilly blue glare. "You just walk back across town to your cottage, go in, lie down, and sleep. There is nothing you can do about your father. If he is innocent of the crimes he is accused of, he will turn up eventually. Now be a good child for once, and leave me the hells alone."

Maybe Lalliard was right, thought Macal. Maybe he should just go home and try to sleep, although he wasn't sure his racing thoughts would let him. For a moment some small voice inside him whispered that maybe, just maybe, in the morning, things would be better.

Yes, Lalliard was right. He had just said the same things Macal was feeling. The boy realized then that he was truly helpless. There was nothing at all he could do to help his father.

Without an invitation he stepped into the cottage. Several cats, two orange ones and a black one, quickly came up to make his acquaintance, eager for affection. At the table in the center of the room, Lalliard was pulling chunks of chicken out of a covered bucket and tearing it apart with his hands, throwing the shreds onto a large wooden plate.

Macal surveyed the dirty room crowded with cats. He counted at least a dozen of various colors, sizes, and shapes. Several windows had been opened to let the night air into the room as an antidote to the musty smell inside.

In one corner a cluttered stairway led to the loft where the wizard slept. Next to the staircase was an open doorway revealing a small room overflowing with high stacks of books, some of them on the verge of toppling over. Even in the main room that acted as the wizard's scullery and common room, the shelves sagged under their weight of thick, dusty volumes. The number of tomes was matched only by the number of empty wine crocks scattered across the floor and piled in the corners.

"I get thirsty," explained Lalliard swiftly. He seemed slightly embarrassed as he noticed the boy eyeing the empty crocks.

Macal quickly changed the subject. "Why do you have so many cats?"

"Why not?" answered the wizard flatly. "And this way, it will be easier when one of them dies; I'll be distracted by caring for all the others."

"Did you name them all?" the boys asked in curiosity as he watched a couple of the cats jump onto the table while Lalliard prepared their dinner.

"No. Don't be stupid!" Noticing the confused look on the boy's face, the wizard added, "You have trees on your farm, don't you?"

"Yes." Macal was uncertain where this was going.

"Did you name all of *them?*"

"No!" answered Macal incredulously. "They're trees. Not cats. You don't name trees."

"You don't? Says who? Who made that rule?"

"I don't know," said the boy helplessly.

"Me neither. But trees are alive, just like cats. They are both living entities. They are born, grow, and eventually die. If you don't have to name one, you don't have to name the other. You don't name trees. I don't name cats. And anyway, how would I remember all their names?" expounded the wizard, as if that explained it all.

Macal looked around, ready to change the subject again. "You read a lot."

Lalliard continued to prepare the cats' evening meal. "Everybody should."

"I don't."

"You should."

"Why? There's no need. I've never needed books yet."

"Yes, and you can be stupid like the rest of the people in this horrible village. Great ambition you have. You've never used a sword before, have you?"

"No," answered Macal, unsure of where this was going or what it had to do with reading.

"I bet tonight, with your hopes and dreams of going out to find your father somewhere in the world, you wish you knew how to wield a sword. Don't you?"

"Yes," the boy said hesitantly.

"Well, there you go. Just because you don't need something right now, that doesn't mean you won't need it later."

Macal was considering this wizardly remark when loud shouts broke out in the village, shrill with alarm and distress. A moment later, cutting across the screams that tore through the night air, an echoing horn began to blow from the distant heart of town, rallying the men of the village to arms.

Macal ran to the window to see what was happening. Flinging open the shutters, he saw with horror his world being ravaged.

CHAPTER 4

F rom the window of the wizard's cottage, Macal could see a herd of massive creatures with long, crooked noses and thick olive skin covered in boils, warts, and scars stalking through the night, pouring out of the shadows of the northwest Rotelen woods.

"For gold and glory!" He could hear the brutes shouting as they lumbered forth.

To his horror he recognized these foul creatures. Although he had never actually seen anything so hideous and terrifying in all his life, he had heard enough to know that the trolls had come.

The monsters moved with amazing speed. Only a few moments before, the night had been quiet and placid; now it was fraught with panic and terror. Some of the creatures had two grotesque heads, some even three. The trolls had massive hands and feet with only four large gnarled fingers and toes. Most of them had tiny twisted plants and damp moss growing amid their rough greenish hair. All were bedecked in an array of colorful trinkets and jewels set in gold, silver, and platinum, hanging on chains, brooches, and bracelets, or set in rings, pendants, and amulets. The trolls looked as if they had raided a king's treasury, so bejeweled were they in diamonds, emeralds, rubies, onyx, pearls, peridot, sapphires, and other stones of every color and value. Macal assumed these were booty from the previous towns they had swept in search of spoils and blood.

He could see that several of the charging monsters only had one gigantic cruel eye centered in the middle of their bulbous dark faces, glaring at the world with a baleful visage while twinkling just like their stolen gems in the light of the large torches.

Lalliard joined Macal at the window, watching the trolls swarm from the forested hills to assault the town.

"They must have been following the troops, pillaging all the towns they've already passed through," said the wizard incredulously. "These are grave times, if the trolls are so deep within our borders."

The trolls were pouring into town just north of Lalliard's house. There were dozens and dozens of the rushing monsters, nearly ten feet tall and carrying large hatchets, notched axes, great cleaving swords, mighty spears, and gigantic clubs. Those who carried torches began lighting the cottages on fire as they charged into the village.

The assault was swift and deadly. Accompanying them were huge beasts, monstrosities that resembled furless oxen, their skin etched with innumerable thick, pulsing purple veins. The trolls and their beasts stampeded through wooden houses, tore down fences, and crushed cattle and anything else that stood in their way.

As the two watched from Lalliard's window, men from the village finally arrived and attempted to fend off the onslaught.

To Macal it seemed obvious that the meager force had no chance of success against the large raiding party. He could see children fleeing. He saw Loment, one of the local farmers, stand up to one of the two-headed monsters, a wood ax in his hand. The invading troll never flinched, paying no more attention to his adversary than a man confronted by an ant. With a great swing of his heavy club, he hit Loment so hard that, as far away as he was, Macal heard Loment's bones break. The sturdy farmer sailed fifteen feet through the air, smashed into a tree, and slumped unmoving to the ground.

Emerging from the rear of the assault force were trolls pulling heavy, wheeled wooden cages that creaked and groaned as they went. Laughing joyously, another of the rushing creatures grabbed Lomant's wife Anguelle and violently tossed her into a cage he was pulling.

Lalliard's cottage was at the very fringe of town, and by some miracle it had escaped the trolls' notice. From the wizard's window Macal watched in bleak fascination as his village was torn apart by the raid. Children and men were dying everywhere. Women were tossed into cages. Cattle and sheep lowed and bleated frantically as terror overtook them, too. Released from their broken corrals, many sped off into the dark night, fleeing from the pandemonium wrought by the trolls.

More and more men were now flocking to the sound of the horrible invasion, some with shabby, poor weapons, and others with whatever they could find: pitchforks, hoes, and scythes. It was obvious that they were no match for the well-equipped invaders.

As the endless stream of trolls rushed down the hill and into the skirmish, their sickly smell became overwhelming. It was as if they had never bathed; even from a distance, Macal nearly gagged at the stench. Soon, however, the smell of smoke and burning obliterated their foul odor.

It had all happened so quickly. Lalliard and Macal could hear horses whinnying around the village, people screaming and crying and calling for help. There were grunts and battle oaths from the attacking trolls, hoarse orders shouted by their troll commander.

The quiet village of Hormul had been transformed into a nightmare of chaos and fear, of unfamiliar sights and disgusting smells and dreadful sounds, now forever unforgettable. Some families, in pure despair, had already begun fleeing east to avoid the unstoppable slaughter.

As Macal watched, only one coherent thought crept in his head. *Was Uncle Melkes all right?*

Abruptly he came to a decision. With no concern for his own safety, without a word, he ran out the door and off into the night.

He had to find his uncle. He had to find his uncle and they would run away together, to where, Macal didn't know. They could go east past Bronel, or even farther if necessary. It didn't matter, as long as they were safe. They could start a new life anywhere, as long as it wasn't here.

"Wait!" shouted Lalliard as Macal dashed past him and ran off into the war-torn night, amid the death cries and the raging trolls. The boy didn't listen. He had only his uncle on his mind. And if there was one thing Macal knew how to do well, it was run.

"Imbecile," cursed Lalliard as he watched Macal disappear down the road, heading into the thick of the fray.

Reluctantly, after a few seconds' hesitation, the wizard gave a great resigned sigh and ran out into the turmoil after the boy.

On the far side of town Uncle Melkes heard the shouts of alarm. He heard the horn echoing through the valley calling for aid. With worry he looked around for Macal. For the first time as the sounds outside shook him from his shocked stupor, Uncle Melkes realized that his nephew had not come back from fetching him water. Not certain what the alarm was about he called out for Macal. He didn't see him anywhere.

Uncle Melkes began to put the pieces together. He realized Macal must have overheard what had been said. He called to him again desperately hoping for a response. He needed to talk to the boy. He wanted to try to explain what might really be happening with his father.

Getting no reply, the old man ran out of the farmhouse and looked towards the town at the bottom of the hill and nearly fell to his knees, stunned by the horrible scene.

The town was ablaze with fire, lighting it up so brightly that is shone like a sun. He looked in disbelief. What was going on? How could this happen here? Who was doing it? And most importantly, where was Macal?

Could he be down there in that carnage?

Uncle Melkes had seen frightful things in his life, back when he was a soldier, but none were more dreadful than the sight of his village being turned into a fiery ruin. Rarely had he ever seen such devastation. He prayed to all the gods, to any god, who would listen, that Macal was nowhere near any of this.

He rushed back into the house and into his room. He threw back the dusty lid of the Elronian military footlocker at the base of his bed and he grabbed his short sword.

Macal is out there somewhere. I have to find him.

It was the only responsibility he had left in this world. When his sister was dying she had asked him, made him promise, to care for her husband and child. It looked like he may have failed her on her husband, he couldn't let himself also fail on Macal.

Hefting the sword into his strong weathered hand he felt the coldness, pain, and blood that the blade had wrought in its years of use. He couldn't remember how long it had been since he had held this forged steel. When he had left the army he had hoped never to need to wield it again. He had hoped never to shed blood again. Bearing arms was something that he had hoped had passed from his life.

Then an old, familiar anger welled up in the passive man; if whatever was attacking his village hurt Macal he vowed he would make them suffer. That boy was his life. The best family he could ask for. He held the hilt of his sword so tightly that only death was going to tear it from his grasp.

He needed to find Macal, he needed to save him, whatever it took.

Standing back up, Uncle Melkes left the house and ran towards town shouting for his nephew.

CHAPTER 5

Macal ran toward the farm. Behind him he could hear Lalliard shouting after him. He ignored the wizard as he dashed in between cottages trying to avoid notice of the town's assailants. Soon Lalliard's futile calls were lost amid the din of the battle. He knew the wizard wouldn't be able to keep up with him, not when hindered by the limp in his leg.

Skirmishes were happening all about Macal. Fires were bursting to life. Screams of pain, fear, anguish, and sorrow had enveloped the place. Man, beast, and troll ran wildly, amidst their many battles.

Macal sped around another stone cottage and, before he could stop himself, right into the leg of a large troll. The impact with the monster knocked Macal off his feet and he fell onto his back.

The troll had two heads, each with only one enormous yellow eye. The monster was heavily bedecked in colorful shiny riches, draped with golden and platinum necklaces and also several bracelets which it wore as rings.

The troll looked down in surprise and howled in pleasure at its find.

Now that he saw a troll up close Macal could see that their bodies were made of more than just flesh and skin, but also of rock or deformed bone. Instinctively the troll reached towards Macal with a slimy hand that had jagged rocks jutting up from its knuckles.

"Come 'ere, good boy," it said with a wicked smile as it bared its large pointed yellow teeth. Its voice was gruff and echoed as if he were bellowing in a cavern. "I want me some boy bones! I want to chew on 'em! Come to me little one. I won't hurt ya much!"

Uncle Melkes' stomach was queasy with worry as he descended the hill and approached the village center. Soon he was close enough to see what was happening. It was unimaginable! *So many trolls, this far into the kingdom?* His blood went cold as he saw the scope of the destruction.

To his right, near Gorn's cottage, he caught movement in a small copse of trees. One of the foul monsters was lurking in the shadows. Certain the troll had seen him too, Melkes knew the creature was waiting for the chance to waylay him.

He needed to find his nephew, but he couldn't leave the monster alive to hurt others. There was no time to waste. He turned and marched directly toward the troll.

"Comin' to me, pretty thing?" The troll sounded astonished; rarely had it been challenged by a human. Melkes said nothing as it emerged from the trees, its full girth and might revealed by the flickering light of the burning village. The troll carried a huge two-handed axe. Several human skulls dangled like beads from its thick leather belt, trophies of its victims.

"If any of those are my nephew's..." Uncle Melkes' voice trailed off as he took in the true size of the monster before him.

The troll laughed as it stalked forward, the horrible trinkets clinking softly on its belt. "I don't fear you, little man!"

Uncle Melkes held his blade confidently in his right hand. He didn't fear the troll either. He had fought many battles against these creatures, and he hadn't forgotten any of his old tricks.

With a great lunge the troll attacked, its mighty overhead stroke aimed directly at Uncle Melkes' head.

By some miracle Macal was able to scramble to his feet and duck sideways as the troll lumbered forward to snatch him up. The boy felt a breeze as the creature's massive swipe swept past his head. He fled around the corner of another building, hearing the thud of the troll's feet behind him, but almost at once the creature seemed to tire of the chase.

Macal was off once more, heart pounding in his chest. He sprinted past more cottages, ran across the Crawlems' fields, and wove through a cluster of apple trees. Emerging from the copse, he saw a group of trolls up ahead.

"There!" shouted one of the marauders to his companions. Macal stumbled on a fallen apple and came to a halt.

"He's mine," snarled one of the two heads of a second troll, lifting his torch high and moving his great bulk in the boy's direction.

"I saw 'im first," shouted the first troll. Immediately he joined the chase, furious at the possibility of losing his meal to another.

"I only want a leg," said the third hungrily.

Macal's eyes widened in terror as the three monsters headed toward him. He turned and raced back the way he had come, searching for somewhere to hide. A few cottages back, an overturned hay wagon offered a refuge and he dove under it, hoping there had been enough distance between him and the trolls to prevent them from seeing his hiding place.

As the trolls came in sight, the second one pointed to a battered cottage across the way. "He's in there." It waited for the others to charge the small structure, then swung its deadly gaze toward Macal. Baleful and yellow, the single eye in each of its two heads locked onto the boy crouched beneath the broken wagon.

"I'm gonna eat your fingers first," announced the first head as the troll moved closer.

"And," the second added hungrily, "I'll eat your little toes."

As the troll closed in on him, Macal looked frantically for somewhere to run. Then, without warning, the troll tossed his torch onto the wagon. Instantly the half-spilled hay burst into flame. "Where ya gonna go now, rabbit?" asked one of the heads maliciously, as its tongue slithered out and licked its grotesque purple lips.

The cacophony of battle was everywhere, but beneath the burning wagon Macal could hear the monster laughing wickedly.

Uncle Melkes barely had time to jump to one side as the troll's axe descended, splitting the earth where he had stood. Seizing the initiative, he swung his aged sword into the troll's unguarded flank. It sliced into the brute's meaty ribs as it tried to pull its axe free from the soil.

The troll bellowed in pain and turned startled orange eyes upon the old soldier. With its savage companions, it had followed the returning army. They had stormed through many towns, destroying each one as they went, and never before had one of the humans so deftly wounded it. Rage and agony overtook the fiend.

"You cannot win! The trolls will prevail! Our borders will grow as your blood spills! None will stop the Troll King!" the monster roared. With a bellowing war cry, it tore the axe free from the ground and sent it swinging at its adversary. Uncle Melkes ducked under the blade, the axe slicing through the air just above his head.

The mighty swing had brought the troll around to face him and the old swordsman attacked again, this time thrusting his sword into the thing's monstrous gut. The weathered blade slid through the slick green skin, bringing a gush of black blood from the wound. Uncle Melkes leaned on the sword, forcing the blade deeper and deeper until he felt it pop out the beast's back.

Howling, the troll fell to its knees. As it tumbled over, the blade was wrenched from Uncle Melkes' hands. Instinctively he reached for it, but the troll batted his hand away, accidentally striking the hilt of the antique weapon in passing, snapping the blade and sending the broken hilt flying.

The troll lay writhing and roaring in pain, the blade of the sword now embedded inside it. Uncle Melkes turned away from the fallen creature's agonized death throes as it bellowed out prayers for salvation to Orktissa, the Troll God. He doubted it was capable of doing any more harm.

But what now? Assuming he could find Macal, how could he save him without a weapon? He considered using the troll's axe but quickly dismissed the idea; it would be far too large and heavy for him to wield properly. Retrieving the remainder of his sword, he saw there were only four or five inches of the steel still attached to the hilt. Barely a weapon, it was all he had.

With no other thought than finding Macal, Uncle Melkes continued warily towards the plaza.

On his hands and knees, Macal crawled out from under the back side of the wagon, where it leaned against the wall of a cottage. He scurried through the shadows, making it around the side of a building just as the troll seized a corner of the burning wagon and hurled it over on its side with a thunderous crash, spilling burning hay everywhere.

Macal wasn't sure if the troll had seen him, but he wasn't going to wait to find out. He had to find his uncle. Once more he ran, desperately hoping that Uncle Melkes was still safely at home and not one of the many corpses lying in the dirt around him. So far he had already jumped over several unmoving bodies. Each time he risked a downward glance, praying not to see his uncle. So far, his pleas to the gods had been answered.

The doorway of the cottage just ahead stood wide open. As fast as he could, Macal ducked into the house to hide from the hungry troll. In one dim corner of the interior, to his surprise he saw two little girls whimpering and cowering in the protective arms of their mother. Although they were several years younger than he, Macal knew these girls. Like their mother, both were rather pretty, slender and delicate, with long red hair and dazzling green eyes. One was named Aloria and the other was Silvellin. Neither had been a friend to Macal. Like the other children in the village, they were intimidated by Menk's fearsome fists.

The boy wondered where their father was. He too had been away at the war in the Amber Dragoons regiment. Could he be one of the many bodies lying dead outside in the fields and on the roads? Suddenly Macal realized he couldn't stay here. He couldn't endanger these people by exposing their hiding place to the troll. He knew he couldn't live with himself if he caused any harm to come to them, even if in the past they hadn't troubled to be kind to him. Outside he could hear the troll stamping across the grass.

Then he heard his uncle's familiar voice calling, reaching him somehow over the commotion of the battle, a harmonious note in the cacophony of warfare. Relief swept over him. His uncle was alive! As quickly as it had come, the rush of relief subsided. Time was running out if he was going to spare these girls and their mother a horrifying fate.

With a last desperate look at their frightened, teary faces, Macal knew what he had to do. What choice did he have? He couldn't let the troll find them.

Ignoring the fact that his uncle was so close, Macal did the only thing he could. He ran back outside, right into the arms of the waiting troll.

Uncle Melkes attacked the first troll he saw as he entered the edge of the plaza. There were plenty to choose from. He kept shouting for Macal, desperate to hear his nephew's voice, but so far only echoes of his own cries had come back to him.

He slashed at the troll, his broken blade only grazing his opponent. It was a monstrous beast even larger than the one he had confronted earlier. Nearly half the creature's body was covered with a rocklike substance that blended with its skin. Melkes had forgotten how foul smelling the vicious behemoths were. He gagged as he withdrew his weapon.

This troll had a thick sword of rough steel, which he swung deftly at the retired soldier. Uncle Melkes tried to parry with his feeble weapon, but the force behind the attack was so great that he was only able to deflect it slightly. Instead of cleaving off his head, the sword sliced cruelly into his shoulder. The blow staggered him back. His free hand reached up to cover the gash in his shoulder. With his sword hand he did his best to hold his weapon in front of him.

"Don't worry, you'll bleed more soon!" taunted the rock-skinned troll, as it raised its sword for another attack.

Had his sword not been broken, Uncle Melkes knew he could have avoided the injury. Without a blade, even the best swordsman in the world was helpless. He desperately needed to find a new weapon if he wanted to survive out here, but right now he didn't think the troll was going to give him that opportunity.

He needed to find Macal soon. Ignoring his adversary's boasting, he raised his voice and called the boy's name as the troll swung its heavy sword again. Melkes had just enough time to jump back, avoiding the monstrous weapon's cleaving arc.

He tried a retaliatory strike against the troll's arm, but the creature was quick; avoiding the feeble stab, it rushed at him again, this time aiming for his legs. He knew parrying with his broken sword was futile, so Uncle Melkes once more tried to dodge the strike, but the attack was too clean and swift. He felt the sharp edge of the sword bite into his calf, through the muscle, right to the bone.

The force of the blow swept him off his feet. The old soldier fell heavily on his side. He cried out in pain as he hit the hard earth. The troll wasted no time. A victorious grin twisted its cruel face as it moved in, sword held aloft, preparing to plunge the blade through the man's heart.

In desperation Melkes thrust what was left of his sword deep into the troll's unprotected calf, inflicting a wound nearly identical to his own. He left the blade buried in the monster as it yowled in agony.

The pain momentarily drove everything else from the troll's mind. Forgetting its attack, it reached down to pull the stinging blade free. Uncle Melkes was waiting. He yanked his eating knife from his belt. As the troll bent down, he slashed the monster's neck with all the strength he could muster. It was a tactic he had used in the past, and he was happy to see the small thin blade save his life once more.

The creature coughed and began to choke on its own blood, shock and horror filling its bulging eyes as it realized what had happened. Clutching its neck to stem the flow of black blood, it swayed on its feet. Uncle Melkes rolled out from underneath just as the monster toppled and landed with a heavy thud.

Melkes rose slowly to his feet and looked around. His calls for his nephew and his battle with the troll had not gone unnoticed. To his misfortune, several other trolls had witnessed his unexpected victory. Their morale fortified by numbers, four trolls surrounded the injured swordsman, whose only defense was his small knife.

CHAPTER 6

G ot ya!" snarled one of the troll's heads as its great hands locked around Macal's arms.

"Remember, I get the toes," reminded the other head with a leer at Macal. "They're so good to chew on."

The first head seemed indifferent. "You can have the whole legs for all I care. I just want the fingers."

Macal struggled to break free, but he might as well have been trying to pick up a mountain. The troll's grip felt like a vise of dwarven steel.

"Let me pull off his fingers first," demanded the first head.

"No," said the second. "I caught him. I get his legs first."

"*I'm* hungry. I haven't eaten in days!" shouted the first head.

"Me neither!" retorted the other. "It's the same stomach!"

Macal cried out in terror as the bickering troll heads struggled for control of their shared body. He was jostled about like a tiny doll in their hands. All his aches and pains from Menk's relentless beating came alive again.

"Uncle Melkes!" cried Macal desperately, remembering he had heard his uncle's voice not far away. "Save me! Please, Uncle Melkes!" His only comfort was knowing that he was sparing the family inside the cottage the terrible fate that he was suffering. It wasn't much, but at the moment it was all he had.

"Fine," the first troll head conceded reluctantly. "Just hurry up and pull the little wiggly legs off. But I get the rest of 'im!"

"Please don't," begged Macal. "I want to keep my legs!"

"Of course you do, but so does he." The first head nodded at the second, which was drooling in anticipation as it started to pull roughly on Macal's right leg.

"But I think," interrupted a gruff, annoyed voice behind them, "the boy might want them just a little more than you do."

"Wha—?" began one of the startled troll heads. The monster spun around to see who was interfering with its meal, bringing the speaker into Macal's line of sight.

Lalliard stood there defiantly, his staff in his left hand, his faded blue robes splattered heavily with black troll gore. In his other hand was a coalescing sphere of pulsing purple energy, illuminating the wizard with its mesmerizing glow. His face was like hard stone chiseled into a permanent angry glare. Above thin, firm lips his sharp nose jutted fiercely from his face. As always, his prematurely white hair was in a state of disarray, and his thick eyebrows hung so heavily that they looked as if they might collapse onto of his icy blue eyes.

"Drop the boy," ordered the wizard.

"We will no—" began the first head in refusal, but it was cut off as Lalliard hurled the magical sphere, striking it dead on. It exploded in a burst of blinding violet that subsided to a hiss like acid on metal.

The second head screamed in unimaginable pain. Macal wondered how many creatures could lose a head and still be alive to deal with the pain. The wounded monster's roaring was so loud it hurt his ears, and the explosion had left colored spots dancing before his eyes. The next moment, released by the distracted troll, he tumbled to the ground. He rolled clear and got to his knees, blinking to clear his vision.

The head Lalliard had targeted was no longer there; the troll's hands groped for its missing companion, finding only empty space, while the remaining head stared in horrified disbelief.

It was all too much for Macal; he couldn't believe what he was seeing. He had never witnessed such magic, only paltry tavern tricks in which a nomadic magician might conjure a common imp. Above him, the troll continued to scream in pain.

Then, behind the harsh screams, came the sound of a familiar voice: Uncle Melkes, calling his name. Once more Macal's legs commandeered his body. Even if his mind was temporarily stunned, they knew what to do. Without hesitation he jumped up and ran toward his uncle's voice.

"*Wait!*" commanded Lalliard, but again Macal ignored him. The troll, recovering from its shock and bent on revenge, suddenly charged the wizard.

"I should have let you rip off the boy's legs," said the frustrated wizard as the troll closed in on him. This level of activity was far more than Lalliard cared for. The more energy he had to expend to chase the boy, the angrier he got. The wizard chose another clay rune from his pouch. Calmly confronting the ravening troll, he cast another spell.

"Natura Gronusiha!" he intoned, extending his hand to touch the approaching monster's chest. The enchanted rune flared and turned to ash, fueling the spell. Tendrils of magic seeped from the wizard's outstretched fingers. As the magic net made contact with the troll, its strands swarmed over the brute's body. What had once been a two-headed troll of flesh, blood, and bone was instantly transformed into stone.

The troll statue retained its momentum. Casually Lalliard sidestepped as it toppled heavily forward and smashed into fragments on the hard-packed earth.

Grudgingly, the wizard turned to see which way Macal had gone.

In the plaza Uncle Melkes finally stopped shouting for Macal as the group of trolls closed in on him. He knew it was too late. There were far too many trolls for him to handle on his own, and he didn't want his nephew to see what was to come.

He couldn't help notice that his ability to singlehandedly destroy one of the marauders had caught the attention of the most powerful and skilled trolls. While he appreciated the compliment for what it was, he now wished he had chosen a different tactic.

As the menacing raiders surrounded him, wielding clubs, wicked axes, and sharp spears, a single tear escaped the weary old man's eye and slid down his stubbled cheek. The tear was not from pain, or fear of what was about to happen to him. It was for his nephew. He loved Macal so dearly that it hurt him more than any physical wound to think that if he didn't get out of this alive, the boy would be alone the rest of his life.

There was still so much he wanted to teach Macal. So much he wanted to say, so many stories he had left to tell. His heart ached at the thought that he would never get the chance.

Suddenly, as if the angels themselves had gifted him with one final glance, he saw Macal burst onto the far side of the war torn plaza. More tears filled Uncle Melkes' eyes as he saw his young nephew take stock of the situation. Of all the things he had wished, he most wished he could have spared Macal this moment.

The first troll attacked, thrusting forward with a long spear thick as man's wrist, its metal head so sharp it could pierce the stoutest mail. Not prepared to die yet, Uncle Melkes sidestepped the attack and slashed the troll's finger with his meager knife, inflicting a small cut. The troll barely seemed to notice the scratch.

Macal's body went rigid as he stared across the plaza. Around the wide-open area there were several skirmishes going on. Nearly all the buildings were on fire. Just in front of the Waywitch he could swear he saw Captain Jengus fighting for his life against a hulking troll beast. Even closer to where he stood, a knot of local men, some with swords and a couple with just pitchforks, were working together to take down a single troll. He saw soldiers who had come home only tonight raising sword and shield against the invaders.

He even saw the fat merchant who had beaten his horse, fleeing the burning wreckage of the Waywitch as it was set alight, only to be caught and slaughtered by a waiting troll.

Everything else was a blur of discord and confusion. It was as if Macal himself were no longer in the plaza, but a shadow, a wraith, invisible and unaffected as he watched the inevitable doom take over his world. He could see his uncle fighting, armed only with a useless little knife. The separate skirmishes were like pieces of a puzzle, and Macal could see the final shape. He knew there was no way his uncle was going to survive.

Another troll, this one with a well-worn axe, was attempting to finish Uncle Melkes off. By now the he was exhausted and weak. The wound in his leg had bled too much, making him feel faint.

But a new resolve suddenly flooded Uncle Melkes, filling him with vitality. He couldn't let Macal see this. He had to win; he had no choice. He couldn't leave his nephew alone in the world. Ignoring the pain of his wounds, he dove under the arcing swing of the troll's axe, rolled, and brought himself up against its legs.

Quickly, desperately, he plunged his knife into the creature's stomach, then pulled it out and thrust again and again. Small as they were, the wounds were painful, and the troll screamed each time the knife penetrated its skin.

He was not going to die here, Melkes vowed. Not with Macal watching. Grimly and efficiently he ducked through the troll's tall legs. As the beast began to turn toward him, he cut cleanly through the flesh of one of its ankles, right through the supporting muscle.

No longer able to stand, his adversary fell with a crash, its booty of jewels and trinkets spilling across the ground. Uncle Melkes kept moving. There wasn't time to admire his handiwork. Although the fallen troll wasn't mortally wounded, it could no longer maneuver. All Melkes had to do was stay clear of its grasp while dealing with the others.

Wanting to run and help his uncle, Macal found that he couldn't make his body move. He didn't know if he feared for himself or for his uncle. As he saw Uncle Melkes take down the troll, a spark of hope ignited in the boy's heart.

Uncle Melkes' success so far had given him a little confidence, and he readied himself for the next troll. The one nearest him was wielding a great club in its meaty hands. He would defeat them one by one, he told himself.

He had another trick in mind for this one. Limping out of reach of the fallen troll, he prepared himself. It was just a matter of timing. Waiting for the creature to wind up its swing, he risked a loving glance at his nephew. The next moment his opportunity arrived. He dashed forward with all the speed he could muster, ready to leap up and stab the troll in the eye.

But this troll was familiar with such tricks. With a speed that surprised the retired soldier, it brought its club hurtling around just as he leapt off the ground. The heavy club struck Uncle Melkes in midair. The attack couldn't have been more perfect. The force of the blow caused the old man's body to break and sail more than ten feet through the air and land crumpled in the dirt.

The other trolls swarmed over the fallen, motionless body, their weapons exacting a quick and savage revenge.

"For gold and glory!" one chanted in demonic pleasure.

"And *skulls!*" another bellowed victoriously.

Macal's heart exploded in his chest. As he watched them kill his uncle he screamed in torment. The anguished sound rose above the battle din, piercing the night as if in defiance of the heavens themselves. For a moment all commotion in the plaza stopped as every being turned to find the source of the powerful, harrowing cry.

Macal stood there, his tear-filled eyes wide with disbelief, his mouth open and his body rigid. His heart beat so turbulently that he could not catch his breath.

His mind screamed. *Uncle Melkes can't be dead! He wouldn't leave me here alone!*

But he had seen his uncle's face as he spun through the air. He had seen his shock, grief, and pain. In shock a comforting gray cloud instinctually rose up from his subconscious and shrouded the boy, and promised to protect him from the trauma of what he had witnessed.

The combat halted only a fraction of a second before the sound of clanging steel, sundered shields, and blows on flesh rose up once more. But Macal's scream had drawn attention to him.

"There is my boy bones!" squealed a troll entering the plaza behind him. Shaken from his dark reverie, the boy turned toward the creature with blank eyes. It was the very first troll he had seen tonight, back near Lalliard's house. The part of his mind that still functioned could only assume the monster had been following him all this time.

"Brought me right to you, you have. Just give me yer bones, that's all I want. *You* can keeps the rest of you." It laughed, revealing a maw of razor sharp teeth.

Behind Macal, Uncle Melkes' blood pooled on the dirt of the plaza amid the burning ruins of Hormul.

The bone-chewing troll charged Macal. Even in the surreal haze that clouded the boy's mind, he knew he had to run if he wanted to live. He forced himself to move, not knowing where he was going, not caring. He had to get away from here. Away from the thoughts and the memories of this night, everything that had tainted his quiet life.

His body aching with bruises, his face caked with dried blood and his heart sinking into a black abyss, he ran north towards the deep woods. At that moment, when all the trolls were in the village, it was the only place he could imagine that might be safe. With every painful stride, images of Uncle Melkes flashed across his mind. Every step brought more tears to his eyes.

After the news about his father, he hadn't been able to imagine that anything worse could happen him. Menk had beat him up, but he could live with that; he was used to it. While it was humiliating and painful, he would endure a lifetime of them if it would take away either the news of his father or what had just happened to his uncle.

It wasn't fair, he said to himself. *How could so many bad things happen in such little time? And why to him? What had he done to deserve this?*

What in his life had ever gone right? He had never known his mother. He was picked on by every child in the village. His father was missing, accused of being a traitor. His village was destroyed and his uncle was gone forever.

It wasn't fair, he cried again with all his heart.

Somewhere behind him, he knew, the troll was still following, he could hear it. As he cleared the cluster of cottages and reached a grassy meadow that led to the woods, he risked a look back. Not only was the bone-feasting troll in pursuit, but it had been joined by several of the brutes that had attacked Uncle Melkes. They seemed determined to leave no survivors. Macal could only guess they wanted to ensure no one was left to warn other towns of future raids.

He didn't know where to go once he reached the woods. He only knew he couldn't stay here any longer. Hormul was no longer the safe place it had always been. His uncle was no longer there to care for him.

The trolls were gaining on him. There were moments they came so close that he could feel their fetid breath on the back of his neck, but the rough field offered uneven footing, and they were already near exhaustion from their indulgence of destruction. Macal, on the other hand, was a practiced runner. He fled across the familiar meadow as he would a smooth road, spurred on by the bellowing war cries and malign oaths of the monsters behind him.

The woods just ahead were dark, the moonlight blocked by a dense canopy of leaves and branches that clustered together to form a sky of vegetation. Blindly Macal entered the rustling darkness.

Arms outstretched to keep from colliding with the trees, he stumbled over brambles and roots. Behind him the sounds of pursuit diminished as the trolls found themselves hampered by the difficulty of navigating their way through the close-growing trees. Macal kept running. He didn't know how much time had passed or where he was going. Did it matter? Only gradually did he realize that the heavy tread of his monstrous pursuers had died away, leaving him alone in the deep woods.

He could only assume that the trolls, upon reflection, had realized a single boy could not do them much harm now. A single boy, lost in the vast reaches of the dense and dangerous Rotelen Woods.

He had to agree. *What could a single small, scared boy do?*

"For gold and glory!" The motto of the trollkin came back to him. They wouldn't want to miss out on the dividing of spoils and village treasures once the final pockets of resistance had been destroyed. Let their greed save him. He didn't care. He ran until he was on the verge of collapsing from exhaustion, then crumpled sobbing to his knees. All his emotions were heightened to a pitch he had never experienced before. He longed for his uncle so badly he could scarcely breathe, a longing he knew could never be satisfied again. He was overcome with pity for himself, for everything that had happened. Scared and alone, desperate for his pain to go away, he wished he could make himself feel nothing at all.

A dark thought slowly crept into his mind. His uncle had been in the center of the village calling for *him!* His uncle had only been there because he was trying to find him. The pieces snapped together like the jaws of a trap. If it weren't for him, his uncle would have never been in town. He wouldn't be dead.

It was my fault! Uncle Melkes was dead because of me!

The realization twisted inside him like a knife. Had he just stayed home and not run off, he and Uncle Melkes could have easily fled the village before the trolls reached their farm. His uncle was dead only because of what Macal had chosen to do. He could have prevented this. The farm would have been lost, but what did that matter in comparison to their lives? Together they could have found out what had happened with his father.

Scenario after scenario played through the boy's mind. Everything that could have been, had he only done things a little differently.

Mustering what strength he could, he got to his feet. He needed rest and time to think. He knew enough about the dreary woods to know he shouldn't stay where he was, easy prey to the hungry animals that made their home here. Searching through a darkness that seemed as bright as the sun compared to the void in his heart, his hands encountered the thick trunk of a tree. He gathered the last reserves of his endurance and climbed until he was high off the ground. At last he found a branch broad enough to hold him safely while he rested. Climbing onto it, he nestled into a kitten-like ball to keep warm.

Alone in the dark, high in a tree, Macal began to pray to all the gods for forgiveness, even though he wasn't sure any were listening.

There were many gods in the world. One for dragons, one for wanderers, another for trolls; one for demons and one for war. As far as Macal could tell, there was a god for nearly everything. Uncle Melkes had taught him that there was a time when the mortals of the world had worshipped the gods, and enjoyed in turn the boons and graces the gods bestowed upon them. That was before the evil Lumar Or'lmar had banished the right of religious practice.

The Lumar Or'lmar were an ageless race that possessed more power than any kingdom of men, goblins, or even giants. The malevolent smile that seemed to be locked permanently upon their faces had no joy behind it. Their skin was the blue gray of a corpse; their legs tapered off below the knee into wisps of abyssal smoke. Their decree against religion weakened the gods. The fewer prayers the gods received, the less their power was fueled. This was the purpose the Lumar Or'lmar had set out to achieve. They wanted to keep the gods weak. Eventually, without their aid to the mortals of the world, the Lumar themselves would conquer all of Aerinth.

Macal didn't care about the Lumar now. It meant nothing to him to break their decree. He didn't care about anything. As he fell asleep he murmured prayer after prayer, hoping that some god out there was still listening. Hoping he could be forgiven for Uncle Melkes' death.

CHAPTER 7

F ar beneath the rich soil of the forest, below jagged cavernous chambers and under ancient tunnels, deep in a dank cave a Morgog slept. Morgogs were creatures of myth and legend. Woodweavers, there were able to bend and command trees to their will.

The Morgog's lower body was that of a hairy centipede nearly twelve feet in length, supported by hundreds of wriggling, malachite-hued legs. His upper body was that of a muscular man. From the forearms down, his arms were covered in thick but supple bark, his fingers hard as the strongest maple. The Morgog's single eye was located at the end of a long, flexible, olive-colored stem that swiveled back and forth, allowing him to see in all directions. He had no nose, save for three small vertical slits in his face that throbbed as the creature's lungs sucked in air. The Morgog's mouth held an array of needlelike teeth and a prehensile snaky tongue. Greasy, snarled black hair covered his head and cascaded the length of its back.

Once, like many of his kin, he had served the Druids of Ish. The Druid priests had employed great incantations and rites to summon the Morgog race across the planes of existence from their homeland in the bowels of Perlemia, the Plane of Wood and Earth. The Druids had hoped to force the creatures to aid in the care and protection of the woodlands and all those within, but their ancient plan had been flawed. The Morgog had become the plague and bane of what they had been summoned to protect.

The Morgog proved to be slovenly creatures. The merest exertion tired and bored them except, it seemed, when it offered the chance to act against their captors. The Druid priests were unable to maintain control of those they had called forth. Dozens of Morgog eventually broke free from their conjurors, slaying what priests they could. Fleeing their imprisonment, they spread out all across Aerinth.

The Druids were still making amends for their folly. It had become part of the initiation into the druidical circle to recapture a Morgog and send them back to the bleak plane of existence from which they came. Once, these strange creatures had been called upon to serve. Now, when the opportunity arose, the Morgog sought to bend and break the will of their would-be captors, reversing the roles of master and servant. They remained in the darkness, biding their time, waiting for anyone they could force into bewitched servitude.

Rel-Jimore, the Morgog below the Rotelon Woods, had slept for countless years. Possessing a nearly endless lifespan, he seldom felt the need to stir from his slumber. But as the trees whispered tales of a presence nearby, at long last the Morgog awoke.

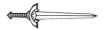

Macal's tired mind was adrift in haunting, distant dreams. A watery image of his uncle's face appeared in waves that rolled over him again and again, threatening to push him under. Each wave drenched him with guilt. The more soaked he became, the deeper he sank into the ocean. He struggled to stay afloat, but the guilt was too heavy and he sank into the depths, the crushing weight bearing him inexorably down.

Now the churning water of guilt became animated with an endlessly repeated scene of his uncle dying. Macal tried to look away, but no matter where he turned the vision followed, even when he closed his eyes. He could see his uncle flying through the air, anguish contorting his face, his body limp as it hit the ground. Over and over the scene flowed through his mind, borne upon the water like debris from a shipwreck.

Macal tried to swim back to the surface of the drowning ocean, to escape its endless torment, to wake and drive the guilt away, but the more he fought, the deeper he sank. The ocean's strength was too great to overcome. His arms flailed uselessly in the current; his legs kicked futilely in the unforgiving abyss. No matter what he did, he couldn't escape his guilt. He was alone. He had come here alone, and alone he would stay. Of all the emotions he felt, trapped beneath the rolling salty water, nothing scared him more than being by himself.

Somewhere deep within his mind, an unknown part of him awoke. Never before had this part of his personality been conscious; never before had it felt the need to come to life. As it awoke, a new vision took over Macal's watery dreams. This one was of his father.

The new voice talked to him, shaping new images upon the churning water, voicing what the rest of his mind had been afraid to say.

"What can possibly be left of the village?" it asked, and Macal knew it was right. His home was no longer the safe place he had always loved. Now it

was like the rest of the world, torn by war, ravaged by greed.

"Hormul is now vulnerable, tainted by war," the voice continued without compassion. Macal bit his lip. Even if the trolls had not come, how long would it have been before the Lumar took over? Whatever sense of safety he had felt had been false. He had never been safe. Never. It had been only a matter of time.

"If you can't go to Hormul, where will you go?" queried the voice. *"What will you do?"*

Macal began to realize where the voice was leading him. He knew it before the words were spoken. His uncle could not possibly have survived. He could not go back to Hormul.

"All you have left," the voice said, *"is your father."*

He knew this newly awakened part of himself was right. "He's all I have left," said the rest of him in agreement. "I need him. I'm too afraid to be alone."

"You have to find him," said the voice.

"I—I have to find him," echoed Macal fearfully. As he came to this realization, the swirling waters of guilt eased their hold. With flailing arms and kicking legs, he fought his way back to the distant surface, finally breaking free of the frigid water. He knew he had found a purpose, but he also knew that even though he was temporarily free of the water, guilt would chill his soul until the end of his days.

And at any time, it could pull him back under.

The Morgog slithered out of his gloomy cave, leaving a slimy trail in his wake. Emerging to the surface, he sniffed the evening air. He had nearly forgotten such freshness existed. In utter silence he crept over the fallen leaves, vines, and underbrush, his bark-covered hands writhing in anticipation. *Soon he would have a servant again.*

The creature could not remember how long it had been since his last servant had died, but it hardly mattered. Spying his new prize slumbering aloft on a branch, Rel-Jimore slithered closer and began an age-old incantation passed down from Morgog to Morgog through eons of existence.

The woodweaver chanted softly in a language unknown to men, the syllables difficult and dizzying in their complex formation. As Rel-Jimore spoke, he curled and twitched his fingers and swung his arms out an odd angles. The tree before him, the tree holding Macal Teel, slowly began to twist and bend in response.

In the crook of the branch Macal slept soundly as the tree gently lowered him down to the Morgog's hungry arms. When he saw his treasure up close, the Morgog would have smiled if he had known how. The pleased eye on the end of its stalk swiveled back and forth slowly, examining the human intently.

It was a very fine prize indeed, Rel-Jimore thought to himself.

The woodweaver's magic was nearly complete when a small branch from a young oak sprout brushed across Macal's bruised cheek. The boy awoke and looked around to get his bearings, shaking off the wet fog of his forgotten dream. Something had touched him. Something had awakened him. Then, in the great darkness of the night, the feeble moonlight struggling through the high forest canopy revealed the dark eerie shape before him.

Shocked by the creature's proximity, Macal screamed, kicked, and punched as the creature bent over him. With arms as strong as the trees they could control, Rel-Jimore imprisoned Macal's flailing limbs.

He began to laugh and cackle in delight at his prize. The sound emerged as a thousand grasshoppers chirping together, echoing dully as if through a valley of bones. Macal could see the strange eyestalk waver forward, studying him. Then he saw the wide mouth slowly open. Like a snake from a dark pit, out crept a long, split tongue.

"A ss-s-servant you ss-shall be." Rel-Jimore's whisper resembled wind through leaves. "The ss-seed will grow and you will forget. The ss-s-seed will grow and you will obey."

Macal screamed again. He didn't know what the creature was or what it was talking about, but he knew he wanted no part of it. The tongue stretched out further and further, slowly approaching the boy's face. He tried to pull away, to get up and run, but he was pinned against a tree branch, held down by immensely strong arms. His screams pierced the night, shattering the peace of the tranquil forest. As the tongue crept closer he turned his face away, but he could still see it. The tip of the tongue had something curled within it.

Releasing Macal's left wrist, the creature grabbed his face instead. The woody fingers pried his mouth open. Macal tried to bite the fingers, but his attempt proved futile against their hard bark. With his free hand he instinctively tried to push the monster off, but he was too weak. The strong woody fingers finally forced his mouth open, and the glistening tongue slid forward, ready to deposit its burden into his mouth. Macal screamed and struggled as Rel-Jimore prepared to finish his rite of servitude.

Behind the Morgog there was a determined rustling in the bushes on the other side of the clearing. A flickering radiance was rapidly approaching.

"Do you have any idea how hard it is to find a lantern in the middle of a raid?" asked Lalliard in annoyance as he broke through the final barrier of underbrush and into the clearing.

Macal couldn't believe it. Lalliard was here! He had followed him!

The creature holding Macal spun at the wizard's approach. "The boy iss-s mine!" the Morgog shouted, defending its prize.

"If anything," retorted Lalliard, setting down his lantern, "after tonight I'm pretty sure *I* own that boy. The gods know I've saved him enough. Put him down and go, Rel-Jimore."

"Never! I hunger! He is my s-ss-servant!" Spittle sprayed from Rel-Jimore's mouth. He hid his surprise that the gaunt man knew his true name.

"Good. I prefer it this way," said Lalliard. Rel-Jimore hissed in displeasure.

Without further dialogue the wizard held up a small rune of brown clay and spoke words of power, *"Aulaer Crorumish Anaer!"* As he finished the incantation, the rune crumbled to ash and a jet of blue fire shot from his outstretched hand, aimed directly at the Morgog.

As the magical searing flame shot toward him, Rel-Jimore dropped his hold on Macal and commanded the massive trees to his will. Forming one hand into a defiant fist, he caused the earth and roots to animate. A massive tangle of roots exploded from the soil in front of him, forming a woven wall of protection.

The blast of magic fire splintered apart as it met the wall, sending up a bright shower of sparks. Having served its purpose, the wooden wall collapsed upon itself as speedily as it had formed. As the burning roots burrowed back into the soil, Rel-Jimore wasted no time launching his own offensive. He had lost count of all the Druids who had come after him, determined to send him back home, or worse, subjugate him to their will once more. He had killed them all, and to remain free he would gladly kill again.

He faced Lalliard, his serpentine body rising to its full height. Upright, he was nearly fifteen feet tall. Calling upon the gifts bestowed upon him by his heritage, the elements of his home plane, he thrust his arms toward the wizard. In the palm of each hand, a small swirling portal from his world opened and out shot a coil of sharp pointed branches.

As soon as he saw the Morgog resist his assault, Lalliard knew there would be a counterattack and he was ready with the one and only defensive spell he knew. Reducing another rune to ash, he called up a magical shield of brilliant, nearly transparent violet. The dweomer centered and adhered its large concave shape to his forearm.

The coil of branches crashed into the violet disc and splintered against its glowing magic. Wooden shards and splinters rained down around the clearing. The force of the impact knocked Lalliard off his feet and back into some thorny bushes. The wizard's momentum was so great that he might have tumbled farther had a boulder not brought him to a jarring halt, painfully battering his unshielded arm.

Everything was happening so fast that Macal could barely follow what he was seeing. Only moments ago he had been asleep, and now once more chaos had invaded his life. He sprang to his feet as the Morgog attacked Lalliard. If nothing else, he knew he had to get away from the creature. With all the speed he could muster, he darted to the far side of the lantern-lit clearing.

Slightly stunned, Lalliard righted himself, shedding leaves and broken branches as he returned to the battle with the Morgog. The power of the creature's attack had surprised him.

The wizard's familiar scowl came across his face. On the far side of the clearing Rel-Jimore was withdrawing his sharp, twiggy tentacles. Promptly Lalliard cast a new spell, ignoring the pain in his injured arm. He flung his pale, veined hand forward, and like a huge, ghostly yellow shadow, a magically augmented hand shot out to grasp the retracting branches.

The ghostly form of the wizard's arm stretched out far beyond his normal one, growing to gargantuan proportions until it was nearly eight feet across. The massive hand latched onto the tendrils, gripping them tightly. Forcefully Lalliard yanked his arm back, pulling the tendrils and hurling Rel-Jimore to the far side of the clearing where Macal now stood.

The woodweaver hissed in fear as he flew through the air. As Lalliard loosened his grip, the ghostly hand shriveled and disappeared. The Morgog struck the ground and tumbled through the brush to collide with a tree. The force of the impact stunned him; he tried to right himself but was too disoriented from the assault. The wizard stared at his foe, knowing he could finish the Morgog off. One spell of lightning would tear through the creature as through a stormy night sky.

Lalliard glanced over at Macal to make sure he was all right. The boy had been watching the fight, huddled against the base of a tree not far from where Rel-Jimore was trying to regain his centipede footing. Sheer terror filled the boy's eyes. Lalliard scowled as he heard him whimpering. *The boy was useless like this,* he thought. *Useless to himself and to the world. If Macal had ever needed strength at any time, it was now, as he faced the task of rebuilding his life.*

Frustrated at Macal's inability, like most people, to deal with his fears, against his better judgment Lalliard allowed Rel-Jimore to rise. He had to do this, he told himself bitterly with clenched teeth. It was the only way he could help the boy.

When the Morgog attacked again, the wizard didn't bother defending himself.

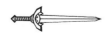

Rel-Jimore attacked from the undergrowth. He knew it would be foolish to use the coiled branch attack again. The wizard would surely use the same counterattack on him. Instead he called upon the trees, bending them to his will again. At the woodweaver's command, roots all around Lalliard burst up from the ground. They writhed like snakes. They coiled, danced, and twitched around the wizard. Everything in Lalliard's nature told him to move. Every instinct warned him not to get caught, but seeing the fear that overwhelmed Macal, he knew he had to do nothing.

The next moment the choice had been taken from him. With the speed of a whip, the roots latched onto the wizard, roughly grabbing his ankles and coiling up his legs, their knotty texture abrading his skin as they snaked over his body. There were dozens of them, wrapping his arms and torso so tightly that the wizard could barely breathe. His advantage in the battle was lost as the roots bound him fast.

Macal panicked as the thick web of roots slowly began to crush the wizard. *Lalliard had been winning! Why was he suddenly losing?* The wizard grimaced in pain as the horrific pressure began to force his bones and muscles into painful, unnatural angles. Macal couldn't believe what he was seeing. *Lalliard couldn't lose!*

He knew the wizard wasn't immortal or all-powerful. Many times he'd seen Lalliard return to Hormul after some long adventure in far worse shape than Macal was now. But each time Lalliard came back, it meant he had won every one of his encounters, or at least lived to tell the tale. The boy could see him starting to turn blue as the roots' strangling grip slowed the flow of blood.

The Morgog hissed in delight. This would be an even better outcome than he had hoped for. One human would be his minion, the other he would eat. He would have the child *and* the man!

The creature started to pull Lalliard closer. The roots ripped through the earth as the Morgog called them to him. At the end of its waving stalk, his eye peered in anticipation at the dying wizard. The struggle was almost over; Rel-Jimore was crushing the life from Lalliard's body as effortlessly as a boy could crush the head of a delicate rose in his hand. Macal flinched as he watched Lalliard about to die. Another haunting vision of horror to add to his collection. *How could this be happening again? And why to him?*

He couldn't let Lalliard die, when the wizard had been trying to save him!

As the thought slammed into Macal like an enchanted hammer, something changed in him.

He couldn't let it happen. *Not again.* He couldn't let another person die trying to save him. Even his mother had sacrificed herself to give him life. He couldn't take any more guilt for causing others to suffer or die. As he stood forgotten and insignificant on the edge of the fight, all the frustration locked up inside him burst to the surface, exploding out of him. His mild face transformed by ferocity, Macal ran forward to save Lalliard.

For my mother! For my uncle! For Lalliard! thought Macal as he rushed at the Morgog, jumped up and grabbed onto the hovering eyestalk with both hands. Using all his weight and momentum, he yanked down on the sensitive limb. The Morgog howled, stunned and wounded by the boy's attack. Blindly, instinctively, he lashed out, his woody fingers sinking into the flesh of the boy hanging from his eyestalk. But the fury burning brightly inside the boy blocked out the pain; again he yanked savagely on the eyestalk as Rel-Jimore twisted and writhed, trying to break the viselike hold. The woods around them quivered in sympathy with the Morgog's distress. Leaves began to fall from the trees like heavy rain. Rel-Jimore's howls echoed through the forest and far off into the valleys beyond.

Tears of frustration filled Macal's eyes. He imagined that the Morgog was Menk, that he was the god who had taken his mother from him, that he was the troll who slew his uncle, that he was the Troll King himself, who ordered the destruction of his home. His anger at a white-hot pitch, he reached out and gripped the eyeball itself, digging his fingers into its slimy surface. He had to do this. He couldn't let the Morgog kill Lalliard. Not *Lalliard* or *anybody else, ever again!*

Rel-Jimore shrieked in pain as his eye was crushed in the boy's grasp. Recoiling, he finally broke Macal's hold and hurled the boy away from him as hard and as far as he could. Macal flew through the air and slammed heavily into the uneven earth a good distance away. Lying stunned in a drift of dry leaves, Macal managed to raise his head. The Morgog, blinded as his eye began to swell and bruise, retreated on silent tentacles into the dark woods, not caring where he went, as long as it was far from these hostile humans.

As the last of Rel-Jimore's centipede body disappeared into the darkness, Macal looked over at Lalliard. The roots that bound the wizard slackened. Lalliard lay on the ground, taking great heaving breaths. His face was still blue and his hands shook from lack of blood flow, but after a moment he shrugged off the remaining root tendrils and got slowly to his feet. Ignoring Macal, he cast a hard glare about the clearing, searching which way the Morgog had run. Then, without a word, he picked up the lantern and burst off through the trees after Rel-Jimore.

"Wait!" called the boy. There was no response, but he could hear Lalliard's gasping breath as the wizard penetrated deeper into the woods. Not knowing what else do, Macal followed. He could guess the wizard's intentions—Lalliard wanted to finish off the Morgog. But for Macal the battle was over. They were alive, and for the moment safe. Right now that was all he wanted.

"Stop!" he yelled, hoping to halt the wizard. The reality of what had just transpired slowly settled upon him. He couldn't believe what he had done. Never before had he stood up for himself or anybody else. His knees were shaking, his heart was beating fast, and his head spun dizzily.

Ahead, Lalliard was running as fast as his bad leg would let him, his gait a cross between a hop and a skip, but with the momentum of a run. Macal could barely keep pace. The wizard kept disappearing through the trees; it was only by the diffused orange glow of the lantern that Macal was able to stay on his track.

Finally Lalliard came to a stop. The lantern, swinging back and forth on its chain, gave off a shifting, spectral illumination. Just behind it Macal could see the wizard's dark silhouette. Lalliard was reaching for his pouch again, pulling out some arcane rune. Macal caught up to him just as he began his incantation.

Just ahead of them, in a ditch near a riverbed, was Rel-Jimore. The Morgog no longer looked fearsome and monstrous. With his long body curled up on itself, he looked feeble, blind, and scared. The creature's posture reminded Macal of his fight with Menk earlier this night. He had curled up the same way, trying to protect himself from the onslaught of kicks and punches. It was a position he knew well, that of the unmistakable loser of a battle.

"Sss-ss-spare me," Macal could hear the Morgog whimpering as his hands tenderly cradled his damaged eyestalk. "Let me be. Let me hunger again in my cave."

Lalliard ignored the creature's pleas. Macal saw his dry, pale lips began to move. In the wizard's eyes burned the determination to kill the Morgog here and now.

Rel-Jimore's cries of distress echoed like wind through a hollow log. Before Lalliard could finish the incantation, Macal reacted without thinking. As the rune started to smoke, he slapped it out of Lalliard's hand, sending it tumbling down the embankment and into the muddy river. The wizard turned on him in surprised anger. "What are you doing? Never touch me!"

"You *can't* kill him!" shouted Macal with so much force that he even shocked himself.

"I can do whatever I want," the wizard informed him bluntly as he pulled out another rune. "This creature is not fit to live. He does not belong in our world."

Before Macal could react again, Lalliard had summoned the magic to use the new rune. *"Litious Forlamorian!"*

"*No!*" cried Macal, but it was too late. The magic had been unleashed. A streak of lightning arced out from Lalliard's fingertips, and like a mighty javelin impaled the Morgog.

Macal stared in horrified wonder at the power of Lalliard's magic. The lightning bolt had burned a large ragged hole through the side of the Morgog's torso and blackened the ground beneath him. The beast no longer quivered, moaned, or pleaded. The hundreds of tendrils on his lower body no longer twitched in fear. He was still and lifeless, like so many others tonight.

Macal had wanted revenge, but not like this. He understood Rel-Jimore was only trying to eat, to find a way to survive. There should have been a way to handle him other than killing him.

As he watched the smoke rise off the dead creature's charred remains, a memory came back to him. A few years ago he had been working in the fields, cutting down the prickly thistles so that he wouldn't scratch his hands while tending the vegetables. His eye had caught a black and white dog traipsing through the rows of growing corn. Already the romping animal had damaged several of the young stalks. Macal shouted angrily at the dog, but it wouldn't leave.

In frustrated fury Macal picked up a rock and threw it. To his astonishment the rock hit the wide-eyed dog directly on the nose. The startled animal yelped in pain. Its nose bleeding, it ran away.

Satisfied that the dog was gone, Macal had begun to cut thistles once more. Shortly thereafter Uncle Melkes emerged from the cottage—he had witnessed all that had just happened. There was a look on his uncle's gentle face Macal had never seen before: a look of disappointment and defeat, as if everything he had tried to do had failed. Slowly his uncle had turned and gone back inside. He had not spoken a word, which Macal found strange for a man who always had a story to tell.

Macal stood there among the rows of tomatoes, cucumbers, and potatoes, realizing he had somehow failed his uncle. He could think of only one thing to do. He dropped his sickle and ran to look for the dog. It took him all of the afternoon and most of the night, but at last he succeeded in finding the injured animal down by the river. He brought it back to the cottage to tend its wound while Uncle Melkes watched in silence, his eyes sorrowful.

Macal kept the gentle dog around the farm, feeding and caring for it as its nose slowly healed. It wasn't until the dog had fully recovered from its injury that Uncle Melkes had started talking to Macal again.

Snapping out of his reverie and back to the present, the boy stared up at Lalliard. "You didn't have to kill him. He would have left us alone from now on."

"You have a lot to learn about the world before you start giving me lectures," the wizard said flatly, unmoved by the boy's words. "If you had begged for your life, he wouldn't have listened."

"No, but all creatures need to do what they have to for survival. They all deserve a chance to live."

"Did you want him to eat you, then? I'm sure we can find another Morgog out here somewhere we can feed you to."

"No! And he didn't want to eat me."

"That is true." The wizard's tone was mocking. "He wanted to make you his slave for eternity, and at the end of time he would finally eat you. Monsters seem to find you very edible. It must be one of the joys of boyhood that I missed out on."

"It's just that I can understand why he was doing what he did. He wasn't being evil, he just wanted to survive. He was being himself."

"So were the trolls back in town. And trust me, Morgogs are evil. Perhaps not as evil as the Lumar, but evil enough. Don't pity that creature. Think of it this way: he died because *you* wanted to survive. Fair is fair."

Macal didn't respond. *No*, he was thinking, *he died because I wanted you to live.*

The two of them stood in the quiet hush of the nighttime forest, the waning glow of the lantern feebly keeping the vast darkness at bay. Lalliard was the first to speak again.

"While we are here, let's get you cleaned up a bit" said Lalliard, pointing to the calm flow of the small nearby stream. Although Macal could tell it was more than a suggestion, but he didn't want to stay near the dead Morgog. Without a word he walked upstream, Lalliard following. Macal could only guess the river was a small branch of the River of Abengroth that ran north and South the full length of Elronia.

After about a hundred yards he stopped and knelt to swirl his hands in the river. The water was cool and refreshing. As he cupped it in his hands and sank his face into it, he began to wake up. Until now he hadn't realized how tired he was, how exhausted.

Lalliard stood silently behind him. Macal was still surprised that the wizard had shown up. He began to realize just how much Lalliard had done for him tonight, yet there was a part of him that wished the wizard had just stayed away from him

If Lalliard hadn't stopped the trolls from killing him, he would be with his uncle right now. He wouldn't be alive to experience this guilt and remorse. He wouldn't be alive to face the painful consequences of his actions. Again he splashed water on his face, rinsing away the dirt and dried blood. After tonight, he couldn't imagine caring how he looked, but he had to admit that Lalliard was right: he felt a little better after cleaning up.

"You cannot sleep just anywhere out here, you know." Lalliard broke the silence that had crept between them. "This forest is an unsafe place."

"*Hormul* is an unsafe place!" snapped Macal before he could stop himself.

"True." The wizard seemed oblivious to the boy's hostility. "But out here it is even worse. You, my boy, have chosen to leave the fringes and walk directly onto the battlefield. All right, you're clean enough. Let's find a safer place to rest for the night. As far as I know, Rel-Jimore is the only Morgog in this region, but I have been wrong before. It's a rare occurrence, but rare occurrences seem to happen frequently around here."

Macal stood in silence and followed Lalliard through the forest. The wizard walked slowly, nursing the arm he had injured in the battle. The sight brought Macal's own aches and pains back into bitter focus. Now that the mere act of survival no longer demanded all his attention, other considerations came crowding forward.

His entire body was sore—arms, legs, chest, everywhere Menk and his goons had struck him. Parts of his face were tender to the touch. He didn't know which injuries came from Menk and which had been inflicted during the fight with Rel-Jimore, but it didn't matter. Compared to what had happened to so many others tonight, he could actually be considered fortunate.

It was then that he realized he was limping. Walking behind Lalliard, it looked like he was mocking the wizard's injured leg as they both lurched through the forest. As they made their way over the uneven ground, the wizard spoke. "You surprised me back there."

"What do you mean?"

"You helped me."

"I was scared, but I couldn't let you die trying to help me."

"It showed you have courage." The wizard pushed aside an overhanging branch in his path.

Macal didn't understand. "But I was scared." The wizard carelessly let the branch snap back, and he barely ducked underneath it. "Courage is when you prevail over being scared." Lalliard turned back to lock eyes with the young boy. For a moment Macal thought he could see a great depth of compassion locked behind the icy blue eyes hovering above the flickering lantern. "Even though you were scared, you acted. To be blunt, I didn't think you had it in you. Perhaps there is some hope for you after all."

Unable to think of a response, Macal walked past the wary wizard. Lalliard wasn't sure, but boy's stride—though hampered by a limp—seemed a bit more confident than it had been a few moments before. The wizard smiled to himself. The change was slight, not enough to be called a swagger, but it was a welcome sight.

Eventually they reached a hill. Without a second thought Macal started up the steep incline, using knotted roots protruding from the ground to help himself up the rise. He was about halfway up when he heard a scuffling and scrambling behind him, followed by the sound of Lalliard cursing in some unknown language. He looked down and saw the wizard was having difficulty climbing the hill.

"Are you okay?"

"I'm *fine!*" Lalliard was lying on the side of the steep slope in a snarl of moss and roots, the lantern fortunately unbroken in his hand.

"Do you want—"

"*No!*" Lalliard's shout cut the boy off as he tried and failed to get back to his feet. "Did I ask for your help? I am pretty sure I did not. Get up the wretched hill and wait for me."

Watching the wizard struggle to right himself, Macal didn't know what to do or say. His own leg was painful, but at least he could bend it. Lalliard's right leg appeared to be stiff, as if bound by a rigid metal splint. As far as Macal could tell, his right knee did not flex at all.

The boy found it easier not to watch the lame man's ordeal, but eventually the crashes and curses stopped, and the wizard regained his feet. A few minutes later Lalliard reached the crest of the slope, brushing past him as if embarrassed. Macal hurried after him, a question popping out of his mouth before he could stop it.

"What happened to your leg, anyway?"

Lalliard turned to face him, an ill temper twisting his features. Looming over the small boy he seemed as dark and forbidding as the surrounding trees. When he spoke, his words were low and tightly controlled, as if a storm had been brewing beneath them for many years. "This is the point where, if you want to stay a healthy, breathing little boy, you will shut up and stop asking questions."

Unprepared for such a volatile reaction, Macal took a step back. What was wrong with asking such a simple question? He had injured his own leg before, much worse than it was right now, and he wouldn't mind talking about it if somebody asked. His left leg still bore the scar from a wound he'd received while trying to pull Germ out of a ditch. The mule had slipped when heavy rains caused the road bank to collapse under his weight. When Macal tried to pull Germ back onto the road, he had lost his own footing and fallen into the ditch as well, impaling his leg on a broken tree limb. Nearly an hour had passed before another traveler finally came along and helped Germ and him back to the village. Although the injury hadn't left him with a limp, he still had a nice round scar to remember his adventure by.

Lalliard's reaction to Macal's question only added to the intriguing mystery of his limp, but the boy knew better than to probe any further. He looked around. The trees here weren't nearly as dense. Up in the star-speckled onyx sky, he could catch a glimpse of the waning moon among the leaves. Macal guessed they'd walked at least a mile through the timberland, and with every step he could feel the weight of his fatigue increasing.

"Do you think there's a chance he's okay?" he asked. He was speaking of his uncle, voicing the question he had been afraid to ask since he had encountered Lalliard.

Lalliard remained silent and kept walking. He didn't want to have this conversation.

Macal was sure the wizard had heard him. "Do you think he's okay?" he asked again, catching up with the wizard and grabbing his sleeve. Lalliard looked down at him, his face stony.

"Is he?" the boy asked one last time. Why wouldn't the wizard answer him? Instead Lalliard fixed him with a glare that was answer enough.

Lalliard had seen the same thing he had seen. He had seen the monstrous troll close in on Uncle Melkes and attack with the full might of its fury. They had both seen him crumple to the ground after the creature's blow, like a scarecrow no longer supported by its post.

He didn't survive, thought Macal. *Nobody could have survived that.* It was the thought that had been recurring all evening, but now the reality had registered in Macal's frantic mind and rapidly beating heart. The more time passed, the more real it became.

His uncle was dead.

Lalliard knew what the boy was thinking. "Come here and sit on this log with me."

In a haze, the boy sat. The log was speckled with moss, its ends rotted away through years of decay. The rough bark made for uncomfortable seating. Lalliard sat down beside him. "I am going to tell you something I have never told anyone before."

Staring off into the dark forest, the man seemed distant, as if remembering some faraway place.

Macal studied the wizard's sharp, crooked nose, his wan features, the overwhelming sorrow suddenly visible in his eyes. In sharp contrast to his usual harsh and overbearing demeanor, the wizard now seemed gentle, broken, and uncomfortable with himself.

He couldn't imagine what Lalliard was going to tell him.

CHAPTER 8

King Orgog strode back through the bleak tunnels below the great Castle Darkmoor. The tunnels wound deeply into the rock of the floating mountain from which the fortress had been carved. He had received word that the traitor had finally returned, and that the news he bore was good. *The wretch better have the war plans in his possession.*

The mighty Troll King lumbered his massive bulk through the tunnels as fast as he could, eager to hear what the mongrel had to say. He hoped it was indeed good news. It would mean everything was going exactly as he had desired. The great cogs of the war machine were grinding into motion, and with each revolution he was forcing them faster and faster. *The war could be won, and it could be won soon.*

His generals had reported that the initial success of the raiding parties was far better than expected. His hope had been that his troops would make it a short way into Elronia before meeting with significant resistance, but evidently the shortsighted humans hadn't caught on yet, and his soldiers had done an impressive job of moving deep into enemy territory. Their swords would soon dull from victorious battle—*a worthwhile trade.*

"For gold and glory."

Then it would be time to start allowing a few of the humans to escape, just enough of them to spread the word of the horrors transpiring within their borders. Fear would spread like a disease, devouring the humans, destroying their morale. That was when he would strike. He himself would march upon Keratost itself, seeking those who sat upon the throne.

At length he reached the cavernous chamber where he always met the shadow. As was the case with all their past meetings, the figure already awaited him.

"I offer greetings to the lord of the land." The shadow's voice was meek.

"I hear a quaver in your voice, snake!" Orgog's icy eyes narrowed. He hadn't remained king by ignoring such clues. "It would be in your best interest to tell me now that you have my war plans back."

"My lord, I tried," the shadow whined. "As you know, there was always a chance of *complications*." As he spoke the Troll King took a step toward him, his large clawed hands flexing angrily. "Please let me explain!"

"You were hired because I thought you were a man who could deal with *complications!* Where are my plans?"

"I don't have them."

The king gnashed his teeth. "That, you fool, I gathered. Where are they?"

"A man took them before I could get to them."

"A human?"

"Yes."

"Can he be bought?"

"I don't know."

This time no amount of begging was going to stop the king. He rushed forward, grabbed the man roughly by the neck and lifted him off the ground. "You didn't ask? You call this good news? You dare come back here empty handed and empty of mouth? I'd have been better off trusting an orc!" His grip tightened.

"I'm the only one who knows who the man is!" The shadow choked out the words with difficulty. "If I die, you will never get the plans. I know where he is!"

Logic slowly mastered the king's rage. He flung his victim away in disgust, watching him smash into the ground and roll across the rocky surface. "Obviously he will be taking them to Keratost, if he is not there already."

"He does not travel as fast as I do." King Orgog knew this to be true. It was why he had chosen this human, as useless as he sometimes was. He could summon wings of fire and speed across the sky faster than a stormy wind.

King Orgog pointed a scaly finger at the enigmatic figure. "This is your final chance, get the plans from him and bring them to me!"

Unable to control his rage and frustration any longer the king lunged as the man was trying to get to his feet. He knew he shouldn't do this. They didn't have time to waste, but his anger and frustration were so strong. He struck at the small human with a mighty meaty fist and knocked the shadow's mind into darkness.

Sitting on the fallen tree in the fading night, Macal waited with anticipation to hear what Lalliard was going to say. He was sure the reclusive wizard had many secrets. Anyone so bitter and cantankerous would have a number of things he wanted to keep private. Whatever those secrets were, he guessed they were probably very dark.

Up until now Macal had possessed no secrets. With no friends to entice him into mischief, he hadn't done anything he needed to hide. For the most part his life had been uneventful, but tonight had changed everything. Now he had a secret—something he didn't want anyone to know. The shame he felt was already more than he could handle. He began to long for the days when he had no secrets.

"At the moment," Lalliard said, "you are blaming yourself."

The words surprised Macal. He had thought this was going to be a story from Lalliard's past. He was hoping it would provide a distraction from his own thoughts; he didn't need the wizard echoing what was going on inside him, exacerbating the shame and sorrow he was trying to suppress. "I thought this was a story about you," he said sharply. "I don't want to talk about me."

"It will be about me soon; just give me time to get there. Right now you probably feel guilt for what happened. And one of the things you will learn over the many years of your life, as wars come and go and kingdoms rise and fall, is that the people who declare war are rarely the people who hold a weapon. Most of the time they never even stand on a battlefield. They are the ones who have no blood on their hands."

"So?" Macal did not understand what this had to do with either of them.

"So, it means that the people who started this war, the people who are to blame for what happened tonight, are actually nowhere near here. The kings are the ones responsible for what happened to Hormul *and* to your uncle. Don't blame yourself. Blame them, both the Troll King and the King of Elronia."

Macal wasn't sure he agreed. While it was true that the two kings had caused the war, the decision to run away from his house tonight had been his. Not the kings', not anyone else's. Regardless of what Lalliard said, he still felt that it was his fault that Uncle Melkes was dead.

"Now, so you can understand what real guilt is, let me go on. But first I want an oath on your family's name that you will never mention this to anybody else. What I am about to tell you is for you alone. I am only telling you so that you can see what properly placed guilt really is."

The boy's soft green eyes met the man's stern blue ones. Of course he would promise not to tell anybody, thought Macal. Who would he tell, anyway? He had no friends, and his uncle was dead. His gaze never wavering, he swore his oath. "I vow, on all those named Teel, to never share what you say to me."

Lalliard looked at him intently for a long moment, as if judging whether he was trustworthy. Then he came to a decision. "I am going to give you the very abbreviated version. First, I was orphaned as a child. I never knew my parents. I must have been about five years old when I was sold into slavery in the Keratost slave markets."

Macal stared in wonder at the wizard. He had known very little about Lalliard, but he had never imagined him either an orphan or a slave.

"Where I was before that, I cannot remember, but it is of no significance," the wizard said. "What matters is that I was bought by a powerful man named Maerick. He was a callous and cruel wizard who thought of me as an insignificant object to serve his will. He only bought me because I was the cheapest slave he could find. He hated to spend money, but he needed someone to keep his tower clean and run various errands for him.

"He was a ferocious old codger with thick black hair and eyes of obsidian. My clearest memory of the day he bought me was the sympathetic look I received from the slave master as Maerick roughly dragged me away. A sympathetic look, from a man whose job it was to sell people's lives!

"The master wizard dragged me by my hair back to his tower on the outskirts of town. Have you ever been to Keratost, the capital city? It sits on a massive island in the center of an enormous lake. There is a single bridge of white stone connecting it to the surrounding land. Maerick's tower was right near the gates that led to the bridge.

"It was the first time I had seen the city from outside a cage. I had heard that it was the largest city in the realm, and as he dragged me callously through the streets, I was mesmerized by the breadth and scope of the place. Over the years I spent in his five-story tower—"

"You were a slave for *years*?" Macal cut in, surprised.

"Yes." The interruption annoyed the wizard. "And that is far from the point I am trying to make. Hold your tongue if you want me to continue."

Macal bit his lip. With a grunt of satisfaction, Lalliard continued. "He beat me for any infraction he could find, and sometimes he beat me for no reason at all. He seemed to take joy in it."

"What do you mean, he beat you?"

"You're not stupid! What do you think I mean? He tried to see how close he could come to killing me without actually doing so. He punctuated his scoldings with beatings that left me unconscious. Over and over again. Countless times.

"The worst beating he ever gave me was when he found I had sneaked one of his magic tomes into the cell that was my room. People think I am turbulent and tumultuous, but I am nothing compared to Maerick. He was a master of anger as well as magic. The night he discovered me with his precious book, he gave me a beating to surmount all other beatings. I didn't regain consciousness for several weeks.

"Years went by under his constant abuse, and eventually I grew into a man. Regardless of the beatings, I never stopped studying all the books in the tower's library. They were all I had to live for. One day I realized I was finally bigger and taller than he was, but there was no doubt the power of his magic was still far greater than the power of my hand. So I let him lash me as he normally did; by this time I had become virtually numb to the blows anyway.

"It was when he turned to leave, that I struck. In that moment I had a choice." Lalliard paused, remaining quiet for a long moment as if reflecting upon the dark day he was describing. "I struck and I killed him. I *chose* to kill him to stop the beatings; I *chose* to kill him to gain my freedom. You, on the other hand, did not choose to kill your uncle. He was a casualty of the war. I chose to kill Maerick. That was a decision I made. I didn't have to do what I did, but I did it anyway. The guilt I feel for that is a guilt I deserve, a mistake I still regret. The guilt you feel about your uncle is undeserved. There is nothing you could have done to prevent tonight's attack. And if there was, do not dwell upon it. You will likely do many far worse things throughout your life that will make tonight's mistakes unremarkable."

The wizard's revelation surprised Macal. Although he had to admit he had expected Lalliard's past to be entwined with dark and morose matters, he couldn't push one thought out of his head. The man who had saved his life numerous times tonight was a murderer!

Or was he? Macal couldn't decide. It sounded as if Lalliard had been defending himself from future beatings. Nonetheless the wizard didn't sound particularly remorseful as he had explained what he had done. He had told the whole tale as if it were simply a matter of fact, not a series of life-changing events. Macal could only think he was using the scenario to make a point. He also guessed there was more to this story than Lalliard was letting on, but the wizard had evidently ended his narration and wasn't going to explain anymore.

Macal did note that nothing in the story explained what happened to Lalliard's leg. After the wizard's earlier reaction to his question, he could only imagine that this was one of the missing pieces of the story.

The two of them decided to make camp where they were. Lalliard instantly fell asleep, undeterred by the absence of amenities such as blankets or straw matting. Maerick's brutal treatment seemed to have prepared him for primitive conditions. Macal guessed that the wizard was intentionally allowing him some time to himself to think. He was a bit taken aback by

Lalliard's attempt to console him. Prior to this night, if he had been asked whether Lalliard could show compassion, he would have thought the question a joke, and the person asking it a fool.

He had been wrong.

Macal was starting to see Lalliard in a different light. He hadn't known the wizard had once been a slave. He hadn't even known he had lived in Keratost. And it was inconceivable to him that anyone had ever been able to beat Lalliard unconscious. As he mulled over what he had been told, his heart ached for the wizard. Their lives were so different. Macal had grown up in a warm, caring family—at least until *now*. Maybe their lives weren't so different after all. Not anymore.

Yet Lalliard's story had not convinced him that he bore no blame for his uncle's death. Of course he did. At the root of the matter was the simple fact that Uncle Melkes had come into Hormul solely to search for his missing nephew. Macal was the reason his uncle had become involved in the conflict. However smart the wizard was, on this point he was wrong.

The boy lay awake a long time, lost in his thoughts. His mind turned to all the townspeople who had probably not survived the trolls' raid. Grunc, the barkeep. The Crawlems, who were blacksmiths. The Hagins, whose ancestors had first settled Hormul. Amorva, a blond girl who lived not far from Lalliard with her father, who was a huntsman for Lord Mentis. Macal even thought of Menk. As each person crossed his mind, he became more angry with the world for their distress and pain.

His rage would not let him rest. He had to do something. He couldn't stay here in the woods, and he knew he couldn't go back to Hormul. As he lay fretting, the dream came back to him—the dream from which the Morgog's attack had awakened him.

Yes, the dream, he thought. *He had to find his father*. If there was one thing Uncle Melkes had taught him, it was that nothing was more important than family. It didn't matter if his father was a traitor or not. He was the only family Macal had left.

Glancing over at the sleeping wizard, he knew he couldn't bring Lalliard with him, couldn't endanger the wizard further. The image of Lalliard battling the Morgog was still vivid in his memory. The wizard had come very close to dying. Macal didn't want to be responsible for Lalliard being hurt again or worse, killed on his behalf. Even though he hated the idea of being alone, the boy decided that for now he was better off by himself. Once he found his father, he wouldn't ever be alone again.

He recalled Captain Jengus saying that the men of the regiment had last seen his father on the borderlands of Xanga-Mor at the Mazzul stronghold. That would be his destination. Even if he didn't know how he would find Bertran Teel once he got there, he knew he had to try. He was terrified of everything that lay ahead, but a single thought gave him the courage to combat his fear.

All I have left in this world is my father.

Silently Macal thanked Lalliard for getting him through the night. With the semblance of a plan forming in his mind, he left the wizard deep in slumber and slipped off into the woods.

Macal's stomach growled as the first golden rays of sun splintered through the forest canopy. He was tired from all the walking he had done, but the fatigue was nothing compared to his growing hunger pangs. When had he last eaten? Hormul seemed so far away, both in time and in space. He realized that he and his uncle had skipped dinner last night in their haste to get down to the Waywitch. At the time, he hadn't even been thinking of eating—just of the excitement of seeing his father again. An excitement that had come to nothing.

It meant his last meal had been at lunchtime yesterday, when he had skipped off to have lunch with the neighboring ploughman among the trees that separated their farms. His empty stomach vividly recreated the meal, his mouth watering. He could almost taste the strips of cold rabbit meat from a hare his uncle had been fortunate enough to poach the day before. Some rings of fresh onion had been layered on top of it. Seasoned with parsley, sage, and other herbs, the sandwich had been delectable. Macal remembered wishing the bread hadn't been so stale, but he and his uncle couldn't afford a new loaf every day. If they got one every week, they were doing well.

A cool breeze brushed past him to rustle the leaves of the great surrounding trees. The amber glow of the morning sun was startlingly beautiful, its divine rays cascading down upon the world from above. Just at dawn Macal had seen a few skittish deer. He found his appreciation for them as beautiful, delicate creatures marred by his desire to make them into a meal, but it hardly mattered, since he had no weapon and no other means to catch one. All he could do was watch them sprint away as he approached.

Macal was used to two meals a day. He had only just stopped having the three that were the norm for growing children. All he could think of now, as he walked through the lush Rotelen Woods, was a mug of sweet cider and a fresh tart made of eggs, cream, and fruit. He was enchanted by the thought of raspberries, blueberries, and apples baked in a flaky, buttery pie shell. Only once before, at the Lord's annual fair, had he encountered such a tart, but it was easily the best thing he had ever eaten.

To force the thought of food from his mind, he tried to concentrate on his journey. If his mental map of the kingdom was anywhere near accurate, he should reach the far side of the woods by the end of the day. His sense of direction wasn't perfect, but he had an idea which way was west. Once he had passed through the woods he would come to the Valley of Ashway. Far west past that were the outer lands of the kingdom that belonged to the powerful Lord Moltess, First Lord of Elronia and devoted second cousin to the great king of the land. Although the King had given Lord Moltess the largest holding in the kingdom, the land hadn't come without the price of great responsibility. This region contained the Keep of Mazzul, a massive fortification nestled in the high, mountain-ringed valley that offered the only direct access into Elronia from Xanga-Mor. There was another way for the trolls to enter Elronia, but it required a long trip north around the nearly impassable mountains and then through the haunted Rashinasti Forest.

The very name of the forest made people shudder. In this forest of nightstalkers, the earth would not let the dead sleep. Instead the haunted soil caused corpses to rise and roam, animated by burning rage and endless hunger. Vile Imps, nasty Ilps, tormented ghosts, and wraiths dwelled in the dread forest. To Elronia's good fortune, the magic of the forest trapped its awakened victims within its borders, forever imprisoning them alive in a land of nightmares. Macal guessed the trolls had used this route to invade Elronia. They had taken chances and very likely paid a heavy toll to push through the dark forest and over the low mountains beyond, rather than confront the defensive might of the Keep of Mazzul, built to control all traffic in and out of western Elronia.

The boy was certain that once at the stronghold, he could find news about his father. He had never been so far from home. Although he was still in the Rotelen Woods, everything looked different—the trees, the flowers, even the sparse grass. Marigolds had given way to bugleweed, poppies to featherbells, and instead of mistflowers, jasmine now filled the air with its fragrance. Never before had he smelled such sweet jasmine. Nothing seemed the same even this far from home, and he imagined the sense of unfamiliarity would increase the farther he went. He had never fathomed the world could change so much from place to place.

Climbing over another fallen log, Macal couldn't help thinking of Lalliard. He was certain the wizard would be fuming when he woke to find his ward had left. For a moment it bothered him; then a thought made him smile. *Could Lalliard really get any grumpier?* What did it really matter if his disappearance upset the wizard? As reclusive and severed from society as Lalliard was, he should understand Macal's need to do something on his own.

As the boy passed through a thick cluster of trees, a noise interrupted his musings. Worried, he stopped to listen. It was off in the woods, not far away. It wasn't the first time he had heard strange sounds in the distance; for most of the night he had been avoiding them. Now, quickly and quietly, he moved away.

It was probably a rabbit, a deer, or even a bear, but he didn't want to take any chances. After his encounter with the Morgog and his realization that the trolls had passed through here, he could only guess what else might lurk in these woods. His ability to run away from trouble and danger was proving valuable; he had never thought his cowardice would turn out to be a useful skill. He reminded himself that this journey wasn't about proving his courage. It was about surviving long enough to find his father.

Stopping to listen after a few moments, he found to his relief that the rustling sound had died away. As he resumed his trek, however, another worry arose. What if he couldn't find anything to eat? The rumbling from his stomach was getting louder with each step he took. Closer to Hormul, he was familiar enough with the plants in the woods to know which ones were safe to eat, but here he wasn't sure about anything. He wished he had brought Germ with him. He would have no food for the mule either, but at least he would have some company.

Was Germ okay? Concern welled up inside him and he forced it down. He couldn't think about that right now. He had to stay strong. He had to find his father. What chance did either he or Germ have without him?

Another sound, filtering through the trees ahead, distracted him from his worries. It was the sound of water rushing over rocks. He hurried forward and came upon a river with rocky banks. Although the rapidly flowing water looked cold and deep, Macal's first thought was to swim across and continue westward. The river wasn't very wide, perhaps twenty yards—a swim he could easily accomplish with a bit of effort. Then a glance upstream showed him a small mill on the same bank where he stood. The water swept steeply past it, spilling downstream over a series of rocky ledges in cascades of white foam.

What was a mill doing out in the middle of the woods? And what had happened to it? Although the structure looked as if it had recently been whole and productive, it was now in ruins. A good portion had been burned to the ground, and as Macal stood there the smell of burned wood drifted toward him. The giant wheel that had once harnessed the flow of the river had fallen over and lay at an angle in the water, charred and scorched from the flames. The top portion of the building had mostly turned to ash and collapsed in upon itself. No more would the pulleys, shafts, and belts of the mechanism work to turn grain into flour that could be made into biscuits, pancakes, muffins, cornbread, and other delicacies, the mere thought of which made Macal's stomach groan with eagerness.

Noting the steady stream of smoke still wafting up from the wreckage, he was certain this was the trolls' handiwork, perhaps performed on their way to Hormul. Such a large wooden structure could smolder for days. Fortunately, since the mill had been built out on the rocky riverbank, the fire hadn't set the surrounding trees alight.

As his gaze shifted past the ruined building, Macal saw a bush he recognized—a raspberry bush growing amid a cluster of unfamiliar greenery. His stomach growled in anticipation at the sight: raspberries were something he knew he could eat. His instinct was to avoid the mill in case any trolls had chosen to stay behind for some unknown reason, but his rumbling stomach would not be denied. He needed to eat. And why would trolls remain in a wreck like this? Wouldn't they want to continue on to the towns where the wealth, riches, and glory were? There was obviously nothing left here or they wouldn't have burned it down. After all, it was only an old mill.

Desperate hunger guiding his logic, Macal moved toward the mill. As he did so, the rushing of the river concealed the sound of the footsteps that stalked him from the trees.

Lalliard slowly awoke in the midmorning sun. He yawned and stretched, coaxing his muscles back into usefulness. He hated waking up. Among the two things the wizard truly enjoyed, cats were one. Sleeping was the other.

The few hours' sleep had been as good as anything he would have gotten at home. As long as he slept, it didn't matter where—but he could use a lot more. The thought that anyone could ever have enough sleep was unfathomable. There were times when he attempted to sleep for several days in a row, and often he succeeded. Sleeping meant he could avoid the conscious experience of life, and that was a desirable result.

Finally his grogginess dissipated and he began to get his bearings. Annoyance rose inside him at the memory of where he was and what had brought him here. *Wake up*, his mind told him. *You've got a plan to formulate.* While birds sang an unfamiliar song on the morning air he lay with his eyes still closed, analyzing all the options for himself and the boy.

Where would they go? What would they do? Keratost was likely the safest place for them. The King was there, and therefore a good portion of the army—but the wizard had no intention of returning to a city haunted by the terrible images of his childhood. There had to be somewhere else. Immediately he dismissed the idea of Fellenlom. Not far distant, it was a small town like Hormul and doubtless destined to suffer the same fate, if it hadn't already.

Lying on the damp, chilly grass, the wizard also dismissed the idea of Avie, a small, wooden-walled town of tricksters, thieves, and vile ratmen, creatures with the body of a man but the head and tail, legs, and paws of a mangy, oversized rat. While Lalliard had never been one to dote on children, he knew Avie was not a place to take Macal. Why did the King even allow such a place to exist? Then again, the current war had made it clear that the King wasn't particularly prone to good decisions. Any city that could pay its taxes would be tolerated.

Fornlin came to the wizard's mind. It was the second-largest city in Elronia; only Keratost was larger. Located on the kingdom's only shoreline on the far eastern coast, Fornlin's success as a port had made it a large and lively city.

Yes, that was where they would go. With the trolls devastating their lands in the west, it was likely the safest place. Only through a complete breakdown of Elronia's war machine would they again find themselves on the front lines of the battle. His decision made, Lalliard finally sat up and opened his eyes to find himself alone in the makeshift camp. Realizing Macal had disappeared again, the wizard remembered why he didn't like children.

Macal crept hesitantly toward the raspberry bush, expecting a troll to jump out from every shadow and from behind every tree. His hunger, greater than his fear, kept him moving forward. He knew the fear was only in his mind. The trolls were far from here. They had passed through this area even before they had invaded Hormul.

He had nothing to worry about.

Although his hunger was paramount, his need for sleep was beginning to make itself felt as well. Last night he had stayed awake, waiting for Lalliard to drift off so that he could sneak away. He was tired from walking and sore from the abuse he had taken yesterday. After he ate, he would find somewhere safe to rest for a bit and enjoy the satisfied feeling of his stomach digesting his meal.

Nearing the raspberry bush, he could see the fruit was ripe and plump, a scrumptious feast ready for his enjoyment. He was just a few feet away, hand outstretched to pluck a colorful berry, when a swift rustling alerted him to danger. In fright Macal jumped back, but he was too slow to evade the large scaly hand that burst through the bushes, its long talons latching onto the front of his tunic. To his horror, a huge body followed the hand, the thick leaves parting to reveal a creature unlike anything he had ever seen.

Its body was shaped like a man that was nearly seven feet tall. It had reptilian hands and slender pointed tail that were covered in thick green scales, but nothing was more fearful than the creature's head—the head of a dragon that seemed too large even for the creature's gigantic body. More scales, hard as steel, descended from the monster's head in a thick array down its long neck.

"Who are you?" the voice of the dragon-headed beast hissed. With the speed of a striking snake, its head darted forward to stop just inches from Macal's.

"M-M-Macal," stammered the boy, trying futilely to break free from the creature's mighty grip. "Macal Teel."

Seated on the same log where last night he had told Macal the story of his youth, Lalliard wondered what he should do now. He couldn't believe the boy had run off again. How many times could he possibly save him? It wasn't as if the boy was his responsibility. Why should he continue to track down a dolt who persistently ran away?

Perhaps it was for the best, he thought. It would definitely be easier not having to coddle the ungrateful whelp. If anyone had a reason to be moody and depressed, Lalliard was sure he was that person. *Let the boy go,* he decided bitterly at last. *It's obviously what he wants!*

An unfamiliar emotion began to unfold inside the wizard. At first he was unsure what it was; then, as left the camp to head towards Fornlin, he identified it at last.

He felt hurt that Macal had abandoned him.

CHAPTER 9

Talons hooked in Macal's shirt, the dragon-headed monster hoisted him high in the air. As the fabric tightened around his small torso, the boy found himself paralyzed by fear. His legs dangled uselessly in the air below him. He had no idea what this creature was, and he was stunned that it spoken to him.

"*Teel,*" repeated the monster slowly, as if fascinated by the name. "It seems that both Devera and Jurnar are at play here."

Macal had no idea what the creature meant. He knew that Devera was the Goddess of Fate, Jurnar the Goddess of Secrets and Riddles. But what did these divine beings have to do with his name? And what did this monster care about the gods?

The creature was scrutinizing Macal dubiously, as if it had been told its prize was worth a good deal more than it appeared. In spite of his terror, the boy found himself curious. Instead of the savage snarl he would have expected, the creature spoke eloquently, with an air of awareness that indicated it knew who it was and how much power it possessed. Its voice was clean and crisp, and it seemed to speak the language better even than he did.

Macal was nearly dumbfounded by the creature's haughty air. His heart was beating fast and his thoughts were racing, but in spite of his fear he was able to note that the monster was clothed—not just clothed, but rather elegantly garbed. Covering its torso was an immaculate piece of shiny plate armor, while its legs were covered with what looked like the bottom half of an enchanter's robe, its long tail escaping from below the hem. Around its neck hung a large gold medallion etched with an artful design of curved lines, a symbol Macal didn't recognize. Over its shoulders the beast wore a long red cloak, and on its hip a sword with a gold decorative hilt. The pommel was set with the largest red gemstone Macal had ever seen.

As if reaching a decision, without a further word the creature tossed Macal up onto its shoulder and began to walk hastily away from the mill. Afraid to imagine its intentions, the boy noted they were heading northwest.

"Where are you taking me? Just let me go," he pleaded, pounding the monster's back with his fists and hurting his hands on the hard plate armor.

"I think you will be far more valuable to me if I don't let you go." The creature leaped easily over a small rocky ridge in its path.

"Valuable? How am I *valuable?*" Macal started to flail his legs as well, finding them no more effective than his hands.

"*Quiet*, boy!" the creature commanded. "Stop kicking me and learn your place."

Macal was baffled. *His place? He didn't know he had a place.*

"Don't eat me!" he begged, suddenly realizing his only possible value to the monster. "You can have that bush of berries back there. It's all yours. All of it. Just let me go!"

"*Eat* you? Don't be disgusting," responded the monster with contempt. "Dragonmeres don't eat humans. If you are this foolish, perhaps you won't be useful after all."

"You're *not* going to eat me?"

"What did I just say?"

"That eating me would be disgusting?"

"Good, you *can* listen. And what did I say before that?"

"Be quiet?"

"So, if you heard me, why aren't you doing it? Speak another word before you're spoken to, and I'll have your tongue splayed."

Knowing he was powerless, Macal fell silent and concentrated on not squirming in discomfort as he was jostled by the creature's rapid pace through the woods. He couldn't guess how far they had traveled already, but the creature's fleetness of foot was astonishing. It did not speak as the trees passed by in a blur. Macal began to wish he hadn't left Lalliard. If the wizard had been with him, he would have been safe. But he had chosen to leave, and now it seemed he was going to pay a high price for his foolish decision.

Eventually the creature's long strides shortened, its pace slowed. They seemed to be nearing their destination—and whatever fate would become him.

As they broke from the trees, Macal realized he was being carried into a camp of some sort. The camp was massive, full of color and vitality, nothing like the destination he had expected; he had thought the creature would take him to some dingy cave where it could slowly feast upon him in glee for the next several hours. He was relieved to find he was wrong. As they moved through the crowded camp, his amazement grew as he realized what he was seeing. This was some sort of an Elronian military camp!

All around him were men dressed in Elronian vestments. Some were in leather armor, while others wore heavy red clothes over plate mail shinier than any Macal had ever seen. Most had long, thick swords on their left hips, short slender blades on their right. The men in leather had matching boots that appeared to be in pristine condition. Macal also noticed they all wore shiny silver rings. As the creature passed close to one of the men, the boy saw that his ring bore a design showing the head of an Elronian horse.

The guards met his gaze curiously as he was carried past them, but did not speak. Instead they bowed to the creature striding nobly through the camp. Macal still couldn't believe where he was. He caught sight of some jotun steeds, horse-like animals nearly one and a half times the size of a normal horse. Two mighty legs in the front and four in the back endowed the jotuns with great speed. Although Macal had never seen one of these mounts from the southern Julabar Highlands, he recognized them from Uncle Melkes' stories. He remembered his uncle saying that in ancient days only the elder elves had ridden jotuns. Now, with the Highlands ruled by Roax the Horse Lord, himself a cross between a jotun and a centaur, others had been allowed to ride these highly sought-after mounts. One thing puzzled the boy. He had been told that one reason the steeds were so coveted was that each one had to be a gift from Roax himself. In front of him now were nearly two dozen.

As his captor carried him through the camp, he also saw cavalier knights, pale one-eyed augurs, and spell casters accompanied by various familiars of toads, owls, and bats. There were aged, bearded sages, and male and female attendants dressed in white robes with gold hems, all of which were taking an interest in his arrival. There was also an aroma of food such as Macal had never smelled before. Each delightful whiff reminded him of the pangs in his stomach. It was some sort of meat, flavored with honey and other wonderful things he couldn't recognize.

They passed even more Jotuns bedecked in full plate armor with thick padding underneath, then an ornate carriage with two unicorns in royal harnesses grazing nearby. Macal couldn't believe it. Unicorns! He was actually seeing unicorns!

As quickly as they had come into view, they were gone. Next he saw several big black stallions, also grazing. Although the beasts were impressive, after the unicorns and the jotuns they barely registered in the boy's mind before they passed a blacksmith's tent that hid them from view.

The soft music of a lute became audible as they approached the largest and most decorated tent in the well-armed camp. Larger than Uncle Melkes' cottage, the enormous red tent was trimmed in elegant gold and black. Here and there along the outside walls was stitched the black dragon head of Elronia. The lute's melody was unfamiliar to Macal, but he found it delightfully serene and poignant, as if the music possessed a heart of its own.

The musician, seated on a fine plush chair just outside the tent, was an elf. His hair was a light mulberry color and hung long down around his face. His skin, matching his hair, was the palest of violets. His eyes were an ice blue that nearly glowed, and he had lips of a dull orange hue. From the stories Macal had been told, based on the elf's skin color he guessed the elf must be from Talorean.

Also in front of the tent were two of the sturdiest and most fearsome guards the boy had seen in the camp. At the approach of his captor the guards bowed and pulled open the tent's red flaps. The creature stepped inside the tent, took a few steps, and dropped Macal roughly to the floor.

"Who is this, Viscount Razz?" Macal heard a sweet feminine voice ask softly as he tried to stand up in some kind of dignified fashion.

"I'm sorry he is so disgusting, My Lord's Jewel," Macal heard the dragonmere answer as it moved away from him. "I found him out in the woods by himself."

Macal raised his head. Seated on an elegant portable throne was the most beautiful girl he had ever seen. Her blue eyes were large and soft, with thick light lashes. On her short blond hair was an exquisite platinum tiara set with glittering diamonds, emeralds, sapphires, and rubies. Her slenderness was accentuated by a silk lavender gown with dainty white frills and lace. All her features were refined and delicate; there wasn't a harsh angle about her. Macal stared, unable to fathom how one person could be so gloriously beautiful. It seemed unfair to all the other women in the world, who could not hope to complete with this girl's surpassing beauty. Gazing at her, he felt his heart stir as it never had before.

Then she said something that left him thunderstruck. It was even more unreal than her divine beauty. The boy was almost sure he had misheard; never had he imagined he would hear those words spoken to him, today or any day.

"Welcome, it is a pleasure to meet you," she said cordially, meeting his gaze. "I am Princess Aeria Stormlion of the Elronian kingdom."

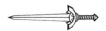

Macal immediately fell to his knees and bowed low. He was unsure if what he was doing was proper etiquette, because he had never before been in the presence of royalty.

"May the Crown stay strong," he muttered in awe, trying to make his voice sound firm and deep. Instead it came out meek and high-pitched.

"It does," replied Princess Aeria with certainty. "On *that* you can trust me; I am an authority on that particular subject. The Crown is strong and shall remain so." Keeping her quizzical eyes on Macal, the Princess spoke to the dragonmere that had carried him in. "Again, who is this, Viscount? And why have you brought him here?"

"We've done no proper introductions, My Jewel, but I think you will find this boy's origins highly intriguing. I found him near the mill when I was making sure the trolls had actually vacated the area. Fortunately for him, they had. But he is very lucky that he did not arrive last night."

Lucky? Macal was pretty sure he was anything but lucky. Everything that had happened to him seemed to indicate that it was Arthanius, the God of Demons, rather than Devera who was watching over him. *And what did his origins have to do with anything?*

"Where do you come from?" asked the Princess after a long moment of silence. She seemed just as intrigued as Macal about the mystery suggested by the dragonmere's words. Her eyes were keen with intelligence and her voice full of confidence.

"I'm from Hormul." In the presence of the enchanting young princess, Macal felt timid and out of place with his disheveled clothing and bruised face. She was beautiful, smart, and poised, and he looked worse than a battered vagrant who had barely survived the pox.

"That is a small hamlet in the northern center of the kingdom, My Jewel," Viscount Razz explained.

"I have heard of it. And what is your name?" she asked.

Macal felt as if he were being interviewed by an angel. His clumsy tongue stumbled over the answer. "M-Macal Teel."

Princess Aeria Stormlion stiffened at the boy's response. "*Teel?* Of the *Bertran Teel* family?"

"Y-yes." Macal was uncertain why his name should spark such a reaction. "Yes, he is my father, and I am looking for him. I was told he was a traitor. Do you know him? Do you know where he is?" He was suddenly filled with hope and excitement. If the Princess knew who his father was, his search might end more quickly than he had thought! *Perhaps his father was here in this camp!*

"Watch how you question the King's Jewel!" Viscount Razz reprimanded.

Princess Aeria ignored the interruption. "*Who* said he was a traitor?"

"A soldier of my father's regiment told us after they arrived in town without him. The new captain of the Amber Dragoons said my father had stolen some important plans," explained Macal. He was still overwhelmed that the princess of the kingdom knew who his father was.

"Should we tell him, My Jewel?" Viscount Razz seemed to be weighing some invisible options. "I shared your current thoughts when he first told me who he was."

"Tell me what?" If they had information about his father, Macal wanted to know what it was. *What do they know that I don't?*

The Princess was silent a moment, then addressed the Viscount. "I think it's best if we talk in private first." Turning back to Macal, "If you will excuse us, Macal Teel, I would like to talk to my Royal Advisor briefly before we continue our discourse."

What? No! Macal shouted in his mind. His feet remained rooted where they were; he didn't want to leave. If these people knew something about his father, he wanted to hear it right now. It was obvious, however, that he had no choice in the matter; at the Princess's command, the two guards waiting outside the tent ushered him out, leaving her alone with the Viscount to discuss the mystery that kept his father from him.

They knew something. As Macal left the tent, the question he kept asking himself was, *Were they going to tell him what it was?*

Outside the tent, the resolute Royal Guards silently returned to their positions on either side of the entry. Macal understood this to mean that he should stand nearby and not wander off. His head was whirling. *Why did the Princess want to talk in private?* He was smart enough to realize that the Princess and her advisor were unsure what they wanted to tell him. That meant he might not be told the whole truth.

He also understood how surprised they were to find him. They were uncertain how to react to the situation and, rather than be hasty, they were taking a moment to regroup and form a plan. He was just a boy, though. Did they really need a strategy to deal with him? And what could be so surprising about finding him? He was nobody important. Obviously it had something to do with his father. *But what? And if they told him anything at all, would it be the truth?*

While he waited outside the tent in the large clearing that contained the camp, Macal enjoyed the bright sun and a cloudless open sky dotted with birds. The smell of cooking food that wafted around the tents reawakened his hunger. If he hadn't been determined to find out about his father, he would have sought out the cooking tent as fast as he could, begged a meal, then sat down to enjoy it in some open space on what under normal circumstances would have been an unmemorable but beautiful day. Standing outside a princess's tent, however, he noticed he was drawing attention again. Now that he understood this was an Elronian military camp, he could see they were all probably wondering the same thing he was. *Why had the dragonmere brought him here?*

Finally the Royal Guards, obeying an order from within, beckoned him back inside the tent. Macal entered nervously. He knew he wanted to hear about his father. He needed to know everything, but at the same time he was afraid of what he might learn. He still clung to the hope that everything would be all right, that he and his father could be reunited and live together happily in a safe place—but he knew there was a strong possibility that what he was about to learn would shatter what little was left of his world.

Resuming his position in front of the throne, he looked into the face of Princess Aeria Stormlion. She couldn't have been much older than he was, but she had an air of maturity and compassion. Standing beside her, Viscount Razz was rigidly impassive.

"Your father is not a traitor," she said at last. "He stole no plans."

Macal was rendered breathless by the brief powerful words. "But they said—the captain of the Amber Dragoons himself said—"

"Your father took the plans, yes," Princess Aeria said. "But he took them because I told him to."

The boy gaped at her. "Told him to? Wh—why?"

"He took them on my orders, and those of my father the King. We needed him to hide the enchanted plans so that only a few of us would know where they were, in order to prevent them from being recaptured by the Troll King. If we wish to survive this war, their value to us is incalculable. We had heard rumors that there was a spy in our midst, and we couldn't chance losing the documents. I will say it again. Your father is not a traitor. And as far as I know, he is still alive."

He had been right to trust in his father's innocence. Captain Jengus had been wrong.

I knew he wouldn't have done such a thing! He loves the kingdom. I knew he wasn't a traitor! The worry that had burdened Macal since last night was washed away by a rush of relief that left him dizzy. He wobbled on his legs. The Viscount took a step forward to keep him from falling, but the boy recovered on his own. A dazzling smile transformed his face, and to the surprise of both the Princess and her advisor, Macal leapt and threw his arms around Viscount Razz in a hug of pure joy. *His father wasn't a traitor!*

The Royal Advisor gazed down in astonishment at the small boy whose face was buried in his chest, dampening his imperial tabard with tears of relief. Hugs were new to him. Uncertainly he glanced at the Princess for guidance. Although she too was surprised, she mimed a comforting pat on the back. The Viscount hesitated. The practice of offering physical comfort was alien to his kind, but as the Princess narrowed her eyes at him, he awkwardly delivered a few gentle taps to Macal's back with his huge, taloned hand.

Recent events had convinced Macal that he would never again have a reason to rejoice, but now the Princess had given him one. In spite of his misery and guilt over his uncle's death, he had accomplished his goal; he had set out to prove that his father was not a traitor, and he had succeeded! He had proof; the word of the Princess of Elronia. *Who wouldn't believe her?*

Maybe, just maybe, he thought to himself, *things might be all right.* Now all he needed was to learn his father's whereabouts so they could be reunited and start a new life. Where would they go? He couldn't imagine returning to Hormul, but his father would have ideas. Once they were back together, they could decide.

Embarrassed at his childish show of emotion, Macal slowly stepped back from Viscount Razz and muttered, "Sorry." He avoided the dragonmere's gaze and instead looked at the Princess, who answered his joyful grin with a smile of her own. She seemed pleased to have been able to offer him this happiness. Although until this moment Macal had never wasted any thought on the royal line, right now he felt proud to have them as rulers. They seemed to mean well and care for those around them. He doubted very much that the Troll King was so empathetic.

"Where is my father?" he asked, eager for their reunion.

"We will get to that," the Princess said. "First, there are a few other things we should talk about."

Although Macal found it difficult to concentrate on anything but the prospect of seeing his father again, he forced himself to listen to the Princess. "Do you know anything at all about the plans?" she was asking.

"Just what the captain told my uncle and me—that some Elronian spy had stolen the Troll King's battle plans. Then he said my father had stolen them from us, to sell them back to the Troll King." Elated that his father was innocent, the boy struggled to keep from smiling. Right now he had to admit he cared nothing for the plans. He just wanted to know where he could find his father.

"The plans contain the complete military strategies of King Orgog," the Princess said. "But there is far more to them than that. Knowing they were stolen, the Troll King could have easily rerouted his troops and altered war strategies. What makes the plans so crucial, both to us and to King Orgog, is that he had them somehow enchanted to continually update themselves. At any given moment, they reflect the actual location of his troops. It was a foolish thing to do on his part. As you can imagine, when we were able to obtain them they proved an enormous benefit to our forces. Of course the trolls want the plans back. Not only do they reveal the location of the troll troops, but of their reserves and all their supplies. Do you understand so far?"

Macal nodded.

"Good. As I said before, once we realized there was a possible spy among us, I ordered your father to secretly remove the plans and take them to my father the King in Keratost. This was several weeks ago."

"So my father is in Keratost right now?" Macal couldn't believe his great change of luck. Instead of being a traitor, his father had been entrusted with an important mission and sent to the safest place in all of Elronia!

The Princess shook her head. "Sadly, no. My father reported that Bertran Teel never arrived in Keratost."

"What do you mean, *he never arrived?*" The boy's voice rose, his worries returning in an avalanche.

"Again, I advise you to watch your tone," warned the Viscount.

"It's okay, Viscount Razz," said the Princess. "He is receiving some very troubling news. An overwhelming sense of emotion is to be expected."

"So where is my father? Please tell me!" Macal's heart was in an uproar. Just a moment ago he had thought his quest was over.

"Your father is a very brave and courageous man," began Princess Aeria. "It is important for you to know that. He has given a great deal for our kingdom, and all those in the realm benefit from his efforts."

Macal didn't like the ring of this; it sounded like an epitaph. Bad as it was not to know where his father was, the thought that he had died was utterly unbearable. As he reminded himself many times during the past night, his father was all he had left.

"That is why I chose him for this mission," the Princess continued. "He is a noble and loyal man. I say this to remind you that you should be proud of him."

Macal heard that. She had said *is. Is*, not *was*. That must mean his father was still alive!

"From what our augurs tell us right now, it is understood that your father may have been captured. Or was. Or will be. With augurs it's so hard to tell. They see so many futures and pasts, it all gets jumbled together—"

"Captured?" the boy interrupted.

"Yes, captured," confirmed Viscount Razz. "And taken to the dungeons of the Troll King's castle."

Captured! The word was like an icy hand clutching Macal's heart. "He *can't* be captured! Not now. Not ever." he blurted. "He *has* to come home. Our town was attacked—my uncle was killed—he's all I have left!"

"If he has already been captured we can only assume that the reason

Bertran is still alive is that he has refused to divulge the location of the missing battle plans to the trolls," the Viscount said. "He must have, or will have, had time to hide them before he was caught. Regardless of when things will happen, we can assume the trolls will keep him alive until they can force him to reveal the hiding place of the plans."

"He would never tell them!"

"Then the interrogation methods will increase in force," the Viscount said bluntly. "And at some point he will die."

"Then you have to rescue him!" shouted Macal. "He risked his life to save your plans!"

"Do not dare to tell the King's Jewel what to do, boy!" Viscount Razz's snarl revealed his full array of sharp teeth.

"They are *your* plans as well," pointed out the Princess, her calm voice easing the tension. "They belong to the kingdom. We will likely all perish if they return to the hands of the Troll King. His forces are far superior in size to ours. They prepared well for this war and they plan to win. Using King Orgog's own battle plans against him has been our best hope; with them we could well prepare for any attack. The Troll King's knowledge of our advantage might have inhibited him; he might even have withdrawn his troops entirely. The reason so many villages—yours and others—have been attacked over the past few weeks is that he is trying to gain a decisive advantage before either side recovers the plans."

"But you can save my father! If the plans are so important, what choice do you have?"

"I agree with you. But the army is already spread thin, and there is no way to advance a whole battalion to the Troll King's fortress, which lies deep within their lands. It would be a wasted effort costing many senseless deaths. Instead of trying to move a large formation of troops to the castle, we have been seeking an individual soldier or hireling to make the attempt. But it is no simple task. Such a person must penetrate Castle Darkmoor and free Bertran Teel—and by doing so, recover the plans and save Elronia."

Princess Aeria Stormlion hesitated, and this first sign of uncertainty filled Macal with doubts. What was she thinking? Viscount Razz stared at him, as if he knew something Macal didn't. Finally the Princess seemed to come to terms with what she wanted to say.

"I am sorry, Macal. Your father has done many great things for Elronia, but right now we can do nothing for him."

A cold knot formed at the pit of Macal's stomach. "Y-you're just going to leave him there? To—to *die*?"

"We will send someone as soon as we find a person capable of the task."

"He could be dead by then!"

"I know that. But all our most qualified soldiers are needed at the front, and no one else has stepped forward to volunteer for what will most likely only be a suicide mission. Time is short; the end of the war approaches quickly. Your father could die at any moment. He may have been forced to tell the location of the plans; they could already be in the Troll King's hands. Or Bertran could die without revealing the secret, and the plans will be lost to both sides. Because we no longer possess them, I ride for Varun on the far side of the Rashinasti Forest, to parley with the hobgoblin warlords for aid in the war. An alliance with Varun is now our best hope of surviving this conflict."

Macal couldn't speak. They were going to let his father die. After everything he had done for them, they were going to let him be tortured to death. A wave of nausea washed over him at the thought that, along with everything else he had lost, he was going to lose his father too. What god had he scorned, that everything he loved in his life should be taken from him? *What god?*

"I will go." He heard the words in the air before he recognized the voice that had uttered them. His own. The realization struck him like a stone. The Princess and the Viscount stared at him.

"What?" They spoke in incredulous unison.

Me? Go to the Troll King's castle by myself? Am I crazy? In retrospect, to Macal it seemed that madness was the only possible explanation for what he had said.

"It falls to me to free him," he began unsteadily. *How could he hope to succeed at such a task?* "All I have to do is go and free him and—and bring back the plans. I can help save the kingdom. I swore an oath that I would find my father. If nobody else will go after him, I will."

"That's insane! You will never succeed! You do not even know how to fight," Viscount Razz said. "You don't even have a knife."

Macal had to acknowledge the truth of these statements. *I'm only good at running away from danger,* he thought. *If you need somebody to do that, then I am the right person for the job.* What had possessed him to volunteer for a mission that would challenge even a brave and experienced warrior, let alone a cowardly boy? *Rescue my father? From the troll lands? Me?*

Macal looked at Princess Aeria. He didn't want to deceive her about his abilities, but at the same time he was reluctant to reveal to her just how weak and inept he really was. In spite of the fact that he had just met her, he already found himself yearning for her approval. If she knew his dubious history as a fighter, she might not let him try to rescue his father.

She was staring at him, amazement still plain on her face. Meeting her sympathetic eyes, Macal felt a jolt of connection. She was just a girl, yet she was doing everything possible to save her kingdom. Why couldn't he, just a boy, do something too?

"I will save Bertran Teel from the Troll King's castle," he vowed, steadily holding her gaze. "I will save him and recover the plans."

"It's not possible," she said at last. "You have no chance of success."

"The Jewel is right," agreed Viscount Razz, although the boy's willingness to take on impossible odds had clearly impressed him. "Your offer shows tremendous courage, but accepting it would be the same as murdering you here right now."

"Come with me, then! Your company is not that large. Maybe a group this size would have a chance of sneaking in." Macal knew he was grasping at straws. The idea of being alone again filled him with terror. He wished Lalliard where here. The wizard would have known what to do.

"We cannot go with you," the Princess said. "We need every man if we are to have any hope of surviving our march through the dark forest. I am sure that the movements of the troll forces have awakened many haunts that we might otherwise have avoided. If we fall, Varun will have trolls on two different borders. In light of the Troll King's desire to claim more lands, the inevitable outcome is obvious. We are traveling with very few soldiers as it is, just enough to protect the emissaries."

"Then I will go alone," Macal said.

The Princess's face softened as she realized how hard it must have been for him to receive all this information at once. Then she seemed to come to a decision. "I promise you this," she said tenderly to the tired, frightened boy. "When I can, if I can find a way, I will send you help."

"You're letting him go?" asked Viscount Razz.

"What choice do I have? I am just a girl, as he is just a boy. Everyone should have the chance to make a difference, especially someone with so much to lose." She seemed to be echoing Macal's own thoughts.

The dragonmere's shoulders sagged as he relented. He was clearly astonished by the turn of events, but he also knew he wasn't going to win. "Then we had better equip you."

"Go, Macal Teel," Princess Aeria said. "You look tired and hungry, and you need time to convalesce before your journey. Relax and heal as best you can. We will need to rise early tomorrow morning if we intend to make a small side excursion on our way to Varun."

Macal became curious. "An excursion?"

"Yes, to the Tomb of the Old King." Her tone said no explanation was necessary, but Macal was still in the dark.

"I've never heard of it. Why are we going? What will we find there?"

"Hopefully," she said as she beckoned the royal guards escort him out, "your destiny."

CHAPTER 10

Volten the Shadow woke up in the meeting chamber below Castle Darkmoor. He rubbed his head gingerly where the king had struck him. His head ached, his cheek was surely bruised, and his vision had gone blurry. As he painfully pulled himself up off the floor, hatred for the Troll King enveloped him. He focused and cleared his mind. Yes, he hated Orgog, but for the moment he needed him.

At first he went slowly, until the dizziness started to fade. Once he regained his balance he moved speedily down through a secret tunnel that led beneath the castle out onto the dark mountain. The Shadow emerged through the exit, concealed in one of the gargantuan support pillars that held the castle in the sky. He looked back and up at the vile fortress. As always, he found the strange, misty emerald glow of the fog that rose about the mountain unsettling.

The castle was an uplifted mountain. Spires, towers, turrets, and balconies had been roughly carved into the archaic stone. The bulk of the fortress appeared to float several hundred feet in the air, suspended by great pillars and irregular masses of rock continually swathed in a haunting fog. He didn't know how they had raised it. *Magic*, he guessed.

All around him bubbled pools of odd green lava. Not far from where he stood a long stairway twisted its way up the thickest and most central of the support pillars, ending in a massive pair bronze double doors at the front of the castle. An entrance he never used. Behind the castle rose another range of even higher mountains.

As always, he watched as the tunnel he had just exited slowly vanished. The black, jagged rock seethed and churned like a rising wave, to seal up the rock of the pillar once more. The king's witch brides watched him closely with their scrying spells, always. When he returned they would again tear the rock open to grant him access. Always watching....

He shook off his unease. His orders were clear and he knew this was his final chance. He did not doubt that if he came back empty handed the Troll king would kill him. *Let them watch. That was not going to happen. Not that I would come back empty handed. I would disappear instead.*

But there was too much at risk. He didn't really care about the Troll King's plans, or if he succeeded in his campaign to conquer Elronia. What he did care about was the future that waited for him at the end of this assignment. One acquisition and delivery. Then he would be done with all the shadow and secrecy.

He wasn't going to succeed because it helped the king. He was going to succeed because it helped him.

His past had been agonizing him more and more lately as he got closer to possibly freeing himself from it. Images of his parents dusted themselves off and came foremost to his mind as he touched the two copper bracelets on his wrists together.

As the wide shiny bands clanked, great fiery wings erupted from his back, giving him the appearance of a dark angel. The grotesque and slimy creatures that inhabited the mountainside nearby scattered in panic as he lit up the night with his wings. With a crouch and jump he launched himself into the sky and streaked across it like a meteor.

His parents had been serfs. Peasant farmers who paid their lord dues in exchange for a small piece of the lord's land on which there allowed to farm food for themselves. As he blazed through the dark sky, the wind rustling his long shaggy brown hair, he could recall wanting nothing to do with that sort of life even in his earliest memories. He hated it as a child. *He hated it now.* He thought that Serfdom was one small step away from being slaves. He had never figured out why his parents had sacrificed their freedom to become serfs.

Protection from poverty, hunger, sickness, and war was what they were promised, but it didn't take long to see they still suffered all that, except now they had also lost the freedom to leave their village of Torvin.

Worse still, he recalled, not only did he and his parents have to work their own small field, but they had to spend several days a week working the lord's fields. Lord Mercious had built his manse several miles east of the village. Volten had spent uncountable days by his parents' side ploughing, planting seeds, weeding, and harvesting another man's farm, working to fill another man's food stores. Of course all the serfs—and the lord—knew that the time spent tending his land meant they no longer had enough time to properly care for their own fields.

All of that traded for a place to live and a meager harvest of vegetables. Their tiny single-room domicile was more like a hut than a house. It didn't even have any beds; instead, as if they were animals, they used piles of straw for bedding. They had to eat out of crude wooden bowls with chunky misshapen wooden spoons and cups.

To make it all worse it soon became evident, even to the lord, that his parents were not adept farmers, so the yield from each harvest was dismal and barely reaped them enough to eat after Lord Mercious collected his dues.

As the dues increased, his parents were unable to keep up with the payment demands of the lord after only a few seasons. With his mounted men-at-arms, Lord Mercious eventually came to their hut and cast them out just as the winter months came. He announced unceremoniously that another family had been granted dominion of their house and lands and that they were no longer welcome there. Lacking all provisions, the three of them were escorted to the borders of Lord Mercious' lands and told they would spend time in the Sheriff's dungeon if they ever returned.

As his past kept flooding through him, reminding him of the importance of succeeding with this assignment, the wretched landscape of Marglamesh came to an end. He could now see the shadowy landscape that was, unmistakably, Xanga-Mor.

Back then, it was Volten who had found them shelter. In the nearby woods from which the lord had allowed them to gather firewood, Volten recalled the location of a cave he had come across. Going there meant going back onto the lord's land, but they couldn't see any other choice. For a while the cave had been a blessing, but with no food, even the best of shelters wouldn't have mattered.

He had snuck back to the village to beg for food while his parents slept, but the other serf families turned him away without even a morsel. They had been forbidden to share their harvests, lest they lose their own place on the lord's estate.

Volten watched helplessly as his parents slowly starved to death in the cold snowy cave. Every time that thought revisited him a volcanic rage swelled. Fiery hot like his wings, fueled by a pain that had scorched his soul.

Only he survived the long winter. He often thought it was his youth that allowed him to persevere. His father had died first, followed within days by his grieving mother. With no shovel to dig into the frozen soil he left without burying them.

He took his father's gloves, the only pair the three of them had, and his father's worn boots, which were still better than Volten's. Lastly, he slid a small knife he had once stolen from the lord's house into the sheath on his belt.

It was that moment, as he prepared to leave, that he had changed his name. He wanted no souvenirs or reminders from this place. It was dead to him. Never would he go back to this world, to this life of subjugation.

The chill wind stung his ears and cheeks as he stepped out of the cave and he immediately wished he had a hat. It was at that moment, as he left his parents frozen in a cave and set out into the world alone, that he remembered that this day was also his birthday.

For the next several years he went from place to place stealing food and clothing to survive. To his fortune, he had found he had a knack for it. With the threat of poverty always looming behind, he knew he needed to take more, regardless of the risks. As his confidence and skills at thievery grew he forced himself onward to purses and pouches.

It was simple—everybody always took from him, now he was going to take from everybody.

This new tactic had worked well, until one day when he was caught in Floirus by the thieves guild. They were not fond of rogue cutpurses working their territory without having first paid their dues and also offering the guild a cut of the take.

Marglamesh passed behind the winged Shadow as he raced over the craggy lands of Xanga-Mor.

The mark Volten had successfully robbed just before the guild enforcers closed in on him was a young noble with a pouch of rare magical baubles, each imbued with a different incantation. Fortunately the enchanted trinkets really impressed the guild master, who kept them in exchange for giving Volten a choice.

The heavyset guildmaster slumped upon his garish wooden throne was direct: "Work for the guild or lose your hands. The choice is completely yours, of course."

Without delay Volten chose the former. From then on, surrounded by people far more talented and trained in the profession of filching, he learned a great deal and refined his skills. He came to also learn that this guild was one of the most prominent and skilled in the region, which meant there were a lot of very profitable assignments to be hired for. He was never sure why this was; perhaps the guildmaster had seen something in him, but eventually the tasks he was hired for stopped being about the acquisition of objects from another person's procession and rather about a much more valuable commodity—information. That was when his life as a spy began.

Several years passed. After gaining enough of a reputation through some successful and prominent assignments, he realized he didn't need the guild anymore. They took half the cut, which he was sure went right into the guildmaster's personal coffers. This arrangement reminded him much of his parents' life as serfs. He had to do all the work and they took half or more of the profits.

With clients coming to him directly, he left the guild and moved to Watermark, and the great and rich port city of Gelvin. One of the most powerful realms in all of Aerinth, Watermark was a vast trading empire that spanned the Formaline Ocean, and thus a good part of the globe. It was not the domain of a king, but ruled by a select group of wealthy and powerful guildmasters.

Shortly after arriving in Gelvin he met a woman named Glendrel, and his plans for the future changed in a flash as he fell for her. But, after a mishap stealing from her father—a rich merchant with even stronger underworld ties than himself—he was compelled to exit the city in haste in the shadow of night. It was one of the only thefts he ever regretted. He had to take temporary sanctuary in Drakenport, another port city, until he could make amends in Watermark.

Volten still mused on the idea of finding Glendrel once he was setup with his new life. Then he would have enough money to make amends with her father. *A small donation to his holdings should take care of that.* He was embarrassed to admit, even to himself, that he missed her more than he did his parents. She was short, with auburn hair and brown eyes. Her face had the perfection of a goddess and her understanding smile always caused his chilly heart to quiver with warmth.

How times had changed. Now he had his own underlings and nearly enough wealth to retire from this second stage of his life. Even now he had his spies watching Bertran Teel, the man who bore the Trolls King's war plans. The man that stood between him and the future he'd been running to since Lord Mercious had thrown his family onto the streets like vagrants.

The last report he'd received was that the soldier was between the riverside villages of Rorenth and Maylan. He was heading south on foot toward Keratost. The spy hadn't wasted time while he went to see King Orgog. His associates had been using that time to prepare a trap for the soldier.

He descended and gracefully landed on the war ravaged land of Xanga-Mor. He reached into his pouch and took out some colorful rune-covered stones and tossed them onto the ground. Soon a ghostly image appeared. The scene in it changed as he directed it to find one of his men.

In a moment he found Lof, a man with skin the pale blue hue of a zombie and nearly the size of an ogre. The behemoth noticed Volten's magical presence immediately.

"Is he still heading south?"

"Yes."

"Are we ready?"

"Yes. He will not get away."

Escorted by soldiers, Macal walked through the afternoon sun in a daze. Although his feet automatically kept moving, his head was swimming. *His*

father was not a traitor. His father was alive. His father was on a secret mission for the royal family. But he had been caught, or would be, and he was going to be cruelly interrogated by the trolls to extract the location of the hidden plans. It was now up to Macal to put things right. He had to find his father and retrieve the plans that would save Elronia from the doom of the trolls.

The boy's fear of the task before him paled beside the thought of his father being tortured. Right now, in the dark recesses of the troll moorlands, Bertran Teal could be enduring terrible pain to protect the realm from destruction.

Macal came to himself with a start as the soldiers halted beside a tent. It was red like all the others, and large enough to house several men comfortably. From within wafted the fragrant aroma of food.

"Is this where I'm supposed to stay?" he asked.

"Yes, sir," replied one of the soldiers. "And I'd like to tell you something, if you don't mind."

Macal looked up. The man was big and muscular, as solid a soldier as he had ever seen. He had dark hair and eyes and his arms were crisscrossed with battle scars.

"I am Mercule Gentris," he said. "I have served with Bertran Teel, as have many men here. It was an honor. He is a great soldier, and it seems that you inherited that greatness. You'll have no trouble succeeding in your quest."

Macal stared in disbelief. *This man knew his father! But how did he already know about Macal's mission?* The soldiers, he decided, must have been listening outside the tent. "You really knew my father?"

"Yes, I was with him at the last battle of Xanga-Mor. I saw him slay the two-headed Troll King and claim the wondrous silver sword Alrang-Dal from the monster's corpse. I was proud to serve with him, and I am proud to meet his son."

Macal didn't know what to say. He couldn't remember anyone ever being proud to meet him, or anyone ever praising his family. He was far more accustomed to gibes, jests, and punches from Menk and his crew.

"Th-thank you," he managed to stammer at last. Gentris nodded and turned away. Macal entered the tent, expecting to find a few tent-mates, but there was only a single cot with an empty military locker at its foot, the lid open. Macal regarded the bed. With fresh sheets, a light linen blanket, and a fluffier pillow than any he had ever seen, it looked supremely welcoming. He wanted to dive into it, snuggle under the blanket, and sleep away the turmoil of the past night and day. Maybe when he woke up, it would all prove to have been a bad dream.

In the center of the tent stood a small wooden table and stool. Set on the table beside an unlit tallow candle was an oversized plate piled with thickly sliced mutton, a bowl of steaming beef stew, and assorted soft cheeses with a strong, unfamiliar smell. There was also a chunk of crusty bread, a mug of crisp apple cider, and a cinnamon-spiced custard tart. Macal could scarcely believe his eyes. He was advancing on the feast when he noticed two large wooden pails near the left side of the tent. The first overflowed with soapy water, suds running down the side of the weathered container; the second held clean water to rinse with.

All this—for him! He had never had his own space before. When his father was at home, he slept with him in the main room. This enormous tent with its luxurious accommodations was no doubt a temporary lodging, but it made him feel like a king.

Overwhelmed by hunger, he rushed to the table and sat down. Cleaning up could wait. As he delved into the delicious meal his stomach sang out in delight. He had never had such a feast before, even on special occasions and holidays. Mutton, stew, bread, and cheese disappeared in a matter of moments. He had just taken a bite of the fresh tart when he heard a small, frail voice just outside the tent.

"May I enter?"

The voice was so soft Macal almost missed it. He swallowed the tart and took a gulp of cider. "M-b-yes!"

Into the tent stepped a tiny man with large brown eyes and a balding head. He was dressed in a simple red robe of silk, with shoes of the same color. Macal had never seen anyone so frail. His body seemed to have barely enough muscle to hold his bones in place. Draped over one spindly arm were several lengths of fabric in gold, white, and red. A bandolier belt over his shoulder sported needles and spools of thread along its length. He carried a slender piece of pale rope marked with numbered lines, obviously a measuring device.

"I am Osiary Rendal, Royal Tailor to the Princess of Elronia. May the Crown stay strong." The voice was as diminutive as the man; Macal had to strain to hear him.

"May the Crown stay strong," he responded automatically. "I am Macal Teel."

"The Princess has sent to me to properly attire you." The tailor was clearly less interested in boy's name than in his dimensions. "Could you step away from the table?"

Macal obliged. The Royal Tailor scurried up to him, shoulders twitching in rhythm with his steps. His bulging brown eyes darted around Macal's body as if memorizing its shape. Quickly he set the fabrics aside and began to measure the boy, muttering numbers to himself in a nearly inaudible voice. He did not address Macal again, and it was obvious he regarded speech as a distraction from his true heart's desire, the crafting of clothes.

"Are these colors to your liking? They are all we have on short notice." Finishing his measurements, the Royal Tailor seemed embarrassed at the small selection, as if he should have known to plan for the boy's surprise arrival.

"Yes, of course," Macal said. The fabrics the tailor had brought were in stark contrast to the bleak grays, browns, and occasional greens he was used to wearing. He had always agreed with Uncle Melkes that brightly colored clothing was far too expensive to be worth the price.

"That is all for now, then." The meek little man quickly gathered his fabrics and started out the door, his shoulders twitching.

"Wait!" Macal said. "Let me ask you something."

Osiary Rendal slowly turned back, his face blank. He was plainly uncomfortable with the idea of a conversation that wasn't about clothing fabrication. He blinked.

"Do you know what the Tomb of the Old King is?" asked Macal hopefully.

"No, I don't." The tiny man shuffled his feet, as if talking was intolerable when there was work to be done.

"Thanks anyway," said Macal, his hopes dashed.

Osiary Rendal started out and then suddenly turned back. For a moment Macal thought the man had remembered something he was about to share, something that would shed light on the mystery of the tomb. But the tailor only muttered, "A sleeping robe for the night will be along shortly." Without another word he turned and left the tent.

"Thanks," the disappointed boy called after him.

After Osiary had gone Macal returned to his tart, wishing he had a dozen more just like it. As he finished it off, his thoughts returned to his conversation with the Princess. He hoped she was convinced he was right to volunteer for this mission, even if he wasn't entirely sure.

He *did* have to save his father. He knew that if he were in danger, his father would do whatever he could to save him. How could he not do the same? He only hoped that the Princess would be able to send the help she had promised. That promise was the only thing giving him strength to attempt this quest.

True to the word of the Royal Tailor, a short time later a plump girl with long dark hair and a round, cherubic face delivered a bright red sleeping gown hemmed in shimmering gold. Judging by the look of it, the gown would be a perfect fit. Either it had been already made, or Osiary Rendal was the fastest tailor in the realm.

His hunger satiated at last, Macal disrobed, washed, put on the sleeping gown, and climbed into bed. Within minutes he was fast asleep. Through the afternoon and into the night he slept restlessly, tormented by dreams. Images of his uncle's body lying unburied on the plaza alternated with specters of the cruel pain his father must be suffering.

Despite his fitful slumber, when he finally woke to the early morning bustle of the camp he was energized. Outside the tent he could hear the soldiers being called to muster and assigned their duties for the day. As he sat up on his cot, he saw that sometime during the night he must have had a visitor. Hanging from one of the tent supports was an exquisite riding outfit made of leather. Next to it hung a thick red cloak complete with a cowl. To Macal's amazement, there also dangled a heavy chain mail shirt that looked small enough to fit him, its hundreds of rings fashioned from brilliant steel.

The footlocker at the end of the bed had been filled. He could see a large backpack, a dagger, and some thick leather kneeboots. All this was for *him?* Eager to try on the new garments, he jumped out of bed and put on the riding outfit. It took a few minutes to figure out how to work his way into the chain mail shirt, but at last he succeeded. Lastly he pulled on the boots. It was surprising how just a change of clothes could alter the way he felt. Confident, almost regal—ready to battle dragons! He was willing to bet Menk had never owned clothes so fine, and he was sure the bully had never owned a chain mail shirt!

Sifting through the supplies in the backpack, he found flint and steel, a tinderbox, some dried military rations, a small length of rope, a roll of bandages, an eating knife, and a bedroll—everything he could possibly need to survive on his adventure! He strapped on the dagger and stepped out of the tent into the first faint rays of rising sunlight.

He was ready to find his father.

As the darkness of night gave way to dawn, Volten descended on a small tract of road that connected the villages of Maylen to the north and Rorenth to the south. The western side of the road bordered a thick wood, and following the road on the eastern side was the massive Abengroth River.

Not wanting the brightness of his wings to alert anyone on the road, he landed a short distance from the trap his associates had set. He dismissed his wings and made his way through the dark to where they waited. The Abengroth forked here, splitting off a small stream, named Laundle, that ran southwestward cutting across the road. His men lurked on the north side of the small stone bridge that spanned the flow.

After a moment searching, he spotted the giant Lof just inside the edge of the woods. He crept up to them unnoticed.

Lof the Keen was staring up the road, his small eyes straining to see in the dim morning light. He had earned the moniker because his size and slow mannerisms were often mistaken for lack of intelligence, rather than the sharp calculated thoughts he always had. The spy had to admit that the large club Lof carried didn't help dismiss this notion.

Next to him stood Jengrul, Lof's older brother. In drastic contrast to Lof's gigantic size, Jengrul was so small and thin he looked like a half folk, with a disfigured grotesque face, narrow eyes, and a dark streak as cruel as a demon. While he shared the same odd pale blue skin as his brother, Volten had found he did not share his brother's intelligence. Amazingly, even with a face like that the horrid man had six wives and over thirteen children. Volten had learned that Lof only did this type of immoral work because he didn't know what else to do with his brother, who had no other skills, and a large brood to feed.

Standing next to the brothers was his final associate, Dalent. Dalent was a drant, a bark-and-branch-covered slight-framed humanoid that was packed with the strength of a giant. Drants came from Asceri, a land of fey folk, and were not common in this part of the world. Volten was not sure why Dalent did this type of work, but he also found that he didn't care, as long as the drant did his part well.

As Volten looked upon them unawares a strange feeling overtook him—he hoped none of them would get hurt. He wasn't in this for violence; that was why he had hired them. They didn't mind mixing a little blood with their work. *That was the trick, making sure you have the right people around you. People who could do what you couldn't. Or wouldn't.*

Lof finally noticed his presence. "Welcome back. He's close." His voice was thick and deep and as if it echoed from the depths of a volcano.

"Good."

Jengrul turned to Volten with a sinister smile as he fingered his daggers. "Yes, it's almost play time. I love this part."

The spy ignored him.

Dalent's moss green eyes allowed him to see in the darkness. He pointed up the road with a branch-like finger. His voice was softer than a whisper. "He's coming."

"Everybody get to your positions." Volten smiled as he saw the oblivious man approaching. *Finally it was about to all be over and he would be richer than he ever dreamed possible.*

CHAPTER 11

Macal stepped outside of his tent. There was a soldier nearby who must have been waiting for him, because as soon as Macal came out the man approached. "I'm to take you to the mess tent, sir."

The soldier set off at a brisk pace and Macal hurried to follow, while still being very conscious of his new clothes. As they made their way through the crowded camp, he hoped for a glimpse of Princess Aeria. Among the dark images churning through his mind, hers kept reappearing like a beacon of light and comfort.

He was starting to think he liked her. He couldn't wait for her to see him in his new attire; he thought he looked dashing and brave, and hoped she would agree. He hoped his military garb would show him in a more impressive light. Perhaps if she had more confidence in him, he would have more in himself.

He had never felt this way about a girl before; it was exhilarating and scary at the same time. He couldn't quite figure out what it was about her that attracted him so powerfully. She was pretty, but he knew appearance wasn't everything. It might be her intelligence. Macal guessed she had a great many learned tutors and probably spent a lot of time in study. He had always been drawn to intelligent people and she seemed very quick. After further thought, he decided that her royal status didn't hurt. But most important of all was the fact that she had been nice to him. It was a new feeling—somebody his own age treating him with kindness and consideration.

He found it to be a wonderful sensation.

Following his escort to the mess tent, Macal fell into a new stride, brisk and proud. Somewhere on the mighty mountain peaks of his cowardice, a shred of confidence had managed to gain a foothold. He wasn't sure if it sprang from the clothes, his new feelings for the Princess, or the fact that he knew he had no choice but to go and find his father. Wherever it had come from, he hoped it would help him make up for what he had done to his uncle.

Again he wondered about the Old King's tomb. He had never heard of it. Uncle Melkes, who seemed to have a story about every place in Aerinth, had never mentioned it. That seemed strange, especially if it was so important and interesting. His curiosity hovered around thoughts of the tomb like a moth around a candle flame. What could it possibly have to do with his destiny?

On their way to the mess tent he wondered why so many people were looking at him. It couldn't be just his new attire. He guessed the rumor of his quest had spread through the camp, making everyone curious to see the boy who had pledged to venture alone to the Troll King's castle to save the once-honored Captain of the Amber Dragoons. Under the pressure of so many inquisitive glances, Macal began to feel daunted by what he had undertaken.

As he entered the tent his stomach rumbled in anticipation. Inside, he scanned the noisy crowd for Princess Aeria but she was nowhere to be seen, and he realized with disappointment that someone of her stature must eat in her own quarters.

"You can sit there." His escort indicated an empty seat with a fresh meal waiting in front of it.

"Thanks." Macal headed to the table, trying to ignore all the watching eyes. The hearty breakfast consisted of porridge and a crust of sweetbread served on a tin soldier's plate, which was accompanied by a battered leather drinking-jack of cider. The meal was blander than last night's, but still better than the fare he was accustomed to, and he ate and drank until his stomach was on the brink of hurting.

As he ate, he noticed the soldiers performing a ritual with which he was unfamiliar. As each man finished his meal, he approached a large decanter of wine sitting on the center table, hoisted the massive jug, and poured a small libation onto the grassy ground. Macal watched in puzzlement as he swallowed another bite of crusty bread.

A hand patted his shoulder. He looked up to see it was Corporal Mercule Gentris, the soldier who had campaigned with his father. "Good morning. Sleep well?"

"Yes, thank you."

"Good, glad to hear it." The Corporal followed his gaze. "Curious about the ceremony?"

"A bit. Why are they doing that?"

"Your father never told you?"

"Not that I can remember." Macal had never really spent much time with his father, and definitely not enough for stories.

No, my father didn't tell me. He wasn't around enough.

"It's a ceremony soldiers perform in hopes that the gods will accept their offering and bless them throughout the day. It's mainly done during wartime, but some soldiers do it every day."

Macal looked up at the man uncertainly. "Does it work?"

"Well, all the soldiers who were here yesterday are still alive today. So take that for what it's worth."

"Should I do it?" Macal blurted.

"That's up to you."

"Am I supposed to?"

"Again, that's up to you. There is no law saying you must. But Elronia still survives and thrives as a kingdom, perhaps solely because of this ritual."

"You really think so?"

"It doesn't hurt to hope."

Macal was still unsure. He hated being the center of attention; he had learned young that he wasn't good at much, and there was no benefit to parading his ineptitude. And on a purely practical note, he wasn't sure he could lift the heavy wine decanter. Nonetheless, the ritual was being performed by everyone who came to the tent. It might be more awkward to abstain than to try, even if the attempt meant making a fool of himself in front of strangers, some of whom, like Mercule, knew his father.

"I think you are worrying too much about it," Mercule said after a moment. "It's up to you; no harm done either way. The ritual is between you and the gods."

It won't be so bad, Macal told himself. *It's not as if everybody is watching. Only a few people will notice.*

Mercule detected the boy's nervousness. "There's no reason to be afraid."

Easy for you to say, thought Macal. *You've done this many times and you can no doubt easily lift the jug.* He knew that if this were yesterday morning, he would have been too nervous and shy to even consider performing the ritual. But somehow today was different. If he was really going to attempt to save his father, he would have to deal with situations a lot more dangerous than a room full of friendly soldiers—and he would need the blessings of all the gods he could enlist.

To his own surprise, without another word he rose from his seat and walked toward the center table that served as an altar. It seemed as if everyone in the tent turned to watch. Panic washed over him. This was going to be like the archery contest in Hormul, with everyone watching as his arrow whizzed off haphazardly, narrowly missing the crowd of onlookers. He didn't want to fail and be ridiculed again. *What would they think if he couldn't manage even this simple task, when he was the one traveling alone to the troll lands of Marglamesh?*

It was too late to back out; he was committed. Clenching his jaw, he stepped up to the table. He could feel their eyes boring into him, scrutinizing his every move. He took a deep breath. *I'm representing my father. These people see the son of a great soldier. I can't let them down, even if they're wrong.*

The heavy decanter of wine was nearly half his size. Trying to imitate the soldiers he had watched, he wrapped his arms around it and attempted to lift it. At first he was confident he was going to be able to do it; then he realized how heavy the jug really was. It contained enough wine for everyone in the camp to take a swig.

Around the tent Macal's struggle had whetted the onlookers' interest; now they were wondering whether he would be able to perform the ritual or not. *He had to do it! He had to do it for his father. If he couldn't do this, he would never succeed in his quest.*

With a mighty effort the boy hoisted the decanter off the table, managing to tilt it just enough to pour out a little of the dark purple liquid as an offering to any god who would listen.

To his surprise, cheers erupted around the tent as the wine splashed onto the grass. He struggled to put the decanter down and looked around in disbelief. They were applauding him. *Him!* They had all watched him try and succeed, and now they were applauding him! He stared back at them, not quite sure what he had done to deserve this, but welcoming the cheers as a great improvement to the booing he was used to. In spite of the fact that his legs were shaking, he felt a twinge of satisfaction as he left the tent.

"Nicely done," said Mercule as he caught up with Macal outside and gave him a pat on the back.

"Why were they cheering?" asked Macal.

"I think because you just proved yourself a soldier."

"Did I?"

"In their eyes you did. Everybody is interested in the boy who has volunteered to go to Marglamesh alone. They wanted to know what you are made off, and you just showed them that you share your father's commitment to our cause."

"But all I did was pour some wine on the ground."

"But you did it like a soldier. As one of us. All we can hope now is that some god accepts your offering."

Yes, said Macal to himself. *Because I'm going to need all the help I can get.*

114

The First Fable

Volten watched Bertran Teel approach the bridge. His heart pulsed with excitement as he prepared to initiate the trap. His only real concern was for the war plans. He didn't care about the man carrying them.

He went over the plan one last time, though he knew it was too late to change anything. It was a trap they had used before. It had been loaned to them to use on the wizard Tereclent the Ageless. He had come across an enchanted artifact, a spellbound mask that Volten's employers had greatly desired.

Their payment for the job had been the ability to purchase the trap. It had cost him a good sum, all the savings he had made over the years. He still felt it was a good deal. If he succeeded now he would be paid far more than he had spent.

Volten had learned through trial and error that people, when carrying something or somebody valuable, always became especially cautious as they crossed a bridge because it was such a good place for an ambush. So he had decided to have his associates bury the trap's five short iron spikes just before the bridge, where their mark would least expect it.

These marvelous spikes would create a cage around the man, and once he was within the cage it would be an easy task to subdue him and get the plans. He figured this was the safest way to deal with the man rumored to have killed the last Troll King in Xanga-Mor. Volten didn't believe the rumor, but he didn't want to take the chance he was wrong.

Volten held in his palm a small cube of blue crystal. He watched carefully as the soldier approached the start of the bridge. The man's mannerisms hadn't changed. *He expects nothing.*

Once Bertran got to the designated spot the spy deftly made a claw and touched all five visible sides with a finger from his other hand.

The ground around the man burst to life in an upward spray of soil. From the earth jetted lengths of thick, rough, jagged black iron. Startled, the soldier took a defensive step backward only to find more quickly snaking strands blocking his way.

The animated bars moved at amazing speed, winding, twisting to encompass the man. With a smile the spy flipped over the cube to touch its final face and seal the cage.

His grin widened as Bertran yanked his sword from its sheath. *It's too late. There is nothing you can do. You are mine.*

The silver sword glinted in the early morning light before it came alight with fire. A mesmerizing azure flame erupted and spread along the length of its blade. With both hands on the sword Bertran hacked at the infernal bars.

Shocked, Volten watched the ensorcelled brand cut deep and hew through one of them. Horrified, he saw that the magic of the Prison of Zaglel was no match for the mystical power and runes etched upon the

115

edge of the fantastical sword. With only a few swings Bertran sundered the cage enough to free himself.

Volten's victorious smile was gone. He hadn't thought it possible to break free from this prison. Not even Tereclent the Ageless has been able to escape. He had underestimated the man. In consternation the spy watched as the remainder of the prison, and all his savings, crumbled useless to the ground behind the soldier.

Another rising concern rose up within him. Now that Bertran Teel was free he looked very, very angry.

As Macal and Mercule stood talking, the boy's escort reappeared with a smile on his face. "That was a fine bit of soldiering you just did. Making an offering like that. Now, if you'll come with me, the Jewel has requested your attendance."

Macal was instantly elated. He'd been quite eager to see the Princess again.

"I'll see you a bit later," Mercule promised as they parted.

"Thank you for the help," Macal called after him.

"It was my pleasure," replied the big soldier as he headed off into the camp.

Following his escort, Macal could see that in the hour or so he had been in the mess tent, most of the camp had been broken down, reverting back to an empty glade in the woods. He was amazed at the efficiency of the soldiers. As they came in sight of the Princess's carriage, he was suddenly attacked by misgivings. *What if he hadn't put on his armor correctly? Would she think he couldn't dress himself?* But it was too late. There was Princess Aeria Stormlion, standing outside her glorious carriage with her entourage nearby. The two majestic unicorns harnessed to the carriage were pawing the ground as if anxious for the coming journey. Amazed as he was by such wondrous creatures, Macal found them far overshadowed by the elegance and beauty of their mistress. Today she was clothed in gold and white silks and she smiled as she saw him approaching.

She smiled at me! Macal's heart began to pound. The Princess looked as beautiful as the sunrise brightening the sky behind her. Trying not to gawk at her, he forced himself to look around at the others present. There were several heavily armed footmen seated on the back of the carriage, resolutely looking off into the distance, pretending to show no interest in the Princess's affairs. Just inside the carriage Macal could see two older ladies whom he assumed were ladies in waiting or some such people.

Just then Viscount Razz arrived, followed by an esquire holding the reins of a black jotun steed. "I have finished the morning inspection of the troops, My Jewel," the dragonmere announced. "We should be ready shortly."

"Very good, Viscount Razz Munin." The Princess gave a pleased nod before turning to Macal.

Overcome by the prospect of her full attention, the boy ducked his head and mumbled, "May the Crown stay strong."

"May the Crown stay strong," she responded lightly, as if sensing his tension. "Did you sleep well?"

"Yes, thank you" he fibbed. "Your hospitality is far better than anything I'm used to." Flustered, Macal added, "And thank you for the new clothes."

"It is the kingdom's pleasure. I hope someday to show you true hospitality inside the walls of a peacetime castle. You look very fine in your new attire," she said with a smile.

Macal couldn't believe it. *She noticed!* His heart sang with pleasure and excitement. Somebody as pretty as *her* had noticed *him!*

Princess Aeria Stormlion reached inside the carriage. "I've had the armiger find a suitable weapon for you. I hope you treat each other well."

In her hand was a thick steel short sword with a slender gold handle and a pommel shaped into a dragon's head, inside an elaborately decorated leather sheath.

"That's for me?" Macal was in a state of disbelief. It was far more splendid than Uncle Melkes' military sword. He had never possessed anything so valuable, much less a weapon of any kind.

"I can't send you off on a royal quest ill-equipped, can I?" the Princess asked, turning the weapon in her hands to present Macal with the hilt.

As the boy reached for it, Viscount Razz spoke. "Protocol states you must be on one knee when taking a sword from one of royal blood."

"Sorry. I didn't know." Macal dropped to one knee.

The Princess stepped forward and placed the weapon's cold, heavy hilt in his outstretched hands. As he felt the weighty metal in his grasp, Macal remembered something his uncle had told him. "If churches were still common, I'd try to convince you to become a priest," Uncle Melkes had said. "A priest's life is safer, or it used to be, than that of a soldier like your father. In the service of the church there are few sleepless nights out in the rain on a rocky battlefield. There is less strenuous labor, and most important, there is little need to wield a weapon."

The boy also remembered being told that weapons were dangerous things, used by far too many people who didn't need them. With the sword in his possession he felt the burden of responsibility. He sensed that he was crossing a threshold beyond which he would no longer be a carefree boy, but someone more mature whose outline was still shadowy and undefined.

In his hands he held the power to hurt. He could hurt people as Uncle

Melkes had been hurt, causing pain to those who loved them. The damage didn't end when the swing of the blade had stopped. With his own sense of loss still fresh, he knew exactly how it felt. Strapping the sword to his waist, he vowed to himself to never use it for any ill purpose.

"I have a few more things for you," Princess Aeria said.

"More things?" Macal looked up at her. What else could he possibly need? "You've already given me more than enough."

"The Royal Jewel is very generous," said Viscount Razz.

"The next two items will serve as proof that you are on a royal mission, and that you have the Crown's blessing if the need should ever arise. The first is the vestment of the kingdom," she said, retrieving a red tabard with a black dragon's head on it, identical to the ones worn by the other soldiers. "This you wear over your torso." She helped Macal, still on his knees, to place it over his shoulders, covering his chain shirt. Then she handed him one last item. "And *this* you wear on the middle finger of your weapon hand. It is a signet ring bearing my personal crest."

Macal was uncertain which was his weapon hand, but he had always favored his left. He held it out, fingers spread apart. As Princess Aeria Stormlion slipped the wide golden ring onto his finger, he looked at the delicate crest it bore. In the center was the dragon's head of Elronia, surrounded by a ring of immaculately sculpted roses.

"Are you sure you want me to have this?" he asked. "I'm not sure I deserve it."

"You embark on a quest to save our kingdom," the Princess said. "These are just trinkets; their value is nothing compared to what you may accomplish, all the lives that you may save if we can end this war. And your humility adds to your worthiness. Now, we have wasted enough time with ceremony. Time is precious; we have very little of it. So let's be off."

The Princess's order spread like wildfire through the camp. Some soldiers moved into marching formation, others mounted their steeds, and some boarded carriages and wagons. At last everyone was ready to ride out. As the Princess climbed into the carriage and closed the door behind her, Macal was unsure what he was supposed to do. Then he noticed that the Viscount, standing beside him, had made no motion to mount the black jotun.

"The King's Jewel also gives you this steed," the dragonmere informed him, motioning for the esquire to hand Macal the jotun's reins.

"You're kidding," the boy burst out. The two unicorns drawing the Princess's carriage were snorting with excitement, their hooves beating an eager tattoo on the ground.

"I'm not known for joking," Viscount Razz said. Macal didn't find that hard to believe.

"But you're sure? I can really have a jotun?"

"Positive," replied the half dragon. Marveling how much his life had changed over the last day, Macal took the reins from the esquire. "Her name is Shelga," Viscount Razz added. "Follow me as I get my mount. You are to ride with me."

Macal was about to obey when he saw the Princess watching from her carriage window, a wry smile on her face. She winked at him. "Don't you just love the dramatics of the royal court? The last gift I have for you lies in the depths of a tomb near the northern edge of Elronia."

"What is it?"

"You'll see soon enough." The mischief in her smile told Macal she enjoyed keeping him in suspense. As he racked his brain trying to imagine what other gift the Princess could possibly give him, the cavalcade moved out.

CHAPTER 12

Bertran Teel smiled with satisfaction as he stepped from the crumbling wreckage of the enchanted cage. A moment before, inside the egg-shaped cage he hadn't felt so confident. The walls forming around him, the gaps in the cage disappearing. *I can't let myself be caught. There's too much to lose.*

He took a moment to feel grateful for his years of experience with the dangers of the world, which had enabled him to quickly recover from the surprise of the assault. *Whomever was hunting him had underestimated the weapon he wielded. This was no simple sword with paltry magic imbued upon it. It was Alrang-Dal, a sword of legend. Held through the ages by untold kings and heroes. And now he, the once Captain of the Amber Dragoons and soldier of Elronia, owned it.* With the aid of Alrang-Dal he laid waste to the trap.

Just out of sight in the shadows of the wood, Volten grimaced as the Prison of Zaglel fell broken to the ground. *That was the problem with this world, too many people had access of magical items.*

He seethed at his loss. All the money he had sunk into this trap was gone. His only choice now was to complete the contract. Fortunately he had a Secondary Plan. There was always the Secondary Plan—the oldest plan there was in this line of work. His associates moved in, weapons in hand.

After witnessing Bertran cut his way out of the prison, Volten was no longer sure he wanted to face him in combat. The part of him that hoped it wouldn't come to the Secondary Plan—the part of him that liked to be alive—reminded the rest of him that this was the man who slew the last Troll King on the fields of Xanga-Mor. *And he had done that before he wielded that famed silver sword.* He decided to let the others engage first.

Bertran felt the earth tremor. He turned to see Lof stomping toward him through the trees with a massive club in hand. Now that the trap had failed, he was not surprised to see somebody approaching to attack, however the giant's pale blue skin and size were unexpected. On his other side the soldier noted a second man, tiny compared to the first, on the approach. He wielded a dagger in each hand.

Jengrul cackled with glee as he closed in on Bertran. "I'm glad you broke the boss' toy. Cause now we get to play with you."

Bertran spun to keep watch on both flanks with Alrang-Dal, alight with flame, held out before him. Leaving some distance remaining between them and the soldier, the two approaching men circled around toward each other, curving inward from a similar angle. Bertran was surprised by the tactic, but he was happy to have both of them on one side. He took several steps backward, off the road into a thin array of trees. The little man's incessant, sinister smile started to bother him.

The brothers increased their strides through the tall grass. Bertran needed time to come up with a plan. He retreated further, past a peculiar tree. As he did so it came to life and with a sturdy arm-branch smashed down on his sword wielding arm. Startled, and in intense pain, Alrang-Dal fell from his grasp. Its blue flame instantly ceased.

"We walked ya' right into that one." Jengrul couldn't help but chuckle. "Always gets 'em. Every freakin' time."

Understanding there were now three foes, Bertran scrambled to pick up his sword with his off hand, but as he grabbed the hilt, Lof stomped his gargantuan foot down on the blade, pinning it in place and crushing his fingers under the hilt.

Lof leered at the soldier. "I don't think you need that anymore."

Bertran grimaced in pain. "I disagree."

Seeing an opening, Jengrul and the strange tree-creature rushed forward. Still maintaining his grip on the handle, Bertran did the only thing he could think of. He willed the blade to burn with conjured fire.

The blade once more exploded into flame. Lof howled in pain as the fire incinerated the bottom of his boot and charred his foot. Responding to the howls and bellows of pain from his brother, Jengrul broke off his approach and rushed to put out the fire that engulfed his sibling's foot.

Thinking their prey distracted, Dalent didn't hesitate. He stepped up behind the soldier and brought both bark covered arms up to deliver a single hammer blow to the crouched man's head. In a blur of speed Bertran spun with sword in hand, a trail of blue fiery tendrils in the wake of its arc. The blade sliced through the air and then through the drant.

The separate wooden pieces of Dalent fell to the ground.

Jengrul, stunned, watched his comrade fall. They didn't normally run into such trouble. With a roar of pain Lof brought down his club. The Elronian soldier dove out of the way and rolled onto his feet. The giant swung again. The club dented the earth as he missed a second time. In a series a fluid motions, Bertran countered and with a double handed strike he chopped through the middle of the large club, retracted the sword and brought it up forcibly toward Lof's head.

The brute failed to escape the keen edge of the sword. Alrang-Dal sunk deep into his wide jaw. Lof, hands clutching at his marred face, fell to his knees in anguish.

In response to this terrible assault on his brother, Jengrul launched a frenzied attack. His daggers flashed through the air, hungry to avenge his brother. To spare himself from being minced Bertran had no choice but to give ground while he parried attack after attack.

From the shadows Volten could see things were not going well. Yet he desperately needed the plans, so reluctantly he entered the fray. He charged forward and threw his body into Bertran's with a crunch. Alrang-Dal flew from the soldier's hand again as both of them toppled to the ground.

The two men wrestled and Bertran finally ended up on top. Volten reflexively pulled out a slender knife and jabbed upwards several times. With each strike he felt warm blood spill onto his hand.

Bertran let out several cries of pain as the knife slipped into his chest and stomach. Amidst more stabs he reached for his own knife. He brought it up to his opponent's throat to end the man. His blade hesitated. "Who are you working for, traitor?" To his surprise the spy looked back at him with impassive eyes.

I'm not a traitor, thought Volten. He had already moved to Gelvin. Elronia was no longer his kingdom. *And what did he care if Elronia fell? Elronian lords took his parents. Let them all burn.*

In that moment Jengrul charged up behind Bertran with a dagger in each hand. In a rage he thrust the blades into the man's back, wider and deeper than the frontal wounds. Bertran screamed in anguish. With great dexterity the thief's finger pressed a mechanism to release poison held in the hollow reservoir of one of the blades. Bertran screamed in even more torment as the poison was injected, burning through his body like acid.

Volten pushed the howling man roughly off of him and got to his feet. A moment later Bertran Teel lay motionless on the ground.

Jengrul stood over Bertran, dagger raised, ready to further punish the man who had grievously injured his brother.

"Stop," commanded Volten.

The slight man looked at him with wild fury. "Did you see what he did to my brother? He's mine!"

"No." Volten didn't see the need for killing any more than necessary. He held his knife toward the grotesque man. "I think you are even."

"Gonna attack me, are you? Cause of him?"

"We need him."

"No. We need the plans."

Volten relented with a sigh and lowered his knife. "Fine. Get me the plans and he is yours."

With practiced hands Jengrul searched the soldier for the war plans. They were not tucked in the man's jacket pocket. Nor did he find them hidden in his tunic. They were not folded up in any of his belt pouches. His pants had no pockets. Next the thief searched the man's boots with no luck.

Panic started to rise in Volten. He raced over to check the pack that had fallen off Bertran when the trap was set off. He emptied its contents onto the ground and with haste sifted through them.

The plans were not there either.

Volten felt his future collapsing as he realized Bertran Teel did not have the war plans.

His first thought was that somebody had made a mistake. He had been misinformed. Bertran Teel was not the bearer of the Troll King's war plans. He mused this with alarm for several minutes until another thought occurred to him.

Maybe Bertran knew he was being watched, so he hid the plans. *If that was true what choice did he have?* Or he had somebody he trusted he could hand them off to.

Yes, that must be it. He must have known he was being hunted and he hid them.

Volten produced a pair of slender manacles from some hidden pocket and attached them to Bertran. "What kind of poison was it?"

"What do you care? He cut my brother's jaw off!"

"You idiot! He can't die. We need him to tell us where the plans are."

Jengrul glared and growled at Bertran like a savage wolf. "You said I could finish him now."

Volten looked at him in frustration. "No! All may not be lost. There may be a way to fix this. I'll meet you back in Drakenport."

"How do I know you'll show up and not just take all the money?"

"What money? He's not going to pay us if we don't give him the plans. And regardless of what they say, there is honor among some thieves. I give my word that if the Troll King doesn't kill me, and somehow gives us something for this man, I'll return with your share of the payment."

There was something about his flat tone that told the diminutive man that Volten was not lying. Jengrul pointed a stubby finger at Bertran. "We're giving the him to the king?"

"What else can we do? Now let's hope he can stay alive long enough to survive the trip." Volten grabbed the unconscious Bertran and his sword, summoned his wings in a fiery blaze and launched himself into the sky toward Castle Darkmoor.

CHAPTER 13

T he cavalcade rode through the better part of the day, traversing a vast part of the forest and stopping only for a brief respite. Quickly and efficiently the camp cooks prepared a vegetable and meat stew, boiled potatoes, and handed out crusty bread. Once everyone had eaten, the caravan wasted no time in moving out once more.

After several hours of riding, Macal was finally getting used to the big jotun. Up to now, the largest creature he had ridden was a slow, decrepit old mare back in Hormul. In contrast, his present mount was young and spirited, with the strength of several horses. Shelga seemed to have a mind of her own, and he suspected she was purposefully testing his riding abilities as he followed Viscount Razz on his inspections of the procession. Fortunately Macal's knack for riding, the knack that had won him the horse race in Hormul and earned Menk's resentment, had not deserted him. By late afternoon he had adapted to the oversized steed and begun to enjoy himself.

He was listening to the faint strains of the minstrel's lute playing when the Rotelen Woods finally came to an end. Ahead of the cavalcade lay the enormous Valley of Ashway, a massive pass running many leagues from northeast to southwest.

Macal reined in Shelga to admire the majestic view. Descending the steep slope into the valley, the trees slowly dwindled and disappeared, giving way to rocky earth in which brambles and weeds struggled to make their home. Far off in the northern distance, beyond the greens, browns, and grays of the valley, Macal could see the lone ridge of mountains that separated Elronia from the Rashinasti Forest, their towering peaks nearly lost in low-hanging clouds, and down below, twisting its way along the bottom of the Valley of Ashway was a deep, slow-moving river called the Drangel.

The royal entourage made its way along a rough trail leading down into the valley. A cool fragrant breeze rolled over Macal as he turned Shelga to follow them. Memories of the destruction of Hormul faded before the grandeur of the world and all the beauty that it held. He had never been so far from home before. He had never known that the world could be so beautiful.

Viscount Razz, just ahead, reined in his brown jotun to ride beside Macal. "Enjoying yourself?" asked the dragonmere. "You seem to have gotten a good handle on your new steed."

"I am. Thank you." Macal then decided to ask the question that had been torturing his mind. "Do you know what's in the tomb?"

"If I did, do you think it would be proper for me to tell you?"

"I guess not."

"But to answer your question, I do not. I do imagine it is something of great import, for the Princess to have chosen to divert herself and all these people from her mission."

That was exactly what Macal had thought. *Why would she go so far out of her way at such a crucial juncture, just to give him something?*

"Do you know how to use a sword she gave you?" inquired Viscount Razz.

Macal was too embarrassed to speak, but the dragonmere read the answer on his face. "It's nothing to be ashamed of. You should feel blessed to live in a kingdom where you do not need to know warfare from birth."

The boy nodded in agreement. *What was the benefit of knowing how to kill somebody?*

"I assume, from your initial reaction to me, that you know nothing of my race," the Viscount continued.

"No, I don't." Another gap in his worldly knowledge. There was so much out there in the world, so many different races, ideals, ways of life— he had much to learn. "Where are you from?" he asked as they continued slowly down the hill.

"From Ermalon, a large kingdom in the far western corner of the southern continent. Have you heard of it?"

"No. But I'd like to go there."

"No, you would not, nor would I if I could avoid it. It is a dark, ancient empire of men, elves, and goblins. It is always night in Ermalon; the realm is covered in a deep, gloomy moss-colored fog that blocks out the sun and causes the wind to howl with rage. The land is ruled by my kind, the sorcerous dragonmere."

It was hard for Macal to imagine the composed, civilized Viscount hailing from such a savage place. The reference to sorcerers had caught his attention and intrigued him. "You know how to use magic?"

"No. I am more swordsman than runecaster or spellweaver."

"Why are you here in Elronia?" asked the boy.

"As the youngest son of my family I have been indentured to King Glagor for a term of twenty years. I was sent here in this service by my father. When I have completed it, in exchange your king will give us the Gemstone of Onarous."

"Onarous," Macal echoed. "That's another kingdom, isn't it? Also on the southern continent?"

"Very good. Onarous borders Ermalon."

"And your kingdoms are also at war, and somehow the Gemstone of Onarous can help you win?" guessed Macal.

"We are eternally at war. It is the nature of my kingdom, as it is the Troll King's. An Onarian legend says that if the gemstone is destroyed, the royal Onarous line will slowly succumb to a dark fate. The nature of that fate is unknown to us, and to the Onarous royalty as well. It was my father's belief that if we obtained the gemstone and threatened to destroy it, the Onarians would fall to our will. Somehow King Glagor recovered the gemstone during a crusade. He claimed to have found it in the depths of a ruined Votabel temple, but refused to say where that temple lies."

Votabel was the standard god of humans, Macal knew, commonly worshiped before the Lumar Or'lmar. "So your father is a powerful man?"

"He was the ruler of Ermalon."

"*Was?* You mean he's dead? And you're the new ruler?"

"Perhaps." The Viscount's response was absentminded; he was gazing down at a ring on the center finger of his right hand. Macal hadn't noticed it before. It was fashioned of platinum and set with a large spherical emerald surrounded by eight smaller rubies. The dragonmere's eyes, normally sharp and attentive, had softened. As if feeling Macal's scrutiny he said, "This is the Ring of Ermalon. My possession of it means that both my father and my older brother, who was the first heir to the kingdom, are dead. The ring was created in the early days of the realm, back in the Age of Heroes. Back when the mountains were much taller. It is enchanted so that when its wearer dies, the ring mystically appears on the hand of the next ruler of Ermalon. That way there can be no doubt as to who has the right of ascension. Now, after many thousands of years, it has come to me."

"I'm sorry." Macal didn't know what else to say to the sullen dragonmere. The two rode in silence as the royal entourage circumvented a rocky outcropping near the base of the valley. Once they had cleared the rocks, Macal started a new conversation.

"Is Onarous a land of men?"

"For the most part, yes." The Viscount had recovered his composure. "They are a cryptic people who have been altered and shaped by ages of dark nights. While they are still human, they do not look like you. Many possess multiple eyes, some of which are said to see the future. The Onarian are powerful augurs and readers of destiny. This is why the legend of a dark fate caused by the destruction of the gemstone frightens them so. They know it to be true."

"How much longer are you indentured?" Macal was starting to like the dragonmere. In spite of his startling appearance, his manner was reassuringly calm and restrained.

"My term of service ended four months ago."

"Then why are you still here?"

"I cannot go home until the war is over."

"King Glagor won't let you go?"

"He has offered the gemstone to me numerous times already, but each time I have refused. I cannot leave while the Princess is in dire peril. For the past thirteen years, since the day she was born, I have watched over her. I will not leave now, not while she and her people suffer such great danger."

The dragonmere's tone hinted at a continuous inner conflict. He must be anxious, Macal thought, to see what had happened back in his homeland, especially after being away for over twenty years. He must want to see what became of his father and his brother. The boy wondered if any other members of the Viscount's family were alive, but decided now was not the time to ask.

He was impressed by the dragonmere's loyalty. Instead of ruling his own kingdom and discovering the fate of his family, he had chosen to stay in Elronia and protect the Princess. Macal knew he wouldn't have stayed, indentured or not, if he had learned his family was in peril.

"Come on." The Viscount's voice cut into his thoughts. "When we stop again, I will teach you how to use that sword of yours."

True to the Viscount's word, weapon practice began that same afternoon, when the cavalcade reached the floor of the valley and stopped beside the slow river. Above them in the distance to the north rose the mountains, resembling a line of broken, decaying teeth. The Viscount ushered Macal towards a hilly clearing where the grass had somehow managed to resist being overtaken by brambles.

"Swordplay is more than swinging an edged blade," began the dragonmere as they made their way toward the clearing. "There are theories and concepts you must learn. Additionally, to become a great swordsman you should also be trained in a fallback weapon like a dagger, and all its attacks, counters, and evasions. In combat you can never rely on one weapon alone. But those lessons will be for another time."

Macal was trying to memorize everything the Viscount said. Even without a sword in hand, the dragonmere moved as if he were carrying one. He had mentioned that he had been trained in swordplay all his life; wielding a sword was his earliest memory. The reflexes and mannerisms from that training had become a part of him, and were revealed in the way he moved and walked. He led the way to the center of the clearing and stopped.

"I believe that all students training in swordsmanship should also learn wrestling and grappling techniques. The drill we are going to do, however, will give you merely the fundamentals of sword-wielding techniques. In every art there are many styles and schools of thought, and swordplay is no different. What I will be teaching you is the way in which all the Lords of Ermalon are taught."

Macal nodded and noticed that several men from the cavalcade had turned to watch.

"For the sparring session," Viscount Razz continued, "we are going to use practice swords. There is no need for us to walk away from this exercise short a finger or three." He handed the boy one of the long wooden swords he had been carrying.

Disappointment seized Macal. Excited by the prospect of learning how to use a sword, he had hoped to use the blade the Princess had given him. It seemed that was not likely to happen, at least not today. The Viscount noticed the sudden collapse of his enthusiasm. "You thought we were going to use real swords? If that were the case, why would we have brought these wooden ones?"

"I don't know," Macal mumbled. "I just thought that if the Princess trusted me with a real sword, you would too."

"When you make a mistake, wood is more forgiving than steel," the dragonmere said levelly. "All in good time. I am sure there will be occasions when you are forced to use that sword of yours against your wishes. Shall we begin? First you must learn what a guard position is. It is a stance from which you can either attack or defend. In a guard position you are not like a statue, rigid and unmoving. You must be like a river, full of constant rhythmic movement. If you can remember that, you might just survive your first fight. Now stand over there, on the up side of the hill, so you will be closer to my height."

Several of the watching soldiers made their way closer to get a better view. Even standing on the hillside, Macal was nowhere near the dragonmere's height.

"You should hold your sword like this." Viscount Razz brought his sword straight up in front of him, its blade slightly tilted towards Macal. The boy did his best to imitate his teacher, but the long wooden sword was far too unwieldy for him to hold with just one hand. He had to use two.

The Viscount considered the small figure in front of him. "Good. I'm sorry the sword is so big. It was all we had on such short notice. Now let us consider that your basic guard position…" He launched into a long lecture explaining various sword positions, feints, swipes, defensive withdrawals, parries, blocks, and other guard stances, and how each could be countered by another. Again and again he had Macal mimic his movements, drilling each position.

Parry. Swipe. Feint. Strike. Withdraw. Over and over again. As the lesson continued, Macal's arms began to ache from swinging the heavy wooden sword. More intrigued soldiers arrived to watch. Macal guessed they might want to see what they could learn from this scion of the fierce Ermalon royalty.

Viscount Razz eventually called an end to the drilling of stances. "Now I will try various attacks, and you will try to use the various defenses you have learned to counter each one. At first the attacks will be slow, but they will increase in speed as I see you becoming more comfortable blocking them."

Without another word, the Viscount swung his practice sword in a wide, lazy arc at Macal's left side. The boy did his best to cross block the attack, succeeding just in time.

"Well done." The dragonmere struck again, this time with a thrust aimed at the boy's chest. With a fair amount of speed Macal withdrew, tapping his opponent's blade to the side as he stepped back.

"Remember, you want to use the counter that leaves you in the best position to attack. That is what swordplay is about, and the person in the best attack position tends to be the one who wins the battle. Withdrawing is good, but it rarely leaves you in a position to go on the offensive."

Viscount Razz continued to strike, cut, and thrust at Macal. Within a short time he had quickened the pace, not to actual combat speed, but much faster than the painfully slow attacks with which he had begun. It wasn't long before Macal grew winded and fatigued. He hadn't realized how tiring sword fighting could be, and he had no doubt it was even worse in real combat, when you were worried about staying alive. He now saw the dragonmere's wisdom in using practice swords instead of real ones; his knuckles were bruised and aching from clumsy parries that allowed the Viscount's sword to slide down his blade and crack his fingers.

"You are leaving your defenses open again," warned the dragonmere as he struck once more. "Whichever attack I use, you must instinctively counter with the appropriate block. And keep your feet moving. Don't stand still. You are a river, not a statue."

Once more an attack came, this time a cleaving strike aimed at his neck, but Macal was already bored by simply blocking and batting away the Viscount's sword. He wasn't sure he agreed that he needed to be able to defend himself before he should learn to attack. If his opponent was already dead, there would be nothing further to block. Inspired by this revelation, he knocked aside the dragonmere's two-handed slice, saw his opening, and counterattacked.

As fast as he could, he lunged forward to thrust the wooden sword into his opponent's abdomen.

Caught by surprise, Viscount Razz froze in mid-movement. Macal stood with his arms still extended, his blunt sword touching the dragonmere's midsection. As he took in the Viscount's shocked expression and heard the collective gasp of the watching soldiers, blood began to drain from the boy's face. What had he done?

With haste he withdrew his sword. Viscount Razz's face was hard to read, but Macal could only imagine that he was far from pleased. The boy took a step back, ready to flee from the dragonmere's wrath.

Then Viscount Razz began to smile. "Well done." He seemed more than a little surprised at the deftness of the attack. "You have a natural aptitude for swordplay, doubtless inherited from your father. I am impressed."

The boy's face lit up. *Me? Good at swordplay?* He had always wanted to be like his father, and now for the first time someone acknowledged a resemblance. This moment brought him an astonishing joy he never imagined he could feel.

"Now let us see how you do against someone who is *expecting* you to attack," the Viscount said, drawing a laugh from the spectators. Macal grinned. He had been enjoying the tutelage, and he had to admit the techniques came easily to him. With the smile still on his face, he didn't wait to be attacked. He swung again, this time with a cutting strike at the dragonmere's right leg.

With an effort that was obviously exaggerated, the Viscount parried the swing just at the last minute. "You will make a fine soldier in the King's Army someday," he observed as the mock swordplay continued with the relentless smack of wood against wood.

The words stopped the boy in mid thrust.

"Never." Macal Teel's voice was hollow as he met Viscount Razz's eyes. "Once I find my father, I want nothing to do with wars, or battles, or even glory."

"I see. Yet everyone dies, and most without meaning. At least a solider dies for a cause he has chosen. He has a chance to give meaning to his death. I pray that you get the life you desire, young boy. But be warned, not many do. Now back to the drills."

To the amazement of those watching, the dragonmere took a deep breath and exhaled a huge cone of fire into the air above his head before launching an attack on Macal again.

Macal had several more training sessions with the Viscount in the days the caravan moved onwards. He was starting to feel confident in his sword-wielding abilities. No longer were they using wooden practice swords, but real swords with dulled blades. Macal had to admit that he had been enjoying Viscount Razz Munin's companionship as much as he did the drills. The dragonmere's knowledgeable manner in some small way reminded him of his uncle.

They had passed far beyond the Valley of Ashway into the Avie province, beyond which were Lord Moltess' land. The Lord's lands were the largest and the farthest west in the kingdom, bordering Xanga-Mor via a narrow, rocky valley. From what Macal had seen, the province was an endless vista of rolling grassy hills and fields.

The Viscount explained to Macal that prior to the recent invasion, the farthest the trolls had ever infiltrated Elronia was the Fields of Garune, near the Lord's citadel to the far west. It was only thanks to Lord Moltess' great tactical abilities that the trolls had never previously reached the heart of the realm. If the king never spawned a male heir, the dragonmere said, it was likely that upon his death Lord Moltess might receive the crown.

The Princess had been taking them in a westerly direction since they emerged from the northern end of the Valley of Ashway. At the moment the caravan had stopped, and they were eating lunch in her tent, erected for the duration of the meal. Blowing in the wind from the top of the tent was her royal pennant, a black dragon surrounded by roses.

Inside, Princess Aeria sat in her plush, high-backed chair while Macal and the Viscount were seated on plainer chairs. In one corner, the Elven minstrel played serene music on his lute. The Princess's handmaidens were present as well, seated at a separate table, and with them sat the caravan's priest—a quiet, aged man called Gloliver of Fornlin. Macal had learned that he was a follower of Malakel, the God of Peace and Truth. Around the priest's neck was the holy icon of his god, a silver tear said to represent the tears Malakel cries over the sufferings of the world he has yet to heal and mend. He thought it brave of the priest to wear a religious relic so blatantly regardless of what the Lumar might do.

To Macal's delight, this afternoon's meal had started with some fruit, cheeses, and nuts brought by a serving boy on finely carved and decorated wooden plates. These were followed by a delicious course of fish and fruit pie called Tart of Brymlent, made of fresh salmon, figs, raisins, pears, and apples minced and washed in wine, then boiled with a little sugar and baked into a flaky pie crust.

By the time the main course was done, Macal's stomach was once again near bursting, but when the serving boy brought in some sweet white bread spread with honey and toasted pine nuts, he couldn't resist.

"How much longer 'til we reach the tomb?" he asked as he swallowed another tasty mouthful. He realized he was becoming happily accustomed to this amazing food, and he dreaded the thought of what he would have to eat once he left the caravan.

The Princess took a sip from a glass of hot water flavored with sugar and spices. "If what I recall is accurate, our journey should take no more than two days, perhaps three."

"If you recall?" Macal was confused. From the Princess's previous mention of the tomb he had assumed she knew exactly where it was.

"I've never been there. But my father used to tell me about it when I was younger."

"How then do we know it is safe to go there? We cannot fail to reach Varun," interjected Viscount Razz. "While I harbor no ill will toward Macal's mission, an alliance with the hobgoblins remains our best hope, even unlikely as it is to come to pass."

"No offense taken," Macal said lightly, seeing the Princess glance over to gauge his reaction to this remark. *What was the point in taking offense?* He was well aware that his chances of success were also slim.

"We will make it to Varun safely," replied the Princess simply. "That is the purpose of your being here, Viscount. With you in charge of our defenses, I have no doubt we will overcome all obstacles."

"Which is exactly why I am voicing my concerned opinion now. Any detour from our predetermined route to the hobgoblin lands is a threat to our security. We should head straight north through the pass in the Ashkath mountains to the Rashinanasti Forest. It is the fastest route."

"We will be fine, Viscount." Princess Aeria seemed confident. "And you should know I would not put our duty at risk if I did not think this detour would help us in some way. If I remember right, what lies in the tomb will be of great benefit to Macal on his quest."

"You're not sure what's actually there either?" Macal asked.

"Again, my knowledge derives from bedtime stories my father told me, and it has been a few years since we were close enough for such occasions. The war has been a great strain on him."

"What do you *think* is there?" inquired the boy.

Everyone in the tent turned toward the Princess, awaiting her response. Her face remained composed; she looked from Macal to the Viscount as if weighing her words. Before she could speak a royal guard rushed through the entry of the tent, his expression concerned.

"My Jewel. One of the scouts has returned and requests an immediate audience with you."

132

"Send him in." Putting down her napkin, the Princess stood and faced the tent opening. The Viscount and the others followed suit except for Macal, who remained seated until he saw the elf giving him a meaningful nod, then the boy jumped to his feet. He was still not accustomed to court procedures; back home he had not been expected to stand when Uncle Melkes rose from the table. He watched his two dining companions, impressed by how quickly their demeanor had altered. In an instant the atmosphere inside the tent had changed from light and curious to tense and grim.

Into the tent stepped a lean, tall man wearing a weathered green hooded cloak over a suit of dirty, mud-covered leather. He had the longest beard Macal had ever seen. Strapped over his shoulder was a heavy crossbow, and hanging from his left hip was a well-worn sword. He dropped to one knee.

"Jewel of the Kingdom." His voice was husky, as if parched. "I bring a warning from several leagues ahead."

"Please tell us in all haste, Kelifex." Princess Aeria's tone was grave.

"I spotted a small brigade of trolls moving southeast. It seems obvious they are coming from the dark forest."

"Probably late arrivals," surmised the dragonmere. "Trying to catch up with the rest of their forces. How many in the brigade?"

"Three dozen, my Lord."

"We cannot let them roam within our borders," the Princess said.

"Did they see you?" the Viscount asked the scout.

The man looked insulted at the question. "No more than they have seen the error of their ways."

"Good. We can catch them by surprise. I agree with the Princess; they cannot be allowed to further molest Elronia," the dragonmere said. "We also cannot risk you being seen or caught, My Jewel. I will deal with them. I will take half of the men and cleanse the world of this filth. Macal, you will come with us."

"Me?" Macal was startled by the Viscount's sudden announcement. "I barely know how to use a sword!"

Noticing the Princess had turned to look at him, he cursed himself inwardly. He didn't want her to see that he was afraid to defend his kingdom from the trolls. As her soft gaze remained on him, he thought he could read judgment in her eyes. In a situation like this, what choice did he have?

"I will go and serve my King," Macal Teel said at last. "If I am to survive my trip into Marglamesh, I ought to be able to stand my ground inside my own kingdom."

"You are braver than you realize." Princess Aeria seemed impressed, and her response pleased Macal. *Now*, he thought, *all I have to do is survive the battle*.

Within a surprisingly short time the cavalry was on its way out of the camp. Mounted on Shelga, in the lead with the Viscount and the scout Kelifex, the boy discovered a small part of himself that wasn't as scared as the rest. This part had taken a few moments to wake and make its presence known, but now that it was conscious, it was signaling its happiness at going out against the trolls.

It wanted to fight.

It wanted revenge.

CHAPTER 14

Castle Darkmoor's vast echoing throne room was the largest chamber in the entire castle. Two rows of pillars supported a vaulted ceiling of such height that the flickering torches below never illuminated it. Large tapestries depicting previous bloody ages of Marglamesh covered the walls and gave the gloomy room its only color.

The great War King sat on his throne, fuming about the war plans. He couldn't believe how foolish he had been in allowing them to be created. The frustration he felt for this inept decision was driving him mad.

Where was that infernal rat. He hadn't heard from him in days. His chance to win this war quickly was slowly decaying. If the humans were allowed too much time they would be able to rally and fortify, causing the war to become a long drawn-out engagement.

Did the spy find the plans? Was the man who had them able to be bought? Or worse, did the plans make it to Keratost? Because if so, all could already be lost.

Perhaps he should communicate with him. That was why he had the witches give the spy the rune stones anyway.

His thoughts were interrupted as one of his advisors entered the throne room. He hadn't wanted to be interrupted. He had made that clear. The king glared down at the troll as he stood at the base of the dais. "What is it?"

The small craggy advisor bent to one knee. "For gold and glory, my King."

"For gold and glor—just tell me what you herald."

"Yes, Great One. I bear good tidings. The large movement of forces into Elronia has gone well. The raids are going according to plan and the troops have moved far deeper into the human lands than expected."

"A plan, unfortunately, that they probably know of," reminded the king. "We should expect a great opposition quickly." His strategy had been to sweep in from the north through the dark forest, regardless of the losses incurred by the forest's residents. Then attack as many villages as he could, knowing that the humans would spread out their troops in an effort to defend all the locations. While that happened the Troll King would redirect his forces toward Keratost, the capital city of Elronia, and with the human troops spread about the kingdom there would be few left to guard the great city.

He knew what the magic war plans told. He had no choice now but to assume that the humans knew his plan. He would have to move now with such haste that even if the humans knew what he was planning it would be too late.

From a side entrance to the room floated in his three witch brides. The tattered gray robes of the witches seemed as ancient as Time itself, as if the slightest touch would cause them to crumble to dust. They drifted to a stop just behind the advisor. "Master, the shadow has returned," spoke one of them.

King Orgog looked at her in surprise. Without a word he got up and stormed from the room. None of them had ever seen the king move with such speed.

As he wound his way down through the tunnels to their meeting place, King Orgog thought, *He better bear good tidings.*

As the force rode deeper into the province, doubt assailed Macal. Surrounded by tough veteran soldiers, he realized just how inexperienced he was. He was beginning to think he had made a serious mistake in coming along when he was suddenly distracted by the scout calling the party to a halt.

The thin, keen-eyed man had reined in his mount, a horse as lanky and haggard as he was. As he spun it on its haunches to face the men, the dragonmere moved his jotun to stand beside him.

"We will be setting up an ambush," Kelifex announced. "There are twenty of us against thirty-six trolls, but do not be disheartened. We have the advantage of surprise; we have more skill and more training. You men were chosen because you are the best. These monsters cannot be allowed to haunt Elronia. They cannot be allowed to harm the Princess. They must be defeated; they must be slain. If they continue to move in their current direction, we will catch them as they pass through a shallow ravine. It is a perfect place for an ambush. We will arrive first and lie in wait. Do you understand?"

"Yes, sir!" the soldiers shouted in unison.

"Will we spare Elronia the gruesome touch of these monsters?" shouted back the scout.

"Yes, sir!" the men shouted again.

"Will we keep the King's Jewel safe?"

"With our lives, sir!"

"May the Crown stay strong!" called out Kelifex as he kicked his horse into motion.

"May the Crown stay strong!" chanted all the soldiers.

Watching silently, Macal saw an unsettled look pass over the dragonmere's face at Kelifex's words, but before he could guess the cause, it had gone.

"You have your orders. Move out!" ordered Viscount Razz.

The soldiers kicked their horses into a gallop behind the scout, and soon they were once more moving at full speed across the grassy hills. Macal was still having doubts about this venture. Even if Elronia's soldiers were highly trained, did it really make sense to attack the trolls with a smaller force? To the boy it seemed more sensible to have used the whole cavalcade. Against their superior numbers, the trolls would have no chance.

He urged Shelga up alongside of the Viscount's jotun. The dragonmere, who at first seemed lost in thought as he rode, finally glanced over and acknowledged the boy's presence with a nod.

"Why didn't we bring more soldiers?" asked Macal over the rhythmic thud of hoof beats that surrounded them.

"Because this way, if we fail," explained the dragonmere matter-of-factly, "the Princess still has a chance to reach Varun."

"How would we fail if we had all the men with us?"

"In warfare, you do not necessarily win just because you think you should. We cannot let the trolls roam free. At the same time we must not jeopardize our mission; the Princess must reach the hobgoblin lords. So this is the safest course." They rode in silence for a few moments before the dragonmere spoke again. "Once we have engaged the enemy, I want you stay away from the heart of the battle."

Relief rushed through the boy. "Then why did you want me to come?"

"I just want you to see real battle. A fight by trained men, effectively using the techniques I taught you."

"So I'm not to fight?"

"I think it would be rather foolish to thrust a young, barely trained boy into such a melee."

"But you're letting me go to Marglamesh."

"You do not go by my choice. I voiced my opinion to the Princess. I said that letting you go alone was irresponsible."

"And what did she say?"

"She said I was right."

"Then why is she letting me go?"

"She asked how we would stop you. If you want to go after your father, she said, you would find a way no matter what."

"Oh." This announcement pleased Macal. "Is that why you're spending so much time training me? You think I have no chance of saving my father?"

"If I thought there was no chance at all, training you would be a waste of time, wouldn't it? It is my opinion that if you are going to make this attempt, you should at least have an idea of what you are doing."

"What were you thinking about back there, when Kelifex was talking to the men?"

"What do you mean?"

"I mean you looked uncertain. Uncomfortable."

The Viscount glanced at Macal. "It is not the way of the dragonmere to lie in ambush and attack an opponent unaware. It lacks honor. In Ermalon we proudly ride out and challenge those who vex us, with no secrecy or deception. But this is not my kingdom, and whatever sway I hold over these soldiers, they are not mine. Who am I to change a tactic that works for them?"

Before Macal could respond, the scout slowed his steed and fell back to ride beside them. "We're almost there."

"Good" replied the Viscount. "I want to finish this and return to the Princess as quickly as possible. If there is one war band about, there may be others. If the Princess's entourage is attacked, I must be there to protect her."

"Agreed, my Lord," responded Kelifex. "If the ambush is successful we should be back with the Princess shortly."

"And if not successful?" asked Macal.

"Then helping the Princess Aeria will be beyond our means," replied the scout.

"Why?"

"Because we will be dead."

The Troll King entered the meeting chamber deep below his castle. In the dim torchlight he could see the vague shadow of the spy across the room. His three witch brides quietly glided in behind him. The shadow shifted uncomfortably as the witches entered the room.

Volten had hoped the witch brides would not be present for this exchange. He hated being near them. He felt like they could read his mind or see his future, and he never got the impression they saw good things for him. To make it worse they always wore dark, knowing smiles, as if they enjoyed his discomfort.

The king stepped to the center of the room, his eyes never leaving the shadow. "Do you have them?"

"No." Volten's voice came out more sheepish than he wanted.

Rage welled in the king. He took another step toward the human, his hands clenching and unclenching in anger. He seethed and bared his long jagged teeth. "How much more useless can you be?"

The spy rushed to explain before he came to physical harm. "The man did not have the plans with him."

The king seared his fiery gaze into Volten. He could feel deep in his scales that this was the meeting, this was the turning point, where everything was changing and he was beginning to lose....

"We followed him through several towns," continued the spy. "He must have known that he was being watched and hid them."

"So you are as incompetent at stealth as you are at the retrieval of items."

"Your Greatness, I have not failed entirely."

"Failure is failure, traitor."

The shadow reached into the deeper recesses of the darkness behind him and with some effort dragged a large bound and limp shape out in front of him. "I brought him. I thought that you might be able to entice him to give us the location of where he placed the plans."

Hope relit within the king. *All may not be lost.* He hid the pleasure from his face. "You brought him here so I could finish the job of finding the plans? So I could finish your job. I don't want him. I want the plans!"

"Through him we can get the plans."

King Orgog stepped forward to look at the unconscious man. Upon seeing the extent of their captive's wounds, the king could barely contain his anger. "He's nearly dead!"

"Only nearly. Not entirely."

"Do you mock me?"

"Never, Lord of the Land. I only wish to say that you have the means to keep him among the living, where as I do not. At least, until he divulges the location we seek."

The king motioned the witches toward the fallen man. "If he dies, so do you. Once he is stable, get the information from him however you need to. Whatever it takes."

The witches started to drag the unconscious man away, but the king recognized something. "Stop!"

He bent down and pulled the sword from the soldier's sheath. "Alrang-Dal!" he muttered. The silver sword glittered like a jeweled moon.

He kicked the man over, face up. He recognized him, too. The man who helped him ascend to the throne by defeating his predecessor. Bertran Teel. An amused smile grew upon his face. "How whimsical the fates can be."

Volten watched as the witches dragged the soldier away. "Shall we now talk about payment for services rendered?"

King Orgog stopped admiring the silver sword to look at the spy. "Payment? You have failed on all accounts."

"I delivered the bearer of the plans."

"And yet, he does not have them and neither do I, which was our deal."

"Through him you will get the plans."

"Only if he lives."

"So some small token would be appropriate."

Even without the plans, the fact that he now held Alrang-Dal pleased the king. He was much larger than the previous king, so it was too small for his own use, but for some reason he liked having it. He decided it would have a place of honor in his trophy room.

"I'll give you half the payment agreed upon. Consider yourself fortunate for that, and not having this sword in your chest. I also consider our business concluded. Never present yourself in Marglamesh again."

"What about when he tells you where the plans are? I could recover them for you."

King Orgog stepped up close to the man and looked down upon him. "You are a waste. A wretch. And an incompetent traitor." He removed a pouch filled with precious stones from his belt and dropped it into the man's hands. "Take this and be gone forever from my sight."

The spy for the last time withdrew from the room, and found as he did so that he was more curious as to the tortures that awaited Bertran Teel than he was about the value of the heavy bag in his hand.

By the time he exited the mountain his thoughts had reverted to the prospects of his new life. He definitely felt it was time to get Glendrel back. He had more than enough wealth now to make amends with her father. Soon he would feel her auburn hair once more against his cheek and be able to look into her deep brown eyes.

He had no desire to go to Drakenport. Part of him felt a little shame that the king hadn't given him Jengrul's share of the payment. But the disgusting man would have to suffer—or if he wanted it, he could come here and ask the king for it.

Volten sprouted his wings of fire and launched himself into the night toward Watermark and his future.

CHAPTER 15

T he sun burned bright in the pale blue sky, warming the soft western wind. Kelifex and the dragonmere had led the way to a rocky bluff divided by a narrow crevice, stationing soldiers on each side of the ravine through which the monsters must pass to continue their march through the kingdom. The surrounding area was covered in gentle hills and dotted with squat trees. Half the soldiers had been ordered to the north side of the crevice, where the scout was in command. The rest were on the south side under the direction of Viscount Razz.

Macal lay down at the lip of the bluff with the rest of the men, hearing a voice to his right say, "This spot is perfect. Raikis has blessed us today." The speaker was a blond, bearded solider. Like all the others except Macal, he carried a short bow and a quiver full of arrows.

While Macal was no expert on warfare he had to agree that, as the only easy way to reach the plateau, this narrow passage did seem the ideal spot for an ambush. Perhaps the god of war had really blessed them with this tremendous advantage over the unprepared band of trolls.

"Something to remember, boy, about soldiering," remarked the blond soldier, his gray eyes on Macal. "It is always better to attack than to be attacked."

As Macal stared at the hearty, weatherworn face, the soldier's words triggered a memory of Uncle Melkes. His uncle had once told him something along the same lines, but the point he had made was vastly different.

He had told Macal that it was better never to need to attack at all.

"Look! Here they come!" As the soldier pointed to the northwest, Macal noticed he was missing his pinky and ring fingers.

The troll war band was moving quickly. Seeing the vile creatures for the first time since the devastation of Hormul, Macal felt his stomach churn.

Monsters just like these had killed his uncle and destroyed his home. This force looked equally deadly. He had the urge to vomit and was barely able to suppress it. Some had a single bulging eye, others two or three. All were covered with spiky protrusions and patches of ochre moss. Their faces were bulbous and disproportioned, and more than a few had several heads atop their meaty bodies. The wide, fat tails that swung behind them gave them a slug-like quality. It looked as if Kelifex had been right about their numbers. At the center of their procession, pulled by a large ox with a dirty, scarred pink hide, was a large, reinforced wagon.

One difference between this collection of trolls and the ones Macal had seen in Hormul was that these lacked jewels and treasure. The boy guessed they hadn't yet had an opportunity for plunder, but they made up for their lack of loot by an abundance of weapons. All bore savage, massive swords, heavy clubs, and thick spears. Several trolls also carried crude stone hammers.

Out in front, striding ahead of the rest, was a huge troll clad in chinked chain armor, with twin axes strapped to its back.

"That's a troll war chief!" The blond soldier seemed taken aback. "You don't see many of them. When you do, it's time to run."

The words sent a spasm of fear through Macal. The muscles in his legs tingled as if eager to follow the soldier's advice.

"Oh, but don't you worry about this one. All we have to do is wait for them smelly buggers to get deep into the throat of this causeway here; then we'll attack. Trust me on this. They won't stand a chance!"

The trolls were pouring into the slanting crevice, beginning their trek to the top of the bluff when suddenly Viscount Razz appeared at the far end of the ravine—riding out to face the trolls alone!

Macal was stunned. He heard rumbles of shock and horror from the soldiers around him. The Viscount was giving away their ambush! Catching the trolls by surprise had been their only hope of an easy victory. Now, even if they managed to win, they would undoubtedly sustain heavy casualties. Even worse, it was obvious to Macal that the dragonmere was doomed to die down there, against the onslaught of the entire troll war band.

From across the way, seeing their opportunity about to be wasted, Kelifex ordered an immediate attack. It was now or never; their advantage was slipping away. If they had any hope of surviving, it was by forcing significant losses on the trolls before they could gauge the situation. At the scout's command, the Elronian soldiers drew their bows and sent a fearsome volley of arrows flying. Kelifex used his heavy crossbow to launch a bolt through the air with deadly precision. All around Macal, the ambush had commenced.

"For the Crown!" some of the soldiers shouted as they let loose their attacks.

"For Elronia!" bellowed others as their war cry.

The first volley rained down with devastating effect, the sharp, thick-shafted arrows penetrating troll armor and flesh. Several of the monsters were slain before they could react. The second volley was already in flight before the slow-thinking trolls began to grasp their plight, and more wounded monsters fell to the ground.

The war chief, more quick-witted than the rest, took stock of the situation and angrily began to shout out orders for his small legion to charge forward. Not wanting to be pinned down, the remaining trolls scrambled to follow their leader's commands.

"For gold and glory!" snarled the trolls as the war band rushed forward. From atop the bluff Macal could see that most of them, even though caught at a disadvantage, seemed gleeful at the prospect of causing pain. Their eyes gleamed as their weapons shifted restlessly in their four-fingered hands. Several closed in on the Viscount, ready to hack him apart, while the rest attempted to reach the far end of the ravine, eager to surmount the bluff and engage the humans.

"He's mine!" The war chief's roar claimed the dragonmere. The trolls charging Viscount Razz hesitated, their bloodlust urging them to disobey. At last they reluctantly turned their attention to the soldiers on the bluffs. As they shambled the length of the ravine, several more fell victim to Elronian arrows. The toll would have been higher if many of the men had not held their shots for fear of accidentally striking the Viscount.

Two trolls had stayed behind with the wagon. Now, with a speed and precision born of familiarity, they quickly released latch pins at each corner of the wagon. Heavy iron rods fell to the ground, freeing the metal-reinforced wooden sides, which fell open to reveal an object on the wagon's open platform.

It was a huge bone-colored jar the size of an ogre, adorned with blood-colored glyphs and held in place by thick wrought-iron chains. Macal had no idea what it was, but all around him the soldiers cried out in fear as they saw it.

One of the soldiers called out in frantic desperation. "They've got a specter!"

"Stop them!" a soldier shouted, but the trolls near the wagon had already readied their weapons to smash the jug. It was too late. Even as the Elronians released their arrows, the trolls used their clubs and axes to shatter the clay jar. It broke with an eruption like a burst of lava from a seething volcano, freeing the specter confined within.

"The gods have cursed us!" shouted a soldier.

The specter that rose from the explosion was an undead abomination. It was a skeletal troll nearly five times the size of the others, its face a fleshless, aberrant mask of pitted yellow bone. Swirling around it was a mist of noxious vapor that radiated a haunting purple glow of vile magic. A grotesque stench as from a field of dead carcasses pervaded the battlefield.

In Macal's worst nightmares he had never encountered such a horrendous beast. He stared, paralyzed with fear. Surprise attack? *Who had surprised whom?*

"Stand your ground! Do not run!" commanded Viscount Razz from down below. The boy could see his companions struggling with their fear. More than half the trolls were still alive, and now the specter had joined their force; but the men responded to the dragonmere and valiantly held their positions.

"I AM FREE!" bellowed the creature of death, its booming voice shaking the ground with an earthquake's force. Glaring around the battlefield, it understood its purpose well. With the strength of a giant, it seized the metal cart it had been carried on and flung it, grotesque ox and all, at a ledge where several Elronian archers stood. The wagon struck the bluff with tremendous force, shattering the earth under the men's feet in a great blast of soil. Men, dirt, and rock tumbled to the base of the cliff with the remains of the wagon.

"I AM FREE TO SLAUGHTER!" roared the specter, snatching up two of the stunned soldiers and hurling them against the wall of the bluff, where they fell in lifeless heaps. The demonic creature stalked forward, its unearthly moan filling the air. *"LET THE FLESH RENDING BEGIN!"*

The trolls who had rushed to the end of the ravine were now circling up to the top, where the soldiers held their positions. The specter, still in the ravine, was reaching up and pulling men off the northern ridge, hurling them through the air a great distance to crash down into the earth. On the south side, a number of trolls gained the bluff. Seeing the ungainly monsters trudging forward, Macal began to back away. One noticed him and turned in his direction. Already at the cliff's edge, the boy had no place to run. As the troll lumbered closer he reached for his sword. The cold steel felt heavy and useless in his trembling hand.

"Whatcha gonna do wit dat? Be careful not to gut yerself!" jeered the troll. It was the leanest troll Macal had seen, with long gangly limbs and a tangled mass of black oily hair. It had an incredibly long, pointed nose and its face was covered with sickly little warts.

"How 'bout I cut out yer guts fer ya?" snarled the creature as it produced its own sword, three times the size of the boy's. Closing the distance between them, it raised the weapon above its head with both hands. Macal found himself unable to move. He couldn't possibly hold his own against such a monster. His sword fell from his numb fingers.

Down below, the troll chief moved to attack Viscount Razz, wielding a battle axe in each hand. The dragonmere, sparing an instant's attention from his own fight to check on Macal, felt his heart sink. There was no way he could reach Macal in time to save him, and the boy was only here because he had insisted upon it.

Back on the bluff Macal stood petrified. He couldn't believe it. He was going to die right here, right now. With each passing second, death came closer. As his mind began to grasp his own mortality, one odd regret came to him. He would never know what was in the tomb.

Before he even had time to say a prayer, the troll was upon him. In another second it would all be over. And then there was a blur of motion from the right, as a soldier leaped in front of him to tackle the huge troll. The impact unbalanced the monster; the battling pair rolled to the edge of the bluff in a cloud of dust and went over.

For a moment Macal saw the man's face hanging in the air. It was Corporal Mercule. Then he fell from sight.

The troll chief stalked forward, eyeing Viscount Razz. In each hand the monster held a double-edged axe. It couldn't believe its witless soldiers had set the specter free. The wretches had no forethought. If they had not already been slain, the troll chief would have slain them itself.

Behind the mighty troll, the Viscount could see the specter continuing to wreak havoc against the Elronians. He forced his mind to focus on his own battle. He was still mounted on his brown jotun, holding the reins in one hand and his sword in the other. Warily the two combatants started to circle each other.

"Ever think you would die in a war that is not even yours?" asked the troll chief provokingly.

"I had not really considered it." The Viscount's response was flat. "I have not spent much time planning how to die. I assumed Death would follow its own dictates."

"It's something you should start thinking about sooner rather than later," the troll growled. Waving its axes at the Viscount to test his reaction speed, it was disappointed to find him remarkably quick. The chieftain did not care for challenges; it preferred outright slaughter, in its favor. "None of you rotters have any chance of walking away from this fight."

"We were actually thinking about riding away," mocked the dragonmere.

"The specter is tearing *your* people apart!" snapped the troll chief.

"And what will stop it from doing the same to yours?" Viscount Razz countered.

The troll growled under its breath. The question was fair. Specters were beasts of uncontrollable chaos and incredible power. The troll captain had been promised all the wealth sacked from the human Keep of Merthor if it could capture the fortress with this small contingent of troops. The specter had offered the assurance of victory in this endeavor, but now it had been wasted, set free in a petty battle. And without the magical skills of one of the Troll King's witch brides, there was no way the creature could be forced back into a Jar of Containing. With the loss of the specter, along with the casualties from this battle, there was no chance that the Keep of Merthor would fall by the troll chief's hand. *There would be no gold and there would be no glory.*

Furious that its greed would not be satiated, the troll mentally commanded its enchanted axes. An inferno of orange flame engulfed the left hand's blade, while the edge of the right axe suddenly hissed with a searing, olive-colored acid. The dragonmere's eyes narrowed as he watched the weapons come alive.

"I think I hear Death coming for you," taunted the chief, baring his pointed yellow teeth. Stepping forward, he swung his fiery axe at the jotun steed in a blazing orange arc.

Viscount Razz pulled sharply on the reins, avoiding the attack by forcing the jotun onto its four hind legs. With the steed still rearing in the air, he leaned forward and thrust his sword downward at the troll chief's shoulder—but the troll flung up its corrosive axe to deflect the blow.

The Viscount forced his adversary back by letting the jotun drop back to all six legs, then immediately kicked his mount into a charge, hoping to cleave the troll chief's head as he rushed by.

Again the troll was quick to react. This time both axes parried the swipe, knocking the sword aside. As the Viscount swept past, the war chief brought both of its magical axes down, hacking into the jotun's flank. The force of the blow caused the big animal to stagger sideways. Twisting in the saddle, Viscount Razz saw the flaming gash left by the fiery axe. Where the other blade had torn the jotun's hide, bubbling acid was eating through its flesh.

As the jotun screamed and stumbled, the troll chief saw its advantage. Before the Viscount could regain control of his fraught steed, it rushed upon him with another vicious double swipe, easily capable of cutting the dragonmere in half. Viscount Razz saw the attack coming and was unable to avoid it; all he could do was to try to survive the onslaught. He swung his sword around in a defensive block just in time, but the strength behind the troll's attack knocked him off his injured mount. He landed hard on the ground at the troll chief's feet.

"I guess I was right; that *was* Death I heard coming for ya," sneered the monster as it brought its axes down onto the dragonmere.

All around Macal, the trolls had engaged with the human soldiers. The advantage the Elronians had hoped to gain by the ambush had not been wholly lost; many men were making quick work of the trolls, some of whom had already been wounded by the volleys of arrows. Macal stumbled to his feet and ran to the edge of the bluff to look for Corporal Mercule. To his relief, the soldier was dazedly untangling himself from the motionless troll he had landed on. As he stood, Macal could see that the corporal's legs were still shaky. He looked astounded to have survived the fall.

Macal was about to call out his thanks to Mercule for saving his life, when suddenly his blood ran cold and his throat closed in fear. The specter had noticed the Corporal.

"COME HERE, MEATLING!" roared the wraith.

CHAPTER 16

The Viscount rolled to his feet just as the troll chief's axes descended, then spun to face his enemy as the troll dragged its blades free from the dirt. The troll and the dragonmere circled each other, suddenly clashing together in a flurry of clanging blades. Even though the war chief had two weapons to the Viscount's one, the latter's speed and expertise with his sword proved capable of keeping the cruel axes at bay. In a furious dance of deadly metal they struck, parried, and countered, locking together at last in a trial of strength.

"I look forward to roasting your eyes for dinner. I hear they're the delicacy of you whelps," spat the troll chief.

"And I look forward to mounting your head on a pike," said the Viscount through his barred teeth.

Using its elephantine bulk, the troll brutally forced its enemy off his feet and onto his back. Strong as he was in comparison to a human man, the dragonmere was no match for the immense troll. The war chief leaped forward with axes raised, determined to finish its stunned opponent once and for all.

Macal found his voice. "Behind you!" he screamed in warning to Corporal Mercule, who shouted a hoarse warning in return. Dread flooded both man and boy, threatening to drown them as each turned to see certain death lumbering towards him.

"THE BLOOD OF THE LIVING FEEDS THE DEAD," groaned the specter as it moved toward Mercule. Lurching toward Macal was a one-eyed troll whose enormous body was heavily scarred from previous battles. One of its pointed ears was missing, apparently lopped off by a dull weapon that had left behind a few flaps of tattered flesh. Instinctively Macal crouched and retrieved his fallen sword. Left arm wobbling in fear, he held the weapon out before him.

"Nighty night, wee one!" chortled the fleshy monster, attacking with an overhead swing of its huge mace.

As Macal frantically tried to remember what the Viscount had taught him about meeting this type of attack, he found that his body had already reacted. Grabbing the hilt of his sword with both hands, he held it up horizontally to block the assault. As the mace slammed down onto the short sword, it took every ounce of the boy's strength to deflect a blow designed to crush his skull into unrecognizable pudding.

For a second he was stunned. Even though the attack had knocked him to his knees and the impact had numbed his hands, he had managed to block it. *He had done it! He had saved himself!* He had never believed it could be possible. The troll seemed just as shocked as he was.

"Da little one t'inks he can fight!" The monster gave a guttural laugh. "Ya can't stop us, little one; yer whole kingdom is gonna be ours. We're gonna kill and eats you all!"

Macal knew he had been lucky. The troll had only been easy on him because it had thought him an inept fighter. Without wasting an instant, Macal did what he did best. He ran, sprinting back across the bluff and down the ravine toward Viscount Razz, hoping the dragonmere could protect him.

Behind him, the rotund troll warrior wasted no time in pursuit. "We're gonna kill you all, but I's wanna start wid' you!"

As his jotun galloped away screaming in agony, Viscount Razz looked up and saw death hovering over him in the form of the two ensorcelled axes. Quickly shifting position, he craned his head forward and released a huge gout of his fiery breath into the troll war chief's face.

The startled troll recoiled, howling in pain as the intense heat seared its skin, melted its eyes and ignited its hair like a flaring torch. The dragonmere jumped to his feet. As the troll chief staggered back, shrieking, the Viscount brought his sword down in a powerful two-handed swing that severed the creature's scaly hands just below the wrist. The activated enchantments of the magical axes faded as they fell to the ground, clutched by the still writhing hands.

The war chief roared and wailed in horrific torment. The flesh of its face was devastated, its arms mutilated and useless. Its cries echoed across the battlefield, momentarily capturing the attention of the other combatants. Reluctant to let the creature suffer, regardless of its origin, the Viscount did what he hoped an enemy would do for him if the roles were reversed. With all his might, he thrust his sword forward with one hand on the hilt and the other pushing on the pommel. The blade slid cleanly through the troll's chest, silencing it forever. As the once formidable war chief slid off his sword into a limp heap on the ground, the Viscount turned to see a terrified Macal running towards him, closely pursued by another troll.

Turning to see the approaching specter, the Corporal wondered fleetingly what god he had so offended, that this should be his fate.

The monstrous revenant wasted no time in attacking. Its claw-like hand, as big as the Corporal's entire body, lashed out in an attempt to seize the man and tear him in half. Mercule was an experienced soldier who had been in many battles, most of them bigger than this one. If he was going to die, he wanted the specter to remember their fight. As the enormous hand came within range, he thrust his sword straight into the palm with all the force he could muster.

"*h-a-a-arRRRRRG!* " A bellow of agony exploded from the undead monstrosity as the sword slid through its hand. Its recoil yanked the sword from the Corporal's grip, and Mercule quickly backed away from the raging phantom. Towering over him, the specter tore the stinging weapon from its hand and cast it away, then charged forward to seek revenge. Corporal Mercule drew his only remaining weapon, a simple dagger.

Then he turned and ran.

Fleeing from the mammoth troll, Macal saw the Corporal charging in his direction while he was running toward the Viscount, who was now just ahead. The dragonmere seemed aware of the Corporal's plight as well as the boy's. Both were easily outpaced by their pursuers.

For a moment it seemed as if the soldier and the boy would collide as they ran for their lives. All around them raged the chaos of battle. No longer did the humans have the advantage; the trolls had recovered from their initial shock and were delivering their retribution.

The enormous troll was so close to Macal that he could feel the murderous beast's breath on his neck. The specter's huge right hand clutched at the Corporal, but he ducked under the grasping fingers. Just as Mercule's path was about to cross Macal's, the specter reached out again. The Corporal dove to the side. Missing him, the massive claw accidentally caught hold of the troll behind Macal.

With a startled yelp, the troll disappeared into the specter's frightful grip. As Macal, the Corporal, and the dragonmere all watched transfixed, the specter stuffed its bleating victim's head and torso into its mouth, taking a large bite before tossing the rest of the body to the ground.

"That should make a meal or two," the dragonmere joked weakly.

"That's good news," the Corporal said. "Can't imagine it'll still be hungry." But even as he spoke, the specter turned in their direction.

"I think it wants dessert," Macal said as the three of them backed away.

There was no doubt of the gruesome creature's intent. It charged forward, skeletal arms outstretched. All around the battlefield, the surviving Elronians darted horrified glances at the coming massacre. Some of the trolls also risked a glimpse, pleased at the prospect of slaughter.

Eyes glowing a hellish violet, ribs protruding through its disintegrating flesh, the specter towered over its three victims. With a victory howl of bloodcurdling rage, it struck.

There was no doubt a single blow from the demon would destroy them all. Everything in Macal's short life shot through his mind like a splintering star. He thought about the courageous father he would never rescue, the gentle uncle who had died to save him, the beautiful mother who had given her life so that he could have his. Now it would all go to waste.

Without a word Viscount Razz stepped forward, holding his arm upright with his hand forming a defiant fist, the royal Ring of Ermalon faced toward the specter. Macal had a glimpse of his face, both resolute and saddened, grim and accepting. The emerald in the ring flared instantly to life, dazzling as a tiny green sun. The sudden brilliant flare stunned the specter into immobility.

Around the emerald, the ring's rubies burst into radiance, shaping the green gem's glow, forcing it into a cone. The enchanted beam lanced out to engulf the specter. To Macal's amazement, the rays of light solidified around the demon, encapsulating it in translucent green stone.

"Nooooooo!" cried the specter as it tried to break free from its new prison. Too late—the magic of the ring had trapped it, and the demon was no match for the ancient wizardry of the crafters of Ermalon. Its bellows of

rage and terror faded as the gemstone prison finished its formation. At last the specter was locked within a faceted translucent cage, unmoving.

Macal's astonished gaze turned from the imprisoned wraith to the dragonmere just as the Viscount collapsed to the ground as if struck dead.

In the great throne room of Castle Darkmoor, King Morgog sat in counsel with his three witch brides. The vast echoing chamber was the largest room in the entire castle. Two rows of pillars supported a vaulted ceiling of such height that the flickering sconces below never illuminated it. Vast tapestries depicting all the previous bloody ages of Marglasmesh covered the walls and gave the gloomy room its only color.

Tension and anger twisted the king's massive body in spite of the opulent comfort of his great throne on its dais. The war plans had still not been retrieved, and the answers he needed were not forthcoming. "Has he confessed the location of the plans?" he demanded again.

"No, my Master, the torture continues." The ghostly voices spoke simultaneously. The witch brides floated inches off the ground in slow, wispy curves about the dais, none of them daring to meet the king's furious gaze.

"And what does your *Void* say?"

Again the brides spoke in unison. "The Void does not speak of them. It is part of the dweomer that protects the plans."

The tattered gray robes of the witches seemed as ancient as Time itself, as if the slightest touch would cause them to crumble to dust. The first bride cradled a blackened human skull in her hands, running her fingers sensually over its hard surface. One eye socket held a large sapphire gemstone, the other a bright ruby. The back of the skull had been smashed away, and in the hole was set what was possibly the largest emerald in all of Aerinth, twinkling like a third eye.

The second bride held a long blackened staff. It too was bejeweled in a variety of colorful gemstones, set at intervals along its knobby surface. The last bride held in her arms a living cat of bones. The skeletal feline purred as she lavished attention upon it.

"You made the plans, yet you cannot find them?" The Troll King's roar echoed through the chamber as he stood suddenly, scattering the witch brides like a harsh gust of wind. He swung his massive head around to glare at them. "What about the assassin?"

The first bride peeked into the emerald on the back of the blackened skull she carried. Together the three answered, "The Void says he closes in. He will have her blood free from her heart. Soon."

"How soon is soon?"

"The Void cannot say. Within days, perhaps."

"She must die!"

"She will, Master. The Void has said this assassin has no equal."

"Then the *Void* hasn't seen me murder. Elronia is almost mine. I will not lose my chance to succeed in an endeavor no other Marglamesh ruler has been able to achieve. My glory will not be stolen from me! I will be Emperor!"

"Yes, Master. The Void has declared that such is the fate to come. The Void has said you will be Emperor," whispered the three brides in harmonic unison.

"If the *Void* is wrong, it means you are wrong, and that means you are of no use to me. Take this as a warning, crones. If I fail to become Emperor, you will fail to exist."

"Yes, Master." The brides continued to swirl just out of reach of the Troll King.

"Go and get me answers. I want the prisoner to speak, and I want to be informed as soon as the assassin strikes. Do you think you and your *Void* can accomplish that?"

"Yes, Master."

Macal and Corporal Mercule ran to Viscount Razz. The dragonmere had fallen forward, his red cloak spread around him. As the boy flung himself down by his side, he saw that the Viscount now looked gaunt and frail. The steely green scales on his head and long slender neck seemed looser, slightly curled and grayish around the edges. His reptilian red eyes were open, but their former sharpness had grown dull, as if the mind behind them was no longer capable of receiving their observations. To Macal it looked as if the Viscount had aged a decade since his courageous act of a moment before.

Around the battlefield, the few surviving soldiers recovered from the shock of seeing the Viscount fall, while the small remnant of the troll forces left standing were still reeling from the defeat of the specter. They had now lost their strongest ally along with their war chief. Taking advantage of their fading morale, the Elronian soldiers attacked with their last reserves of strength, bravery, and courage. It was all or nothing. If the dragonmere had given his life to spare them a horrifying fate at the specter's hands, his sacrifice would not be in vain. In spite of their anguish they chopped, struck, and cut into the remaining trolls. Some of the monsters stood stoically for a moment, but most began to flee realizing they had lost. Within another moment the battle was over. The proficient soldiers of the black dragon left no survivors.

Kneeling beside Macal, Corporal Mercule gently turned Viscount Razz onto his back. The dragonmere's head hung limp at the end of his long scaled neck. His shiny chest plate was battered and marred from his battle with the troll war chief, his white robes covered in filth and mire. Macal was shocked by how fragile he looked.

"Is he alive?" he asked as the Corporal examined their fallen comrade.

"I don't know." Mercule's face was grave, his eyes sorrowful.

"Is there *anything* we can do?" The boy's voice was shaking. He didn't think he could bear the death of someone else he cared for.

"We don't even know what happened to him!" The Corporal was becoming overwhelmed by the situation as well. "How can we fix what we don't understand?"

"I don't know! I figured maybe you had seen this before."

"Trust me." The Corporal glanced at the gemstone prison encasing the specter. "I have *never* seen anything like this before."

The soldiers who had survived the melee approached their fallen leader. Macal noted that there were only five of them; the rest of their force lay slain on the battlefield. Glancing up to the southern bluff, he saw that even the gray-eyed scout Kelifex had died. The man's blood dripped over the edge of the cliff, wetting the rocks below. Horror and sadness engulfed the boy. *So many had died. So many good men were now dead.* All the happy memories he possessed were being drowned by new, darker ones filled with corpses and blood, pain and decay. First Hormul, and now this. *What kind of world were the gods watching over?*

The surviving soldiers clustered around the motionless figure of Viscount Razz, muttering in confusion.

"What happened?"

"How was he able to do that?"

"I've never seen anything like it," a soldier said, staring at the green stone prison.

"He saved us all," marveled another.

Macal looked at the bodies of the dead. "Not all of us," he whispered.

"You're right, boy, it is a grim day," one of the survivors said. "It shouldn't have been like this."

"That's right! He brought this on us. He gave away our ambush!"

The angry words came from a neat, fit man with cropped blondish hair, clad in thick mail. Macal had talked to him before; his name was Drennin of Rellemore, or something similar. The boy was taken aback by the way the man was speaking of the dead dragonmere. Back in Hormul his uncle had taught him never to speak darkly of the dead, because they could hear you. It was their time to rest, not to wallow in the failings of their mortal existence.

"You better watch what you say," shouted Corporal Mercule, standing up to face Drennin. "Without him we would all be dead right now. The trolls would have loosed the specter whether or not he had ridden out by himself against them. He was the only one of us able to stop that thing."

"I disagree, *sir.* There's a good chance we could have stopped them before the specter was released, had we not ourselves been surprised and our initiative lost because of his sudden appearance in the *damn* valley." Drennin made a sweeping gesture at the littered battlefield. "Many of those men had been my friends for years. Now they are dead! For *what?* To stop a random raiding party? They died for nothing. This battle was inconsequential!"

"They were my friends, too." Corporal Mercule stood rigid. "It was the trolls who killed them, not Razz. Do not forget that."

"I'm glad he's dead!" shot back the exhausted soldier. "If he wasn't *I* would kill him myself." His face twisted as he prepared to spit on the fallen dragonmere.

"Do that, and you will join the rest of the dead on the ground," warned the Corporal, stepping between the angry soldier and the dragonmere's body.

At that moment, a groan from Viscount Razz stunned them all. It was only then that Macal noticed that of the eight rubies on the Ring of Ermalon, one was no longer radiant but had blackened to coal.

All the men jumped back as if they were seeing the dead rise.

"Kill me now, Drennin." The dragonmere's voice was scarcely audible, his strength spent. "Here is the chance you desire. I'm barely able to move. You'll never have a better chance for vengeance than now."

Drennin's hand moved instinctively to the hilt of his sword. As the dragonmere's eyes closed in exhaustion, all the men turned to watch Drennin. The bitter man's threat had been answered, and now they waited to see if he had spoken empty words or a true oath of revenge. Macal couldn't imagine they would allow him to slay Viscount Razz. *Would they?*

Drennin was clearly torn, his hand trembling on his sword hilt. Then, to the company's shock, he pulled his weapon from its scabbard. Macal caught his breath. No one moved, not even Corporal Mercule. *Would they really let this man slay the Viscount?*

Sword in hand, Drennin stepped forward to stand over the dragonmere.

"Do what you think is right." Exhausted and wounded as the Viscount was, pride was still audible in his voice. The soldier looked down at his supine adversary with hate in his eyes. He was trembling; to Macal it was clear he had meant every word he had spoken. He was about to strike. The boy couldn't fathom why nobody was trying to help the dragonmere. As Drennin raised his sword to plunge it through the dragonmere's chest plate and into his heart, Macal flung himself forward and shoved the man aside.

"No! Get away from him!"

While not enough to move Drennin far, the unexpected assault knocked his sword aside. Rage swept over the soldier. *Who dared stop him from seeking the vengeance that was rightfully his?* Instinctively he raised his mailed fist to backhand Macal, a blow that would have knocked the boy unconscious if Corporal Mercule had not seized Drennin's wrist.

"You're pushing your luck today. Devera will turn against you if you do not master yourself. He's just a boy."

"Keep your *child* in check, then."

"Back off," ordered the Corporal. To his surprise Drennin obeyed, stalking off toward the place where the soldiers had hidden their horses before the skirmish. The others had already turned back to the dragonmere, who seemed to be rapidly regaining his strength.

"How many are alive?" he asked in a steadier voice as he sat up.

"Five, sir, other than us," Corporal Mercule said.

The dragonmere's shoulders sagged. "Five?"

"What happened?" asked one of the soldiers.

The Viscount glanced at him. "The Power of Ermalon happened."

"What do you mean?"

"The Ruler of Ermalon is granted the power of this ring, which channels the power that resides in my kingdom. Unfortunately its power is limited for each ruler. And each time it is used—"

"—it ages you," interjected Macal, beginning to put the pieces together. "And you can only use it seven more times."

The Viscount nodded, impressed at the boy's cleverness. "Something like that. The ring will continue to serve me, but only at the cost of my life." He paused a moment before asking, "How do I look?"

"Older," answered Macal. "Much older."

"That's how I feel."

"But it's better than being dead," Corporal Mercule said. "And you saved us."

"Perhaps." The dragonmere's response was noncommittal. "Drennin does not seem to think so."

"It's been a bad day for us all," one of the soldiers said. "He's taking it pretty hard. Who would have thought they had a godforsaken specter, sir?"

With the help of the Corporal and Macal, the Viscount regained his feet. "We must get back to the Princess. If there are more such troll forces, I must be there to protect her."

Mercule nodded vigorously. "Yes, sir. I agree."

"What about that thing, sir?" A soldier indicated the green gemstone prison, dazzling now as sunlight splintered through it.

"Leave it." There was still a thread of exhaustion in Viscount Razz's voice. "When moonlight strikes it, it will decay, taking the specter with it."

"Decay?" asked Macal in disbelief.

"Yes, the conjuration will fade. It will crumble into disappearing wisps and motes of magic. Now, we must hurry back to the caravan to ensure the Princess's safety."

"Wait." Macal was still curious. "If moonlight destroys the magic, what would have happened if you tried to do it at night?"

"You don't want to know," replied the dragonmere cryptically.

Corporal Mercule was surveying the field. "What about the dead, sir?"

"We don't have time to bury them. Leave them where they are. If we succeed in our mission to Varun, the gods willing, we will return and offer them a proper burial."

"Are you *sure*, sir?" Clearly the Corporal was uneasy about simply leaving their dead.

"You have your orders, Corporal. The Jewel must come first. If she dies, all is lost, and there will be more dead here in Elronia than we can ever attend to. Now let's get our horses and ride out."

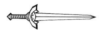

Soon they were all mounted and heading back to the caravan. Unable to recover his frightened and seriously injured jotun, the Viscount now rode a regular horse that had belonged to one of the soldiers killed in the battle. The other horses had been gathered up and were being herded back as well. Macal rode in silence beside Corporal Mercule until finally the soldier spoke.

"Your father would never forgive me if I had let one of these monsters kill you. Practice is good, but there is nothing like an actual melee to increase one's understanding of the blade. In that one battle, I think I witnessed the birth of a true swordsman."

"What do you mean?" Compliments were so rare in Macal's experience that he wasn't sure he was receiving one.

"What I saw today up on the bluff; you against that troll. A troll, mind you, three to four times your size. You should be proud of yourself."

Macal gulped. The few simple words gave him a warm, unfamiliar feeling of confidence. "How long have you been a soldier?" he asked as they crested another hill and passed through a small copse of trees.

"Since I was old enough to sign up and get paid for it. Didn't have much of a choice back then, after my father forced me out of the house."

"Why did he do that?"

"Not worth talking about, really. Let's just say that by the time he kicked me out, I was already more of a man than he would ever be. No real man would ever sell his daughters into slavery just to make a few coins for drink." The Corporal paused and then added, "I think you're making the right decision about not being a soldier. After this war, even I'm going to leave the military. No more battles for me. And you know, I think your father was thinking the same."

"Really? After this war he was going to quit the Legion?"

"War has a way of aging you. Making you tired, resentful. I think I've given enough, and so has he—more than twenty years now. It's time I start enjoying some of the fruits of my labor. That is, if any of those fruits survive this war."

"You don't think we'll win?"

A forlorn look crossed the Corporal's face. "Well—if we lose, it won't be for lack of trying. Right?"

"I guess," Macal said without much conviction.

A short time later they reached the camp. It was a relief to find their companions unmolested and the Princess unharmed. Dismounting, Viscount Razz headed on unsteady legs for the Jewel's tent, ordering Corporal Mercule to follow.

Macal was left alone. At loose ends, he climbed down from his jotun and started toward his own tent, but he had taken only a few steps when a Royal Guard ran out of the Princess's tent, shouting orders. The cavalcade would be moving out within the hour.

Finally, the boy thought. *Finally I'll find out what's in the Tomb of the Old King.* He wasn't sure why the Princess was creating such an atmosphere of mystery about the tomb. His own curiosity obviously entertained her, but she was keeping the secret from everyone else as well—even from Viscount Razz Munin.

CHAPTER 17

Macal watched in a daze as the soldiers speedily and efficiently collapsed their camp for transportation. He couldn't stop thinking about the battle. How could these men do it? How could they repeatedly engage in such actions, risking their lives in a melee of steel and blood? In the midst of this introspection he was sure of one thing: he knew *he* never wanted to be in a battle again.

But they did it, didn't they? They had to, in order to save Elronia. My father does this all the time.

Even though the fight had been over for more than an hour, he was still shaking from head to foot, helpless to control the waves of trembling that passed through him. The persistence of his fear was crippling, causing him to doubt himself again.

Could he really go to Marglamesh to find his father?

So many soldiers had died on that battlefield. Veteran soldiers, older men, all skilled warriors, part of the Royal Guard. Many of them had been the elite of the kingdom, and almost *every one* of them had died!

I'm only twelve. I shouldn't be involved in this. If I go, I'm going to die.

But what about my father? If I don't try to save him, there's no one else to send. The trolls are ravaging our land. The king can't spare a single man at a time like this. If I don't go, nobody will.

If only I had Alrang-Dal.

His father's magical silversword. Corporal Mercule had been with Bertran Teel when he claimed Alrang-Dal—when, leading the Amber Dragoons, he had slain the last Troll King. Macal had never heard the full story, but he was proud of his father's legendary feat. How many soldiers could say they had defeated a Troll King?

What few facts Macal did know had been told to him by Uncle Melkes. His uncle the storyteller had said that the two-headed Troll King had been

159

tricked into taking part in the battle by one of his subordinates. This underling had promised an easy victory on the Xanga-Mor lands, one that would boost the failing morale of their troops by showing their leader glorious and victorious in battle.

In truth, it was no small battle; the Amber Dragoons led one of the largest forces ever assembled on one front, and the overmatched trolls stood no chance. With the great throne of Marglamesh rendered vacant by Macal's father, the troll underling, Orgog, had become the next king. That had been more than a decade ago. In that interval the new king had rebuilt and strengthened his army, and now he had started the war anew.

After that fight, the King of Elronia had offered his father a small fortified keep and chests of gold as a reward. He could have been rich, Macal and Uncle Melkes would have been taken care of, but his father had turned that all down, asking only to be able to keep Alrang-Dal. He also said that he was not a soldier for the rewards, but because he wanted to protect those who couldn't protect themselves. That is what gave his life value.

If only I had Alrang-Dal, Macal thought again. The sword had magic powers that could help him. Along with the Viscount's training, it would at least offer him a chance. The pommel was set with a beautiful ruby, and the wide, gleaming silver blade was etched with ancient, unreadable words. Macal had always thought the mysterious script must tell the story of the sword's fashioning; but Lalliard, although he couldn't read the characters, insisted that they were runes of magic from which the sword drew its power. At Bertran Teel's command, the blade would dance with brilliant azure flames. The magic of the runes also kept the enchanted silver edge keen and allowed it to cleave an opponent with ease.

Yes, thought Macal. *I wish I had Alrang-Dal. Maybe then I wouldn't be so afraid.*

Deep inside him, an insidious little voice spoke. *What good would the sword do you? It obviously didn't help your father.*

He was spared the necessity of answering by a gentle touch on his arm. Princess Aeria Stormlion stood beside him. "Are you all right? You don't look well."

Macal shook the haze from his mind and blinked at her. "I'm all right."

She didn't seem convinced. "Are you sure? We're leaving now, but if you need to rest—"

"I'm fine. Really, I am."

"Are you sure you want to go through with this?" The question was filled with concern, as if she could read his thoughts. "You don't have to do it."

In the face before him, so beautiful, intelligent, and brave, Macal suddenly found fuel for his courage. He was inspired by her willingness to endure anything for her people. More than that, he didn't want her to see his own weakness and inadequacy. His reasons might not be noble, he thought, but they were the best he had.

"I have to go," he said at last. "Someone has to save my father."

Her carriage stood nearby, the white unicorns tossing their heads. Macal escorted the Princess to it, and within a few moments the cavalcade was once more on its way to the Tomb of the Old King.

To Macal's delight, as they travelled northwest he was able to squeeze in one more training session with the dragonmere. He had discovered he enjoyed learning new things. All he had to do was forget that the true grim purpose of these lessons was to learn to shed blood. So far that hadn't been that easy, but even so he was making significant progress in the rudimentary skills of swordplay.

At long last they reached the place not far from the Rashinasti Forest, in the far north of the Avie province, where Princess Aeria insisted the Tomb of the Old King was located. Macal saw Viscount Razz, ahead of him in the procession of men and horses, making his way over to the Princess's carriage.

"Where do we go from here?" the dragonmere asked the Princess as he matched pace with her conveyance.

"From the stories my father told me, the tomb is part way up the base of a mountain."

The Viscount scanned the horizon, where rolling green hills were spotted with trees. "I see no mountains nearby. Perhaps he meant one of those knolls. Stories have a way of exaggerating facts."

"Possibly." Princess Aeria pointed. "Do you see that hill?"

"The large hill flanked by two smaller ones?"

"Yes. Let us make camp there and send out an exploration party."

"And will you be joining that party?"

The Princess favored her advisor with a wry smile. "Of course."

Her orders traveled quickly through the entourage, and in what seemed like no time at all they had once more set up camp. Shortly afterward, the exploration party was assembled. Macal was invited to join them. The dragonmere insisted on coming as well, "for The Jewel's protection." Corporal Mercule was also a member of the force, along with several other soldiers Macal didn't know.

The group set off to fulfill its mission without delay, the Princess leading with the Viscount by her side. According to the Princess, she had been told that the entrance to the tomb was marked by a three-headed rock. All they had to do was locate the rock. From there they could enter the tomb.

A three-headed rock, mused Macal. He assumed that the heads had been carved into the rock, but after all the strange things he had encountered recently, he wasn't willing to bet on it.

At first an air of anticipation animated the search, but as the hours passed it began to dwindle. The exploration party combed the highlands, finding only barren hills, tall grass, a variety of odd flowers, and random formations of granite thrusting up through Aerinth's soil.

"The King's Jewel." Corporal Mercule was having difficulty concealing his frustration at their fruitless search. "Are you *sure* it was this range of hills your father spoke of?"

The Princess seemed annoyed. "Are you doubting the memory of a royal heiress? One with the upbringing I have had?"

"Of course not, Princess." The Corporal raised both hands to show he meant no harm.

"I think what the Corporal is trying to say, My Jewel," the dragonmere said, "is that we have searched every hill around the camp, and so far not a single one even remotely resembles the location you describe. With that in mind, is it possible that we have come to the wrong area, even if by only a few leagues?"

"I suppose so." Princess Aeria seemed insulted by the doubts of those around her. She glanced at the sky. "It's getting dark anyway. We will head back to camp, and in the morning we will start the search anew."

At first there was only darkness. Then slowly two hungry eyes emerged from the abyssal black. One was ocean blue, the other murky green. As the eyes moved through a lone beam of moonlight, the assassin himself became visible. He was a goblin, tall by the standards of his race. His nose and ears were long and pointed, his skin the color of ochre. His thick black hair resembled a snarl of seaweed.

Once more he vanished into the black night, creeping noiselessly through the trees on the hillside. Murky darkness had just fallen over the land, and he welcomed it as an ally. They had done much work together, the night and the assassin. It was where he felt at home, where everything was easy and his dreams came true. In the night, he felt alive.

Hungrily he scanned the darkness once more. He knew his prize was close. Once he had reached Elronia it had taken him over a month to find the trail, but since then he had been following it with ease.

His mismatched eyes brimmed with obsession, as they always did when he was on the hunt. He was overwhelmed by his desire to fulfill this contract for the mighty Troll King. For now it was the purpose of his being; nothing else mattered. His success was his reputation, and his reputation was the most valuable thing he possessed. It all came down to his standing in the Guild. He had an inborn need to be a master of his art, better than any who had preceded him. He cared nothing for the goblins' reputation as the best wizards and runecrafters in the world. His family needed to be shown there was more than one path in life. Magic was nothing, their obsession with it nothing more than a racial quirk. It was not the life for him. His success in his chosen path exceeded anything they would ever achieve in theirs.

Killing was an art, and he was an artist. His choice had been the right one. With the termination of this victim, he would become the most famous assassin in Aerinth. Then his family, back in the goblin kingdom of Ozgar, would know that there was more to life than magic, that there were other paths to great success. Then, if they still kept him outcast, it wouldn't matter. Very likely, very soon, he would have a guild to run. A Guild of Assassins.

He was the best there was; he knew it, and none doubted it. Masters of the craft looked to him for instruction. Only he had trained in Frostmoor, the land of the ice giants; only he knew the boons the cold could bring, the benefits yielded by frigid conditions.

As he moved up the hill, searching, his delicate, green-skinned hand with its claw-like nails fondled the hilt of his magical dagger. He was anxious to hold it, but for now he restrained himself. The time would come soon enough.

He could feel Nilelurdar, the God of Death and Disaster, with him tonight, as on so many nights before. Once more the skeletal god had blessed him. He was Nilelurdar's tool in the mortal world; it was his task to send souls to Narekisis, the Plane of the Dead, for the dark god to receive. The assassin prided himself on sending one kill a month to his god in homage. Nilelurdar would never be wanting and Narekisis never empty as long as he could wield his dagger.

This assassination was to be the turning point of his life, the culmination of years of work. Everything he had worked for would come to fruition. All he had to do was bring back the head and signet ring of his victim to receive the rewards and adulation he had earned.

It was nothing personal. This was not about liking or disliking his victim; it was about completing a job for which he was being paid. The equation was simple: money for blood.

And if by completion of the job all his dreams came true, who was he to complain? How difficult could it be, after all? Princess Aeria Stormlion was just a little girl.

CHAPTER 18

"Wake up!"

The urgent summons roused Macal from a deep sleep. Imagining an attack by a troll brigade, he sat bolt upright, astounded to find Princess Aeria kneeling next to his cot. She was dressed in leather traveling gear that he had never seen before, a fitted jacket and trousers, and thick, knee-high boots.

"Shhh!" She placed a soft hand over his mouth. Macal couldn't help noticing how sweet it smelled. "We're going to the tomb right now." She glanced over her shoulder at the tent's closed flap to make sure her presence hadn't been noticed.

Macal gaped at her. "You *know* where the tomb is?"

"Of course. Do you think I would travel so far, risking our trip to Varun, if I didn't know the tomb's precise location?"

"Then why did we spend all day searching for it?"

"Because I want to go there alone, and I knew Viscount Razz wouldn't let me. And by alone, I mean just you and me."

"So you knew where it was the whole time?" Macal still couldn't believe it. His body ached from hours in the saddle. Had all the day's hard riding really been for nothing?

"Didn't I already say I did? I couldn't believe how long it took them to start questioning my memory. I didn't want to end the search too quickly, in case they suspected I knew more than I was telling them."

"So you were lying?"

The Princess sighed. "Can we move past this? I'm a Princess; I'm allowed to lie. It was pretty good acting though, wasn't it? Didn't I seem offended?"

"You had me fooled," Macal admitted.

She stood abruptly. "Come on. Let's go."

164

"Just the two of us? Who will protect us if we run into trouble?"

"You can protect us!" the Princess said airily, as if they were playing a game.

"Me? I think you might have me confused with somebody who knows how to fight."

She produced a gold-hilted saber and flourished it. "Don't worry, I have this!"

Macal looked at her in bewilderment. She was behaving as if she couldn't wait to begin this exciting adventure, while his feelings were the exact opposite. It was the most insane thing he ever heard—two children venturing alone into a mysterious, ancient tomb. He cleared his throat.

"I just want you to know that I say this with no offense intended, but I think you're a bit touched."

"I prefer eccentric. Now come on, we need to get started. Don't you want to see what awaits you inside the tomb? I think you'll like it."

"It might be easier if you just told me what it is."

"What fun would that be for me? Seeing you uncertain and curious is so much more entertaining. Are you coming or not?"

"What if I refuse?"

"Then I'll go alone."

"You would go into a dark and scary tomb all by yourself?"

"Who said it was scary? I never did. What makes you think it's scary?"

"Have you ever heard a story about a tomb that wasn't scary?"

"Well, no—"

Macal let his silence speak for itself. The Princess frowned. "I am going into the tomb with or without you, Macal Teel. This is the final time I will ask you. As a Princess, to be forced to ask even once is already more than I am accustomed to. Are you coming with me into the Tomb of the Old King, or not?"

Macal sighed deeply, thinking how stubborn she was, and how pretty. "Of course."

As quickly and quietly as he could, he readied himself for the expedition, making sure to bring his soldier's backpack and sword. Then he and the Princess set off for the tomb, careful to stay in the shadows as they crept through the camp, waiting for the guard patrols to pass before moving on. Their progress was slow but steady; in a few moments they had reached the edge of the camp.

"That was easier than I thought it would be," commented Princess Aeria.

"Wait," Macal said. "What's *that?*"

Up ahead of them on the dark hillside, an approaching silhouette was just visible in the night gloom.

"*Run!*" The Princess sounded urgent. "Before they see us!"

"If we run, they're bound to see us," Macal whispered. It was already too late. The flickering light from the camp revealed the figure of Corporal Mercule closing in on them.

"Uh…umm…" A stammer was all Macal could manage as the Corporal came up to them.

The Princess spoke up, but she sounded uncharacteristically nervous. "Hello, Corporal."

"What are you two doing up and about so late?" Even in the poor light they could see the Corporal's eyes had narrowed with suspicion. Macal tried to think of a good excuse.

"We were just, um, um—watching the stars."

"Yes," Princess Aeria said. "We were just seeking a better vantage point."

Corporal Mercule nodded. "Ah, I see." The Princess and Macal had begun to relax in relief when he added, "There's just one little thing—and that is I don't believe you. So why not tell me what you're really doing?"

"We're going to the tomb," Macal said. The Princess shot him a sharp look and he shrugged. "I'm no good at lying."

She rolled her eyes, "That much is obvious."

"The tomb—ah. You know where it is, don't you, Princess?" said the Corporal putting the pieces together. "You knew all along."

"I am the Princess," she said. "I can keep secrets, and I can do what I want, when I want."

"Actually that's only partly true. You are indeed a Princess. But while you can do what you want, you *can't* put yourself in danger. In such matters, your father's orders supersede yours."

She made an impatient gesture. "We are going to the tomb, just Macal and myself. I am ordering you to stay here and tell no one."

"And I cannot obey your order."

"I command you!"

"I still cannot oblige you, My Jewel."

"Just let us go." Macal was surprised by his own unexpected plea. "She knows all about the tomb; her father told her everything. We'll be in no danger."

"Yes. Please, just let us go. What could really happen to me in the tomb of my ancestors?"

The Corporal stared at the two children long and hard, his eyes shifting back and forth between them, then he sighed. "All right, go. But be back soon, or I will have no choice but to inform the Viscount."

Before he could change his mind, they set off up the dark, tree-shrouded hill.

"I thought you said you didn't know how to lie," the Princess said, once they were out of Mercule's earshot.

"I said I wasn't any good at it, not that I couldn't do it."

"Well, you really came through this time."

Macal had known he had to save the day for her. Their excursion seemed to offer her such a sense of freedom and excitement that he could not have let her down. Hesitantly he said, "But you do know all about the tomb, right? It wasn't a complete lie?"

"I wouldn't exactly say I know *everything*, but I'm sure we will be fine."

"You're sure?"

"Oh, very sure."

Back at the base of the hill on the outskirts of the camp, Corporal Mercule remained motionless, weighing the wisdom of his decision. Suddenly he cursed himself and ran off to wake the Viscount.

Within moments the whole camp had been roused and every bleary-eyed soldier mustered. The fuming Viscount paced back and forth before them, his green-scaled brow knotted with fury. His hands gripped each other as if to refrain from strangling someone.

"Let it be known that King Glagor himself will hear of your ineptitude if the Princess is not recovered quickly and unharmed!" His eyes were blazing. "As for those on guard duty and those supposed to be watching her, I will deal with you *later!* Right now I want every man out looking for the Jewel. If the gods owe any of you a favor, now is the time to claim it. If she is not found, you will quickly learn the price of such incompetence in Ermalon— and trust me when I say you cannot begin to imagine the depravity of my realm. Now go! All of you! Find the Princess and bring her back to safety!"

There was a thunder of footsteps as the soldiers stormed out of camp in haste to follow the dragonmere's orders.

Macal stopped to listen to the commotion behind them. "I think they're following us!"

"Of course they are. I'm surprised it took them this long." The Princess continued to climb. As they neared the crest of the steep hill, the trees had begun to thicken. "Don't worry. I think we're almost there."

"They're gonna find us." Macal could hear the soldiers getting closer.

"Not if we hurry!" The Princess spoke sharply. "Stop being so slow!"

"I'm only slow because I'm following you. You don't really seem to know where you're going."

"I do know, and it's just up ahead." As proof, a small, hidden clearing opened in front of them among the close-clustering trees. Macal caught his breath. Set into the steep hillside were three large heads sculpted from granite, each resembling a noble, crowned king with angular features and a heavy beard. Created by masterful craftsmanship, they had endured through the centuries, since the time of the first kings, somehow untouched by time. The heads sat in a row, each facing a slightly different direction. The mouth of the middle one, unlike the others, was open wide; it might have been an entrance except that it was blocked by a solid granite slab.

"See, I told you," said the Princess triumphantly.

"Wow," Macal marveled at the enormous stone heads. "You were right."

"Apology accepted." The Princess's smile vanished as she heard the soldiers approaching. They didn't have much time.

"We have to get in!" whispered Macal as they ran forward to the heads. "How?"

"I don't know! You're the one who brought us here!"

"I know, but as I said, I don't remember everything!"

"This must be the door." Macal moved close to the middle head and put his hand on the stone slab that blocked its mouth. "Your father never told you anything about this?"

"I don't think so."

"Well, they're going to catch us if we don't get in right *now!*"

"I know that!" the Princess nearly shouted in frustration. This was her chance to have an adventure out in the real world, not just in a book, and she didn't want to miss it. Time was short; the soldiers were closing in. Running up to the middle head, she pounded on the granite slab. "Let us in!"

To their surprise, with a great grinding of stone against stone, the granite door slowly slid into the ground. They stared at each other, astounded. They were going to get inside!

Or were they? Their jubilation drained away as the stone barricade revealed another door behind it, this one a massive working of cogs and gears fashioned of gleaming metals, dizzying in its complexity. Macal was reminded of the insides of a wind-up clock Uncle Melkes had once shown him. The mechanical door was a hundred times more elaborate.

"You've got to be kidding me. How do we get past that?" he asked.

"Stop asking questions you know I can't answer," the Princess snapped.

"I'm only asking you because this was your idea. You dragged me out here. Normally when people do something like this, they have a *plan*. And besides, there's nobody else to ask."

"Well, stop asking and just try to solve it."

"Solve what?"

"The text."

"Text? What text? What do you mean?"

"The text! We have to read it! Why else would it be there?"

"Read it? Read what?" the boy said.

"The writing, stupid! It must mean something."

Macal was bewildered. "What writing? I don't see anything but gears and cogs."

She looked at him. "You really don't see it?"

"No, I don't. Where is it?" Macal squinted at the door in a desperate effort to see what she was talking about. At the same time, he was secretly glad he couldn't see the writing. He didn't want to admit to Aeria that he didn't know how to read. Behind them the soldiers were crashing through the trees, every step bringing them nearer. "What does it say?" he asked hurriedly.

"It says 'The second eye.' What second eye?"

"I don't know. It must be mean one of the eyes of the statues," then she paused for a moment. "Wait, I just remembered. King Ferance, the first King of Elronia, before he came and settled this land here, he came from the North. And there was a battle somewhere on the way here. I forget with what, but I remember being told he lost a good deal of men, but more importantly for this moment, do you know what else he lost?"

"His eye?"

"Yes! He also lost his left eye. Okay, so the second eye the writing refers to is the right eye of the statue, that makes sense."

Macal stood up and examined the statue's right eye. It looked like plain sculpted granite. "I don't see anything. I still don't understand why I can't see the writing."

"Don't worry about that now. It doesn't matter. We have to hurry."

"But it may matter. If I can't see the writing, maybe there are other things I can't see. Like something on the eye."

"Oh," she said. "That makes sense. Let me look." So the princess got up and examined the same eye that Macal had looked at. "I don't see anything either. Let's check the other statues."

Knowing they were running out of time, they ran to the statue on the left. The princess scrutinized the statue's left eye, which was the second eye in the line of eyes.

"I don't s—" then she stopped and quickly jumped back. "Oh wow! Do you see that?"

"No," said Macal curiously. "What is it?"

"It's strange. At first it just looked like plain rock, then slowly as I looked at it, it began to glow. How do you not see it? And now writing is appearing around the edges of the eye."

"What does it say?" asked Macal.

"Give me a second," she said as she moved closer to look again. "It says 'Gaze into me.'"

"Do it. The soldiers are getting closer."

"Why don't you do it?"

"Because it's not asking me. It's asking you."

"Fine, fine. Okay." The Princess got up close to the eye and craned her head forward and gazed into its glowing depths.

Macal watched in fascination as suddenly he too could see the stone eye glowing blue, the light shooting out as if from within a hooded lantern. Even more amazing, the same glow started to emanate from the Princess's eyes.

He jumped forward to pull her away from the ensorcelled statue, but as he grabbed her she shouted, "No, don't!"

"What's going on? What's happening?"

"I don't know," she said, her eyes still matching the glow of the statue's. "But it doesn't hurt."

Then before they could discuss it further, the mouth of the statue animated as if alive and opened into a scream. Once the mouth had stopped moving the glow from the Princess's and the statue's eyes faded away. Princess Aeria stepped back to stand beside Macal.

"I've seen more magic in the past few weeks than I ever thought I would see—or even thought was possible," said Macal in awe. It seemed like every day he was alive he was learning more about the world and just how small his view of it had been since he left Hormul. "I always thought the stories my uncle told me were just fantastical stories to entertain me. I'm starting to think it's possible some of them may have been true."

"If I was you, I might start expecting this to be a normal thing. Especially with your chosen quest on the horizon."

"I'm not sure I like the idea of that."

"Just wait until you see what's inside this place for you. You may change your mind," she said with a wry smile. Without saying anything more she stepped up to look into the mouth. It was a little taller than she was. Macal moved up with her.

They each took a quick scared step backward; as they looked into the shadowed recess they saw it was a churning mass of irregular needles. Each row of needles was moving rhythmically in and out. In alternating fashion one row would move out as the adjacent rows went in.

"What is that?" Princess Aeria asked.

"I'm pretty sure I'm okay with never finding out," replied Macal.

"What do we do?" she asked.

"Again, I have no idea."

"Well, I'm not putting my hand in there."

"Either am I," Macal agreed. "But we must have to do something to it, so we can get inside and we don't have much time. Maybe you should touch it."

"What? No! Why would I do that?"

"You said you like magic and we should expect it."

"This isn't magic, it's a thousand needles! And what if they are poisoned?"

"It just seems strange that there was writing that only you could read, and it told you about this eye and to look into it. Something is helping us get inside. How much do you want to get us inside the tomb?"

"Fine, I'll do it."

"What? Really? I was only thinking out loud," explained Macal.

"I know. But we are out of time. Can you hear them? They'll be here in a minute."

"How about if I do it instead?" offered Macal.

"We could both do it. We could both prick a finger with one of the needles."

"Yes, only a finger," agreed Macal. "Are you ready?"

"Yes," she said. "Okay, let's do it."

Together they stepped forward and each reluctantly inched their finger forward to the churning array of moving needles. They paused for a moment and looked at each other. Both a little excited, but both very scared. Then they did it—as the next set of needles came out they held their fingers in position and the aged metal penetrated the skin of their fingers and drew blood.

Suddenly the ground shook. As the head on their far right unexpectedly rose up out of the ground, Macal and Princess Aeria jumped back. Clumps of moist earth fell off the head as it broke free from the soil, revealing a wide column of stone. Beneath the stone king's chin they saw an open doorway with a rounded arch on top.

"It's a secret entrance!" said the Princess excitedly. "The door in the middle was just a decoy."

"Well, it worked on me," admitted Macal.

"It worked on both of us."

"Viscount, over here! I've found them!" As the shout broke from the edge of the clearing, they saw a soldier running swiftly toward them.

"Come on, we have to go now." The Princess grabbed Macal's hand and pulled him toward the doorway. Together they plunged into the tomb. They were only a few steps beyond the threshold when the great king's head began to descend back into position.

As the entry closed, Macal looked back in time to catch a glimpse of the soldier's surprised face. An instant later Viscount Razz appeared beside him, the two of them watching helplessly as the tomb sealed itself shut, locking the children in and the dragonmere and his soldiers out.

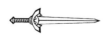

The assassin knew the Princess's camp was near. As night fell, he saw campfires flicker to life on a neighboring hillside, warming the gloom of the darkness.

The goblin had not smiled in years, but when he saw the firelight a malicious grin twisted his features. His target had just revealed itself. Thanking Nilelurdar for this gift, he sprinted downhill and headed for the camp in the distance, bearing death with him. Even moving at great speed he made no sound. A dog lying directly in his path wouldn't have noticed him.

CHAPTER 19

Inside the tomb, the absolute darkness lasted only as long as it took Macal to fumble around and find the flint and steel in his pack and light a torch. By its flickering glow the children were able to take in their surroundings. Outside they could hear Viscount Razz shouting infuriated orders as the soldiers pounded on the king's head, trying to open the tomb.

"Do you think they'll be able to get in?" the boy asked.

The Princess shook her head. "I hope not."

"The good news is, at least it's not likely there are any trolls in here."

"Exactly. I don't know why Razz is so concerned. We'll be fine."

They stood in a narrow passageway built of precisely fitted blocks of stone. Smelling strongly of earth, the tunnel was just wide enough for the two of them to stand abreast. It led in only one direction; off into the darkness.

"I have another question." Macal started cautiously along the tunnel, the Princess close behind him. "Do you think we can get *out?*"

Before she could respond, there was a loud groan over their heads, followed by the sound of stone grinding on stone. They looked up. In the torchlight, dust was sifting from the edges of the large stone block directly above them.

"Move!" shouted Macal. They flung themselves down the passage, deeper into the tomb. Behind them the block fell free in a hail of dust and mortar, smashing down with a jarring force that shook the tunnel and cracked the stone floor. Thunderous echoes reverberated around them.

Lying flat in the passage, Macal coughed on dust and looked back. The stone block had barely missed crushing them. "Uh...did your father tell you about that?"

The Princess was visibly trembling. "Actually, I think he did. I remember it *now.*"

"Well, I guess that answers my question, that block just sealed us in. We'll have to find another way out, or eventually starve to death in here."

Recovering her composure, the Princess got to her feet. "At least there's no way Viscount Razz and the Elronian Elite can follow us anymore."

"They can't follow us." Macal rubbed his nose, which was still full of dust. "But they can't *help* us either. Viscount Razz must be really angry you left him behind."

"His time of service is over anyway. I'm old enough to take care of myself."

"All right, come on. I think I see an opening up ahead." Macal sneezed as the dust overwhelmed him.

"That's a good sign," said the Princess as they started to move forward.

"What?"

"Your sneeze. According to the old ways, a sneeze meant the gods had just blessed you."

"Then we may be very blessed. I tend to sneeze a lot around damp soil." The boy proved this remark with two more sneezes.

Continuing down the stone passage, they came to a curved stone archway of a rough, antiquated design.

"Do you see the writing this time?" The Princess was examining words neatly engraved into the arch.

"Umm, no, I don't." Macal lied. He could actually see the letters this time, but he was still too embarrassed to admit to the well-educated Princess that he had never learned to read.

"Really? You can't see it? It's carved into the stone around the door."

"I can't see it," he lied again.

"That's strange. The writing outside was glowing; the letters were moving around like snakes. It was obviously magical. This writing looks ordinary."

"I'm sorry, I can't see it!" The boy was having difficulty hiding his discomfort. "Just tell me what it says."

"No need to get angry." The Princess sounded hurt. Scanning the archway, she recited: " 'All those who enter this tomb in impurity, Zarn shall lay upon you a divine justice to crush your bones and lay still your heart.' "

"A 'Get out of here or die' sign! In every story my uncle ever told me about such warnings, the people in the story never listened to them, and you know what happens?"

"Let me guess. They died?"

"Exactly. We shouldn't be doing this alone. Maybe Viscount Razz is right."

"Maybe you should stop being so afraid."

"I'm—I'm not afraid," the boy said. "But do you really want Zarn, the Ruler of the Gods, to curse you?"

"You don't have to lie to me. There's nothing wrong with being afraid. I have read about fear and bravery, and everything you are experiencing is perfectly natural."

Macal stared in bewilderment. "*What* are you talking about?"

"I have been taught by the greatest scholars and sages in the world. They all fled Calastine after the Black Wizards War destroyed the City of Knowledge, and they have all remained in Keratost ever since. My father wanted me educated so that I would be more than just *a rose in the royal court.*" The Princess uttered this phrase in a gruff voice, as if mimicking her father. "I try to read every book I can get my hands on, because I agree with my father. I want to be more than just an idle princess. Among other things, I have read about fear. Being afraid is nothing to worry about. And besides, since this arch was inscribed, Zarn has disappeared from the heavens. It has been documented that he is no longer considered an established deity, even though he was the original Creator God."

Annoyed, Macal pointed through the archway to a small chamber beyond. In its far wall was a circular door with stone faces carved all around it. "Did any of those books tell you how to get past that door there?"

Princess Aeria looked where he was pointing. "I don't think so. I'll go first through the archway; I'm not worried. My intentions are far from impure."

"I'm not worried either," Macal hastened to assure her, even while his legs refused to carry him through the archway.

"Of course not," Princess Aeria said absently as she entered the room. Macal watched as absolutely nothing happened to her. The Princess glanced back at him. "See? Nothing to be afraid of. My bones aren't powder and my heart still beats."

"For the final time, I'm not afraid!" Against his better judgment, Macal stepped through the archway to stand by her side. "See?"

She ignored him and approached the portal. "I've never seen a door like this, surrounded by faces. Have you?"

"No." Macal's hand moved to his sword hilt; he had no idea what to expect next, but the touch of his weapon comforted him. Closer up, they could see that the ring of carved faces filled a one-foot border around the door. Each of the dozen different faces was carved and assembled from numerous pieces of stone. The eyes were one piece, which fit perfectly against a piece with a nose carved in it. The cheeks had their own pieces, as well as the mouth, chin, and forehead, each precisely sculpted to interlock with all the surrounding pieces. The door itself was a piece of smooth, solid granite with no visible handle.

"Any ideas?" asked Princess Aeria perplexed.

"We could just try pushing it open?"

"You think that will work?"

"Not really. But it's worth a try."

"Okay. I'll do it."

"No," said Macal. "I will."

"All right." Surprised, the Princess stepped back from the door. Macal took her place. His hands shook as they hovered over the door. What if he triggered a trap, like the stone block back in the hall? *Just be prepared to jump again*, he told himself. Placing his hands on the door, he pushed with all his might.

It didn't budge.

"Maybe I should help." Princess Aeria joined him, adding her weight to his. Still the door held fast.

Macal gave up and stood back. "There has to be something else to it. It must have to do with the faces."

"Like a puzzle?"

"Or a riddle. In a lot of the stories my Uncle Melkes used to tell me, there was some sort of riddle the hero had to solve if he wanted to continue on."

"Really? I never got to read many stories, and nobody told them to me. Most of what I studied was politics and history, theology, and a bit of astrology. That was my favorite, and I had to beg my father to let me learn it."

"Well, besides farm work, most of what my uncle taught me were stories with meaning."

"Meaning?"

"Yeah, *meaning*. Every story he told me had some moral meaning in it, some important lesson he thought I should learn. Like a fable."

"Interesting. So there is another riddle or a puzzle here we have to solve. What could it be?" Princess Aeria gazed thoughtfully at the door.

"Obviously it has to do with the faces, maybe with how they're fashioned in odd pieces. I wonder if they move." Macal stepped up, placed his hand on the nose of one of the faces and gave it a slight push. The nose slid in several inches. Intrigued, he pushed again, and the piece returned to its former position.

Princess Aeria was clearly impressed by her companion's intuition. "So we just have to push in one of the pieces, and it will unlock the door. Which other one should we try?"

"I'm not sure."

"There are only a dozen faces. Can't we just try all their pieces?"

Macal looked uncertain. "Anybody could figure that out in a matter of minutes. It ought to be more complex. If this really is a lock, there should be something more to keep people out. I think it must be some sort of combination of the different features."

"Like pushing in the eyes of one of the faces and the mouth and nose of another one?"

"Exactly. At least, I think so. It's the only thing I can think of."

"We can try that. But what face are we trying to make?"

"Maybe one like the face of one of the three stone kings outside?"

The Princess shook her head. "I don't think so. Since this is one of the only stories my father did tell me, I *do* remember some of it. I remember him telling me that the heads outside were sculpted to look like the sculptor himself, because he had no other model. He died just after they were completed, before any of the inside work had begun."

"Wait!" Suddenly it became clear to Macal. "I think I know what to do."

The Princess caught his enthusiasm. "What is it?"

"Wait and see," the boy said. "Just wait and see."

"Are you going to tell me how to open the door or not?" Princess Aeria demanded.

Macal smiled at her, "Of course I am." He found he enjoyed knowing something she didn't. "Do you remember how, when we were outside, only you could see the writing on the false door?"

"Yes."

"Well, maybe the whole tomb is like that. Maybe it was designed so that only those of royal blood could find a way in. That would explain why I couldn't see the writing and you could. And maybe the needles were there to check if the person trying to enter had royal blood. In which case I pricked my finger for nothing."

"What does that have to do with these faces?"

"I think the puzzle is connected with having royal blood. I think that by choosing different features, we have to create the face of the first king, your great-great-great grandfather, or however many 'greats' it is. If I'm right, the door will open only for someone who can figure out what the king looked like."

"But I don't know what he looked like. I've never seen a painting or a sculpture of him. And it's seventy-four 'greats,' to be exact."

"We don't need to know exactly what he looked like, because we have you. Your features are your family's features; you're the key to the puzzle! Replicating his face would be difficult for anyone not of his bloodline, especially if they didn't have a Stormlion with them. But we do."

The Princess nodded. "Oddly, that sounds logical. The builders wanted to keep tomb raiders out while allowing members of the family entry if they desired it."

"Let's give it a try," Macal said. He examined the faces, paying more attention to their various features than to each one as a whole. He didn't need to look at Aeria to study her features; they were already emblazoned in his mind. Among the stone faces, he looked for her narrow nose, soft brow, and high cheekbones.

"I guess it's a good thing I look like my father," she said. "I think those are my eyes. Well, they look more like my father's than mine, but my grandfather's were the same."

Macal studied the wide serious eyes. "I agree. Push them in." Next he chose a sleek, straight nose. "And what about this?"

"That looks like his," the Princess agreed.

Now that they had come up with a plan, the pieces seemed to fall into place. Most of the features could be eliminated on the grounds that they bore little or no resemblance to Aeria or any Stormlion she could remember. Within a short time they were ready to choose a mouth.

Macal pointed to one on the upper right side of the door. "I think it's that one."

"Really? I'm not so sure."

"It looks just like yours!"

"Yes, but I have my mother's mouth, not my father's."

"Then which one looks like his?"

"I think that one." She indicated the face directly below the one Macal had suggested.

"You would know better than I would." He reached up to push it, but then withdrew his hand. "Suppose something bad happens if we get this wrong?"

"Do we have any other choice than to try? If we can't move on, we'll sit here and starve to death."

"Good point."

"And besides, my father always says to expect losses. Actually he says, 'We expected losses.' Usually just after a battle."

"That's inspiring."

"That's the harshness of war."

The boy sighed. "Are we going to do this?"

She nodded, and he pushed in the final piece of the puzzle.

In the darkness of night the assassin stalked the perimeter of the camp, seeking the best way in. The camp bustled with activity, soldiers scrambling in every direction as if an alarm had been sounded and they were struggling to deal with an unexpected situation.

The goblin knew he was not the cause of the alarm. If he did not choose to be seen, he was invisible to all. But he could take advantage of the chaos. It was obvious the soldiers had not been called to arms, so the situation did not involve a physical threat. Their defenses were down; they seemed to be searching for something. Suddenly he pricked up his ears. Ahead, approaching him along the perimeter, was an Elronian soldier.

This was his chance to get some answers. Quiet as a spider, he crept up on the soldier and at long last drew his dagger. This was no ordinary weapon. Its heavy hilt was made of enchanted obsidian, its cold, wicked blade of blue ice. Procured during his time in Frostmoor, the legendary dagger was unique, its magic too rare to exist twice in one world.

Now that it was drawn, it had to shed blood before being nestled back in its sheath. The assassin was not a creature who wasted effort. If he drew a weapon, he would use it. He had his own rules for his art, and he followed them religiously. Before the soldier so much as sensed his presence, the tall goblin was upon him. Agile and swift, he thrust the man against a tree, leaning into him with the dagger's freezing point against his throat. Where the tip of the magical blade touched the soldier's skin, the assassin could see ice slowly spreading outward.

"Where is Stormlion?" demanded the goblin in a whisper. Light from the newly risen moon glanced off his pointed teeth.

"*You!*" The stunned soldier was struggling to comprehend. "You took her!"

The assassin was surprised. "Took who?"

"Where is she?" demanded the soldier.

The assassin's mind was racing. *The Princess is missing. That is what they are looking for. If she is missing, she is unguarded. And unguarded means my task is that much easier.*

"Do you worship Nilelurdar?" he whispered in the soldier's ear. The man was of no further use to him.

"No!" The soldier seemed offended by the implication that he was connected to the evil god.

"Your loss." The icy dagger penetrated the man's chest, its frigid point lodging in his heart. Quietly the goblin withdrew the blade and laid the slumping body on the ground, keeping his hand over the soldier's mouth so that any dying moans would not be overheard. In the dark the soldier's sudden disappearance went unnoticed.

In the dying, dimming eyes the assassin saw a familiar pleading look. The man had something to say. Not one to be needlessly cruel, the goblin removed his hand from the bloody lips. When the soldier whispered, the assassin bent lower to hear the fading voice.

"Who are you?" The dying man's eyes welled with tears of death.

The master assassin did not answer. He stared blankly, then leaned over and roughly twisted his victim's neck until it snapped.

He had many names, a different one each time he was hired. At the moment he was Izgar. Nobody outside his family knew his given name. It was just as well. He no longer needed a name; he was known by the magical ice-bladed dagger he wore. Those who wanted the best hired the one who wielded the blade of ice.

The goblin rose from the still body and continued his hunt.

CHAPTER 20

T he stone passageway still echoed with the muffled shouts of the soldiers outside, ordering Macal and the Princess to return, as the boy pushed in the final piece of the puzzle. For a moment nothing happened. Maybe they had done something wrong. Maybe his guess about making the face of the first king had been off the mark, or maybe they had chosen the wrong features. If the door failed to open, what sort of horrific trap might they have set off? As the possibility of defeat loomed in his mind, the round stone door began to move. Elated, they watched it eventually roll to the left. A grinding sound reverberated throughout the cavern.

"We did it!" shouted Macal in joyful surprise.

"*You* did it," said Princess Aeria. "You're the one who figured it out."

The boy blushed, at a loss for words. Looking through the doorway, he saw a short passageway beyond. They stepped into it, the torchlight throwing shadows on the stone walls.

"I think we're getting close," the Princess said as they walked along.

Macal glanced at her, confused. "What do you mean? I thought this was it. How big is this place? It's only supposed to be a tomb."

"A *king's* tomb."

"He's only one man. How much space does he need?"

"You'll be able to judge that for yourself, won't you?"

A few more steps brought them to another cavern twice as large as the last. In the shifting torchlight they could see stalactites hanging from the ceiling like large stone icicles. At the very edge of the light Macal could see small orange salamanders scurrying across the stone floor among the pillars that had formed beneath the stalactites. There were also some pale, shriveled spiders that appeared to be eyeless. The musty stench they had smelled at the tomb's entrance was much more prevalent here, an almost physical presence through which they had to wade.

The chamber appeared to be a dead end. Against the far wall was a pool in the shape of a half moon. The water was an unnatural cyan, its glow partially illuminating the cavern. Covering the pool like an inverted bowl was some sort of transparent mystical barrier, a phosphorescent dome that resembled a jellyfish membrane of dazzling azure.

The marvelous sight drove all other thoughts from Macal's mind. "What is *that?*"

"I don't know." The Princess seemed to share his fascination.

"Why is it here? And where do we go now? There's no way to get out." Macal moved deeper into the chamber, toward the pool and its strange barrier.

The Princess followed him. "Our continuing on must have something to do with this pool. But what's that thing covering it?"

Macal approached the barrier. "That's what I'd like to know." From here he could see the pool was very deep. His hand moved as if possessing a will of its own, yearning to touch the shimmering blue membrane.

"Maybe you shouldn't do that," said the Princess suddenly.

"Why? You just said that to continue on, we have to do something with the pool. Don't worry; nothing bad happened in the last chamber."

"Because we didn't do anything *wrong!*"

The Princess's warning shout was too late; overwhelmed by curiosity and its strange beauty, Macal had already laid his hand on the enchanted dome. Suddenly the whole chamber shuddered as if from an earthquake. Chunks of rock shot like corks from the walls around them, revealing hidden channels that began to spew a thick, hazy aquamarine gas. At the same time, down the passage behind them, they heard the round door of faces roll back into its closed position.

"*See?* I told you!" Watching the gas close in on them, Princess Aeria seemed more angry than afraid.

"I…I'm…I'm sorry!" Fear began to overtake Macal as the reality of what he'd done became clear. "I think that's poison!"

The noxious cyan cloud slowly filled the chamber and began to envelop them.

"We're going to die!" shrieked Macal.

"Now I remember!" As the poison fog surrounded them, the Princess choked out the words.

"Remember what?" Gagging on the horrendous taste of the poison, Macal could feel it convulsing his lungs.

Princess Aeria choked, unable to respond, her blue eyes widening in panic as the fast-acting poison began to strangle her. Macal watched in horror as she fell to her knees. Her strength fading, she reached out and touched her signet ring, the black dragon surrounded by roses, to the azure barrier above the pool. Instantly the barrier disappeared as if it had never been.

"In!" the Princess managed to gasp.

"Into the water?" Too weak to hold the torch any longer, Macal dropped it, it still flickered and he saw her nod feebly. As she tried to crawl into the pool, she collapsed. The boy's eyes were watering and he was wracked by nausea, but he managed to shake off his pack, seize the Princess under her arms, and drag her toward the pool. With the second rough tug, she was at the edge. Macal's lungs burned as he rolled himself over its foot-high lip. Keeping a firm grip on the Princess, he kicked off on the inside of the pool and pulled her in.

Underwater, he could see an opening in the depths of the pool, a passage leading through the wall. He had no idea where it led, but it couldn't be any worse than being in this room. The water had revived the Princess; she exhaled an explosion of bubbles and flailed her arms wildly, grabbing onto Macal. Looking into her terrified eyes, he guessed she didn't know how to swim. He too was almost out of air, but he nodded reassuringly at her, trying to communicate that he could swim.

There was no time to waste. He put his arm around her and swam downward, taking her with him. His practice swimming in the ponds back home proved valuable. Once they were in motion, the Princess seemed to relax. At first Macal thought he had managed to calm her, but then he realized she had lost consciousness again. There was even less time than he had thought.

Down he went further into the radiant pool and entered the opening. He was thankful that he hadn't worn his chain mail tunic; its extra weight would have made swimming impossible. The underwater passage was short, opening almost immediately into what appeared to be another half-moon pool on the other side of the wall.

In desperation the boy swam upward, hungering for breath. As they splashed to the surface, he gulped in air, his lungs savoring every gasp, then swam to the pool's rim and pushed Princess Aeria out of the water. His whole body shook with weakness as he climbed out beside her, rolled her over and gazed at her pale face. *Had he been fast enough to save her life?*

All at once she stirred, coughing up the water that had entered her lungs. Relieved that she was alive and breathing, Macal collapsed beside her. In less than a moment, unconsciousness overtook them both.

Macal didn't know how long he had slept, and he didn't really care; it was the most blissful sleep he could remember. Beside him, Princess Aeria was waking as well. Slowly the two of them got to their feet, still dizzy from the effects of the poison gas but much revived by their rest.

"Are you all right?" he asked.

"Yes." She gave him a grateful look. "Thank you for saving me. You really are the hero I thought you would be."

Feeling himself blush, Macal quickly changed the subject. "How did you know what to do back there?"

"It was just a part of the story I suddenly remembered. I recall my father saying something about touching an enchanted force field with the Stormlion coat of arms."

"Well, that's what saved us. So thank *you*," Macal said. Scanning their new surroundings, he saw that the passage in the pool had led them into a room three times the size of the last. The smell in here was equally earthy, rancid, and dank, but the cavern was dimly lit by the gleaming surface of the far wall. After a moment the boy realized it was an enormous mirror, so vast he guessed a full-grown dragon could easily fit through its glorious silver frame. Set into the top of the frame was an gigantic red garnet easily the size of a soldier's shield. To the left of the mirror stood a mountainous stone statue of a thickset humanoid knight holding a huge stone sword. The sculpture was easily the height of several men. Macal shifted his gaze from the statue to the girl at his side.

"So, I guess you didn't learn to swim from any those books you read."

Princess Aeria shot him an indignant look. "My parents never allowed me to go near water! They said it was too dangerous, and it seems that they were *right!*"

"I was just joking." He couldn't keep from grinning, and after a moment she answered with a smile. As a loud crunching noise sounded from across the room, their smiles faded and they turned toward the sound.

The stone guardian was coming to life.

The assassin's fingers tingled with excitement. This was to be the crowning achievement of his career. What bigger game would he ever hunt? Princess Aeria Stormlion would be the jewel in his crown. He couldn't wait to watch the life seep from her limp body. He had promised himself that he would cherish every moment, savor every detail, truly appreciate what he had worked for and accomplished. Those who were unexceptional were not hired to kill royalty. Only the outstanding, the excellent, the best, were considered.

She was so close he seemed to smell her. She was in the air. He wanted to breathe her in, swallow her down, and choke the life out of her.

In his cautious exploration of the camp, he had reached what must be her royal tent, the handsomest one there. Staying in the shadows, indistinguishable from the darkness, he crept closer. The soldier had said she was missing, but he needed to be sure.

Just ahead, at the edge of the darkness, another soldier was standing guard. With the speed of a gusting wind the assassin was upon him, one hand covering the man's mouth, the other holding the ice dagger to his throat.

"Do you worship Nilelurdar?" he whispered.

"N—no...." The soldier's body had stiffened at the cold touch of the dagger against his skin. The cruelty in the goblin's mismatched eyes made him pale in terror.

"Sorry to hear that." The assassin's tone belied his words as he deftly drew the dagger across his victim's throat. Catching the slumping body, he quietly laid the man on the ground to let the seeping blood enrich the grass and soil.

Then, hidden by the surrounding structures, he cut a small vertical slit in the cloth of the tent wall, just big enough for his slender frame.

Inside, he could see that the first soldier had not been lying. The tent was empty. His prize was being elusive. Instead of upsetting him, that fact excited him. He preferred a challenge.

Stepping back outside through the hole he had made, the assassin continued his search.

CHAPTER 21

Across the room from Macal and Aeria, the stone guardian moved. Each motion of its heavy limbs produced a cracking sound like rock being broken as the guardian wrenched itself away from the wall and took two lurching steps forward. It seemed to be finding its bearings. Its boulder-like head swiveled slowly on its thick neck while its blank, unmoving eyes stared and its hand flexed on the hilt of its massive sword.

"This is not good," Macal said. The guardian had finally noticed them, and now it took a step in their direction. "What are you going to do with *that?*" Next to him the Princess awkwardly unsheathed her golden sabre and waved it menacingly at the approaching statue.

"Fight!"

"That thing is made of stone," Macal pointed out. The guardian took another great stride toward them.

"Don't worry; I've read all about swordplay!"

"You're not going to stop that thing with a sword!"

As the guardian took another step forward, Princess Aeria flashed a resentful look at Macal. "Razz gives you a few lessons and now you're an expert?"

"It's made of *stone!* Your sword won't hurt it!" In spite of his fear, a sense of injustice prompted Macal to say, "It's not very fair, making a guardian of stone."

"Well, he doesn't need feeding."

"How convenient for you royals!" the boy shouted. The statue was now only a few steps away.

"Stop mocking me! I'm a Princess!"

"I don't think the stone man knows that!"

186

"Good point—run!" shouted Aeria. They dove out of the way as the stone monster brought its sword down right where they had been standing, shattering the rocky floor and sending shards of stone flying.

"What about 'we expected losses'?" Macal asked breathlessly, running to the far right of the chamber to put as much distance as possible between himself and the statue.

"I didn't expect us to be among them!" the Princess replied from the other side of the room.

Lifting its sword, the guardian turned and slowly moved its massive body in her direction. Macal eyed its clumsy progress with apprehension. "What do we do now?"

"I don't know. You're the one who says we can't fight it."

"Because we *can't!*" Something caught Macal's eye as he glanced around the chamber in search of escape. He pointed to the top of the mirror's frame. "Look up there! There's writing on it."

"What does it say?" The Princess was backing into the far wall to avoid the looming guardian.

"I don't know. I can't read."

"What?" she replied in astonishment. "You can't read?"

"No! No, okay? I can't," Macal finally admitted, embarrassed.

Aeria didn't have time to respond as she stabbed her sabre at the statue's leg and it bounced off harmlessly.

In response, the massive guardian swung its mighty fist gracelessly at the Princess's head. Macal felt his heart stop. In spite of Aeria's lack of skill with the sword, she was quicker than the oafish statue, ducking its fist to roll safely to the side. The stone fist smashed into the wall, and sent out another shower of rock shards.

Macal began to breathe again. He was glad to see that the guardian wasn't very accurate, but he also realized accuracy was not an important trait for such a creature. It never needed to eat or rest. If it had them trapped in here, it would eventually catch them.

Taking advantage of her momentary escape, Princess Aeria ran toward the mirror to examine the writing on the frame. The script etched into the silver was thin and elegant; she recognized it as belonging to the older Elronian language. Fortunately, that was something she *had* learned in books.

The guardian had recovered and was in pursuit, its steps thundering on the ground like an avalanche of boulders. As fast as she could, she read the words and interpreted them just in time to elude the stone sword that slammed into the ground where she had stood. This time she did not escape unharmed. As the cavern floor exploded in rock fragments, a number of stones tore through her leather shirt and pants and into her skin. She stumbled and fell. Behind her, the statue moved closer and raised its weighty foot to crush her.

The shadow of the massive foot fell over her as it began to descend. Aeria looked up, wide-eyed with fear. About to be crushed into oblivion, she felt something knock her out the way—Macal, rolling over and over with her across the stone floor.

There was no time to thank him for saving her life again; the untiring, unyielding statue was already renewing the chase. The two of them scrambled to their feet and sprinted away, the Princess wincing in pain. The rocky debris had peppered her back and legs and Macal could see blood soaking through her clothing. Gritting her teeth in pain she said, "The inscription says, 'Only the pure may enter.' I think we have to pass through the mirror to get out of here."

"Pass through the mirror? How?"

"I don't know. Magic? Is it any stranger than anything else we've seen in this place?"

Macal didn't respond, because the significance of her words took a moment to register on him; then his flare of hope that they might get away from the animated statue gave way to dismay. *Only the pure may enter,* she had said. *I'm never going to leave this room. I lost all my purity back in Hormul, when I got Uncle Melkes killed.*

"I can't go through," he said flatly. "You have to go alone."

"Can't go through? Why not? I'm not leaving you here!"

As the guardian closed in on them once more, they retreated in opposite directions. It stood stupidly for a moment, its heavy head following one and then the other, before fixing on Macal.

"You have no choice," the boy yelled as he ran. "Just *go!* Now's your chance!"

The Princess stood her ground. "Not until you tell me why you can't go."

Macal glared at her. If he didn't go with her, she was going to stay here. He had to tell her the truth; maybe then she would go. "I killed my uncle," he admitted.

"You *what?*"

Macal continued to dodge the statue, staying just out of its reach. "I got him killed. Back in Hormul. When the trolls attacked. He came to find me and the trolls caught him."

"So how *exactly* did you kill him?" The Princess hadn't moved.

"He only came out there to find me. Otherwise he would have been safe. He could have easily fled without being caught."

"You're being stupid. We're not going to survive in here for very long. We have to go now, or we are going to die. You didn't kill your uncle!"

"I can't go!" he shouted back in frustration. He realized he was getting exhausted and slowing down, while the animated statue was not slowing at all. He felt its grasping stone fingers graze the back of his head as he dodged away in desperation. "Go without me! I'm not pure!"

"No! I need you to help me get out of here! You can't leave me alone!" There were tears in Aeria's eyes and a fright in her voice. "Whatever's in the mirror can't be worse than this!"

Macal couldn't resist her plea. "All *right!*"

They both sprinted towards the magic mirror. The guardian understood the intruders were trying to escape. In a last attempt to stop them, it hurled its huge sword end over end. The blade made a whickering sound as it spun through the air.

Macal thought the sword might overtake them before they reached the mirror. They both stretched forward to touch its shimmering surface. The sword spun closer. The tips of their fingers made contact with the mirror. The sword came closer still. Their hands magically pushed into the glass as if into a vertical sheet of water. The sword was just inches from cleaving them apart. As their bodies disappeared into its gleaming plane, the sword made full contact, shattering the mirror into a million sparkling fragments.

Continuing his search, the assassin was having as poor luck as the soldiers about him. It was becoming obvious that the Princess was not in the camp. His search would have to lead elsewhere. Where, he didn't yet know, but his hunger for his victim's blood was growing to overwhelming proportions. His eyes were beginning to glaze with obsession.

As he stood in the shadows, something caught his attention; a lone figure with a purposeful stride descending the hill through the trees. The goblin stayed where he was and watched the man. Once the soldier reached the camp, he began calling out orders to stop the search and gather around him.

This man had important news; the assassin could feel it. As the soldiers gathered, he listened closely, straining to hear every word. It was difficult, even with his keen ears, but it sounded as if the Jewel had been found.

"All right, now get back to your posts! And no more mistakes!"

"Yes, sir, Corporal!" replied the soldiers in unison.

As the soldiers dispersed, the goblin realized this Corporal hadn't said where the Princess was. That was disappointing, but if there was one thing he knew, it was how to get the information he needed. *That man knows where I can find my prize.* Slowly he slid his ice-dagger from its sheath.

The weapon had been drawn; now it must be used.

CHAPTER 22

T hick, swirling darkness surrounded Macal. As if from a great distance, he heard a muffled sound like breaking glass. His body felt as if it were being stretched forward and backward like a piece of dough, growing longer and thinner with every passing second; then suddenly his legs and feet snapped forward to catch up with the rest of him and he felt himself back on solid ground, no longer adrift. Around him, everything was still black, as if light had never ventured to wherever he was.

There was a nervous whisper beside him. "Macal? Are you there?"

"I think I'm right next to you." He found her hand and took it softly in his. "Are you all right? You were bleeding."

"I'm okay. It's not as bad as you might think. I've read that the mind often makes an injury seem much worse than it is."

"The blood looked pretty real to me."

"I said not to worry about it. I'll be fine. And see? The mirror agrees with me that you are not to blame for what happened to your uncle."

"That depends where we are. Maybe this is my punishment. I can't see anything."

"Maybe this will help."

A shimmering, pearly light suddenly banished the darkness. Blinking, Macal saw it was emanating from Aeria's sabre. She held it high, the blade glittering with iridescence as she moved it back and forth. By its light they could see they were in a cavern. Releasing Macal's hand, the Princess walked around and used her enchanted sword to illuminate the space, growing more excited as she explored.

"I think we did it. We made it in. We succeeded in our quest!"

Looking around, Macal had his doubts. "Are you sure? There's nothing here. This place is as bare as an old bone."

Regardless of the Princess's excitement, he was disheartened by the vacant cavern. Had everything they had endured been for nothing? This chilly chamber was as large as the last one. From end to end and side to side, there was absolutely nothing in it at all. Not even an exit.

At the sight of his dour face the Princess gave a knowing smile. *"This* I remember! Everything you're looking for is *invisible.* Only those who speak the Word of Power can make it visible."

"Word of Power? What are you talking about?"

"Trust me, I did not bring you here for nothing. I just hope my memory of the treasure is accurate; otherwise you might not get *exactly* what we came for. But I'm sure we can find something else for you."

"What?" Macal was alarmed.

"Just joking." She gave a mischievous grin. "I know exactly what was left here."

"Are you finally going to tell me what it is?"

"In a moment you will see for yourself." The Princess seemed exuberant, as if she enjoyed breaking free from the restraints of her duties, as if this adventure, with all its fear and danger, was the most enjoyable experience of her life. *"Brinizarn!"* she shouted.

Instantly the room began to change, its illusion of emptiness broken by the Word of Power. Delicate coils of hyacinth-hued smoke swirled up from the floor. As they rose through the room, the previously bare rock walls suddenly revealed tightly-fitted blocks of pale stone that cascaded down in a circular pattern from ceiling to floor.

On the far side of the chamber a massive formation emerged; a raised platform with several steps leading up to it. On the platform stood eight thick, square pillars, intricately carved. The carvings depicted gorgeous angels wielding mighty weapons. On top of the pillars rested a small peaked roof. Across the base of the pediment was another stone carving, this one of a great black dragon.

Within this elegant stonework structure rested a wondrously ornate sarcophagus, its sides carved in deep relief with a long line of intricately detailed, sword-wielding angels tightly packed against one another. The cover of the sarcophagus rose in a pointed peak along its length, echoing the design of the platform's roof.

As the colored smoke dissipated, Macal could see that the Black Dragon, the Elronian coat of arms, was carved into the center of each step leading to the platform, and emblazoned as well on an ancient red tapestry on the back wall.

Filling in the rest of the space were jeweled vases, delicate and extravagant mirrors, richly decorated chests of stone and wood, and a plethora of detailed sculptures of different gods. In the middle of all these stood a great throne of gold.

Macal was too awed by the spectacular sight to speak.

"Welcome to the Tomb of King Ferance the First, the Old King, the First King of Elronia, the Dragon of all Dragons," declared the Princess.

The boy nodded mutely, overwhelmed by the richness and glory of everything around him.

Princess Aeria pointed to the largest chest in the room. Resting at the foot of the sarcophagus, it was made of wood and lavishly decorated in jewels along its platinum support bands. "Open that and see your treasure. It's finally time for your reward."

Macal gulped. It was almost like stealing from a dead person, and a king at that. The sheer wealth in this chamber was more than he had ever imagined could exist in all of Aerinth. He knew that by selling a single treasure from here, he could live like a noble for the rest of his life.

"I don't think I can," he said at last. "It's not right taking from the dead."

"I'm saying it's all right," the Princess said firmly. "The King is of my bloodline. He would want you to have this, if it can help save Elronia. Go on. Open the chest and take it."

Macal had to admit that they had come a long way and almost died entering the tomb. It would be a great waste to leave empty-handed—and besides, he was extremely curious about what was in the chest.

Finally, with great trepidation, he climbed the steps to the platform and respectfully approached the elegant chest. He knelt, fumbled briefly with the jeweled latch, and hoisted the heavy lid. At long last, here was his treasure.

After returning his troops to their posts, the Corporal headed back up the hill. The goblin assassin watched from the shadows. Within a moment the man was lost to the darkness. The assassin knew he couldn't lose this man; the Corporal was the one who could lead him to the Princess. Checking his surroundings to make sure his presence was undetected, he moved swiftly and quietly out of the camp, following the Corporal.

The man moved rapidly up the hill and the goblin hastened to catch up. He had to take his prey before he reached the company of his comrades. For each step the Corporal took, the assassin took three, like a wolf stalking an unsuspecting hare. The stalwart soldier was completely oblivious to the creeping doom in the darkness behind him. Closer and closer the assassin came, silent as a void. Soon he was close enough to smell the Corporal's sweat. With an ease born of long practice he matched the rhythm of his steps to the soldier's, the ice-dagger poised to strike.

When he was ready, he launched his attack with the speed of a snake lunging to swallow a rodent. Wrapping his arm around the surprised Corporal's neck, he clamped a hand over his mouth and roughly yanked the man's head back to reveal the tender flesh of his throat. The Corporal struggled to break free, but the goblin's grip was as strong as iron. Gently he leaned his head close to the terrified man and laid the frigid edge of the dagger against his neck. His whisper was no louder than the night breeze in the grass.

"I hope you worship Nilelurdar."

As Macal knelt before the open chest, the word *Brinizarn* came back to him. When Princess Aeria had uttered it to reveal the treasures of the tomb, he had recognized the word. He knew he had heard it somewhere recently. Hadn't Uncle Melkes used it in his story about Greykus the Hero and his great white horse? Hadn't he said that Greykus was a vassal to the King of Brinizarn?

Why would Brinizarn be the Word of Power here in Elronia? He would have to ask the Princess later; for now, she had brought him here to retrieve a treasure that would help him find his father. His father, who wasn't a traitor, but a hero like Greykus. He had been captured trying to keep the dweomered war plans out of the hands of King Orgog.

Now, with this gift, it was up to Macal to free his father and bring back the hidden plans.

The boy thought of what it had cost to get where he was now. He thought of all the soldiers who had died during the ambush in the ravine. That skirmish, with all its deaths, would probably not have taken place if the Princess had not insisted on coming west to the tomb for Macal's sake. While he understood the necessity of stopping the trolls, the task could have fallen to a different company, who might have managed it with fewer casualties. Then again, if Uncle Melkes hadn't died he wouldn't be here either. He would be in some safe place, probably far to the east, smiling and laughing as his uncle told him another story.

And what of Lalliard? If the bitter old wizard hadn't kept rescuing him, he would have been killed either by the rampaging trolls or the sinister Morgog. But Macal had abandoned him, left him alone in the night as he slumbered.

Until recently, Macal had led a completely unremarkable existence on a shabby old farm back in Hormul. Now so much had happened so quickly. No longer was his life boring; it was rife with warfare, travel, royalty, hidden treasure, and death. The realization descended on him like a heavy weight.

All he had ever wanted was the quiet life of his little hamlet, perhaps a friend or two, with Uncle Melkes always by his side. Now he would never have that again. That life and hope was over. Dead. Macal told himself to bury it in the depths of his mind and never dwell on it again.

Just breathe, he told himself, trying not to choke on the misery swelling inside him. At last he gained enough control to let his eyes focus on what was inside the deep chest. This treasure, he knew, was the key to his new life. The old one was gone, but now he would find his father and they would be together, as he had dreamed.

His heart beat faster. Neatly folded in the chest was a garment of a rich lilac color, resting on a red silk pillow. Unable to restrain himself, Macal reached for it. The first touch of the durable, velvety texture told him it was made of moleskin. As he lifted it, it unfurled into a billowing, full-length cloak with a deep hood. A thick band of gold cloth decorated the hem, matching the cloak's fine stitching. Attached to the front was a large gold brooch set with a pair of magnificent pale blue opals as big as his eyes.

"You must have this," explained Princess Aeria, mounting the platform to stand beside him, "because I cannot trust the safety of the kingdom to you alone. Go ahead, put it on."

Macal looked at her and then back at the cloak. He didn't know if the Princess had noticed, but it looked far too big for him.

"Don't worry," she urged. "Just put it on."

Macal obeyed, but a question nagged him. *How was a piece of clothing going to help him find his father?*

In the moonlit trees, the assassin held Corporal Mercule in his deadly grasp. Although the soldier continued to struggle, he was unable to gain an advantage over the experienced assassin, who anticipated and countered his every move.

"Where is she?" growled the goblin. He held the dagger close to his victim's throat, but loosened his fingers so the man could speak.

"She who?" It had taken Mercule only a moment to understand what was happening and what this wretch's purpose was. He was not going to give up the Princess.

Izgar answered him with a quick cut to the neck, painful but just shy of a fatal slice to the jugular. The assassin was a professional; he had done this many times before. "Your life is on the line. Where is she?"

"She went to Mazzul Keep," said Mercule.

In a flash the assassin removed the dagger from the Corporal's neck and plunged it into his side, sliding it expertly between his ribs to puncture his lung. Mercule's eyes widened in agony, strength draining out of him as his lung collapsed.

"No more lies. This is the last time I ask. *Where is she?*"

Mercule fell to his knees in shock, blood seeping from his lips. He could feel the blood starting to pool painfully inside his lung. Only the assassin's grip prevented him from falling over. The blade was back at his throat.

Visions of Aeria and Macal flickered through his fading mind. The Princess, so spirited and beautiful. Macal, so much like his father, although he didn't know it. Tears welled up in Mercule Gentris's eyes as he realized he was going to betray them.

He spoke in a raspy weak voice. "...she...is...in...*tomb*..."

"Is the tomb up the hill?"

"...*yes*..."

"Do you worship Nilelurdar?"

Mercule could only spit up blood in response.

"I didn't think so." Without another word the assassin threw the Corporal to the ground and rendered him unconscious with a kick to the head. Leaning down, he whispered into Mercule's ear, "Trust me, it is best not to feel the life draining from you. Enjoy Narekisis, and please, offer Nilelurdar my regards."

"THIEEEEEEF!"

The sudden shout nearly deafened Macal as he donned the heavy lilac cloak. He turned on the Princess angrily. "What?"

"Watch your tone," she said curtly. "I am a member of the royal family! And I didn't say anything!"

"Thief!" Macal heard again.

"What?" He looked around in puzzlement. If the Princess was not shouting at him, who was?

"So, you are stupid, as well as a thief," came the voice again. *"You don't even know what you're stealing."*

"Where are you?" The voice was so loud it was giving him a headache. Then he realized what it had said. *What you're stealing.* Startled, he looked down at the cloak draped heavily around his shoulders and realized that it had somehow shrunk to fit him. Meanwhile the Princess was regarding him with troubled curiosity.

"Whom are you talking to?"

"This cloak." Macal said in confused disbelief. "I think it's talking to me."

"Talking to you? How can a cloak talk to you?"

"Of course I can talk, Thief," said the voice in Macal's mind. *"What kind of magical cloak would I be if I didn't talk? Now put me back before the king's guardians come for you."*

"We've passed all the guardians," the boy said. "And I'm not a thief."

"You're stealing property that is not yours. You are a thief, Thief!"

"I am *not.*" Macal pointed to the bewildered Princess, who was watching him conduct half a conversation with himself. "See that girl? She is of royal blood, a descendant of this king you speak of, King Ferance the First. She is the Princess of Elronia."

"A thief who can lie!" mocked the cloak. *"Oh, I'm surprised!"*

"I'm not lying. She is the Princess. Ask her!"

"I can speak only to the one who wears me."

"So I'll put you on her." Macal prepared to remove the cloak and give it to the Princess.

"Don't you dare! Being on your dishonorable shoulders is already enough filth for me."

"I'm not filthy *or* dishonorable."

"All thieves are dishonorable!"

"I told you, *I'm not a thief.*"

"Then put me back in the chest!"

"Macal, what's going on?" demanded the Princess.

"The cloak thinks I'm stealing it!"

"It's still talking to you?"

"Yes, and it won't stop calling me a thief."

"Thief!" said the cloak.

"He's not a thief!" confirmed the confused Princess.

"Oh good, the Thief's companion says the thief is not a thief. Now of course I believe you. Ha!"

Annoyed by the cloak's abuse, Macal yanked it off his shoulders.

"About time!" he heard the garment say, assuming he had come to his senses and was going to replace it back in the chest. Instead the boy threw the purple cloak over the Princess's slender shoulders.

"Arghhh! The filth, the further stench of thieves!" the Princess heard as it landed on her, shrinking further to fit her smaller frame. She could scarcely believe it. Macal wasn't joking or going insane. The cloak really talked!

"Put me back, Thief!" it was shouting. *"I belong to the First King of Elronia. Any other than one of royal blood who dares take me from this tomb will be cursed with the legs of worms, the arms of snakes, and the head of a cow for all eternity!"*

"I *am* of royal blood," she declared proudly.

"You are n—" shouted the cloak before abruptly choking off its words, as if it had somehow detected her royal lineage. *"You...you are! You are of royal blood!"*

"I am well aware of that." The Princess sounded impatient. "I have come here to give you to him. He is my vassal."

"Your highness, I beg forgiveness. Of course. Anything you wish. I expected to be awakened eventually; I simply imagined it would be by treasure hunters, rogues or other dark-hearted, thieving scoundrels."

"Serve him as you served my great ancestor. He is on a royal mission. If he fails, there will likely be no more descendants of the royal line for you to serve." The Princess removed the cloak and handed it back to Macal. "Maybe you'll find it more cooperative now."

"Hello, Thief," said the Cloak of Brinizarn as Macal donned it once more.

"My name is Macal, not Thief," the boy said in exasperation.

"We'll see about that. She says you're not, but I still have my doubts about you, Thief."

Macal began to wonder how useful such a cloak was really going to be. He knew the Princess meant well by this gift, and he had not forgotten how much effort it had taken them to obtain it. But was it really as special as she had been led to believe?

"I can hear what you're thinking, you know," said the cloak. *"And she is right. I am special, Thief."*

Izgar the assassin moved up the hill through the dark coppice, seeking the tomb of which the Corporal had spoken. He had no idea whose tomb it was, or why the Princess was in it, nor did he care. Such trivial details did not matter.

Perhaps for her, he thought, *it does matter. These are, after all, the last moments of her life.*

Stealthily moving through the thicket, the goblin's skin prickled with excitement. These were the moments that defined and fulfilled him. To watch life escape from a once healthy body, a body that he had weakened to a state of failure, was a beautiful, wondrous thing. His pace quickened at the thought. Surmounting another steep slope, he saw torchlight in the distance off to the east and eagerly moved closer.

Soldiers were everywhere, swarming about like ants on an anthill. Most of them were gathered around a crevice in the steepest section of the rise; something was attracting all their attention. Princess Aeria was nowhere to be seen.

This must be the entrance to the tomb, the assassin concluded.

From somewhere close behind him came the sudden snap of a broken twig. The goblin spun around, dagger flying into his hand. Two soldiers were coming up the hill. At first he wasn't sure if they had seen him, but as they closed the distance he realized he had to act.

By the time the soldiers recognized the threat, the goblin was already in motion. There was no time to shout an alarm; he lunged forward, thrusting his dagger into the throat of the first man. The victim fell to the ground, choking on his own spurting blood.

These soldiers were no match for him. It was like fighting children, he thought pleasantly.

The second soldier was trying to draw his sword, but as he fumbled with the hilt, the assassin's blade sank into his heart. Like the first, he fell to the ground and died.

Nilelurdar will be pleased with tonight's work, the assassin mused to himself. *So many are going to join him.*

Scanning the area, he saw no sign that the two deaths had been noticed, but as his gaze lingered on the crevice, something caught his eye. A dragonmere! He had been informed by his employer that the royal dragon-beast was the Princess's personal escort.

He will know where she is, he thought. It was all so easy. Like following a chain, one link to the next, until he found the one he was looking for.

CHAPTER 23

M acal was still getting used to the idea of the magical cloak talking to him all the time. He found it disconcerting. He voiced an internal question. *"I don't need to talk to you out loud?"*

"Unfortunately, no. Everything you think, decide, or wonder about, I can hear."

Any time he wanted to keep his thoughts private, Macal realized, he would have to remove the intrusive garment.

"I heard that," it commented.

"So, what can you do?" asked Macal inside his mind. *"Do you have any special powers?"*

"I can talk. For an inanimate object, I think that's pretty special."

"I mean, what else can you do?"

"That's not enough? Times have really changed. Back when Ferance was around, people found my ability to speak impressive."

"It is impressive. But I don't see how it can help me free my father."

"Free your father?" mused the cloak. *"I haven't been told about that. Just give me a second."* As it fell silent, Macal began to feel a strange sensation, as if the cloak were sifting through his memories—like someone rifling through a drawer in search of two matching socks.

"What are you doing?" Whatever it was, he didn't like it.

"Trying to find out about your father, so that I know what you're talking about."

"You can't do that!"

"Yes, I can. I'm doing it right now."

"No, I mean, I won't let you do it. Not to me. What's in my head is private. It's mine."

"Not to worry," the cloak said airily. *"I found what I was looking for. I understand I am to help you reach the Troll King's castle in Marglamesh and free your father."*

Displeased at having his private thoughts ransacked, the boy didn't answer.

"*So, you're angry. All right, Thief. But how was I to know you were so touchy?*" said the cloak.

"*Do you have powers that can help me or not?*"

"*Maybe.*"

"*Maybe? You're not going to tell me?*"

"*Why trust a thief with secrets?*"

"*How many times do I have to tell you? I'm not a thief!*"

"*In time, perhaps I'll believe you. Right now, I don't.*"

The Princess spoke up. "Are you two done in there yet?" She had been standing next to Macal during this silent exchange, growing increasingly anxious to move on. "I would like to change into dry clean clothes and have these cuts ministered to."

"Sorry," the boy said. "Yes, I'm done. It just won't stop talking to me. Do you know how to get out of here?"

"No, which is why we need to get going. Who knows how long it will take to find our way."

Inside Macal's mind the Cloak of Brinizarn whispered, "*They hid the exit behind the tapestry. I'm only telling you this, Thief, so we can get her attended to. Royalty must be cared for, first and foremost.*"

"*What about me?*"

"*You're not royalty. You don't count.*"

"There's an exit behind the tapestry," Macal explained aloud to Aeria. "The cloak told me."

A pleased smile lit her face. "See, it's helping you already!"

Macal nodded, although he was still dubious about the cloak's usefulness. Did its advantages outweigh its disadvantages?

"*Remember, I can still hear you,*" came the disapproving comment inside his head. All Macal could do was sigh.

As the Cloak of Brinizarn had said, behind the thick tapestry was a passage, angling upward in the darkness. Princess Aeria led the way with the pearly glow from her sword. Several minutes of walking along the short rounded tunnel brought them to what seemed to be the final room of the tomb.

It was the smallest natural chamber they had seen so far, less than ten feet across and just tall enough for a man to stand upright. The only object of interest lay in the center of the room—a circular slab of granite stone about a foot in height. Carved on its top in six concentric rings were a series of delicate runes.

"*All you have to do,*" explained the cloak to Macal, "*is step onto the stone disc one at a time, and you will appear outside where you entered.*"

"*Are you sure?*" After the ordeals they had undergone, Macal was skeptical. "*What if it's another trap or something?*"

"*You asked me for help. I reluctantly give it to you. It's impolite to start demeaning my efforts when you requested them.*"

"Fine," Macal said aloud for Princess Aeria's benefit. "We just have to step onto the platform and we will appear outside."

"*One at a time,*" the Cloak reminded him.

"One at a time," Macal repeated. "I think I should go first, in case something goes wrong."

"*Still don't trust me, Thief?*"

"No more than you trust me, Garment."

"Are you sure?" The Princess seemed touched by Macal's chivalry, impressed by how much he had changed from the timid boy of a few days ago.

"Yes." Macal hid his nervousness and walked forward, drawing his sword in case he needed it. Stopping in front of the stone disc, he hesitated and turned to the Princess. "We expected losses, right?" he said with a wry smile.

"We just don't want to be part of them," answered Aeria with a warm smile of her own.

Macal turned back to the rune-covered slab. "Wish me luck."

"May your heart stay strong," she said.

Without further delay, Macal set a cautious foot on the cold granite disc and moved toward its center. As he entered the inner ring of runes, it suddenly flared to life. Blue light shot up through Macal to reach the low ceiling. Once the inside ring was alight, the one beside it burst into the same blue scintillate glow. The third, fourth, and fifth followed, hissing with sparks that filled the air of the small stone chamber.

The boy had just enough time to throw Aeria a worried look before the sixth and final ring lit up.

Somewhere deep in his mind, he heard the Cloak of Brinizarn say, "*This should be fun.*"

Then Macal disappeared from sight.

Izgar was trying to approach the dragonmere, but there were too many soldiers around him. He knew his only hope was for his target to move off alone. The assassin skulked along the edge of the torch lit area where the men had gathered. He wanted a better view of what was in the crevice, and now he could see the three carved heads—the entrance, he gathered, to the tomb. From here he could also see that the majority of the soldiers were trying, without success, to open the mechanical door.

Izgar scowled. How could he enter the tomb and find the Princess if her soldiers could not? The crowd inhibited his movements. He would not be able to interrogate the dragonmere, nor to enter the tomb. A change of plan was called for. He would wait for the Princess to emerge from the tomb, then finish what he had come to do.

Biding his time, the goblin forcibly quelled his lust for blood and crept back into the night.

The soldiers were now using hammers to smash through the dense metal door. Loud clangs echoed through the night. After several grueling minutes of pounding, the door showed barely a dent. The men stopped and the largest soldier turned to the dragonmere.

"It's impenetrable, sir."

"How could two children walk in with ease when we cannot find a way to enter?" shouted Viscount Razz in frustration. Angrily he snatched the hammer. "Give me that thing!"

As he stepped up to the door and raised the huge mallet to swing, there was a blinding burst of bluish light behind him. It lasted only a moment, as if a star had exploded into existence and then immediately winked out, leaving behind a faint, curious scent of jasmine.

Everyone, including the startled dragonmere, turned to stare. There in front of the mechanical door stood a weary Macal, wearing an elegant purple cloak. The soldiers eyed him with astonishment. The boy looked just as surprised to see them.

Viscount Razz strode up to him, fuming with rage. "Where is she? Do you know what a fool you've been? If she has perished, you need not fear the King, because I myself will deliver all the retribution you deserve."

"She is—" Macal began, but a second flash of dazzling blue interrupted him, heralding the appearance of a battered Princess Aeria. Awestruck, the soldiers fell to their knees. Viscount Razz stared at the girl in horror. How could she be so careless, risking her life by entering the tomb and playing with magic?

She looked pleased. "That was fun. I might want to go back and do it again some time."

"Not as long as I live," snapped the Viscount.

"Stop worrying. I'm all right."

"You are wounded! What happened? And *how* did you get inside this forsaken tomb?"

"Entry to the tomb is a secret I plan to keep."

The dragonmere shifted his questioning glare to Macal.

"By royal decree I am sworn to secrecy," the boy blurted. As Viscount Razz's expression darkened further, the Princess spoke up.

"You are right. I do have wounds and I would like them attended to as soon as possible."

"Of course, My Jewel." The Viscount bowed and turned to his soldiers. "All of you, quickly! Escort the Princess back to camp! Where is Corporal Mercule?"

"I don't know, your highness," a soldier replied. "I haven't seen him for a while." None of the others seemed to have a better answer.

"He's probably back at the camp," guessed the Viscount. "Find him and tell him I wish to speak with him. Now that we are done with our little excursion here at the tomb, we must bid farewell to Macal and make haste for Varun. Now all of you, go."

Still hidden among the dark trees, the assassin watched the torch-bearing entourage head downhill toward their camp. *That is where it will happen. The Princess of Elronia, the budding rose of the human kingdom, will die in the heart of her camp, right in the middle of her veteran force. It will be a magnificent night.*

For the first time in years, Izgar smiled in happiness.

The soldiers had escorted Princess Aeria and Macal at a rapid pace back to camp, where the two had been taken directly to the healer's tent. Lady Alonia, a lithe red-haired girl who served as the Princess's primary handmaiden, was sent for. After examining the Princess's wounds, the Elven healer had quickly concocted a medicinal poultice, using sage to reduce the inflammation, adder's tongue to soothe the wounds, and chamomile to hasten the healing.

Lady Alonia helped the Princess out of her torn clothing and applied the balm to her wounds with utmost care. Gloliver, the resident priest of Malakel, entered the small tent. In his hands was his god's holy icon, the silver tear. Quietly he gave thanks for the Jewel's safe return, then began to pray to the God of Peace for sanctuary so that the Rose of the Kingdom might fully heal and fulfill her mission.

Macal had been kept waiting outside the tent. At last the Princess, newly bandaged, emerged with Lady Alonia close behind her.

"Are you all right?" asked Macal.

She seemed pleased by his concern. "I will be fine. The wounds are not serious, and what we gained was well worth the price, don't you think? Actually, I don't feel bad at all now."

"That would be the poultice working, my lady," explained Lady Alonia.

"It is working well, then. Macal, will you walk me back to my tent?"

"Of course."

"Good. Lady Alonia, I would like to talk to Macal alone."

"Yes, my lady. I will see to our departure."

The Princess turned to Macal. "Shall we?"

As the two of them made their way back across the camp toward the Princess's tent, Macal couldn't help echoing the handmaiden's last word. "Departure? Are we leaving already?"

"I must continue on to Varun. And you have your own journey ahead of you."

Macal's stomach twisted as she spoke. He didn't want to leave the Princess, nor did he want be all alone again. He wasn't ready.

"Don't you need to rest?" he asked desperately, hoping to buy more time.

Princess Aeria smiled at him. "I am well enough to travel."

"Well, how am I going to get to Marglamesh from here? I still have to travel through the rest of Elronia, and then cross Xanga-Mor before I even reach the border to the troll lands. Maybe it would be best if your force escorted me, at least to our border...."

"I have already used up crucial time bringing you here to the tomb," the Princess said. "I must reach Varun while an alliance may still prove helpful. As to how you are going to reach Marglamesh, the answer to that question will be my final surprise for you."

"What do you mean? You said this cloak was your final surprise. How many more tricks do you have up your sleeve?"

"Enough to keep you guessing for a while! But don't worry; shortly you'll understand what I'm talking about. The caravan should be ready to move out within the hour. By that time, you will already be on your way to find your father."

The Princess's words knocked the wind out of Macal. *Within the hour? So soon?* He had started to become attached to all these people. He felt as if he belonged with this cavalcade; they had battled together, bled together, shared meals together. He had learned so much from them. And even though Viscount Razz was angry at him at the moment, Macal didn't doubt that the dragonmere would soon return to his role as mentor and instructor.

Then there was the Princess. More than any of the others, she had found her way into his heart. Spirited and clever, beautiful beyond dreams, she made him feel things he had never felt before. Her confidence in him gave him confidence in himself; she made him feel that he could actually save his father—that somehow, against all odds, he could succeed. Most important of all, he knew she actually cared.

Looking into Aeria's clear blue eyes, Macal asked himself why he had to leave her.

The Cloak of Brinizarn spoke suddenly inside his mind. *"What did you think would happen, Thief? That you two would grow up, get married, and live happily ever after? That will never happen. She is a princess and you are just a peasant."*

The boy had forgotten the cloak could hear his thoughts; it was something that was going to take a while to get used to. *"I don't know what I thought was going to happen,"* he answered in desolation. *"I know I have to find my father. I just didn't expect to leave so soon. I thought we'd have more time."*

"We're at war. There is no time to spare. War means it is us or them. If we want it to be us, we have to do everything we can do to make sure we win. Right now, that means not wasting any more time."

"Are you okay?" Aeria's voice cut into Macal's thoughts as he was about to respond to the cloak. "You're being very quiet."

"Sorry. The cloak was talking to me again."

Aeria smiled at him. "Being helpful, is it?"

"Careful how you respond here!"

"Oh, definitely," lied Macal.

"Good. I'm sorry we have to leave you. I just wanted to say that to you myself. I can't imagine what it would be like to go so far from home all by myself. I have faith that you will succeed, but I want to ask you now, while we are alone—are you *sure* you want to do this? You don't have to go. If my parley with Varun goes well, we may still all survive this war. Nobody would think you a coward if you changed your mind. They might actually think you had somehow gotten a little wiser."

They had stopped walking and now stood staring at each other under the dark, starry sky. Around them, the camp was filled with preparations for departure, but the bustle was lost on Macal as he gazed into her serene face. Even if he wanted to, he could not have looked away. He didn't know what to think. The Princess said she had faith in his success. Why then ask him if he really wanted to go?

"Because, you fool, she cares about you!"

"And she thinks I might die?"

"With good reason. There's a strong possibility that you will."

"Well?" Princess Aeria was awaiting his answer. "Are you sure you want to go?"

Macal swallowed. "I have to. He's my father. I can't leave him there if I have a chance to help him, even if it's only a small one."

"Are you *sure* you're sure?"

"Yes," he said.

"I just want you to know you wouldn't lose any honor if you changed your mind."

"I didn't know I had any honor to start with."

Aeria touched his arm. "You have much more than you know."

Macal blushed. He was thankful when Aeria turned and headed for her tent. They walked together in awkward silence until they reached their destination. They found the tent unguarded, with all the soldiers busy packing up the camp. Aeria went inside and Macal followed quietly. As soon as they entered, they saw a long slash in the heavy fabric of the far wall.

"Who did that?" asked the Princess alarmed.

"Not me," said the cloak quickly to Macal. Since its creation, it had frequently been blamed for anything bad happening in its vicinity.

"I don't know," said the boy aloud. "And I'm pretty sure I don't want to find out."

Hasty footsteps sounded behind them and they turned to see the blond soldier named Drennin. Stern and deliberate as always, he bowed briefly and reported, "Princess, we found Corporal Mercule. He has been attacked."

"Is he all right?" Macal asked.

"He is barely alive. Several other men have also been assaulted. They are dead."

"By whom? Or what?" Princess Aeria demanded.

"We don't know, Jewel. Viscount Razz sent me to protect you."

"Too late for *that!*" The new voice rang out without warning, followed immediately by the rasp of metal links being sundered. Macal and Aeria watched in horror as Drennin's eyes rolled back in his head. He lurched forward, staggered, and fell to his knees, his arms flailing behind him, seeking the grievous wound just inflicted upon him through his chain mail vest.

As the soldier fell, Izgar stepped over him, his ice-dagger dripping with blood. Aeria and Macal backed away. Ignoring the dying soldier, the goblin followed them, eyes gleaming as he saw the end of his long road. Here was his prize.

"Finally, Princess of Elronia, I have found you."

"Who are you?" The authority in her voice faltered as the goblin came closer.

"A legend that is about to be born." A menacing smile twisted his face; the dagger was hungry in his hand. "I promise to make this quick."

"I'm thinking this isn't good!" wailed the cloak.

Macal didn't know what was happening or who this creature was, but fear overwhelmed him as it had so many times before. He wasn't the goblin's target, but that made no difference. As the assassin moved closer, the boy retreated step by step until his legs struck a padded stool behind him and he lost his balance and toppled onto his back. Lying petrified, his body refusing to react, he watched as the murderous creature closed in on the Princess.

"Coward!" screamed the cloak. *"You're going to let her die? What curse has been*

laid upon me that I should crest the shoulders of one such as you, Thief?"

Macal heard, but could do nothing. The fear was stronger than he was.

Aeria had now run out of room to retreat. "The King of Trolls offers you his regards," whispered the assassin. He raised his dagger of ice. Behind him Drennin now lay still.

Desperately he wanted to help the Princess, but Macal was paralyzed by his fear. His mind joined the cloak, screaming at him to save her. He wanted to help, but he couldn't. Immobilized, he could only watch in terror as the gloating goblin prepared to slay the Princess of the Land, the Rose of the Kingdom, the love of his heart.

"You are more lowly than the worms who feast on rats!" cried the cloak, but there was nothing the boy could do to stir himself.

The tent flap was torn open and Viscount Razz stood in the threshold, transformed by ferocity as he took in the scene before him. "Goblin wretch!" He drew his sword and charged forward with a savage roar. "It is time for you to join the denizens of the nether world!"

The goblin spun to face the Viscount. Princess Aeria and Macal watched as the two squared off in combat.

"Ah, the King of Ermalon," sneered the goblin. He had recognized the Viscount immediately; the ring on the dragonmere's hand was as significant as a crown etched with the kingdom's standard. "It seems my fortune is growing. Slaying you this night, along with the Princess of Elronia, will raise my repute above that of any assassin in the world!"

"I am not the king." Viscount Razz made a thrust with his long sword, but the agile goblin easily parried the assault.

"Your ring says otherwise, my lord," mocked Izgar.

In fury the dragonmere grabbed the hilt of his sword with both hands and swung the blade overhead, directly down on the assassin. Izgar deftly sidestepped the attack and lashed out with his dagger, slicing the unarmored dragonmere across the ribs.

The Viscount roared in pain and retaliated with a mighty kick to the assassin's chest. The force of the blow knocked Izgar backward off his feet. Viscount Razz lunged forward to thrust his sword through his enemy's torso, but the goblin responded with equal speed. As the great ice giants had taught him, he activated the magic harnessed by his blade.

Instantly a blizzard erupted inside the tent. Thick snow, sleet, and hail diminished visibility to almost nothing. A glacial chill enveloped them, threatening to freeze them where they stood. Numbed by the cold, Macal finally managed to crawl to his feet.

"Aeria! Where are you?"

"I'm here," she called over the sound of the galeful wind. Macal could barely hear her over the whipping storm. He couldn't tell if she was right beside him or across the tent. Viscount Razz was turning around and around trying to keep his defenses up on all sides.

Izgar though, by the power of his weapon, could still see as if it were the clearest of days. As he watched the three of them flounder in the wintry snowfall he imagined how pleased Nilelurdar was about to be when the dark god received his latest offering.

Slick ice formed on the ground inside the tent. The Princess was finding it difficult to keep her footing; the Viscount had better luck, able to gain some purchase on the ice with his clawed feet. Macal wondered where all the soldiers were. Then he realized how fast everything was happening—Drennin's arrival, the appearance of the assassin, Razz, the storm.

Even if the soldiers came, what could they do in this frigid mess? He could only hope that the Viscount had scared away the foul goblin, that the assassin had used the storm as a means to escape. *But what if he was still here?*

"Why don't you do something?" he demanded of the cloak.

"ME? Why don't you do something for a change? What am I supposed to do, anyway?"

"Aren't you supposed to help me find my father? Don't you have some power other than talking? What good are you?"

"I am the Cloak of Brinizarn! I was made by the Sorcerers of the Three Towers during the Age of Dreams! I have been in existence longer than your kingdom! Do not dare to doubt my powers!"

"Then help me!"

"No."

"What do you mean, no?"

"There is nothing I can do here."

"But you just said you were the Cloak of Brinizarn and older than time, and not to doubt your powers and all that."

"All of which is true. But none of my powers are relevant here."

"So you do have powers."

"Did I deny I did?"

"What are they?"

"You doubted me. I won't tell you now."

"Doesn't matter anyway," the boy grumbled, pelted by sleet and hail, *"They're probably useless."*

"They're not useless!"

"Sure they aren't. Now just shut up and stay out of my head."

"If you are wearing me, I can't do that, Thief."

"Try."

"Macal!" The Princess shouted over the wailing wind.

"I'm here." Immediately he regretted this announcement. *What if he and Aeria had just alerted the assassin to their whereabouts?* Feeling a touch on his arm, he jumped.

"It's me," came Aeria's voice, barely audible above the storm. Macal's body was freezing, but his soul was warmed by her hand on his arm. "What's happening?"

"Some sort of magic, I think. We have to get out of here. It's so cold I can't feel my hands or feet."

"Me either. But which way is out?"

"Any. Let's just go in one direction 'til we get out of this bewitchment."

Huddled together, they felt their way forward, hoping to escape the mystical storm before it killed them. Macal had spread his cloak wide, wrapping it around Princess Aeria to give them both some protection against the frigid elements. Their vision almost completely obscured, they did not see the slender figure in front of them until it spoke.

"I didn't say it was time to leave yet. Did I? You leave when I say to leave."

Terror swept over the two children as they recognized the voice of the goblin assassin. Immune to his own magic, he had come to them.

"And Princess," came the hissing voice. "It *is* time for you to leave. Not just from this tent, but from the world! By any chance do you worship Nilelurdar?"

"Run!" shouted Macal, trying to push the Princess away, but it was too late. The goblin lunged forward and thrust his ice dagger at the Rose of the Kingdom.

Aeria screamed in pain as the assassin's blade sliced through her. Macal heard her cry out but, unable to see her, he could not tell how badly she had been wounded.

"No!" he shouted. He fell to his knees, searching blindly. "Aeria? Aeria!" His words were lost in the howling, snow-choked wind, but his hands encountered her body almost immediately. He felt a slickness on his fingers. *Her blood!*

"Aeria?" He moved his face close to hers and heard a faint gasp of response, enough to convince him that she was still alive. Glancing through the open tent flap, he could see guards coming, bearing hooded lanterns and striding through the stormy gale like lit ships sailing through a foggy night at sea. *Finally.* Relief flooded him, only to drain away as a silhouette blocked his view of the rescuers.

The goblin assassin's dark shadow loomed above the two children like a bloodthirsty warlord ready to claim a new throne. Snow blew through the air about him, catching the hazy glow of the approaching lanterns. On the ground beside Macal, the Princess cried in pain.

"Now we end it all," they heard the assassin intone. "Nilelurdar, please accept this most bountiful offering. May she inhabit your kingdom till the death of eternity!"

Seeing the shape of the goblin raise his weapon for the final strike, Macal reacted without thinking. His heart pumping harder and faster than he had ever felt it before, he threw himself at the assassin. His body struck the slender creature's legs, knocking him off balance. Izgar stumbled, but managed not to fall. He reached down to tear the boy's grip free, but Macal held tight. If he wanted the Princess to live, he couldn't let go.

They struggled, and the goblin was on the verge of prevailing when a hulking figure rushed forward and crashed into him. Viscount Razz had also seen the assassin's silhouette against the backdrop of lantern light. The force of the impact sent both goblin and dragonmere to the ground with a jarring crunch that knocked Izgar's Frostmoor dagger from his hand. The obsidian hilt slipped from his slender green fingers and slid out of reach across the ice-coated ground.

As soon as the dagger left the assassin's hand, the magical tempest ceased. Being separated from his weapon was like having his soul torn from him, but Izgar had no time to mourn; the dragonmere rolled his massive body onto him, pinning him down. Izgar Grym had just enough time to look up into a pair of infuriated yellow eyes before Viscount Razz loosed a searing gout of flame from his mouth at him.

The battle was over.

Now that they could see, Macal and the Viscount ran to Aeria's side to check if she was alive, or if the assassin had succeeded in his fell quest. The soldiers followed suit, except for a few who surrounded the goblin's charred corpse.

Macal was the first to reach her. The snow on the ground had already started to melt, but what remained was stained crimson with the blood of the Princess of the Kingdom. Her skin was pale and cold. Macal reached out to touch her, aware of Viscount Razz at his side. "Please," the boy prayed to any god who might be listening. "Please…."

Aeria's right side was soaked in blood. It was hard to see where she had been hit, but as the boy gently moved her, she grimaced and cried in pain.

"She's alive!" Macal shouted.

Viscount Razz gathered the Princess in his arms. "We need to get her to the healer." He stood and started across the camp, carrying her as fast as his long legs could take him. Macal scrambled after him along with many of the soldiers.

A few moments later they reached the healer's tent where the elder elf, needing room to work, ordered everyone except Lady Alonia to leave. Macal and the Viscount left grudgingly. As they paced restlessly outside the tent, impatiently awaiting word from the healer, an occasional murmur of pain from the Princess reassured them that she still lived. Time passed slowly until at last the bent elf emerged from the tent to greet them.

"Will she live?" demanded the dragonmere. His normally ferocious face was twisted with grief, his piercing eyes wet with tears. Macal was sure he looked no better.

"It's a grievous wound, have no doubt about that," began the healer. "What sort of wicked blade could inflict such an injury I am sure I don't know—"

"Enough of your ramblings! Will she live?" The Viscount appeared to be on the verge of seizing the healer and shaking him.

"That she will, my lord. Wicked was the injury as I have said, but it was only to her arm. Sore and painful and a long time healing it will be, but the Princess of Elronia, the light of our lives, shall live beyond this day!"

Macal was so overwhelmed with relief that he couldn't prevent himself from throwing his arms around the healer and then the dragonmere. Then he remembered something else. "Where is Mercule? Is he going to recover too?"

The elfin healer's pleased expression faded into sorrow.

"I'm afraid that the gods have granted us only one miracle today. I fear that Corporal Mercule Gentris will not live through the night—"

"Where is he?" Macal interrupted. "I must see him!"

"He's just inside—"

That was all Macal needed. He raced into the tent, hearing the elf say, "—behind the second curtain."

Throwing aside the second curtain, the boy saw Corporal Mercule lying pale as a dove, a blood-stained bandage wrapped around his bare chest. His faint breathing came with a rasp. He opened his eyes with difficulty as Macal came close to him.

"Sorry...Aeria..." The dying man's lips formed the words, his voice a mere thread.

"She's safe," Macal assured him. "The assassin is dead."

Cheered by the news, the Corporal gave a smile that almost immediately faltered from weakness. A moment later he struggled to speak. "Ma—Macal...."

"I'm here," the boy whispered, wishing the Corporal wouldn't waste his strength by talking.

"Save...Bertran."

"I will," said Macal. It was plain that what little life Mercule had left in him was moving toward the heavens. "I promise."

In the night, at the base of the small mountain containing the Tomb of the Old King, Mercule Gentris, Soldier of Elronia of the town of Fellonon, offered his last words in the mortal world. "You...are everything...he wanted you to be...."

Then the Corporal died.

An air of mourning lay over the camp as the Elronian force finished making ready to travel again. Mercule Gentris had been well liked, as had many of the assassin's other victims, and the survivors were haunted by a sense of guilt and failure. One enemy, alone, should not have been able to perpetrate such losses against the Royal Guard of the Jewel of the Crown. But it had happened, and their folly and ineptitude were to blame.

Tended by the healer, Princess Aeria was now conscious and managing the pain. Viscount Razz had refused to move from her side in case the assassin had an accomplice. Macal left them only briefly to gather his belongings from his tent before it was dismantled and packed onto a wagon.

The caravan seemed so much smaller than when he had first joined it. Then it had been whole, full of life and unscarred by malevolent encounters. Now more than half the men had been lost, the Princess herself assaulted, and the morale of the remaining soldiers beaten almost to nothing by the prospect of what lay ahead—the nightmare journey through the dark forest of Rashinasti.

As the time for departure drew near, the Princess was moved into her carriage, with Lady Alonia at her side. Viscount Razz stood outside the conveyance, alert to the possibility of further attacks. Joining him, Macal was handed a new soldier's backpack to replace the one he had lost in the tomb. The boy had resumed his chain mail vest and Elronian vestments; on his hand was the golden ring emblazoned with Princess Aeria's personal seal. Off to the side he saw an esquire holding the reins of two steeds, Shelga and the Viscount's brown jotun, apparently recovered following the battle with the troll force.

"Macal." Princess Aeria's voice emerged from the carriage. "Come in here and speak with me a moment."

Macal saw Viscount Razz eye him curiously, but the Princess's request left him as much in the dark as the dragonmere. Who was he, a lowly peasant, to deny a member of the royal family? He climbed into the carriage to join her.

"Lady Alonia, a minute alone, please."

"Of course, my lady." The Lady stepped down from the carriage, closing the door behind her.

Princess Aeria reclined on the bench opposite the one on which Macal had seated himself. Her arm was heavily bandaged by soft lengths of linen, but she looked much improved by the ministrations of the healer and Lady Alonia. "Macal, please shut the blinds." Slowly she sat up. "I have one last thing to tell you and one last thing to offer you."

"You don't have to give me anything else," Macal protested as he closed the blinds.

"Yes, I do."

She placed a hand on his. "First, do you remember when I said the augurs sometimes have a hard time telling what has happened and what is about to happen?"

"Yes," he admitted with trepidation. He wasn't sure he liked the soothing tone she was using. He hadn't ever experienced that sort of tone when something good was about to be said.

"I have to tell you," she continued gently. "That the augurs are now sure that your father has been captured and is in the Troll King's castle."

Macal had known this was going to happen. The augurs had already said so, but they had been unsure if it had happened, so there was a part of him that had hoped that they could be wrong or that the future could be changed. Now, hearing those words from her, it was all real. He really was going to go to Marglamesh to find his father. His father really was in danger. He might be the only hope his father had.

"I'm sorry," she said. "And like I said I do have one last thing to give you."

As the Princess leaned toward him, he was filled with uncertainty. "But what else is there?" he asked.

"This." She kissed him on the cheek. "May you be as brave as you are kind."

In Macal's confused state it took a moment for the gesture to register, and then he found himself blushing like a rose. *She kissed me! The Princess of Elronia kissed me!* His heart pounded so hard he thought it might burst from exertion. *She kissed me!* He had to catch his breath; the blue-eyed angel before him seemed to have stolen it with her lips. *She kissed me!* He stared at her. She was the most beautiful girl in the world. *She kissed me! She kissed me! Maybe I'm not such an imbecile after all. She kissed me! Did Menk ever get kissed by a princess? I doubt it!*

As he climbed out of the carriage on weakened legs, his face bore the biggest smile it had worn in years.

She kissed me!

CHAPTER 24

King Orgog descended the spiral staircase down past the undercroft to the dungeons. Without a word he walked past the gaoler along the hall until he came to an ancient stone door in the corner. He pushed the door open and entered the room.

In the center of the octagonal chamber was a strange black iron contraption that held many clamps and restraints. Currently, it securely held his prisoner in the air several feet off the floor. The human now wore only a simple loincloth. His body was covered in scars. One set of metal clamps went under his arms and up over his shoulders. Others held him in place by his wrists, ankles, and his waist. Fastly bound in the device, Bertran Teel was unable to move.

The witches hovered around the held man. Their hands drifting over his back and arms, their fingernails searing his skin with their touch. The soldier's head hung limply with his eyes closed.

"So, this is the man who stole my sword," grumbled the king as he studied his unmoving captive. "Though I owe you thanks for killing my predecessor." Bertran didn't move or respond.

"We were able to mend his flesh," said the witches together. "He lives."

"You point out the obvious. What has he told you?"

"Nothing. He refuses to speak."

The king grabbed Bertran's chin, his claws cutting into the man's skin. "Did you give them to somebody?"

Bertran slowly and weakly opened his eyes, but didn't reply. He stared at the king emotionless and uncaring. He knew the instant he told the king where the plans were hidden he would be killed. *No, he had to make the king think the plans could still be used against him. But how?*

King Orgog turned back to the witches. "What else have you found out?"

"We have scryed, my Master. He's protecting his son. These thoughts are clear to us, he believes if he gives the plans his son will die in the war."

"Find the son then," ordered the king. "And if he is not already dead from the massacre being wrought on the tainted land, kill him. Then our poor proud father here will have nothing more to protect."

Bertran's eyes flooded with emotion.

"Your boy is going to die anyway," taunted the king. "There's no saving him. Why not end your suffering? Tell me where the plans are and I will put an end to your pitiful life."

Getting no response, the witches cast a cantrip in unison to summon their familiar. Upon completion of the spell a floating shape materialized in front of Bertran. The demon's head was a skinless skull that rested atop a boil covered, bloated green slimy body. It had a rotund belly and frail scrawny legs.

The small demon hissed and squealed at all of them. "What's it that you'es the wants?"

"Rinaskul, we need you to find a human boy," chanted the witches together.

"No!" shouted Bertran, speaking for the first time.

The witches gave him a malicious smile. "Yes."

Rinaskul looked from the witches to the captive man. "Finds a boys? Which boys? There is lots of the boys."

The witch carrying the black jeweled staff pointed it at Bertran. "His son."

The demon looked back to the witches excitedly. "And what's I get to does onces I finds the vomit bag?"

The king made sure he had Bertran's attention before he spoke. "Anything you want."

Rinaskul clapped his tiny clawed hands together in excitement. "Oh the goods! The goods! Such funs I wills the have making the offsprings do the crying before he stops the breathings."

"No!" cried Bertran again.

King Orgog brought his face close to Bertran's. "Tell us where you hid the plans."

Bertran clenched his mouth shut.

King Orgog gave a frustrated growl. "Go demon on your errand!"

Laughing and in great mirth Rinaskul flapped away on little leathery wings. As he disappeared down the hall they could hear the demon talking to himself in glee. "Oh the funs I will have doing the pains to him!"

Bertran did not want to believe this was happening. "If you kill him I'll never help you."

"You'd be surprised what men with nothing left will do," replied the king. "Your other option is to tell us now and spare your boy what Rinaskul is going to do to him."

"I…can't."

"You can. And you will in time. You have until the demon finds your son—what was his name?"

"Macal," informed the brides.

"You have until the demon finds Macal to save his life. Tell us and I'll recall the demon." The king then turned from him and left the cell.

As the witches began to torture him again all Bertran could think of was Macal, and as the pain inflicted on him increased he didn't know how much longer he could protect his son.

"So now it begins, eh, Thief?" The Cloak of Brinizarn spoke in Macal's mind, interrupting his warm reverie of Aeria's kiss.

"What?"

"Our quest."

"Oh, right. Begins. Wait—isn't that what I've been doing all this time? Questing?"

"No. All that was preparation for the quest. Trust me, I know about quests. I have been on as many quests as a dragon has gold coins. So far you have only been properly attired, partially trained, and somewhat readied for battle. Now comes the real test, the real quest, and it only gets harder from here. From now on, you'll be all alone. Well, all alone except for me."

"That's not helping. And you're not raising my confidence."

"I'm not here to do that."

"I'm still unsure as to why you are here."

"Are you ready?" Viscount Razz's voice interrupted Macal's exchange with the cloak. The dragonmere still stood beside the carriage. The vehicle's curtains had been opened and Lady Alonia had returned inside. "It is time to leave. Time for us to part ways."

"Oh." It was all Macal could manage; he had been dreading this moment. He couldn't imagine a worse feeling than being left alone.

"From here we head north through the Rashinasti Forest and on to Varun. You must go southwest to reach Marglamesh."

"Do you have enough support to make it through the forest?" Macal asked. "Perhaps I should stay with the force and help."

"You must go your own way from this point," the Viscount said. "We will persevere; we must. Do not fear for us. Nothing further shall happen to the Princess as long as I breathe."

"How will I know where to go?" asked Macal.

"Head slightly left of the setting sun," said the dragonmere. "Always follow close to the path it burns through the sky, and you will come the

Troll King's lands."

"How long will it take? Is it even possible for me to get there in time to save my father?"

"That is something only the fates can answer," said the Princess from the carriage window. With a wry smile she added, "As for how long it will take—that will be the fun and interesting part!"

After his adventure with her in the tomb, Macal was wary of the excited look on her face. Her sense of fun was very different from his.

"Have them gather," she ordered one of the guards. As the man saluted and hurried away, Macal looked after him uncertainly.

"Have *who* gather?"

"The casters of Xazarnth. They are potent wizards in service to my father."

Macal had seen them around the camp—aged men of great intellect, sages who had long ago studied at the grand school of magic called Xazarnth. He had once heard Lalliard mention attending the school as well. As far as he knew, they were the only three casters in the cavalcade.

Mounted on their skeletal horses, the three ancient wizards soon arrived. They dismounted stiffly and bowed to the Princess.

"King's Jewel, we are ready to serve." Clad in the regal red robes of the kingdom, they spoke in unison with their heads bowed low.

"Thank you." She turned to Macal. "You are about to do something I have desired to do all my life. It will require a great effort from these men, so tremendous that once they accomplish this feat they will be rendered incapable of working magic for a full cycle of the moon. Even so, their efforts will not send you all the way to Castle Darkmoor. But it should greatly shorten the distance of your journey and thereby increase your chance of success."

"What do you mean? What are they going to do?" Macal was starting to worry. The Princess's excited smile was a warning sign, and now there was magic involved. Glancing at the dragonmere, he saw an expression of amusement on his face.

"You are about to see," the Princess was saying. "Now please mount your jotun." She beckoned the three red-robed wizards closer.

As he mounted Shelga, Macal mentally consulted the Cloak of Brinizarn. *"Do you know what they're going to do?"*

"Not a clue, but how bad could it be?"

"Maybe I should tell you everything she had us go through in the tomb."

"Perhaps now is not the best time to think about that."

The Princess was speaking again. "The means with which you are about to travel, Macal, is the means by which I initially wanted to travel to Varun. But my father would not—"

"Nor I," said the Viscount.

"Nor Viscount Razz; neither would allow me travel to such a place without a host of defenders. You see, this magic is effective only for a small amount of weight. Although not useful for an entire force, it is perfect for your needs." Her smile sparkled with mischief. "At least one of us will get to try it."

"What exactly am I *trying?*"

The eldest wizard answered him. "By use of the Flow, the magic of Aerinth, we are going to send you soaring through the sky, arcing over the world with the speed of a shooting star. Not even the fastest of dragons will be able to catch you. With luck, you will clear the borders of Elronia, and likely those of Xanga-Mor, before you land."

"F-flying?" Bewilderment made the boy stammer. "And when you say *land,* you mean safely—right? I won't be like one of those shooting stars that crashes into the earth, will I?"

The old wizard smiled at him. "Your fear is misplaced. When the spell's duration comes to an end, you shall descend from the sky as lightly as a feather. You need fear only the possibility that your landing point will be in the Dark Troll's realm. Once you land, you must make the rest of your journey on foot. But the magic shall spirit you across this realm and the next before night falls again upon us all."

"It is time to go," said Viscount Razz. Since the assault on the Princess he had grown impatient, wanting to finish this venture and return her to safety.

Princess Aeria nodded. "Yes, our journey won't be quite so speedy. Now, Macal, I gave you a promise and I will repeat it now. I will send help when I can. Have faith in that. If at all possible, you won't be alone for long."

"Thank you," the boy managed to say. As he spoke he saw the crowd of onlookers move back, leaving him at the center of an empty circle. The three wizards moved into the emptiness to form a triangle around him. Each produced two finely carved gray clay runes and held them aloft.

"Goodbye," the Princess said hurriedly. "May you succeed in your quest."

The wizards began to chant. As they did so, green light seeped from their fingers.

"Go with the blessing of Ermalon!" shouted Viscount Razz.

The wizards' intonations grew louder. Green radiance flared out to encompass their arms.

"Here we go, Thief!" said the Cloak of Brinizarn.

The wizards were nearly shouting now, the brilliance blossoming to obscure their robed figures.

"For the Crown!" shouted all the soldiers in attendance.

As the runes at last burned to ash, Macal felt himself and Shelga lift from the ground. There was only time to take a firm grip on the reins before he shot into the air and off over the countryside, leaving the royal caravan far behind.

The world whipped below Macal in a blur as he sped through the air. The ground was a rolling carpet of green far below; clouds burst apart as he tore through them, soaring higher than any bird.

He could feel Shelga shivering beneath him. Even with the hereditary fearlessness of her breed and the strict training she had endured, she was terrified by this ordeal. Macal could feel his own courage wavering. His knuckles were white from gripping the leather reins as he flew high over Elronia. He was not sure why the Viscount had told him to follow the setting sun; even if he were to try changing course, he didn't think he would succeed. It must have been the magic that was guiding Shelga. The jotun seemed to know where she was going, and nothing was going to deter her from that destination.

As the landscape fell away and he rose higher and higher, a dark blur on the ground caught his eye. Not far distant from the cavalcade he had left behind, there was an army on the move. The massive force, larger than any he had even seen, moved over the earth like a swarm of ants. At first Macal assumed they were Elronian soldiers on the march, possibly heading to the Keep of Mazzul under Moltess' lordship, but he quickly realized his mistake. These were not human soldiers. They were trolls heading away from the Keep, deeper into the ravaged land of Elronia.

His heart fell at the sight of the huge force. Their presence could only mean one thing—Lord Moltess' defenses had fallen and Elronia, his homeland, was now entirely open to invasion!

Worse, the troll force was traveling northeast, in a line that would intersect the path of the Princess's entourage. A sickening despair filled the boy; there was no way the small complement of soldiers guarding the Princess would be able to stand against such bloodthirsty opposition.

He had to go back! He had to warn them!

He yanked on the reins, but Shelga remained true to her original course.

"Turn, damn you! We have to warn them!" His shout had no effect, and regardless of how hard he pulled, the jotun did not respond.

"She can't," explained the Cloak of Brinizarn. *"It is part of the magic. Once a direction is chosen, it cannot be altered."*

Macal's frustration boiled over. "How do *you* know? Are you a wizard?"

"No, but I have served many of them. And you—how many have you served?"

Macal was too angry and sickened by helplessness to answer. All he could do was look down uselessly as he passed over the troll army below. In his heart he knew the monsters were going to annihilate the only friends he had ever had.

CHAPTER 25

The Princess and her small army rode northward with haste towards the Rashinasti Forest. Even though they had used several days helping Macal, Aeria still hoped there was time to get to Varun so that she could request an alliance with the hobgoblins.

She didn't regret her decision to help Macal. She did admit to herself, more than once, that she wished he hadn't gone away so quickly. She had only just started to know him and something in her wanted to learn even more about him.

She looked out the window at the passing landscape of hillocks and continued her wistful musings.

Viscount Razz rode at the front of the cavalcade, leading them in the most direct path he could toward the forest. He had spent the ride planning how best to navigate safety through the dark forest with the reduced number of soldiers that remained.

Too many strange things lived in the nefarious forest. For reasons lost to the ages it was now overrun and haunted by the risen dead. It was a place of fell creatures and doom to those who ventured in without caution.

In addition to the vengeful animated skeletal remains of innumerable creatures, there were many other hazards. There were the foul ilps, strange vine-like creatures that had long agile stems that ended in bulbous spheres. From these spheres protruded flailing tentacles ending in dark pink poisonous suckers. Razz had heard prior to leaving Keratost that the tentacles allowed the ilps to feed off the dreams of those they latched onto, draining them painfully out of their victim's mind—and as a side effect, tearing away part of their victim's intellect.

The depraved forest was also filled with natural hazards. One was the Ever Sinking Marsh, and all who entered the area were rumored to be pulled to the core of the world. There were also stories that the earth itself was alive and wicked in places. He had heard that it could rise up and mold itself like clay attacking all who dared trod upon it.

He didn't know how many of these stories were true, as not many people dared venture into the forest, but to be safe he tried to view them all as truthful. Bearing all that in mind, he hadn't come up with any plan of merit that would offer them safe passage through. And he had no idea how they would make it back through the forest after their errand was done.

As he swept his gaze over the horizon in routine survey the Viscount saw a rider fast approaching from a line of trees to the West. It took a moment for the shape to become recognizable to his red reptilian eyes. It was the scout Fenral.

The scout was riding toward him at great speed, his grimy olive hooded cloak fluttering behind him. Fenral had been appointed Drennin's replacement by the Viscount. He was not as sturdy a man as Drennin was, but the dragonmere thought he did his job well.

I'm running out of scouts, thought the Viscount as the rider came closer.

Viscount Razz couldn't tell whether or not he should be concerned. He tried to read the man's face as he approached, but it was of no help. Fenral's face always had a dark and solemn, if not grave, expression.

"I have a dire report," he announced. His horse turned about to keep pace with the Viscount's.

"Then speak it quickly," ordered the Viscount.

"A host comes from the west," Fenral replied.

"How large of a force?" asked the dragonmere.

"Massive."

Viscount Razz knew that Fenral was not one for exaggeration. He lacked the imagination for that kind of thing. The Viscount's face grew grim. "We must change course. We can't let the Princess come to harm. Come, let's inform her."

As the dragonmere turned his horse around the scout said, "I fear we may to be late for that."

The Viscount paused. "For what?

"For changing course."

"Why?" asked the Viscount, afraid of the answer.

"I think they saw me," Fenral admitted in shame.

The flying magic swept the boy and his steed along at great speed. Small forests appeared on the horizon and swiftly fell behind to be lost from sight. To the south a large blue-green disk passed by, surrounded by evergreen trees in a basin of rolling hills—a lake many times larger than the one Macal had swum in back home in Hormul.

His thoughts were in turmoil. *How many people in this world was he going to lose?* He had lost his uncle, Corporal Mercule, and countless soldiers of the Royal Guard who had befriended him; now the trolls would likely kill even more. He knew they would; it was what always happened. The trolls had taken everyone from him except his mother, but he had lost her too. With each passing second his hatred for the trolls grew. He had never imagined he could feel such fury, such hatred for another living creature, but he hated the vile creatures with his entire being.

"That is why you have to continue forward," declared the Cloak, cutting into the boy's dark thoughts. *"The trolls have your father, but he still may live. He can be saved. He can be the one the trolls don't take from you. There is also a possibility that the Princess's cavalcade may reach the forest before the trolls cross their path. They are a smaller force and can travel much faster. There's a chance they will never be seen."*

"Didn't you see how near those monsters already were to the caravan?" Macal shouted aloud. "As soon as we were aloft I could see them. That's how close they are! If the Princess does not ride in all haste, troll scouts will surely spot the caravan, recognize its insignia, and know who is in the procession. Once they realize it is the Princess of the Kingdom, do you think anything will stop them from giving chase? After the King and Queen, she is the ultimate prize for them."

"Viscount Razz will let no harm befall her."

"What?" Macal would have given the cloak an incredulous look if he had thought it could see his face. "He has already let her be harmed once. And she snuck away from him to enter the tomb. You give the Viscount too much credit; he is not powerful enough to protect her from a huge army of murdering trolls."

"I'm just trying to make you see the other side of things, Thief! You could be wrong."

"I hope that I am. But I know my luck, and the danger it brings those around me."

Silence fell on this exchange. A short time later Macal caught his breath as the Fields of Garune, located on the eastern side of Lord Moltess' Keep of Mazzul, came into view. The boy was so high in the air that he could barely make out details, but even so it was evident that carnage had been wrought on the plains below. Fallen bodies both troll and human, lay scattered everywhere.

Lord Moltess' fields, once green, were now red with blood. This was as far as the trolls had ever managed to penetrate in their attempts to pass into human lands through the stone valley blocked by the Keep. This time they had come through the Rashinasti Forest and attacked the back side of the fortress, opening the main conduit into Elronia for the rest of their forces. Macal recalled his uncle telling him that it was King Orgog who had given the trolls craft and intelligence in their strategies. Their army was still chaotic and cruel, but their former lack of discipline had been exchanged for cunning.

It wasn't long until he passed over the great fortified keep, normally bristling with numerous spires and towers. Evidence of its fall could be seen everywhere. Countless spires had been toppled, walls had been razed, and smoke from innumerable fires billowed from the remains of once magnificent structures. The pearly clouds through which he had flown only moments earlier became black with hot smoke from the smoldering fortress.

Macal's eyes stung as he flew clear of the choking darkness and left the ruined keep in his wake. On the southwestern horizon he could make out the barricade of mountains that defended Elronia from Xanga-Mor and the territories beyond. Soon he passed their high gray peaks and flew into a foreign land for the first time in his life. He was amazed at how fast and how far he had gone.

Although the slaughter he had seen on the Fields of Garune had shocked him in its atrocity, it paled in comparison to the gruesome sights that met his eyes as he passed over Xanga-Mor. This new land of ashen, chalky grasslands, lowlands, and marsh contrasted sharply with Elronia, where the terrain was lush and green with trees, grass, and flowers. Xanga-Mor was dismal, bleak, and gray, as if all color and life had been washed from it and drained into Narekisis itself.

Surveying the landscape below him, the boy recalled some of what his uncle had told him about this kingdom, where his father had frequently been stationed. It was a country torn and conquered by the trolls, who had destroyed most of the major cities. Only a few villages had escaped harm, the rest falling victim to the whims of the savage monsters.

Evidence of the troll occupation was everywhere. This was a land ravaged by war. As Melkes had explained, Xanga-Mor had not seen peace for several hundred years—not since the trolls had begun to desire more power and territory. Marglamesh was like a hammer that kept pounding this land, crushing all hope of life and happiness. Since the Troll Kings decided Elronia was their next prize, things had only gotten worse. Humans were now all but extinct in Xanga-Mor; most had fled the brutality of their troll masters to other realms. The remainder had been forced into submission by their new lords, treated like slaves, starved, and tormented. The trolls were merciless conquerors. Macal shivered in his saddle at the thought that this terrible fate would befall Elronia as well, if his people lost this war.

Xanga-Mor was now merely a scarred roadway between two warring kingdoms. How many battles had been fought here? How many people, how many soldiers from distant kingdoms, had died in this foreign land?

Macal was relieved to know he wouldn't have to set foot down there, so wretched did the place look. As far as he could see, everything was in ruins.

In this fallen land he was unlikely to find succor from its savage conquerors.

He had never been so far from home, so far from the world that he knew. The vista below him was beyond anything he had ever imagined could exist. From his uncle's stories he had known that the world held places of true splendor, but not that it harbored sights so abominable as this.

This was where the world came to die, he thought.

What few trees he could see were lifeless and skeletal. Nowhere was there even a scrap of green. It was as if the mountain range he had just crossed was more than a barrier to keep out enemies; it seemed to keep life at bay as well. This was where his father had fought so many battles, defending his homeland as the head of the Amber Dragoons. In this bleak land Bertran Teel had defeated the last Troll King and claimed the enchanted silver sword Alrang-Dal as his own.

He turned for a final look at his homeland diminishing behind him. As he looked upon its beauty he hoped to the gods that he would see it again.

Viscount Razz rushed back to the Princess's carriage. On the way he called out orders to the men to ready for battle. He called another to pull down her standard, so that if they were attacked the enemy might not know who they had come upon.

Hearing his shouts Princess Aeria opened her curtain and looked out. From the look of his stern countenance she didn't expect good news.

"My Jewel," he began in even more seriousness than usual, "a large troll force marches upon us from the west. It's very likely that they are aware of our presence."

Her face went pale. "What do we do?"

The dragonmere looked up and down the file of men. He shook his head. "I don't know. We are too few already."

Before further comment could be made an alarmed shout came from the front of the procession. The Viscount craned his head on his long neck for a better view. A swarm of hulking trolls were stomping out of the copse Fenral had emerged from just moments earlier, crushing and snapping the foliage with an eager ferocity for battle.

"To arms!" he commanded. "To arms!" Drawing his sword, he kicked his jotun into action, and rushed toward to the approaching enemy.

The Princess watched him go. "Get me my saber!" she demanded of her two handmaidens.

"Your what, Princess?" asked Greseldal, one of the aged ladies.

"My saber. My sword! I need it."

"For what?" asked Dreseldal in bewilderment, sister to Greseldal and another handmaiden.

The Princess gave them an equally puzzled look. "Didn't you hear? We're being attacked. I have to help!" Outside they could hear the two forces come together in an initial deafening clash. Screams, howls, and the sound of armor being rent suddenly filled the air.

"I know," Dreseldal replied. "But you can't help. It's dangerous."

"Stop talking to me and find my saber!"

Reluctantly, Greseldal pulled the Princess's weapon out from underneath their seats. Aeria snatched it out of her hand, kicked the carriage door open, ready to jump out.

Instantly it was slammed back shut. "Stay in there." Viscount Razz came riding into view again. "We are outmatched. More and more of them continue to spill from the woods. If we are to have any chance of survival we must retreat." Sounds of war, weapons and pain rose even higher. "We must go now or we will all be lost."

The Princess looked out the window facing the battle. Her hand went to her mouth in shock. She snapped back the curtain not wanting to see anymore.

"There are so many," she muttered.

"And more still come. We must go."

"Yes," she agreed shakily.

Many soldiers were dying, unable to defend against the overwhelming number of opponents. The trolls swarmed out into a misshapen crescent line hoping to encircle their foes. Even with the troll army's lack of discipline the circle was already closing around the humans.

"Retreat! Retreat!" roared Viscount Razz. Nearby soldiers, relieved to hear the command, took up the call and echoed it up and down the line.

A third of the Elronian soldiers had already fallen in the initial clash. The luckier ones fled on horses. Others ran on foot. Those unable to retreat fast enough were quickly hacked apart by the monsters.

The dragonmere noticed Fenral nearby. "Where can we go?" he asked.

"There's Lord Vrex's small stronghold several miles to the east. If we hurry we may be able to defend ourselves from there."

Princess Aeria overheard the exchange. She had composed herself again. "Let's go to the keep," she commanded. "That will draw the trolls away from whatever they were sent to originally target. The longer we keep them there, the longer they are not commencing this sort of slaughter all over Elronia."

With Fenral leading the way, the soldiers jumped to follow her orders.

Razz gave the Princess a solemn look. He would rather the trolls pillage the entire land than let harm come to her, but it was too late. The order had gone out. Now all they could do was try to survive. Hopefully Lord Vrex had a significantly sized host he could quickly muster.

They also both knew that this encounter, because of the cost of men, also meant it was unlikely they would ever make it through the Rashinasti Forest and to Varun for a parley with the hobgoblins.

"Retreat! Retreat!" Viscount Razz growled again. By now the whole force had received the order. The dragonmere, dripping with sweat from the exertion of battle, stayed by the Princess's carriage as it pressed eastward. Several times already he had to fend off trolls who had hacked through the line of men, drawn to the elegance of the carriage, a prize among the cavalcade.

"For gold and glory!" they shouted just before the dragonmere cut their greedy bodies down.

Fenral was in the front, leading the men to Lord Vrex's stronghold. He had informed the Viscount that it was not far to the east, over several hills and through a thin line of trees.

Maintaining vigilance from the rear the dragonmere was forced to watch the slaughter continue. Many of their soldiers were unable to withdraw from the line of battle, too engaged for a chance to escape. Others couldn't outrun the pursuing monstrosities and their long striking range.

He watched as some trolls aimed their vicious blows at the mounts, causing the steeds to crumple to the ground and render their riders prone. The trolls then swarmed upon the fallen soldiers, putting them to merciless ends.

Orders bellowed from the back ranks of the troll force. Their leader had finally emerged from the woods. The dragonmere didn't understand the words, but he quickly learned their meaning.

Heeding their leader's commands, the trolls withdrew from their combatants and in an organized frenzy charged forward toward the Princess's carriage, stomping on the injured human soldiers not fast enough to get out of the way.

The dragonmere's heart went still. Even without their standard flying, the Troll Chieftain must have surmised who they had come across, and now the knowledge of the Princess's presence gave the brutes insane fervor and vitality. A crazy blinding lust for glory filled their sick amber eyes as they glared hungrily at the carriage.

Dreams of glory quickly filled their horrid minds. The troll who struck down the Princess of the Elronian Kingdom would be honored above all, except King Orgog himself. The only greater achievement they could fathom would be striking down the human king himself. The troll to slay the Princess would likely be granted a castle full of gold, be granted a station of honor, would live out the rest of his days with eighteen wives, along with the adoration of Marglamesh.

In greedy madness the horde of trolls yelled war cries as they bounded toward the Princess's carriage.

Razz rode forward and urged the Princess's unicorns and horses faster. His heart was frozen in his chest. Each glance backward diminished any hope of Princess Aeria's survival. He avoided her gaze. He didn't want to see the fright in her blue eyes.

As the trolls bound closer and closer, the dragonmere realized that, for the first time, he might not be able to protect his charge, and that he could fail the King in his duty to keep Princess Aeria safe.

As night set in the remnants of the Elronian army fled for their lives, hoping to find sanctuary and reinforcements at Lord Vrex's stronghold. Without extra soldiers and a strong defensible structure, Razz knew there was little hope of their survival. With great effort they had managed to put some distance between themselves and the trolls. Viscount Razz had not left the perimeter of the Princess's carriage as he continued to protect her from the more fleet trolls who were able to draw near.

Finally the humans broke through the line of trees and saw a small castle that lay in the midst of the lake at the base of a long slope. What little hope the dragonmere had that they might survive the day disappeared as his eyes fell upon the place.

It wasn't a castle full of men with a great fortified wall for defense. Instead it was in ruin, collapsed into rubble and overgrown in ivy. The castle sat upon a great expanse of flattened rock a hundred feet offshore of a wide, still lake. The top quarter of the rough limestone walls on the north and east sides of the once great fortress had collapsed and crumbled into the water. What the ivy didn't cover was taken over by weeds, moss, or other growth.

At one time Castle Vrex had five peaked towers, but three were now toppled over, worn away by time and weather. All the balconies and gables were also sundered. It was obvious to him that the place had long ago been thoroughly ransacked. It was now just a disintegrating husk of the great structure it had once been. He couldn't even find a single stained glass window left that had not been smashed apart.

A once elegant archway led to a stone arced bridge that spanned the majority of the way from the shoreline to the small island castle. The final portion of the dilapidated bridge was completed by an open drawbridge.

Viscount Razz didn't know the history of the place, and at the moment he didn't really care. He just needed to safeguard the Princess. He had hoped to find reinforcements here. Fenral hadn't explained the state of the place when he mentioned it as a place of refuge. It was no longer a formidable bastion of safety, but they didn't have any other options. Looking at the survivors of the company he calculated that they were down to a fourth of the men that had left Keratost on this journey.

He could see morale fading on the faces of the soldiers as they to examined the castle, and heard the harsh battle cries from behind. At the moment, he had no words of inspiration for them.

"Get in and close the drawbridge!" he ordered as they rode down the slope toward the castle. The men heeded his orders, hurried up over the bridge, and hacked their way through ivy blocking the gateway.

Princess Aeria looked out her window again. She had never seen so many trolls. She wondered if this might be the largest host of them to ever march within Elronia. There were hundreds and hundreds of the monsters charging forward in dark glee as if they knew they had already won the battle. How she would she be able to send help to Macal if she couldn't even help herself?

She could hear the brutes laughing and mocking their prey as they continued to pursue and slay stragglers.

A voice, magically enhanced to the volume of thunder, issued from the rear of the troll force. It spoke in the common tongue of Elronia. "These fiends and demons ripped apart the great Keep of Mazzul stone by stone. They crushed it to dust. This place won't save you. Your blood will spill. You will die on this ruin!"

Viscount Razz looked back to see the Troll Chieftain, a smile of merciless pleasure upon his grotesque face. He rode high upon a massive great beast. It was shiny and black like an eel, with three serpentine heads on long scaled necks. It trod forward on thick stumpy legs, its claws tearing up gouts of grassy soil with each step.

Even from this distance the dragonmere could see clarity and sharpness in the Chieftain's eyes. He realized the Chieftain was more intelligent than most of his race. If he had taken Mazzul Keep there was obviously a cunningness about him, and his words now were spoken to inspire his troops while also further demoralizing the opposition.

Soon they were across the bridge. Men ran to the gate towers and immediately began turning the winches to raise the drawbridge. Slowly it began to rise.

The Viscount looked up at the portcullis as he crossed into the courtyard. It was the castle's second layer of defense behind the raised drawbridge. It was bent, rusty and mangled up in its chute. *It wasn't going to be of any use.*

To quicken the pace of closing the drawbridge, the dragonmere sprang off his steed and ran into northern tower to help turn the winch. The top half of this tower had long ago snapped off and was now half sunken into the lake. The inside of the place was filled with rubble and debris. Fortunately they found that the winch was still accessible.

Even with his strong arms helping the drawbridge still rose too slowly. The rusty gears and lack of care made the task nearly impossible to do with any sort of speed.

The bridge was only half raised when the trolls got to it. Many of the creatures leapt up, grabbed ahold of the bridge with their thick brown and green fingers, and dangled their weight on it. Others, who were taller, simply reached up and tried to yank it back down.

Inside the castle the Elronian soldiers struggled mightily to raise the drawbridge, knowing it was the only thing that might save their lives. As many men as possible grabbed a hold of the winches and tried to help wind them up.

Other men had made their way to the crumbling parapets and were volleying arrow after arrow at the trolls pulling on the end of the drawbridge. Several of the pierced creatures fell heavily into the rocky water.

Even so, three trolls were able to pull themselves up over the edge of the drawbridge. They charged down it and into the castle, wielding large stone-edged axes and bloodstained clubs, cutting down a few men in surprise.

"For gold and glory!" they howled as they struck at more of the soldiers.

"Now where's da' Princess?" growled another, his club collapsing the skull of a nearby man. "I ain't ever eaten royal meat before!"

The soldiers quickly rallied, as they had the three trolls outnumbered. Without further loss, a moment later the castle was once more theirs.

Inch by inch the drawbridge continued to rise. It was now over halfway up. As it rose so did the hopes of the soldiers that they might survive the onslaught.

Inside the northern tower, as Razz and the men strained to reel up the drawbridge, the rusty chain on the winch suddenly snapped under the stress. With trolls still hanging from its edge, the men in the southern tower couldn't hold the drawbridge up by themselves. It snapped open, crushing several trolls beneath as it crashed down.

Seeing their good fortune, a host of trolls ran forward over the drawbridge. The men in the southern tower attempted to raise the bridge again, but now with the weight of the trolls upon it they couldn't make it budge.

"Hold the entrance!" shouted the soldiers as they ran to block the threshold.

Standing near the back of her force, on the collapsed remains of the castle proper, Princess Aeria had just confiscated a bow and quiver of arrows from a nearby soldier when the chain broke and the bridge fell back open. Her mouth became a thin firm line, her jaw rigidly defiant, as she notched a green feathered arrow and let it fly. It sunk deeply into the lead troll's chest. Without a faltered step the creature continued forward, pulling out the arrow as if it was just a minor annoyance. She ignored the pain in her arm that still remained from where the assassin had stabbed her and drew another arrow.

Viscount Razz emerged out of the north tower and took in the deteriorating state of the battle. He could see everything was going wrong. He could see they were going to lose. He could see they were going to die. *He could see the Princess was going to die.*

Drawing his sword, he glanced over at Princess Aeria Stormlion long enough to catch her gaze. Once he had it he gave her a slight solemn nod. Then Viscount Razz Munin, Royal Advisor and Ruler of Ermalon, turned and charged out of the castle alone and into the writhing and seething sea of rampaging trolls.

Macal didn't know how long he had been flying. He passed over a bleak landscape studded with desolate, ruined temples and shrines to long-dead gods. There were barren fields, murky rivers, an endless succession of battlefields. The sun had begun to sink below the horizon ahead when Macal, who had just awoke from an exhausted doze, felt Shelga give a sudden jolt as if she had hit an invisible bump in the sky.

Racing out of the darkness came a small disgusting looking demon, "Yer magic is fer the wimps'es! No mores the flying for you's! Down you goes, down to your dooms'es!" Its voice shrieked like a banshee.

Macal could barely see the maroon-colored creature in the dimness. It was no bigger than his backpack, with a big bloated pink stomach.

"Rinaskul's magic is the most powerfuls of alls!" The creature smiled wickedly—even in the low light its grin was easily visible. Macal, Shelga, and the cloak felt the power behind their magic flight dissipate as the spell was cancelled by the infernal demon. They rapidly began descending toward the ground.

"No! No! No!" Macal couldn't believe what was happening. "We can't go down here. We need to get closer!" The words were barely out of his mouth when he, Shelga, and the cloak crashed down into Xanga-Mor.

CHAPTER 26

The Viscount, hoping to buy the army enough time to close the gate, charged forward into the mad monstrous horde. His sword sliced and cut in a shiny red blur. He had to force the trolls back off the drawbridge before it was completely lost to the enemy. Even if he succeeded, he didn't know if closing the bridge would save the men and the Princess. *But what choice did he have?* he thought. *Some chance was better than none.*

He could see the front line of trolls were surprised by his insane charge—it was evident in their eyes that even they understood this wouldn't end well for the dragonmere.

But these trolls and their Chieftain had never fought a dragonmere, he thought. *And most definitely not the would-be King of Ermalon who bore the ring of his kingdom.* The Viscount smiled grimly as he hewed into another reeking brute.

It didn't take long for the trolls to recover from the shock of his valiant assault. They swelled and came down on him like a crashing wave, overwhelmed with hunger for slaughter and blood. While they didn't know who he was exactly, they did realize he was a person of importance, a leader of the humans. With his death the humans would fall all the easier.

The dragonmere continued to cut, stab, and slash as the trolls surrounded him. To his rear, one of them struck true—the creature's axe sheared through the dragonmere's scaled thigh. A cheer of malevolent joy rose from the beasts as the Viscount fell to one knee.

"Down da' lizard runt goes!" jeered the troll who had struck the blow.

"And soon the rest of 'em!" added another, the fattest, heaviest of them all.

"Today Marglamesh wins the war!" laughed a third one-armed troll.

"Yeah, today, the humans begin to fall," growled a fiend with three eyes and a sickly violet tongue long enough to reach his sternum.

"Let's kill dis' worm, den gets the rest of 'em!" added another.

The trolls furiously attacked the dragonmere. They landed a series of blows that cut, stabbed, struck, and bludgeoned him. The stunned soldiers couldn't believe the dragonmere had left the castle and ran into the troll force. As the assault on the Viscount continued they watched as he fell to both knees.

The men in the southern tower continued to try in vain to raise the drawbridge, even though the trolls and the Viscount still stood upon it.

Princess Aeria watched, opened mouthed, as the Viscount disappeared from sight, swarmed by the murderous war band.

"No! No! No!" she shouted as she unleashed arrow after arrow through the castle's gateway into the troll horde. The cut on her arm the assassin had made opened and began to bleed, but she didn't stop firing arrows.

"My lady," said an anxious voice next to her. Aeria tore her eyes away from the trolls to see that it was Lady Greseldal. "We must flee now! We can escape over the fallen wall at the rear of the castle while the trolls are distracted. We can get you away from here."

Aeria paused and gave her a frigid look. "No. I'm not leaving these men. And I'm not leaving Razz."

"But My Jewel," begged Lady Dreseldal, who also stood nearby. "We must. Look at the men. They know they're not going to win. Their morale is gone! The Viscount is doing this to save you. Don't let his sacrifice be wasted. We must run!"

"I told you, I'm not leaving!" The Princess let fly another arrow. "Now go and find me more arrows. Quickly!"

Razz had been struck so many times he had lost count. He was weak. He felt the black dizziness coming upon him. No longer able swing his sword it fell from his grasp. Blurry though they were, he could see the trolls smiling cruelly at him.

As he fell to the ground he used the last of his remaining strength to raise his hand, to feebly hold aloft the Ring of Ermalon. The ring of the king. The trolls looked at him curiously. Several of them eyed the ring greedily.

Then the ring burst to life like an exploding emerald star and the trolls saw no more.

Macal was hurled to the ground. His backpack fortunately absorbed some of the impact. Shelga careened across the ground beside him. She was fortunate to be able to glide them down before the magic completely wore off, preventing their descent from being a deadly plummet.

Before Macal could fully recover himself he heard the demon's voice again. "So much the funs to have with the you. They tolds me to do's whatsevers I wantses!"

The boy turned toward the sky and saw the creature descending upon him. In its tiny slimy hand was a coil of black smoky magic, which it hurled at Macal. He was able to just roll out of the way as the mystical spear disintegrated the patch of ground where he just was.

Macal scrambled to his feet and clumsily yanked his sword from its sheath. He saw Shelga jump up and disappear into the gathering shadows of the night, the magical flight and aerial attack too much for her to take. *At least she's okay.*

Macal had no idea what the creature attacking them was. He hoped the cloak did. *"What is that thing?"*

"Something trying to kill you, of course."

"Well, that I got. But why?"

"Why are you asking me? I'm not the one attacking you. Ask him. Or it. Or whatever it is."

"I could have sworn the Princess gave you to me because you would help me."

"She may have been wrong."

"Obviously."

Rinaskul threw another smoky bolt, obliterating the ground near Macal's feet. The boy ran and hid behind a formation of rocks. When he dared to peak out Rinaskul sent another bolt, shattering the rock in front of him. The boulder burst apart and hit him with a spray of rock.

"Watch it!" the cloak shouted at him. *"You're going to get me torn!"*

"What does it matter. You don't do anything anyway."

"You're going to be the deads!" taunted Rinaskul in a singsong voice. "So very deads."

Macal looked around for a new place to hide. As he looked behind them something caught his eye and he blinked. In the gathering gloom he thought he could see a structure not far away. "I have an idea," he muttered.

"Oh, this should be good."

Macal didn't bother to respond and instead turned and ran. As he got closer to the shape that he had seen he could see it was the ruin of a manse, its tall outline barely visible in the darkening night.

"The chases!" laughed the demon in merriment. "I loves the chases." Behind him the demon flapped its tiny wings in pursuit, throwing bolt after bolt at him.

Macal got to the manse and squeezed through the crumbling entrance as magical blasts tore into the walls around him. He moved down the hall to a less dilapidated part of the building. The heavy dust of death and decay lay on everything. He backed into a doorway and waited for the demon to come. He knew that outside the creature could easily hover out of his reach; if it really wanted to kill him, now it would have to come down within range of his sword.

Several minutes passed as he watched the doorway and nothing happened. His breathed rapidly and could swear he was sweating, but he was so numb with fear that he couldn't feel it.

"Here's he is!" said a malicious voice behind him. "We founds him!"

In fright Macal spun about looking for the demon, not knowing where it was. Then he saw it. Rinaskul was flying down from the upper floors through a rent in the ceiling behind him. Without thinking he slashed out with his sword. The demon panicked and flapped its wings backward.

"What do you want?" shouted Macal as the demon retreated to safe distance.

"You. The deads."

"Why?"

"Becauses it's the funs. Well, and becauses we was asked to."

Asked to? thought Macal bewildered. "Who asked you to kill me?"

"It doesn't the matters." Rinaskul launched an attack with another mystical projectile. It missed but hit the wall behind Macal, causing part of it to disappear in black smoke. The rest of the wall, now no longer supported, fell. Macal was hit by several pieces of falling masonry. One piece struck his forehead just over his eye, and blood started to drip down his face.

He knew he was running out of time. If he was going to survive he had to attack. Wiping the blood from his eye with his sleeve, he charged forward toward the disgusting demon.

Rinaskul was taken by surprise, never expecting the young boy to be so aggressive. He tried to retreat again, but it was too late. The boy was too close. Macal swung his sword and its edge sliced true, right across the creature's bloated belly.

With a terrible scream of pain, and dark, pulsing magic bleeding from the wound in his belly, the demon faded to nothingness as he retreated to the Abyss.

After taking a moment to catch his breath and bandage his forehead, Macal went outside into the night to find Shelga. Not long after he exited the manse she trotted toward him out of a line of blighted trees.

He looked around, had no idea where he was, and came to a terrible realization. With the magic flying spell broken, he was going to have to travel the rest away on foot.

The Viscount's ring exploded with power, unleashing the magic of Ermalon. In a spinning disk of emerald light the energy surged out from the ring and sliced through every troll on the drawbridge.

Dozens of trolls fell and disintegrated into radiant ash as the force cut through them. The Viscount watched as a second ruby on the ring surrounding the emerald went dim, its magic forever spent.

All who were still alive to bear witness to the battle were stunned by the dragonmere's incredible assault.

Even from her position at the rear of the castle Aeria could see the grave state of the dragonmere's body. Seeing him like that made her want to cry, but she refused to let tears escape her eyes. Even if the battle ended now, she couldn't see how he could possibly survive the grievous wounds he now bore.

The trolls didn't advance further across the bridge. Suddenly they wanted nothing to do with the strange creature upon it. From his position at the back to the troll ranks, upon his monstrous steed, the Chieftain saw them hesitate.

"March or die!" shouted the Chieftain, his voice a thunderous boom. "March for glory or die by my hand!"

Upon hearing their commander's threat the trolls reluctantly advanced. The dragonmere was about to collapse; already his head had lowered to the ground. No longer did he have the strength to lift it.

I could save him, Princess Aeria thought. *There had to be a way.*

"Raise the drawbridge!" screamed Aeria as an idea came to her. The Viscount still lay on the drawbridge—if they closed it now he would slide down and be inside with them. *Yes*, she thought, *we can save him. I can save him.*

Fortunately the soldiers inside the tower were already doing as she bid. They also saw the chance that Viscount Razz had given them.

Razz, though, had other plans. Realizing he was being lifted away from the battle, he mustered the strength to roll painfully off the end of the drawbridge and onto the bridge, toward the trolls. The Princess shrieked in disbelief as he disappeared from sight over the lip.

She couldn't see what happened next, but the men on the wall could. They saw the dragonmere land heavily on the stone bridge and then, weakly fluttering his eyelids to regain some clarity of vision, he aimed his ring at the approaching army. Three blinding bursts expelled from the ring. When the soldiers could see again the entire bridge was clear of foes. Nothing was left of them but ash being carried away on a soft wind.

The third, fourth, and fifth of the eight rubies of the Ring of Ermalon went dark as death.

The Elronians erupted into cheer as a hope sparked to life in them that they just might survive this battle.

Rest. That thought was uppermost in Macal's mind after their hard landing and the fight with Rinaskul. While the flight had been more or less effortless, he was still exhausted from the previous night: his adventures in the tomb, followed by the goblin's attack. Since then there had been no time to rest. If he was to gather his strength for the final leg of his journey to Marglamesh, now was his only chance.

By the light of the rising moon he tied Shelga to one of the blighted trees. Then he went back into the manse and found an empty room that had a large window from which he could see the jotun. Wearily he slumped to the ground and removed a packet of soldier's rations and the water canteen from his backpack. While the meager meal was not particularly appealing, at least it satisfied his hunger and thirst.

Out of the window he could see the moon hanging full and bright in the sky above. Macal spread out his gray wool bedroll and lay down. The Cloak of Brinizarn was pulled tight about him for warmth, but sleep would not come. Regardless of what had just happened to him, only thoughts of the Princess filled his mind. The knowledge that he had left Princess Aeria and the dragonmere behind, with the invading trolls so close, brought pangs of guilt that swarmed around him like stinging insects.

What else could I do?

He hadn't expected an answer, but one came. *"She had the dragonmere with her,"* said the small voice inside him that wasn't afraid to be optimistic, a voice that wasn't the cloak's. *"Viscount Razz would die before he let harm befall her."*

"There were just so many of them," Macal said to himself.

"There's always a chance. Look at how far we've come already. Never did we think we could have done this, but we have. Anything is possible in this world. There's always a chance." As the voice fell silent, Macal dozed for a few moments and dreamed of Uncle Melkes.

He could see his uncle's face clearly before him. Gentle, caring, and loving. Not dead, but alive. The two of them were sitting on their porch back on the farm. The overhang of the roof blocked the scorching sun, offering a pleasant refuge on the hot summer day.

Macal had been here before. He had lived this moment, and now once more it was coming alive. His uncle turned to him, a twinkle in his wise eyes. "Want to hear a story?"

"Is there going to be a moral to it?"

"Of course. Why else would we tell stories?"

"Because they're fun? And to pass the time?"

"Time should never be passed just to be passed. It should be enjoyed and appreciated, because every person gets only a little of it. Besides, there are plenty of chores we could do *just* to pass the time."

"Well, I *appreciate* the fun of the story, if that helps."

Uncle Melkes' smile was like a spring day, brimming with light and beginnings. "I'll take that as a yes. This is a story about Kelspar—a young boy, maybe just a little older than you are now, who lived in a small village at the base of the largest volcano in the land. That was the great Mount Ash in the land of Garrubia, just south of the Ascerian Forest, home of the fey folk. Garrubia was a quiet magical kingdom much like the others on the eastern continent.

"Kelspar was an orphan. He had no family he could call his own, nor any that he could remember. He lived on the streets and felt hunger every day of his life. He longed to be like the other children, happily living on their great estates or in tiny houses surrounded by caring families. All Kelspar wanted in the world was a family of his own.

"Every day he would pray to the gods, begging to be welcomed into a family. At last Sarya, the Goddess of Wisdom and Learning, took pity on the boy who seemed so desperate and alone. She flew down to him from the heavens, right in the town plaza where all could see. In her majesty she resembled a young and beautiful elfin woman with dark hair and intense blue eyes. So miraculous was the coming of the Goddess that all the townspeople fell to their knees before her, revering her with downcast eyes.

"Her voice drifted over them like a whisper in a dream. 'For the lonely suffering you have endured, Kelspar, Orphan Son of Garrubia, I grant you the power to change your world. Your desires will be born to truth; by the power I bestow upon you, they will become reality. Be warned, though, mortal boy. This gift comes at a price. Each truth and dream you create will take youth from you. Use the power sparingly and well, so that you will have years to enjoy the happiness you create for yourself.'

"As unexpectedly as she had appeared, the Goddess disappeared from sight, returning to the white tower in the heavens where the gods reside. Once she had gone, the townsfolk rose from their knees and stared longingly at the blessed Kelspar. Before the goddess had come they had noticed him little and cared less, but now they eyed him like a sacred relic. Now they wanted nothing more than to be in his good graces.

"A quick-thinking maiden was the first to react. Running up to the thin, dark-haired boy, she fell to her knees before him and seized his dirty tunic with both hands.

" 'My father is ill and near death. Please, I beg of you, use your blessed power to save his life, so that he will still have years to grow old.'

"Kelspar stared down at the lovely girl, speechless with confusion. Only a few moments before, he had prayed to the gods to change his life, and unbelievably they had answered. Now he was being asked to use his new power before he had time to understand it. He stared into the maiden's beseeching green eyes, seeing the pain of her impending loss. It made his heart ache. Knowing so well how it felt to suffer, how could he not help her? It would take a little of his life, as Sarya had said, but he would be giving life to someone else. How could he refuse? No person should turn his back on another in need, he thought.

"He took the maiden's hands in his and pulled her to her feet. 'Bring your father to me, and I will expel the illness from him.'

" 'Oh, thank you, sire!' She threw her arms about him in a grateful hug and ran to get her father. The whispering crowd around Kelspar grew as they waited for the girl to return. Everyone wanted to witness the magic the goddess had bestowed.

"In a few minutes she came running back, followed by a strapping man who carried another in his arms—middle-aged, so thin and weary that it seemed Death's great black carriage might arrive for him at any moment. The crowd parted to let them through. 'This is my father,' the girl said.

"Kelspar hesitated, not knowing how to use his new power—but seeing the anguish of the dying man, he knew his decision had been the right one. Suddenly, it was as if he had always known how to harness the gift of Sarya. Placing one hand on the man's forehead and the other just above his heart, he felt the divine power pour through him. To the onlookers it appeared as a soft golden glow, an endless array of angelic feathers. As it entered the withered man he was instantly revitalized, full of vigor, healthier than he had ever been.

"The crowd gasped. Many shouted out prayers to Sarya, hoping she would grant them this extraordinary power, but as they all turned to look at Kelspar they gasped again, this time not from reverence and awe, but from shock. He was no longer a boy but a full-grown man. Everything about him had aged. He was much taller; his long brown hair hung down his back, and the lower part of his chiseled face was covered in a beard a foot in length. In that one instant, he had gone from child to adult, all the years in between forever gone.

"Kelspar looked down at himself, his consternation slowly subsiding. The transformation wasn't so terrible. Now he was big enough to do a man's work; he could get a job and no longer have to endure the pain of hunger. As the maiden's father ran forward and clasped him in a strong hug of gratitude, his lingering doubts vanished. He had given this man back his life, and it was worth it.

"Perhaps he would use the power again, just once more, for himself—to give himself a family and a home in which to share their comfort. But no

sooner had the maiden and her father departed to enjoy their blessed
fortune than a young man gently grasped his arm. Kelspar recognized him
as a local shepherd.

" 'Please, angel,' he began. 'You have much life left within you. Can you
find it within your blessed soul to help me as well? You are still young, with
plenty of vitality left in your life. You shouldn't fear using your power to
help me.'

"Kelspar was taken aback by man's use of a holy title he felt he did not
deserve. 'I am no angel.'

" 'But you are! You work miracles on mortal men for your god. What
else could you be but an angel?'

" 'I am just a boy—well, a man now. A citizen of Garrubia, just like you.
I am no more divine than the cattle in the fields over there. But tell me,
what is it you wish?'

" 'My farm has been consumed by fire, and along with it, all the wool
from my sheep. Without the money from selling the wool, my homeless
family will not be able to survive. We will slowly starve to death. Please, I
have two daughters and a wonderful wife. Will you use your powers to
spare us this undeserved sentence of poverty and death?'

"Kelspar could see a pattern developing. Although the man was
desperate, like the woman who had begged him to save her father, he was
not asking something for himself. He was trying to save those he loved.
The fire had not been his fault; the Goddess of Nature was sometimes
whimsical and cruel.

"And it was true that Kelspar was still fairly young. If he gave a little
more of himself, this family wouldn't perish. Knowing the pain of hunger
and the slow withering it brought, how could he let this family suffer when
he had the power to save them?

" 'Your family shall not waste and wither,' he said. 'I shall grant your
wish. If it is wool you need to survive, then every night you shall pray to
Sarya, and when you do, the tears of faith and love that fall from your eyes
shall be threads of the purest wool. The more you pray to her, the more
Sarya will give.'

" 'I will pray every moment of every day!' swore the Shepherd, realizing
his great fortune.

" 'Then you shall have more wool than a king could buy.'

" 'Oh thank you. Thank you, Angel of Sarya. And when I pray I shall be
thinking of thanks for you!'

" 'Then let it be done!' and with that Kelspar raised his palm toward the
man. From his hand shot the divine yellow light that all had witnessed a
moment before. Arcing through the space between them, it lanced down
into the Shepherd's eyes, setting them aglow. Then the feathered light was
gone.

"A murmur grew among the watching townspeople as they turned back to Kelspar. No longer was Sarya's Chosen a young man; now he was middle-aged, his frame less robust and a slight bend to his back. His brown hair reached nearly to the ground. Seeing them staring at him, he smiled. He knew he had done the right thing in giving the shepherd the ability to spare his family from suffering.

" 'All praise Kelspar!' shouted an old woman. The rest of the crowd immediately took up the chant, but Kelspar raised his hands to silence them.

" 'Do not praise me. I've done nothing. These miracles are from Sarya herself. Let your praise fall upon her; she is the one who deserves it. Now I shall be going.' He began to make his way through the crowd. With the power to live his own life as he wished, he could still have what he needed. But he had gone only a few steps when a bent old woman slipped her bony hand into his, looking up at him with sorrowful eyes from underneath a nest of ragged gray hair.

" 'Oh, Celestial Being, oh, Great One, you must help me as you helped those others. Your bountifulness and generosity are unmatched in any land in Aerinth!'

"Kelspar's heart sank. 'What is it that you need?' He had already given up much of his life's essence to help others. How much was left? He supposed the least he could do was hear the old woman out.

" 'My son, the Huntsman—oh, Angel of Benevolence, he has disappeared. A week ago he went into the Ascerian Forest to hunt the accursed nine-headed wolves who plague that twisted place. He should have returned six days ago, and still I wait for his return. I know something has gone amiss; I fear that the wolves, rather than my son, have done the hunting. Please, oh, Divine Saint, help me find my son. You have already given more than half your life for others. Why not give a little more so that a mother can reclaim her only son?'

"Kelspar stared at her for a long moment, torn by indecision. He knew if he had lost a child of his own and she could help, he would have asked her. She was too old to go seeking her son on her own. How could he refuse? Yet the two wishes he had granted had already taken so much from him....

"As she saw his hesitation, the old woman's eyes welled with tears. This was her last hope; if it failed, she would lose her son forever. Kelspar's resistance crumbled at her look of desperation. 'Old woman, bring me a painting, any painting of oil on canvas. And do so quickly, for I fear your son is nearing oblivion.'

" 'Yes, Great One!' Hobbling back to her house, she returned with the painting he had asked for. Kelspar saw it was an ocean scene depicting merfolk, the elves of the water.

" 'I shall make a map for you and others to follow,' he told her. 'It will lead you to your son, but you must hurry if you wish to spare him the death you have so accurately foreseen. The wolves have nearly prevailed.'

" 'I will, oh Blessed Mortal,' cried the woman.

"Kelspar held the painting in front of him and waved his hand over it. As his fingers swept across its surface, the familiar yellow glow appeared. Glowing feathers danced over the paint, changing the image to one of the local landscape. A red line led into the magic forest, directly to the beleaguered Huntsman.

"By now the crowd held its breath to see what price the magic had exacted from Kelspar. They saw a bent and aged man with a great curve in his bony spine. The long hair coiling on the ground beneath him had gone gray; his bushy eyebrows were white. With a shaking hand he offered the painting to the woman. In a croaking voice he said, 'Take a few hearty men with you, and be quick. You have only until the sun begins to wane to rescue your son.'

"Several strong men equipped with swords and axes stepped up to the woman and offered to accompany her. She hastily accepted, and soon they were gone, riding off to the north and into the woods. Kelspar knew they would be successful in their quest. As for himself, he felt strange, his body gnarled and frail with age when only a little while ago he had possessed the body of a boy. Briefly he regretted using his powers, but these regrets faded. He knew he had chosen the right course in saving the lives of those who had asked him.

"He began to wonder if he still possessed enough vitality to grant his own wish of a loving family. He needed to go on his own way, to ponder what had been bestowed upon him, and whether he should use his divine power one last time, to attain his heart's desire.

"Just then the ground began to shake and the earth was torn asunder beneath his feet, heaving as if it were taking deep breaths. The panicked townsfolk screamed in terror. Many of them were hurled through the air as the land convulsed beneath them, scattering debris. On every side buildings crumbled and collapsed; in mere seconds, only wreckage remained.

"Then came a thunderous boom that deafened them all. The few who had remained standing were knocked down by the cataclysmic explosion. Dazed and cowering, they saw that the great Mount Ash had awakened. From the mouth of the volcano burst black plumes of smoke, followed by a spray of searing magma that shot thousands of feet into the air. A vast flood of flaring lava spilled down the steep slope and rushed toward them. All was lost; they had no chance of escape. Then the villagers remembered Kelspar.

" 'You must save us!' they cried. 'Only you can spare us this death! Since you have so little time left, why not use it to help others before you perish and the power is wasted? Otherwise all in the village will die!'

"Kelspar stared at them blindly. Things seemed to be happening in slow motion. The fiery discharge from the volcano hung in the air above them, a rain of red and orange that blotted out the sky. In a moment they would all be dead. The life force he had already expended had left him old and feeble. He had wanted to save his last bit of strength for his own wish—but if he did not save the town, everyone would die, himself included. He had to exercise the power again. What choice did he have? He would save all of them, himself as well, even though it meant sacrificing his own dream.

"Reluctantly surrendering his desire to love and be loved, Kelspar raised his hands to the rain of fiery death obscuring the heavens. As he turned his palms to the sky, from them sprang a mammoth cone of feathers, spreading to form a radiant dome over the village, protecting all within. The falling magma struck the divine shield, disappearing as it touched the surface. Safe within the dome, the townsfolk watched in awe as wave after wave of gushing lava was turned aside.

"The eruption was short-lived. As Mount Ash subsided, the angelic dome of feathers faded from sight. Kelspar fell to his knees, too weak to stand.

"Cheering, shouting, hugging one another in joy at their salvation, the townsfolk finally noticed him lying on the ground. They gathered around him, speaking in hushed voices. It was hard to believe that this gray, shriveled being was the boy they had known. Kelspar could no longer see them; he lay there weakly, his head lolling blindly back and forth. 'I just wanted a family,' he whispered.

"One of the townsmen knelt and lifted the ancient man's head from the hard, rocky ground of the plaza to rest on his thigh.

" 'I just wanted to be loved,' mumbled Kelspar. 'Loved.'

" 'You are loved,' the townsman said. Behind him the crowd murmured agreement. 'From this moment forth, never will there be a man more loved in all of Garrubia than Kelspar the Orphan.'

"The words brought a smile to the lips of the Chosen of Sarya. Then Kelspar, the boy who became a man to save his people, died."

Uncle Melkes' battered rocking chair creaked as he turned to look at Macal. "And that is the story of Kelspar of Garrubia."

"It couldn't have happened," Macal declared. "I don't believe it. Sarya really came to him and gave him the power to grant wishes?"

"It is not about whether you believe it or not. The truth is still the truth," Uncle Melkes countered good-humoredly. "Do you understand what the story's trying to say?"

"I don't know. All he did was help the people of the town. They just kept taking more from him, not caring what it did to him, as long as they got what they wanted."

"And what does that tell you?"

"Sometimes you can't help others, even though you want to."

"Exactly!" Uncle Melkes smiled. "You're a very smart and wise little boy; your mother would be proud of you. Kelspar's heart was in the right place. You should always help others, but sometimes you need to help yourself a little first. You have to make sure your own life is enjoyable and full."

"You mean, you can't always help everybody, but it's nice to try? Oh, and people will take advantage of you if you give them a chance?"

"Correct."

"Would you have given your life to save all those people?" asked Macal.

"Oh, I know I would have. I just might have used the four wishes differently, so that everybody got what they wanted."

"What do you mean? Give me an example."

"Well, Kelspar didn't have to use his power to help the Shepherd. If he had given himself what he wanted, a family and a home of his own, he could have sheltered the Shepherd and his family until their own farm could be rebuilt and they got back on their own feet. That would have been one wish that solved two problems." Uncle Melkes paused, looking lovingly at Macal before repeating, "Sometimes you need to help yourself a little first."

As Macal's dream ended, his uncle's story lingered in his mind. The conflicting voices inside him began to speak in unison. *"Nothing else matters now. You have to be strong. If you are leaving your friends behind, then you had better succeed in your quest. If you are not going back to save them, you'd better make sure you save your father instead. After all, you may be the only hope your friends and Elronia have left, if the Princess is captured by the trolls and an alliance with the hobgoblin warlords is not made. It's time to grow up. It's time to stop being afraid."*

"Wake up, dolt!" The scream broke into his sleep, jarring him awake. *"Wake up!"* shouted the Cloak of Brinizarn again.

"Wha—what? What is it?" The boy drowsily opened his eyes. Outside he could hear Shelga rearing and plunging beside the tree where he had tied her; the next moment she snapped her reins and galloped off into the darkness, snorting in terror.

"Trolls!" shouted the cloak. *"They're surrounding us!"*

The drawbridge of the crumbling castle finally closed. The men on the wall looked over the edge to see the Viscount, alone on the bridge, his life fading. He had turned a dull gray hue, the vitality of his green scales stripped away by the magic he had wrought upon their enemies. He looked decades older. His eyes were closed and his limp body lay unmoving in a pool of blood.

Princess Aeria rushed and mounted the west wall to see him. She was awed to see that nearly half of the trolls had been wiped out. The soldiers around her with bows continued to unleash volleys on the trolls along the shoreline. None of the monsters now dared approach the dragonmere.

The Chieftain exhorted them forward again. He was not going to let a prize like the Princess of the Kingdom escape his grasp. None of the trolls followed his command. Angrily he thrust his spear through several of the nearby cowards.

He urged his mount briskly forward, occasionally crushing his own cowardly soldiers in his progress. He didn't give them a second thought. They were useless and weak. They didn't want the glory like he did. They didn't deserve it like he did. He rode forward onto the bridge.

The archers, including Aeria, all focused their fire upon him. With a grimace he charged onward ignoring the stinging pricks of the tiny arrows. He would end the dragonmere and regain control of his shaken army. Then the rest of the enemy would fall.

Viscount Razz felt the tremors of the approaching Chieftain reverberate through the stone bridge. He forced his eyes open a slit. He had nothing left to loose. He knew how this was going to end, but he had power still to use before he let that happen.

The Troll Chieftain sped toward him. He tried to aim his ring at the approaching foe, but he was too weak and his reaction was too slow. The Chieftain was upon him.

Without a word, without a malicious smile, without acknowledgement, the Chieftain hurled his massive spear through the dragonmere's chest.

"Get up, you idiot! Trolls have found us! We have to run!"

Macal finally woke enough to realize what was happening. He felt like he had only slept a few moments. The cloak was telling him to run, but instead he stood up and pulled out his sword. *Hadn't he just sworn to stop being afraid? To finally stand up for himself?*

The cloak could still hear his thoughts. *"You really are an idiot. This is the moment you're going to choose to be brave? There is nothing to prove here! Save your bravery for a battle that matters!"*

"Stay out of my head!"

"Unfortunately I can't. Let me just say I have been in more battles than the most veteran soldiers, more than you, more even than your father. I was at the Skirmish of Wrengle and the Battle of Orfitz and the Fall of the Golden Tower. Trust me when I say that fighting this battle will yield you nothing."

"Do you ever stop rambling?"

"Just run!"

"I'm not afraid anymore!"

"Yes, you are. You forget I can read your mind! You're very much afraid. You're the same boy you always were; it's just that now you feel you have something to prove!"

"I left my friends behind!"

"You had to. You have your mission and they have theirs. And you are right. If they do get captured, then the rescue of your father and the plans are Elronia's only hope. Be brave, but don't be stupid. If you die here, right now, and the Princess is captured, all is lost. Do you understand me?"

"Yes," replied Macal reluctantly. Outside he could see the trolls hunting around for the owner of the jotun.

"Then run! And oh, leaving a jotun tied to a tree outside may not have been the best idea."

The boy scrambled out of the house and dashed into the trees. He wasn't sure which way he was running, but he hoped it was west. If he had to run, he wanted to make every step count. He had to find his father.

His escape had not gone unnoticed. The troll force followed, their footsteps thundered behind him. Once more their horrid stink was in Macal's nostrils; he had to suppress the urge to retch. They were gaining on him, taking one step to every three of his.

"They're catching up!" cried the Cloak of Brinizarn.

"I'm aware of that!"

"They're going to catch us!"

"Then shut up and do something!"

Macal raced over the rough terrain, the purple cloak streaming behind him. He darted into another copse of trees hoping to find a place to hide, the pursuing trolls were too close. He could hear their brutish talking.

"It's beens a while since we's had boy meat," laughed one of them, who sounded winded from the pursuit.

"I jus' want to hear 'is bones snap!" growled another with a menacing swing of his gnarled and knotted club.

"He is from the stinky human place, where dey all lives. He might make us sick if we eats 'im. Dey are dirty over dere!" added a third as he shambled through the trees.

"Fine," said the first. "I gets your share of the meat."

Macal tried not to listen. They were getting closer. He couldn't outrun them and he couldn't find a safe place to hide. He was out of options.

Suddenly there was a quick painful tug at his neck as one of the monsters caught hold of his trailing cloak and yanked him to a halt. Macal tried to pull free, but the huge troll's grip was like a vise.

"I gots 'im!" it announced. Its fellows ringed around Macal, cutting off all avenues of escape.

The first troll smiled cruelly. "And just in time for breakfast."

More of the hideous brutes emerged from the nighttime shadows, and soon there were nine of them. The troll holding his cloak released him and joined the others in the circle. Surrounded, Macal kept turning, trying impossibly to keep an eye on them all. In his hand Macal held his short sword as Viscount Razz had taught him. His feet moved fluidly, staying in constant motion, obeying what training he could remember.

Macal hoped the cloak had an idea of how to get out of this. *"Is it time to start praying?"*

"I think even prayer might be too late. You should have run when I told you to!"

The circle of trolls closed in. The monsters smiled in anticipation of feasting on their catch. Macal lashed out at the nearest ones, trying to keep them at bay, but they didn't seem to fear the little human boy.

"Oh, looksey," one said. "He's got a wee little weapon! How cute." All its companions laughed.

"What should I do?" Macal asked the cloak as the trolls took another step closer.

"Listen to me from now on when I tell you something! That would be a good start!"

The ring of trolls tightened more. Macal continued to turn, trying to defend all angles at once. *"You're not helping."*

"Nobody can help us from the mess you've gotten us into."

It was obvious to Macal that this was the end. He couldn't fight nine trolls. In a second all their ferocious weapons would be put to use—swords and axes, clubs and spears.

As the trolls raised their weapons to cut him down, to the east there came an angry snort, followed by the beat of galloping hooves. On instinct they all turned toward the noise.

Macal saw Shelga thundering toward them, bearing down on the ring of trolls. As the monsters scattered from her path, the cloak shouted, *"Hurry! Now! Run!"*

This time Macal listened. He dashed through an opening in the troll perimeter and sprinted away.

"Get 'im!" came the order from the biggest of the monsters. "If you don't catch 'im, I'm going to eat one of you instead!"

In fear the others resumed their pursuit with haste. None of them wanted to be breakfast, any more than Macal did.

As Shelga sped through the clutch of the trolls, several of them struck at her. The jotun was a large target, and two of the attacks landed a serious gash upon the right side of her rib cage, and a bludgeoning strike to her left flank. She staggered, recovered, and in panic and pain sped off into the distance. With her went the rest of Macal's supplies.

Macal ran, begging and praying for assistance from any divine being who might be listening. The courage he had gained in the dream was fading;

slowly he was reverting to his old petrified self. The sight of the grotesque monsters leering as they surrounded him had eroded his confidence. Once more, reality had shown him that he was insignificant. He was nothing. How could he have believed he could stand against them?

As the trolls closed in again, both he and the cloak knew they weren't going to be saved twice. The monsters panted close at his heels; he could feel them reaching out for him.

This is it, he thought. *I can't outrun them.*

The cloak yelled at him. *"You're going to die!"*

"I know, I'm going to die! And that means my father is going to die. My father is going to die, because I failed him again!"

"You can't die! I don't want trolls touching me, Thief! They're even filthier than you!"

"I don't want them to touch me either! And do you ever stop yelling?"

"Only when I'm not with a thief, Thief."

"The Princess told you I'm not a thief!"

"And you expect me to believe her?"

"I can't outrun them!"

"That's becoming obvious!"

Macal thought he heard the cloak sigh, as if resigning itself to something it didn't want to do. Then it spoke. *"I'm doing this for the Princess, Thief."*

Macal was fed up. *"Whatever, and stop calling me that!"*

"Do you want to live?" asked the Cloak of Brinizarn.

"That's a stupid question! Why else would I be running?"

The cloak gave another long sigh. *"Then just say the following: 'For the Crown I shall bear the strength of the kingdom.' "*

"What?" Macal blurted out loud as the ground shook beneath the heavy lumbering tread of the trolls pursuing him. He was nearly within their reach again.

"Just say it. Hurry!"

"Say what?"

"What I just said! 'For the Crown I shall bear the strength of the kingdom.' "

"Why would I want to say that?"

"Just do it. And it's 'bear' as in the animal and not 'bare' as in naked."

"What are you talking about?"

"Just say it!"

"Fine!" shouted Macal. "For The Crown I Shall Bear The Strength Of The Kingdom!"

As he spoke, his skin began to tingle. The Cloak of Brinizarn glittered with motes of brilliant golden light that burst from the spellbound cloth in hundreds of tiny, glorious explosions.

Macal had never seen or felt anything like it. The light was almost blinding in its brightness, as if millions of fairies swarmed around him with glowing wings. A strange sensation coursed through him. As the twinkling motes faded to nothing, he realized the Cloak of Brinizarn had transformed him into an enormous brown bear.

CHAPTER 27

Noooo! Aeria wanted to scream, but nothing came out of her mouth. There was nothing left inside her to release. She stood horrified as she watched the Troll Chieftain pull his spear from Viscount Razz's chest.

She tried to jump down onto the bridge and thrust her saber into the Chieftain's eye, but several of the soldiers grabbed her and held her in place.

She went limp and fell to her knees, but she refused to let herself cry. The soldiers around her renewed their efforts and launched more missiles from the wall.

Razz was dead. Her mentor. Her protector. Her friend. *Her Razz.* How could he be gone? Why did he have to die? Why didn't he let her save him by staying on the bridge?

Why did there have to be this war?

She was scared. Petrified. She didn't want to die as well. *But who did?* she thought. *She was needed though. She wanted to help her people. Help her kingdom. Help Macal.*

She blinked.

In a flash her fear was gone, expelled to a far-off abyss. She was not going to die today. Not after Viscount Razz. Not after all these men fought and died to save her. In that moment she realized that she was no more important than any one of them. She wondered if they knew that.

She wasn't go to die today, because she was not going to give the trolls that victory. She was not going to let them use her to demoralize Elronia. She would fight until every last one of them fell lifeless before her.

Today would not be her final day in Elronia, it would be theirs. With clear eyes and a stern resolve she rose back to her feet with purpose.

"For Ermalon!" she shouted. The soldiers took up the war cry and its chant erupted around the castle.

Princess Aeria readied her bow and focused on the Chieftain. Each arrow she loosed was shot with anger and pain. Again and again, she let loose arrows at him until her quiver was empty.

Not every one of her arrows hit, but that didn't deter her and only made her angrier. Archery was something she had read about, but never practiced.

Each arrow flew from her bow bent on revenge. She wanted a thousand things right now. She wanted to lay down and cry. She wanted to run to Razz's body and hug him, but mostly she wanted all these trolls to die.

Under the relentless volley of arrows the Chieftain's mount crumpled to the ground. No longer afraid of the dragonmere, the rest of the trolls marched across the bridge. Their leader, as he waited for them, stepped off his fallen steed and kicked the dragonmere's body into the rocky lake.

Another arrow missed. She cursed herself for her inability. She notched another one and let it fly. It missed its intended target but struck true into the calf of one of the approaching brutes.

The archers continued to focus on the Chieftain with their arrows, but his hide was so thick that they barely did any damage.

Now that the drawbridge was completely closed, the soldiers without bows barricaded it with the abundance of rubble that lay within the castle.

For the moment, at the cost of Viscount Razz's life, they were safe.

With the gate closed and reinforced, a minor sense of relief washed over the humans. They knew they were not entirely safe behind the decaying castle walls, but at least it was now a more fortified and defensible structure.

Outside in the darkness, the trolls beat on the drawbridge door with fists and clubs, some hurled rocks and stones, while some hacked away at it with mighty axes.

In a roaring voice the Troll Chieftain shouted an order in the guttural troll tongue. The soldiers upon the wall, still raining arrows down upon their foes, saw several of the beasts come forward from the rear of the company. They carried great harpoon-like spears that trailed long lengths of coarsely-crafted rusty iron chain.

"You think your tiny human door will stop us?" began the Chieftain, switching back to the common language. "Ask the ghosts that now haunt Mazzul Keep how much their gate helped them. Launch the Door Breakers!" he ordered.

The horde made space for the handful of spear-carrying trolls, who ran forward and hurled their massive barbs. With great velocity they flew over the gap toward the upraised drawbridge. The Elronian soldiers watched in terror as their bladed edges sparkled with silver light.

The mighty spears struck the wooden door with such force that the foundation of the castle shook. Several of the soldiers lost their footing, one even falling over the outside edge of the castle to his doom on the rocks below. The Door Breakers pierced through the drawbridge with ease.

In practiced fashion the trolls formed two lines and grabbed ahold of the heavy linked chains attached to the spears. In unison they pulled, their enormous muscles flexing and straining with exertion. The pronged heads of the spears that had splintered through the wood now pulled back tight against the inside of the drawbridge. The tips of the prongs bit into the wood like fishhooks.

The trolls yanked again on the chains. The drawbridge gave a great groan as the brutes heaved. Inside the tower the soldiers grabbed ahold of the winch and struggled to keep it locked.

The archers on the wall were running low on arrows. They had given up on aiming for the Chieftain since their attacks were mostly ineffectual on his thicker hide; they were now focusing on the trolls pulling on the chains. Several of the monsters near the front fell under the concentrated fire.

The trolls heaved again. The drawbridge gave another loud groan. The men holding the winch were knocked aside as it gave way under the strain and unreeled several links of chain before they were able to recover.

Princess Aeria, also out of arrows, watched the drawbridge creep open several degrees. Her heart had never beat so fast. She looked around at the soldiers. Only a couple dozen remained, along with several of her maidens and various other caretakers and aides.

She didn't know what to do. There didn't seem to be a way to stop the trolls from getting in. She could see it was only a matter of time. *And then what?* she asked herself. She didn't know. She didn't know what to do. She wasn't a soldier. She was a girl. She needed Razz.

The troll army pulled the drawbridge open several more links.

She looked back to the Chieftain as he shouted more orders in the troll tongue. Heeding his command, the trolls not busy pulling on the chains swarmed out and waded into the lake. Without understanding his words she understood his plan. He had ordered his soldiers to swim around and climb onto the rubble and through the broken walls that were sundered aplenty on the north and east sides of the castle.

Next to her an archer shot the last arrow the company had.

She didn't need Razz, she thought. *She needed a miracle.*

In Xanga-Mor, Macal was still marveling at the fact that the cloak had turned him into a gigantic bear. Still upright, he skidded to a halt, his great claws tearing the dusty soil. He had never felt so big or so powerful. He was huge! Packed with rippling muscle, he was practically as tall as the trolls who were chasing him.

Unlike the rest of his garments and possessions, only his sword and the cloak had remained unaffected by the spell. His tunic and pants had become russet-colored fur, shaggy and dense. His ears were small and rounded and he had a lengthy dark brown snout. Of his former self, only his lustrous green eyes remained—a clear sign that this was no ordinary bear.

Behind him five of the pursing trolls stumbled to a halt, astonished by the boy's sudden transformation. No longer was their prey a tiny weakling, but a ferocious snarling bear as large as they were! Macal threw back his head and let out a savage roar that contained all the pent-up frustration of his life. He wasn't going to be pushed around. He wasn't going to be chased. He was going to fight!

In a fury he had never felt before, he lunged at the largest of the trolls, slashing it across the face with a mighty swing of his great paw. The force of the attack sent the troll spinning through the air, leaving five deep claw marks in its ugly visage. Reveling in his newfound power, Macal roared again and faced the next troll, which wisely retreated.

The bear leaped forward, collided with the brute, toppled it over and raked it with his claws. The two rolled over and over in a chaotic tangle of brown and green, until at last the troll was still. The next troll tried to flee, but didn't stand a chance. Macal roughly grabbed the front of its chain vest and hurled it at one of its companions. There was a bone cracking impact, and the two beasts collapsed to the ground.

Macal let out another roar. He couldn't believe what he was doing, but it felt wonderful. In this powerful body, the trolls were nothing to him.

"Why didn't you tell me you could do this?" he asked the cloak in his mind.

"Do what?" asked the cloak innocently.

"Turn me into a bear!"

"What, and reveal my secrets to a thief? Never!"

Macal was not going to start that conversation again. *"What else can you do?"* he asked as he lashed out at the next troll with his huge paw.

"Nothing," said the cloak a little too quickly. It seemed to sense the boy's disbelief. *"I can still hear you, you know. Whether you believe me or not, the truth is still the truth."*

"Sure it is. I've been hearing that a lot lately."

"Probably, because it's true."

Emboldened by his new powerful form, Macal charged the remaining two trolls.

The first of the trolls able to swim around the castle began to mount the debris of the broken walls and towers. The drawbridge was now halfway opened. Princess Aeria could see that in another minute the trolls would be able to grab ahold of the drawbridge with their hands, and once they could they would wrench it the rest of the way open.

She now wished she had run when she had the time. As that thought occurred to her, she wanted to slap herself. She couldn't run and leave these people alone. These people who were only here and in danger because of her. No, she had made the right decision, whatever the outcome.

With a great whining snap the chains that held up the enormous wooden portal broke under the strain and the drawbridge slammed down and open.

"Retreat to that tower!" she yelled pointing to the one in the southeast courtyard. "Run! Now!"

It was the most undamaged of all the structures left. They had a little time because of the debris they had filled the gateway with, which the trolls were rapidly hurling out of the way.

More trolls were now cresting the fallen walls. The beasts on the drawbridge continued to struggle through the rubble, but the Elronians knew it would only be a moment before they too began to pour into the castle.

As Princess Aeria darted toward the tower several guards came up behind her to offer their protection and light the night with makeshift torches. Across the rubble-strewn courtyard they sprinted as death chased them. With a handful of trolls now over the walls, the slower soldiers were hewn down as they fled.

Some of the monsters charged toward the unicorns still harnessed to the Princess's carriage, drawn by the allure of their enchantments and the rare and delectable meat on their bones. But the unicorns, petrified, used their innate ability to teleport away. The humans looked longingly at them as they vanished, wishing they had the same ability—or at least wished the unicorns could take them away as well. The other less fortunate mounts, jotun and horse alike, had no such magical abilities and were put to their ends by the monsters.

Most of the Elronians made it into the tower before the Princess. Once she was in the survivors attempted to slam the thick wooden door shut, but one of the trolls stuffed his meaty hand through the opening and gripped the door, holding it fast.

Without hesitation Aeria pulled a long sword from a nearby soldier's sheath and brought it down decisively on the creature's fingers. The boil-encrusted digits fell severed to the ground, dripping bluish-black blood. With a nightmarish howl the troll recoiled its hand and the iron-bound door to the tower slammed shut.

Once again for the moment they were safe, but none of the humans had any doubt now how this was going to end.

"May the Crown stay strong," Aeria whispered to herself.

Both trolls had recovered from the shock of the bear's sudden appearance and his monstrous assault. One had a spear at the ready, the other a big two-handed iron mace. As the bear closed in, the mace-bearer swung its heavy weapon and its attack struck true. The spiked weapon slammed into Macal's right shoulder, making him stagger. The second troll saw its opening and thrust its spear forward, hoping to catch the animal in the center of the chest, but Macal recovered in time to bring a paw down on the approaching shaft, slamming it into the ground and snapping it with his great weight.

He barreled into the troll with the mace, stunning it before leaping on top of other one. The bear's body seemed natural, as if he had lived in it all his life. He instinctively knew how to fight, how to use his natural weapons, and he was enjoying every moment of this fight. Pinning the spear-wielder to the ground, he flung away its broken weapon and raked the monster's lower extremities with his rear paws. The troll howled in pain as it was torn apart; then Macal silenced it by dropping one of his front paws on its head, crushing its skull.

The mace-wielder recovered itself and struck once more, hitting him on the back. Macal roared again, this time out of pain. With a ferocious snarl he turned and lashed out at the troll, but the monster used its mace to block the strike. Macal howled in frustration, saliva pouring from his jaws as he and the creature circled one another. This troll wasn't the usual fodder. It was a fighter, a soldier, a warrior. It wasn't going to fall as easily as the rest.

All at once his keen bear's hearing detected a noise in the distance. The other four trolls were approaching, drawn by the sound of battle and probably his roars.

"*We don't have much time,*" observed the cloak.

"*I can take them!*" growled Macal. "*All of them!*"

"*No, you can't.*"

"*Look at what I've already done. I'm unstoppable!*"

"*The first ones were surprised by your transformation. Don't get me wrong, you're doing well, Thief. But when the others get here, they'll attack as a combined force, trust me. Which reminds me, did I ever tell you the story of the time I was in the Mordine with the King of Balentia? Well, we were fighting—"*

The boy-bear interrupted the cloak's ramblings. *"I don't have time for your story right now. I'm a little busy."*

"Fine. As I said, we have to get out here now."

Macal was still full of bloodlust. *"After I finish this one."*

"No! We have to go now!"

"I said, once I'm done!" Macal ducked under a ferocious attack by the troll with the mace. As the brute took time to ready its weapon again, he sprinted toward it on all fours, launching himself into the air. He landed on the troll with his full weight, knocking the mace from its hands. He raked the dazed creature with his claws. Its scaly hide shredded and bloody, the troll went limp. Macal glanced up to see the remainder of the force entering the clearing.

"Can we go now?" The cloak sounded worried.

"Yes." Macal jumped off the troll and headed west, running as fast as a bear could. He could not remember ever having so much fun.

Back in the clearing, the troll who had held the mace struggled to its feet. It was drenched in blood from the countless deep gashes that covered its face and torso. Even so, it smiled, pleased that feigning death had worked. It wasn't sure how much more punishment it could have taken.

As the rest of its companions gathered around, it knew this encounter had left it permanently scarred and deformed. Retrieving its mace and shaking it at the heavens, the wounded troll swore an oath that it would travel to the ends of the earth for its revenge. This fight marked the day of its disfigurement, but it also marked the imminent death of the strange boy who could magically transform himself into a bear.

A few minutes later, the troll war band set out in pursuit.

The tower was mostly empty. Strangely, even though it hadn't collapsed there was a large mound of rubble. They could only guess that at some point in time somebody, or something, had started to clear the courtyard and for whatever reason had placed the gray stone from the broken walls in here.

Trapped and desperate within the tower of Lord Vrex's crumbling castle, Princess Aeria tried to remember everything her father, mother, and Viscount had taught her about leadership. What they had said all seemed trivial and obvious at the time, and now as she tried to remember their advice she couldn't recall anything. She didn't have any idea what to do. This was not something she had come across in any of her books. *I must have missed the chapter on how to survive a troll horde.*

Why hadn't they taught her how to remain calm? She was scared, but she pulled herself together yet again.

She was going to be strong to the end, whatever that may be. These people were looking to her for guidance. They were all afraid, just like her, but looking to her for some sign of hope. She knew she didn't deserve this responsibility. She had never earned it. She had only been born into it. Which didn't seem fair—such responsibility should go to those who had the relevant experience.

There was no use worrying about that now. Things were what they were.

Then she remembered something her father had told her. Her mind, frantic as the trolls continued to pound on the tower's door, couldn't remember when he had said it, but she did remember what he said.

"You must always evaluate and use the resources you have at hand," he had told her in his gravelly voice.

Resources, she contemplated. *What did she have? A tower? Cavalry without mounts? Footmen with swords and various armaments?*

She looked around the dim tower, feebly lit by the persistent rays of moonlight that pierced through the high gothic windows. *What else did she have? Who else did she have?* Looking around she could see Xalefar the minstrel, Jenz the messenger and Faroe the animal handler. But she didn't see Lady Dreseldal and Lady Greseldal or even Osiary the royal tailor. She couldn't see any of the cooks, any of the porters, or any of another dozen others she looked for.

Then an idea occurred to her.

"Where's Rilena?" she asked quickly to those around her. She couldn't see her. "Did she make it?"

Aeria prayed that Rilena was okay. She knew it wasn't likely, not with her condition.

"I'm here," she heard a voice say from over on the rubble. A moment later out of the shadows Rilena was carried over in the arms of a young stocky soldier. Her legs were missing from just below her narrow waist. The Princess was not surprised that her wheeled chair had been lost during the retreat. It probably now lay splintered outside in the courtyard, crushed under a troll's foot.

The girl was young, nine years of age. Her dark hair fell just down to her shoulders and her large glassy blue eyes looked as scared as the Princess felt. She wore an elegant red dress hemmed with lace that was now torn and grimy.

The Princess was happy to see that she had somehow survived the onslaught.

Outside the tower the trolls continued to hammer on the door, causing it to shake and rattle on its hinges. For a moment the Princess was distracted watching the soldiers inside try to reinforce the door with rubble from the pile. With an aching heart she counted only fifteen survivors, besides herself, of the entire company that had left Keratost.

"I'm so happy you live, Princess," said Rilena in her soft sweet voice.

The Princess returned her attention to the girl. "And I you. Are you okay?"

"Yes. For the moment," replied Rilena ominously.

Princess Aeria's eyes narrowed with concern. "What do you mean?"

"Nothing, Princess. I was just saying, I don't know, I'm scared. I don't know what to say or do. I can't run, I can't do anything against them. I can't defend myself. I wasn't using my power, if that's what you mean."

"You will be fine. You don't need to worry—"

"But all those men," stammered the girl in tears. "So many ghosts. I can see them all."

"So, you can still use your powers?" asked the Princess.

"Yes, Princess."

Aeria smiled. "Good. Very good."

As she looked at Rilena she felt a flicker of hope—because Rilena was an augur. She was not only blessed to have a mild ability to read the portents of the gods, but she had also been granted the ability to control slyphs—minor air spirits, invisible creatures of wind. And she could control them like the elves could.

As an infant the girl had been stolen from Iceward—a land of sorcery, dark mystics, and augurs—to be sold as a common slave. Several years after being sold to a master in Keratost she had contracted the Worms of Slithereth, a sickness that had eaten away her legs. Only by her master severing and burning the infected limbs had the infection been stopped from spreading through and eating the rest of her. Now useless as a slave, her owner had cast her onto the streets. Caked in mud and dirt, crawling along an alley by only the strength of her arms, she had been found by one of the city's orphanages. Over time they realized the power of her gifts and promptly sold her for a sizable profit to the Royal Court, who they knew could find many uses for her.

The trolls attacked the door with more force now. The Chieftain could be heard issuing orders and his host tried many different tactics, but so far the sturdy iron-bound door continued to hold in place.

Princess Aeria thought she may have found a resource at her disposal that might be able to help. "Good," she said again. "Then maybe there *is* something you can do against the trolls. Can you use your powers now?"

Relina looked at her nervously. "They don't always work, Princess. Especially when I'm scared. I normally do it in a quiet place."

"Make it work," ordered the Princess. She knew she had to be stern with the girl. *But what choice did she have? Use every resource.* She had to make the girl focus. She knew because of Relina's young age she was only beginning to learn how to use her talents. "You may be the only chance we have to get out of here. Use your powers now and see if anybody is nearby who can help us."

The augur looked at her doubtfully, but eventually said, "Okay. I'll try."

CHAPTER 28

T hroughout the night the trolls continued to bash and batter the door to the tower, which shook more measurably with each assault.

Princess Aeria had marshaled the rest of her small force to make sure all who could help were aiding in barricading the door with whatever they could find. All the debris from the tower was now in place against it, except for small lengths of wood they used to make more torches. Several of the knights and soldiers were doing their best to help hold it in place. She noticed one guard near the back of the tower still held the red banner with a ring of roses on it. She told him to throw it on the barricade.

The trolls shouted their hatred of the trapped humans while they attacked the door. Aeria wondered how many other legions of trolls like this were in Elronia now? How could they possibly win? *But more importantly, even if we don't get help in time, at least through Rilena others will be warned.*

The bolts holding the door in place were now loose in the stone and after another blow one of them fell out. The clink it made as it hit the floor sent a shiver through all their hearts. Panic overtook some of the men as they watched it fall. All soldiers not already doing so raced over to hold the door in place.

"Death will take us all," cried one of them. He looked at the Princess, his eyes glazing over with dread. His grimy face showed the emotional fatigue of watching so many of his friends and companions fall to the beasts today, and now he knew he would be next.

"No," shouted Aeria, hoping to quell the rising frenzy within the tower. She gave them all a long, calm but unrelenting stare. "It won't. And I don't want to hear that said again. Don't waste your energy worrying about dying, spend it finding a way to survive."

"But how long can this door keep them out if they can take down the great drawbridge?" countered the soldier, still not mollified.

"I may be able to help," interjected Xalefar the minstrel stepping forward. All eyes turned to him as the door was struck several more times. His ice blue elven eyes glowed in the dimness of the tower. "I can play a tune with my lyre. It's enchanted. And it can strengthen the wood of the door as long as I continue to play."

Princess Aeria was stunned by this revelation. "Why didn't you do that to the drawbridge?"

Xalefar looked sheepish. "I was in the rear of the courtyard. For the magic to work I must be near the wood I strengthen. And we didn't know they had those Door Breakers. I thought we were safe. I didn't think they could tear down the bridge. I'm sorry."

"Forget about that. Start playing now."

The minstrel pulled his lyre from his pack. It was the lustrous deep violet of rosewood. Without a word he started his tune. It was oddly lively and didn't fit the direness of the moment, but nobody said anything. He guessed he could have played a wedding tune and they would have welcomed it as long as it kept the monsters outside. As he plucked the strings with his delicate fingers he harnessed the power of Yenidree, Goddess of elves, animals, and nature. Arcane shapes of magical energy swam out from the lyre, as if dancing to the music, then towards the door where they burst apart like tiny colorful exploding stars.

As he played, a prismatic glow came into being and encompassed the door. Howls of rage rose from the monsters outside as they found their weapons could no longer strike the portal, now buffered by the magical barrier. Dumb as the trolls were, they understood the power of magic and what it meant for them in trying to get to their meal.

They heard the Chieftain's voice rise from the courtyard, ordering the Door Breakers pulled from the drawbridge for use against the tower door. A few minutes later the tower shook from their impact, but the door itself was unmoved. With the aid of the minstrel's magic the door withstood the strike the same as it would a soft breeze.

The power of the magic Xelefar wrought bolstered the morale of all witnessing it within the tower.

For several more hours the Trolls buffeted and hammered on the door to no avail. Everybody inside the tower relaxed slightly as Xelefar repeatedly played his protective song. Most of them now sat on rocks, were spaced out up several levels of stairs, or were leaning against the wall at the base of the tower.

Despite the relentless attacks on the door, several of the injured and exhausted had slipped into a doze. Eventually Rilena came out of her mediation—which had caused her to float fifteen feet upwards in the center of the tower—and startled them with a shout. "I've found them!"

Princess Aeria stirred from thoughts of Macal. "Who?"

"An Elronian regiment! I'm sorry it took so long," she explained as she descended gracefully back to ground level. A soldier stepped forward to help hold her upright.

Relief filled the chamber. If the regiment could get here quickly they could be saved. They guessed the Chieftain was just waiting for the magic on the door to lapse so he could finally break in.

Princess Aeria knelt down before the augur. "How far away are they?"

"From what I'm told they said they are two days east of here."

In her fatigue the Princess couldn't recall what was two days to the east. There were troops moving around all throughout the country. Since starting the journey to Varun, she had been out of touch with the state of the war, so she had no idea who they might be. Or what forces her father had sent to the area.

Princess Aeria Stormlion looked over at Xalefar. "Don't stop playing unless your fingers fall off."

Together the Cloak of Brinizarn and Macal ran through a once-majestic and glorious temple that now lay fallen and crumbling. All the wonderfully carved columns had toppled over and broken apart on the gray basalt foundation. Intricately chiseled borders of elegant swerving lines were carved upon the once white marble walls, now dark gray and covered with grime and moss. The place was in complete ruin. The statues had been destroyed and their pieces scattered about, leaving no clue to which god the temple had once been dedicated.

"So, I suppose I should probably tell you this," started the Cloak of Brinizarn as they continued running over the battle-scarred land. *"But you can't stay a bear forever."*

"What do you mean I can't?" growled Macal the Bear aloud in a loud fierce voice. Shocked as he was by this new information he was still pleased to know he could continue to talk even in this shape.

"I meant exactly what I said. There is a maximum duration that my powers will keep you transformed."

"And how long is this *maximum duration* going to last?"

"Until, about now, I'm thinking."

"Wha—?" Then it started to happen. The cloak, like it had before, began to glitter with little twinkling lights. Macal's skin began to tingle once more. First his large claws retracted, then his long bristly fur receded as he started to shrink back to his normal boy size and then, in mere seconds, Macal the Bear was again Macal the Boy.

"Why? Why did that happen?" demanded Macal suddenly in a surprised stammer. He would rather be the bear than himself. As the bear he was somebody, he could do things, he could get stuff done, and as a bear he knew he could save his father. "I'm just going to change back right now."

"You can't do that, Thief."

"Why not?"

"My magic for the bear form needs to regenerate first."

"And how long will that take?"

"Well, it normally depends on how much magic was used by how long a wearer stayed a bear. Since you stayed in form till the magic depleted, it could be a while."

Macal threw his hands into the air. "Great."

"Hey, Thief! I saved you back there. Stop being so whiny. Appreciate what you got."

Macal stood silent for a moment looking at the lonely horizon, a gentle breeze tickling his tired face. "You're right," he said aloud. "I'm sorry. I just can't handle all of this. I can't handle everything that has happened. My uncle. All the encounters with trolls. Knowing that my father's probably dead—or if he is alive, that he is being tortured. Turning into that bear was the first time since I started this quest back in Hormul that I didn't feel helpless—that I really had a chance of succeeding."

"And that is why the Princess gave me to you. I can be of great help. Like, once I was with the Prince of the Dragon Lords up in up in the Mortik Dires fighting the Dark Witches of Hallowgrove, who were in service to Mulbalis, the mischievous God of Magic, when—"

"—What other powers to do you have?" asked Macal telepathically.

"You never let me finish my story. Perhaps in one of them you might learn something useful about me."

"I'm sorry, we don't have time for that. I need to find my father. What other powers do you have?"

"None."

"You're lying. Tell me!"

"No. I'm not telling you now. Maybe if you listened to one of my stories you might find the answers you are looking for."

"I'm sorry about cutting you off. Please tell me your story."

"No."

"Want to tell me a story now?"

"No."

"How about now?"

"No."

Macal growled in frustration at the lilac cloak. "Fine. Don't. We have to get moving anyway."

The two of them continued their journey, trying to stay clear of structures or any hamlets or villages. It was nearing dawn when Macal began to get hungry and he realized for the first time that he didn't have his backpack or his bedroll. All he had was just his sword, his clothes, his waterskin, which he just happened to be wearing when he fell asleep, and the Cloak of Brinizarn. Without his backpack, which he left at the manse, he had no rations, and therefore nothing to eat to sate the growing yearning of his stomach.

Perhaps Shelga will find me again, he hoped as he tried to quell the twinges of hunger that his grumbling stomach kept reminding him of.

Eventually they came to a wide riverbed that bore water at a swift current, splashing it vigorously against a few gray-spotted rocks and turning it to a light foam. Macal stopped to fill his waterskin, then surveyed the river. Even though he was a fairly good swimmer, he wasn't sure if he would be able to swim across it. Then he remembered how good bears were at swimming.

He looked up and down the river. There didn't seem to be any easier way to cross it. "Got enough power recharged for me to swim across this river as a bear?"

"I suppose we can manage that," replied the Cloak of Brinizarn. Its tone indicated it was still angry at Macal's treatment.

Within a moment Macal was transformed again into the great animal. As he swam through what should have been chilling water, he didn't notice the cold at all and soon left the river behind.

Their passage for the rest of the day was uneventful. Macal had been keeping a keen lookout for something that he could eat, some berries perhaps, like he had found way back at the mill where he had first met Viscount Razz, or nuts, or roots, anything at all. After unknown hours of expedient walking and hiking he was ravenous for sustenance. He even contemplated eating some of the lichens he had seen, if only he knew which ones weren't poison, but as the sun fell away from the world and darkness took over he still hadn't found anything to eat.

Once night came and with the moon waning from full, he found he could no longer see well enough to travel. He decided to lie down and sleep the darkness away, and hope for better luck finding something to eat in the morning.

All alone in a foreign land, the boy pulled the hood of the cloak up and wrapped the rest of it around him. Then he curled up into a ball and leaned against the bole of a large knotted and dying tree on a small hilltop and drifted off to the only place he knew he could find happiness—the world of dreams.

Macal slept through the uneventful night until the warm bright rays of the late summer sun fell down upon him, stirring him from his slumber.

"I'm so hungry," he said aloud, voicing the first thoughts that came to him.

"You should be, you haven't eaten in well over a day," commented the cloak.

"Have any idea what I can eat?"

"Not really. This place is just a wasteland now, perhaps if we can make it to Marglamesh, the climate and environment there will offer something edible for you."

"Yeah, maybe," replied Macal, stretching his muscles and very wearily getting to his feet. His hunger was taking its toll. "I hope Shelga's all right."

"You should. She was a good mount. But your incompetence lost her, along with the rest of your supplies."

Macal ignored the cloak and its whiny high-pitched voice. He looked around to get his bearings and saw something in the morning sunshine that startled him and caused him take a deep intake of breath.

Down in front of him, off in the distance, the world changed. No longer was it the despairing landscape of Xanga-Mor, but something far worse, more frightful and revolting than anything he had ever imagined.

"Marglamesh," he mouthed in horror.

Beyond the border of Xanga-Mor the land changed into a realm of dreadful moors, foul bogs, putrid swamps, dire black cliffs, and gnarled abyssal trees, all of which made their home on obsidian black soil and rock.

As sickening as the ghastly view was, at least most of the details of the dark shadowy land were washed out by a wispy green foggy gas that shrouded the entire horizon. Even in one of his nightmares he doubted he could have come up with a place more ominous and wretched-looking. This was the place bad dreams came to get inspiration.

The majority of the land appeared to be a mucky swamp that looked more like a flooded forest of mold-covered drooping cypresses, tupelo, and ash. The lower trunks of the bleak looking trees were all submerged in the shallow filthy tea-colored water.

Formations and huge shafts of dark marl rock jutted up from the ground and the disgusting pools of water, at precarious angles like the jagged spikes of hideous stone. There were also a likewise amount of large cloudy white quartz rocks that took an eerie glowing radiance from the aberrant fog.

Macal stared at it in revulsion. It looked like a place only a troll could live, like a place only a troll would *want* to live.

"I have to go into *there?*" he said at last. It was even more vile than Xanga-Mor. "How could the gods let such a place exist?"

All through the day the trolls never ceased their barrage upon the tower. The only illumination now was from the magic of the lyre as it sent its essence out to protect the door. The occasional brief flashes of colorful light gave the darkness of the tower a surreal atmosphere.

Everybody trapped inside the tower listened intently as the minstrel kept endlessly repeating his tune. They had all lost count how many times it had been played as the melody burned forever into their minds.

Rilena, once more in meditation and floating up high, was trying to stay in touch through her wind spirits with the approaching force. So far she had little luck reconnecting with them.

In the last few hours the trolls had started launching fiery projectiles through the windows to rain down upon them. Aeria had rallied the soldiers, ordering them to dismantle some of the upper stairs to use the planks to block the majority of the windows, except the highest ones that faced the water.

In the courtyard the troll force continued to make a commotion. The tower continued to shake, as they assailed the door, but so far the portal had held. More than once they heard the Troll Chieftain shout and curse in frustration.

Some of the more daring Elronian soldiers dropped rocks they collected from the rubble onto the trolls outside from the windows above—after which they were quick to replace the windows' barricades before the beasts returned fire.

With nothing to eat, hunger assaulted the captives. When retreating to the tower nobody had time, or the wherewithal, to grab anything. Aeria placed her hand on her stomach as it growled and ached. Selfishly she wished one of the enchanters had survived. *They could have conjured food enough for all.*

It had only been a day; they still had another day to wait.

She looked at Xelefar. "Do you know a ballad or hymn that can make food?"

"Such a song is not in my repertoire," replied the minstrel as he continued his refrain. His fingers ached, cramped, and hurt worse than they ever had. "There were melodies the ancients used to know that could create such things, but those songs have long been lost. Plus, I would need to stop this song to do so."

It was obvious from everybody's sudden uncomfortable shifting that nobody liked that idea. Time went on with nobody saying another word about food, lest it encourage deeper cravings and pangs of hunger.

Hours later it was Xelefar who broke the near silence that was filled only by the tune of the lyre. "Princess, I'm not sure how much longer I can play."

Princess Aeria sat, leaning against the wall near the door, with her knees up and her arms crossed atop them. She lifted her tired head from where it had rested on her arms and looked at the minstrel. "Play as if your life depends on it."

"But Princess—"

She cut him off. She swept her arm about the tower, indicting all the people inside. "Play as if all their lives depended on it."

"But Princess, my fingers—"

"Play as if *my* life depended on it."

All expression, even that of exhaustion and cramping fingers, left Xelefar's face. Without further word he closed his eyes, lowered his head and continued to play his song.

Just past midnight, a knight shook the Princess awake with a strong gauntleted hand. Even in the dim light she could see the man's face had a grave look.

"What?" she asked.

"Our time is running out," he answered in a hollow tone as he stood up and pointed at the masonry around the door.

Aeria couldn't see what he was indicting, so she crawled over and by the glow of the magic on the door she saw what he meant. While the door under magical protection had withstood the relentless bombardment of the trolls, the masonry around the door was not as fortunate and had started to crack.

She went pale. The hope she had cultivated that they might live was slowly dying. The door was going to fall. *There was no way they could hold off the trolls for another day.*

Standing there transfixed by the landscape of Marglamesh, Macal heard a noise. Fearfully he looked behind him down the other side of the tiny hill. He saw them. Through the skirts of brush and from a copse of trees the trolls trudged forth.

He recognized the lead troll. It was the same one he had fought just yesterday. He was surprised to see him alive. Macal had thought for sure he had defeated the creature and was certain that the monster would never be able to bother him again. But as he saw the gash-ridden monstrosity, bearing its large black mace, he knew he was wrong.

The trolls noticed the boy at the same time he noticed them. The disfigured leader let out a ferocious roar at the sight of its prey.

"For gold and glory, and that boy's head!" it bellowed up the hill as it ordered its band of soldiers to charge. "We've found him! Kill him! Kill the boy!"

"*This, I think, is where we run,*" offered the Cloak of Brinizarn as the monsters clamored speedily up the slope.

Macal didn't need any more prompting than that. He spun on his feet and sprinted down the other side of the hill, running as fast as he could toward the one place in the world he would never want to go.

Behind him the large monsters gave pursuit.

As he ran for his life Macal thought he could feel the earth shaking under the trolls' mighty stomping feet. He didn't dare look back. He didn't dare do anything but run.

"Bear?" he gasped between breaths, hoping the cloak had recharged itself enough by now.

"*Yes?*" replied the cloak, who didn't need eyes to tell that trolls with their longer strides were closing in on the boy. "*But you have to say the words! You have to say them aloud!*"

Macal wasn't just running, he was sprinting as fast as he could, and that wasn't good enough, because the thunderous steps behind him were getting closer.

Macal's breath was ragged. "For The Crown—I Shall Bear The Strength—Of The Kingdom!"

"*As you wish,*" replied the cloak and the magic began anew. In a flash of dazzling light Macal again grew to mammoth proportions and was soon a great brown bear.

He chose not to take his chances. He fought down his impulse to turn back and attack the brutes, though he yearned to feel the power of the bear swarm through him as he tore through the ranks of his enemies.

Once more the trolls were startled and appalled by the magical transformation, likening it to some sort of witchcraft. But that didn't matter, in his new form Macal was able to easily outpace those behind him. As his claws tore into the soil he gathered all the speed he could muster and ran for the Marglamesh border. Soon he had lost his pursuers again.

When he finally stopped worrying about the trolls behind him he hadn't realized how far he had already traveled. He noticed that he was almost at the border to the dark kingdom.

Without hesitation, without a choice—for his father—Macal didn't stop, and a moment later he had crossed into the final kingdom of this journey.

CHAPTER 29

N ow up close, Marglamesh was even more foreboding than Macal had initially realized. His large bear paws sank several inches into the wet soil. From afar he couldn't really smell the place, but now that he was here, the pungent rotten stink of Marglamesh reminded him of a decaying deer corpse he had once come across while playing in the woods north of his house.

Puddles and pools of dank water surrounded large pillars of towering black rock, offering no safe passage. The haze of green fog washed out the details of the forbidding land, and in some places completely obscured his vision.

A gust of stale wind blew by, briefly clearing the fog. In the far distance Macal could see his goal—the Troll King's enormous floating citadel. It loomed over the land, a mountain of solid rock shrouded in a dark fog of its own.

He stood there for a moment still in his magical bear form, silent and unmoving, taking it all in. Who would have thought he would have made it this far? Would his father, his uncle, believe he could have made it here by himself? Would anybody? Then he remembered the Princess. She would believe it. She was the one who sent him here. She thought he could do it.

But what of Viscount Razz? Had he ever believed that this little boy had a chance of making it into the heartland of the enemy? Did the Viscount ever think he would really be successful in saving his father? Macal had always felt that the dragonmere had great reservations about sending him on this mission alone. As he looked around the dark land, he thought maybe he should have followed the Viscount's instincts.

"*But,*" began the cloak, listening as always to Macal's personal and private thoughts. "*Viscount Razz didn't know the Princess was going to give you such an amazing prize...me! He might have thought different had he known the Princess's whole plan, and known of my powers. And now is not the time to wonder whether you should have come, you are here now after all. You have made it this far, now it's time for the final leg of the journey. You should be proud of yourself for making it this far, Thief. I can't imagine that many boys would face what you have faced to save their father. Now, it's time for the hardest part. And it's important that we keep moving."*

"Alright," growled Macal the Bear somewhat comforted, but still swelling with fear. With each new step he took he fought down his trepidation by thinking of his father. He had to do this, because if he didn't, who would?

As they moved deeper into The Marg they passed numerous vile altars and uncountable grave mounds, where the trolls buried their dead in piles, heaping as much soil as they could find upon those that had departed to create small hills of rotting dead.

Hunger continued to plague Macal as he walked on. Eventually he returned to his normal shape, to preserve the cloak's energies. Back in human form he stumbled more frequently, overcome by the lack of food and the sheer exhaustion of the entire trip. Relentlessly, with visions of his father driving him on, he continued forward.

By staying on whatever dry patches of evergreen bush-covered heath he could find, Macal slowly worked his way through the moors. Unfortunately his thin clothing wasn't enough to protect him from the prickly low-growing vegetation and soon he was covered in bleeding little scratches. As painful as it was, he thought it was better than the alternative of stepping off the dry land.

He did his best to remain alert and circumvent the quagmires and deep pools of mud and water filled with strange creatures he didn't recognize and didn't want to meet. Whatever they were, they churned the ooze-like water with their movement.

He passed by many dark cliffs of black rock, a crumbling green stone temple to Orktissa the Troll God, and a half sunken tower dedicated to Raikis the God of War, who the trolls also honored with worship.

More than once he stumbled in his fatigue and slipped on wet soil and slid down deep wide gullies where he had to expend energy he couldn't afford to waste to climb back out.

He walked for hours, he and the cloak covered in putrid muck, working his way through the bogs, always moving in the direction of the great bleak castle that ominously looked down upon the cruel kingdom.

Scrambling over a large fallen slimy log, and slapping at a swarm of insects that seemed keen on feasting on him, he wondered how anything could live in this filth. He already had endured more bites on his arms, face, and neck in the past hour than he had in his whole life.

Eventually he found an area where he had no choice but to wade through the waters of the moor, much to the horror of the Cloak of

Brinizarn that howled in his head about having to touch the grimy, sickly water. Macal pulled out his sword and held it tight and tense in his hand. He ignored the cloak's whining and trudged forward with caution in the murky water, eyes alert for the hunting tentacles of unmentionable creatures.

He had only taken a few dozen steps when he heard a loud splashing behind him. He spun to see the troll war band, the same one that had been chasing him, burst over the dry ridge he had just left, lurching forward after him. Macal couldn't believe they had found him again! Throwing caution to the wind, he turned and ran with the dozen monsters in close pursuit.

The Cloak of Brinizarn felt now was a good time to point something out. *"Perhaps, you shouldn't have left the one with the mace alive."*

"If you recall, I wanted to stay and fight but you insisted that I leave!" snapped Macal as he ran pell-mell through the water.

"A suggestion I would make again, under the same circumstances, but—"

"—But nothing. What are we going to do now?"

"I don't know. Just don't stop running, Thief."

"Oh, thanks. Lot of help that is. Why won't they just leave me alone?"

"Umm, perhaps, because you're a human?"

"You know that you don't have any legs or any way of moving, right? I could just drop you here in this muck and let you rot in this disease-infested filth!"

"I am the Cloak of Brinizarn! I have been donned by kings! You can't leave me!"

"Then you don't know me that well."

The cloak was silent for a second. *"You know you're doing a wonderful job of running. You're incredibly fit and an excellent runner. I bet all the boys wish they could be like you—"*

"—Oh, shut up, you liar."

"Sorry, just trying to help and be more positive, as you requested. Please, just don't let me get wet again! I don't even have a nose and I can still sense how horrible I smell at the moment."

The trolls were closing in fast. His short legs could barely make any distance in the waist deep water.

"Now he dies!" he heard the disfigured troll leader shout in anticipation.

Macal didn't waste time looking back again. He knew he wouldn't like what he saw. He could almost feel the trolls upon him.

The cloak began to panic. *"Hurry!"*

"I can't! The water is too high. I can barely move—" Macal felt a harsh yank at his throat.

"He has me! Oh, by the gods, its grimy hands are touching me! Help! Ick! Help!" wailed the cloak as it and Macal were hauled backwards.

In the sudden motion Macal was pulled off his feet, falling backwards under the green water of the mire. Flailing about, Macal dropped his sword as he floundered to get to his feet and raise his head up out of the muck, sputtering brackish liquid from his mouth.

The troll leader laughed at him, enjoying this comedic prelude to its imminent victory over the irksome boy. Instinctively Macal reached back and grabbed onto the cloak and yanked on it. The wet fabric slipped from the troll's gnarled fingers.

The beast bellowed in fury and attempted to bring its mace down on Macal's head, but as soon the boy was free, he leapt forward and the mighty blow splashed into the water, missing him by only inches.

"Get him!" The troll leader glared in hatred at the fleeing boy. "If he gets away, one of you will die in his place!"

Knowing this was no idle threat, the war band began their frenzied pursuit anew.

To Macal's rare fortune, just a few steps away the earth rose out of the water and in a couple more steps he was on solid ground. He picked up speed as he sprinted forward. He knew he had to find someplace to hide. His panicking eyes scanned the environment. To his right was a huge formation of black rocks rising out of the earth. Ahead of him and to his left was the endless sea of the gloomy mire. He knew that entering the water again would surely be the death of him, so he darted into the tall field of jagged rock.

Exhaustion and hunger were becoming overwhelming. He wanted to give up, to cry, to lie down and never move again. This was all just getting to be too much for him. How many times was he going to be able to escape these creatures? Were they ever going to stop following him? And what could he possibly do to these beasts now that he had dropped his sword, now forever lost into the silt of the mire. By the time he could turn into a bear again it would be too late.

"You're going to die, boy!" shouted the leader as it stepped up on the dry land.

"And I'm a gonna eat ya!" added another, who sounded even closer.

"And looks, he dropped his wee sword!" laughed another.

With the footsteps of the pursuing trolls pounding in his ears, Macal scrambled through the labyrinth of black rocks, some of which were taller even than the trolls. He took a random path through the obstacles, hoping he could lose his followers, but they were so close they never lost sight of him. At least for now his smaller stature was an advantage, as he was agile enough to make sharp quick turns that the trolls couldn't, increasing the distance between them.

As Macal ran on the black rocks on either side of him began to get closer and closer together, rising up higher and higher, and soon his choices narrowed until there was only one path left. Out of breath and running as fast as he could, he didn't give up. He was finally starting to lose the beasts. Up ahead of him was boulder directly in his path, and as he ran past it at full speed his heart stopped in mid-beat.

"That's not good," said the cloak.

"No, it's not!" cried Macal aloud as he frantically tried to skid to a halt.

Just beyond the boulder the pathway ended in a high cliff overlooking leagues and leagues of the Troll Moors.

Unable to stop his forward momentum, Macal Teel slid forward over the cliff and plummeted to certain death on the hard jagged rocks below.

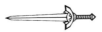

Most of those trapped in the tower slept. It was an uncomfortable and uneasy rest, but for some the exhaustion was so great from all the recent events that they had collapsed into slumber. Others slept as a way to hide from the pangs of hunger.

The Princess had found it impossible to sleep. Instead she sat on the floor, leaning against the wall with her eyes closed. She had been counting the blows upon the door for hours. As time passed they had slowed. *It's no surprise to find that the trolls are not very disciplined.*

As they fell in and out of sleep, one thought went through the mind of every captive. *Help was on the way, but would they be here in time?*

After the cracks first started to show in the masonry Princess Aeria had asked Xalefar if he could do anything about the damage. "Could your magic also protect the walls?"

The minstrel looked at her, ashamed. "No, the walls are stone, not wood. There is nothing I can do for that."

As they watched the cracks grow, they guessed they had only a few hours before the door broke free from the wall. The minstrel played all through the night while the trolls continued to slowly force their way in.

In the wee hours of the morning, a great din and clamor suddenly erupted outside, crashing through the night with the speed and volume of a thunder storm. Everyone immediately woke up.

Startled, Princess Aeria opened her eyes and got to her feet. *What new horror could this be?*

Macal tumbled over the edge of the cliff. Mist and gas rose up around him, shrouding the jagged rocks he hurtled toward.

"I suppose you want to live?" asked the Cloak. Eyes wide the boy didn't speak. He couldn't. He was petrified about what was going to happen to him when his body made contact with the fast-approaching rocks. *"I'll go out*

on a limb and take your silence as a yes. If you want to live, you should probably say: 'For the Crown I shall lift the glory of the kingdom!' And if you could do that soon, that would be especially great. Thanks."

Overtaken with fear of imminent death, he barely heard a word the cloak said.

"Um, hurry. We are getting kinda close to the ground now. Repeat after me, child! 'For the Crown I shall lift the glory of the kingdom!"

Macal numbly mouthed the words. "For the Crown I shall—" his unblinking eyes never left the rocks below.

"Lift the glory of the kingdom!"

"Lift the glory of the kingdom."

Just like when he turned into a bear, when he finished speaking the words an explosion of motes of light burst out from the Cloak of Brinizarn. And then he was flying! He immediately pulled up from his fall.

He was flying. Really flying! Without a Pegasus, or griffon, or anything. Just him and the Cloak of Brinizarn. He couldn't believe it. It was wonderful. It was freeing and exhilarating. It felt more magical than the magic it was.

"Why didn't you tell me you could do this? I could fly straight to the castle! Why were you making me walk so far in that grime?"

Then his smooth flight sputtered and became erratic. The glittering of the cloak winked on and off, and each time the motes of light disappeared he began to free fall until once more the cloak lit up and kept him aloft.

"Umm, what's happening?"

"What do you think is happening?" The glittering nearly faded completely as the cloak slowly lowered him toward the ground. *"Again we go back to the fact that I have limited power and without recharging I can't do very much. And anyway, flight lasts only for short distances."*

"But I was able to stay a bear awhile."

"Like I said flying only works in short bursts. It takes more power. You're not very grateful, do you know that?"

As soon as Macal's feet touched the ground he tried to fly again, but nothing happened. The cloak didn't even glitter.

"Weren't you listening. I have no power left. None. But, hey, you got away from the trolls—"

Macal turned and looked up the cliff he had just fallen from. At the top stood the trolls, staring in disbelief at the boy who continued to do wondrous things to escape their grasp.

Even down here he could hear faint wisps of their shouts and angry calls. Finally the disfigured leader made a harsh gesture to his band and the trolls retreated the way they had come.

"Do you think they're leaving?" asked Macal.

"Do you?"

"No."

"Neither do I."

"We should get moving then. Try to keep as much distance between us and them as we can."

With that Macal set off through the moors, disappearing deeper into Marglamesh.

Everybody inside the tower was awake from the commotion. It sounded like a massive battle had erupted out in the courtyard.

"For gold and glory!" She could hear the trolls bellowing, along with other guttural war cries.

The soldiers on the stairs up near the windows pulled the planks aside and dared to glance out.

"It's the army!" one exclaimed.

"Yes, a large company of horsemen!" added another.

Princess Aeria watched the first soldier's mouth open in wonder. "And they've got grurts and zygysts!"

Aeria's heart rose, because she knew what grurts were. It was hard not to, because they were famous. Great armor-scaled beasts with poisoned tails and a minor acumen in transforming the earth—they could cause it to swell up over their foe's lower legs and bind them in place. Once held, the grurt would charge forward and ram into them with its great curved horns. In battle they were devastating.

Zygysts were small little wisp-like creatures that were released on the field of battle from an enchanted branch of a Drelenor tree. They swarmed over the battlefield into the eyes of the enemy, temporarily blinding opponents with their brilliant starry light.

The soldiers looking out the window could see the zygysts flaring with brilliant brightness. Their vibrant lights blinded the trolls' sensitive eyes. They could also see that, along with horses, some of the knights also rode jotuns.

Princess Aeria didn't hesitate with her orders. "Xalefar, you can finally stop playing." The minstrel sighed with relief. "The rest of you able to bear arms go out and join the battle!"

Aeria followed after them out the door. *If those soldiers were going to risk their lives to save us, the least we can do is help!*

The battle in the courtyard at Castle Vrex was remarkably short. The trolls had been taken by surprise by the incoming force and by the time the captives of the tower were able to remove the rubble and open the door to come out to help, the skirmish was nearly over.

The incoming infantry and heavy cavalry attacked with maces, morning stars, flails, footmen's axes, and broadswords. It was obvious to the survivors that this was an elite troop. A few of them, great soldiers, cut across the field of battle like legends with supernatural abilities, or with the ancient magic weapons they wielded.

One of the heroes, heavily armored and nearly eight feet in height, swung a great two-handed sword, its edge etched with many fantastical runes. The blade of the weapon was transparent, almost invisible to the eye, and it cut through the troll ranks like a scythe through wheat.

They noticed another of the great soldiers was a sorcerer. She was levitating over the courtyard, teleporting here and there and shooting lances of lightning down on the trolls from a yellow garnet in the center of her crystal crown.

Several female winged elves also came to their aid, flying over the castle walls. Princess Aeria recognized them as elves of Ralastania, the only one of the three kingdoms of elves whose inhabitants had the gift of wings. From their magical jade bows they launched arrows of flame, two at a time, into the troll masses. The arrows seared through their targets with the heat of lava.

The incoming host came down on the trolls like an army from the heavens. Their assault was like a cleansing rain, obliterating the filth that invaded their land.

Aeria marveled at the power of her saviors. The company was far more seasoned and potent than her own, even when Viscount Razz was with her.

She looked for the leader of this army as she stabbed the nearest troll in its fatty leg with her saber. She recognized the emblems sewn onto the men's tabards and painted onto their shields. The coat of arms, all in black and white, was a female angel over an upturned crescent moon. One of the angle's hands had been transformed into a mace while the other became a six-eyed snake. She immediately recognized it. *Lord Wreyghul.* She should have guessed it was Lord Wreyghul. Unless she had lost her bearings over the last several days his territory was not far to the east of here.

It took a moment to find him in the melee. He was calling out orders, surrounded by a throng of men that hung near him to aid in his defense if needed. She noticed that he didn't look like the typical warlord. He was small and his golden plate armor hung loosely on his thin frame. The gorget around his neck was bejeweled with large round blue sapphires. Despite his size there was an air of bravery about him. He waded into the center of the chaos and swung his mace with enthusiastic, if not wild, force.

Just as she recognized Lord Wreyghul some of his soldiers must have also recognized her, because before she could engage another troll at least ten of Lord Wreyghul's men rushed to surround her, joining her soldiers in her own ring of protection.

Within moments the trolls were routed and destroyed. Those that fled were chased down and ended. No more would they ravage Elronia.

On his way toward the Princess, Lord Wreyghul called out commands with firm authority. "Set up sentinels on the wall walk. Also at each of the breaches in the wall. If there are any other marauding hordes in the area I don't want them taking us by surprise."

Arriving at her feet he fell to one knee. "My Princess."

Aeria looked at him. She had heard of him, of course, but had never met him. "Please rise. You have saved my life—our lives today. We should be kneeling before you."

Lord Wreyghul rose and removed his golden helm. Seeing his face for the first time, she liked that he had a soft empathetic face and caring brown eyes. Because of these features his men must respect him even more. *Or maybe that was because of his bravery.* "It was our duty and our pleasure to aid your highness in her time of peril."

Princess Aeria looked toward the tower as Xalefar and several others in her retinue exited now that it was safe. Her eyes fell on Rilena for a moment as she was being carried by a soldier. Aeria turned back to Lord Wreyghul.

"How did you get here so quickly? We were told you were two days away."

"I can't explain it any more than we were… apparently…closer than we thought." Lord Wreyghul noticed Rilena as well. "Is that her? The one who sent the slyph?"

"Yes. How did you know?"

"The wind spirit told us much about all of you. It was surprisingly talkative."

"I'm glad it was. You have my thanks again."

"No need to mention it. It was fairly easy and our losses were minimal. Fortunately the scouts I sent forward reported back that these trolls had become overconfident. I'm guessing this came from previous victories and the size of the horde, and because of that they didn't bother setting a guard. They probably thought, who would dare attack them?

"So we waited for night to come. The footmen snuck in and started the attack. Half of the wretches were dead within minutes along with their Chieftain. Then horsemen and other mounted riders charged in across the bridge that the trolls hadn't bothered to close and then you saw the rest." As he finished the lord noticed that Princess Aeria seemed distracted.

"Can you give me a moment please?" she asked. The lord nodded his head, indicating he was there to do as she wanted. To everybody's astonishment Princes Aeria then walked across the courtyard, through the gate, and onto the drawbridge.

Lord Wreyghul watched her with curiosity as she knelt down to reach for something in the water. Not knowing what she was up to Lord Wreyghul called out orders and a couple dozen of his men ran to guard her. *Who knows what else might be about?*

Aeria looked down at Viscount Razz. She couldn't reach him from up on the drawbridge. He was ten feet down, lying on his back on the sharp rocks, half in and half out of the water. Several of the fallen trolls, still spiked with arrows, lay around and partly on top of him.

She couldn't stand that there were trolls touching him. *Resting upon him!* She wanted them off him, wanted to pull him up here, but she couldn't reach. Instead she grabbed ahold of the edge of the bridge and swung herself over. She let go and dropped the rest of the way down to the rocks. Above her the soldiers called out in alarm as she disappeared from sight.

Princess Aeria pushed aside the limbs of the trolls that covered him. She heard the footsteps of the soldiers above her, their heavy boots thudding on the wood. Then she heard splashing and saw some of the men lowering themselves down to help her. A few had weapons in hand, ready for the unknown.

With their help she was able to raise Viscount Razz Munin out of the water and up onto the drawbridge. After hoisting the Princess up as well, the Viscount was carried in solemn silence back inside the castle.

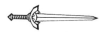

One of the empty carriages was, miraculously, still mostly intact. After turning it back upright, they placed Viscount Razz's body inside. Aeria went in with him and closed the door behind her. She crossed his arms, straightened his cloak and pulled it up over him.

All she did then was sit in the quiet and hold his hand, and went through her memories of him. It was then she noticed what was different about him. Tears came uncontrollably down her cheeks again. *His ring was gone.*

After a short while she emerged from the carriage. Not far away, Lord Wreyghul stood alone with his back to her, his helm under his arm. She noticed that the bodies of the fallen Elronians had been collected. Her ladies, Dreseldal and Greseldal, Osiary the royal tailor and many others were among them. Emotionlessly she ordered them buried back up on the slope near the thin lines of trees.

The lord also offered her the services of his clerics for any of her wounded, which she accepted. Aeria felt guilty that she hadn't even thought of those that were hurt. *I'm too busy thinking of the dead.*

As Aeria looked around at the massive force moving about the castle, up on the walls, in the gate towers and in the courtyard, she formed a plan. *Why don't I go to Varun now that I have an army again? So that Razz didn't die for a failed mission.*

She approached the lord. "Now that we are safe, I have another mission for you."

Lord Wreyghul turned toward her and gave her a curious look. "What Mission, Your Grace?"

She was about to say that she needed an escort through the Rashinasti Forest, but the words couldn't escape her mouth. Instead she heard herself saying, "I need you to go to Marglamesh."

"What?" Lord Wreyghul looked at her incredulously. *What good could possibly come from that? One company against all of Marglamesh. Is she insane?*

Princess Aeria noted his shock, and that of the men nearby who heard his exclamation. "Maybe we should talk in private."

"Shall we go into the tower?" he suggested.

Princess Aeria looked over at the empty tower. "Anywhere but there." Instead they walked to the vacant far side of the courtyard, where she told him all about Bertran Teel, the war plans, and Macal. Their conversation went on for several long moments. Lord Wreyghul had heard of Bertran before and he asked many questions. Hearing her out, Lord Wreyghul sadly shook his head. "I'm very sorry, my Princess, but I can't help you. I can't walk my men into Marglamesh."

Now it was Aeria's turned to be dumbfounded. "You won't do as I ask?"

"I'm sorry, no."

She gave him an angry look. "I order you to help me!"

"You have no military power over me. I answer to the King only."

"And I am his daughter."

"Again, I say this with respect, you have no military authority. And I beg your forgiveness, but I will not risk the lives of these men, who have sworn fealty to me, on a chance that's as likely to succeed as it is that a god will come down from the heavens now and kiss my boots.

"It is fortunate that I was able to come save you here. Can't that be enough? We had only just mustered this force to defend against another marauding troll army like the one you came upon here, when your sylph found us. Those trolls are moving east now into my domain. Some of the reports I've received indicate they even have a few specters with them."

More than the shock that Lord Wreyghul wouldn't do as she commanded, Aeria couldn't believe how many trolls were currently in Elronia. It also struck her hard how unprepared they were for these assaults. *This was probably what King Orgog had been counting on.*

The fact that Lord Wreyghul had only just now mustered his forces, as great as they were, was testament for how ill prepared her father, and therefore her and the rest of the kingdom, had been.

Wreyghul paused a moment, as if trying to figure out how to explain something. "I have six daughters back there I have to protect. And even though my castle is in better shape than this one, if hordes like these can take Mazzul Keep, they will take my home if I'm not there to protect it. Already we will have to catch up to them, because of the time it took to come here to save you. Already they trample my lands, crushing the beautiful wildflowers that fill our colorful meadows."

He looked at her, sorrow plain across his face. "Had it been anybody else but you, or the King or Queen, we wouldn't have come. Who knows how many of my people have now died because of this diversion."

Aeria didn't know what to say, as the guilt of the statement hit her. *If the army goes to stop the troll force how could I help Macal? But more people will die if they don't go. How many? Hundreds of people? Thousands?* She paused as more guilt took hold of her. *But I made a promise to Macal....*

In that moment, looking back at Lord Wreyghul, she realized that she didn't have anybody to send to help Macal.

He was on his own.

CHAPTER 30

Aeria tried one last tact to convince Lord Wreyghul to help her. "You understand that if Macal fails and we don't find the war plans, we will lose the war and we will all die. Even if you go now and defeat the horde in your territory, the trolls will eventually win with those plans. We have nothing to lose and everything to gain by helping him."

The lord was moved by her statement, but held firm to his decision. "My daughters have already lost their mother, I will not let them lose their home, or each other. If so much rides on Teel's son and these plans, why did you send only him? Why not a regiment? I say this with respect, but to put the fate of the kingdom into the hands of a child, it's like—it's like, sending you to parley with the hobgoblins for aid. Your father has made some terrible choices."

Again his words stung Princess Aeria. "I had Viscount Razz Munin with me. The heir to the Dragonmere Kingdom. I was not alone on my errand. And when Macal left we had more options. It was very possible the hobgoblins would have aligned with us against the trolls, if only for their own welfare and the treasures we could promise them. At that point we didn't know the trolls would be invading in such numbers..." her voice trailed off, but then she said, "And there was no stopping Macal, he was going to find his father regardless of the war plans."

"Does your father know about this new plan? About the Teel boy?"

"No. This has all happened since I left Keratost." She turned to him. "You do think it's a good idea, don't you?"

He looked at her, and for a moment she looked like the young girl she really was. He couldn't imagine being that age and charged with this much responsibility. He doubted his own daughters would be doing as well.

Lord Wreyghul then said something that surprised her. "If you really think this could win the war, then after my region is safe we will go to Marglamesh. Because if you are right about what will happen if he is not successful, we, including my daughters and everybody else in Elronia, are all sure to die anyway."

Princess Aeria smiled and jumped forward to give him a very undignified hug.

Wreyghul eventually pulled her away and gave her a warm smile, the first one she had seen since Macal had left her. "After we deal with this scourge we will go and help your young boy."

Her fear for Macal was evident on her face. "I just hope you're not too late."

The Princess and the lord stood together talking. They had paused only a few moments so Lord Wreyghul could step away to issue more instructions. They would be leaving within the hour.

Returning to her he said, "I can provide you with a small compliment and some provisions to get you back to Keratost. You don't have enough men to safely get you back that far south."

"You won't need them?"

"I do and I will, but I need my head as well. And if something happened to you on your way back home, the King would have my head for not protecting you."

"Thank you." Then an idea struck Aeria. "Maybe I should go with you. Help you with the horde, and then in finding Macal."

Lord Wreyghul gave a hearty laugh that shook his thin frame. "I'm sorry, but no. Again we go back to me needing my head. The things your father would do to me if I brought his daughter into the Marg...." Still laughing he turned away to check on the preparations.

All the soldiers moved about, efficiently preparing for their separate journeys. Carriages were given new mounts from the lord's collection. From his entourage she was also given a small contingent of experienced men to bolster her forces.

Then after brief goodbyes, knowing they might never see each other again, the two companies rode out. Lord Wreyghul headed east in haste to save his people and lands, and Aeria's cavalcade rode south to the capital city of Keratost.

Her home.

And her family.

Macal was delirious with hunger. He didn't think he had ever gone this long without food before. On top of that he'd been rationing his water as much as he safely could, but unless he came across another viable stream, he was going to be in real trouble. He was swaying on his feet every few steps. He was now traveling through another formation of jagged obsidian pillars, the thick emerald fog swirling about him as he passed through it.

As he made another turn the monolithic rocks opened up and were replaced by a field of violet bushes on which grew large cerulean berries. Interspersed among the bushes were short white crystalline rocks that were a stark contrast to the black soil.

Macal saw the berries and his heart and stomach filled with joy. He didn't know what they were and he didn't care. He needed food and that was all that mattered. He gathered his remaining strength and stumbled forward to the nearest bush. With a clumsy hand he plucked a berry from it and stuffed it into his mouth.

He was about to bite down, clench his teeth upon it when he heard a voice to his right.

"Um, I wouldn't eat that." The voice sounded like it echoed up from the earth.

Macal refrained from biting down, but didn't spit out the berry. He wasn't ready to give up the first food he had come across in days easily. He looked around for the owner of the voice.

A few feet to his right one of the crystalline rocks blinked its milky white eyes at him.

The boy jumped back in surprise. That rock just talked to him!

The rock smiled. As its face changed shape it made a sound like gravel being crushed. "Um, I said, you shouldn't eat that. Cause, um, you won't like what happens next."

Macal's eyes never left the creature. He spit the saliva-covered berry into his hand. "Why? What happens?"

"Well, um, you turn into me."

"I turn into you?"

"Well, um, not me exactly, into a rock like me. Of course, but, um, if you would like to be a rock, then yes, go ahead, eat it, but it's definitely not the life for everybody. Being a rock."

"I don't think I want to be a rock."

"I didn't think you would, anyway, um…."

"Is that what happened to you?"

"What? Um, oh, did I turn into a rock? Oh no, um, I was like this since the world had two suns."

Macal had never heard of there being a second sun. "Two suns?"

"Oh yes, it was quite a thing to watch the first one disappear. Um, I think you would have liked the world better back then. There was more color. Um, not like now, where it's all blacks, greens, and grays. It's rather kinda drab."

とおり

"There is color in the world. In other places. Where I come from its bright and beautiful and full of color."

The rock was intrigued. "Um, there are other places? You can imagine as a rock I don't ever move terribly far. Um, where are you from?"

"The Kingdom of Elronia. It's two kingdoms northeast of here."

"Never heard of it. Maybe someday I should try to find it, um...."

With more sounds of breaking stone the rock creature sprouted tiny squat legs and arms. "Well, um, I must be going to tend to the fountains now."

Macal's throat reminded him of how dry it was. "Fountains?"

"Oh, um, you wouldn't want to drink from these fountains. Not if you like standing upright and not being a pile of jelly. Um, it was nice meeting you. Off to tend to the fountains I go. Cause, um, if not, who will?"

"Does anybody need to tend them?"

The creature stopped, turned back, and gave Macal a quizzical look. "Um, yes. Why else would I be doing it? Oh, and um, remember, don't eat the berries."

The rock creature turned and waddled away north into to the field. Macal didn't want the rock creature to go. He was glad to have company and he didn't want to be alone again.

"You're not alone. I'm here."

"But I wish you weren't."

Leaving the berries behind Macal turned west and continued toward King Orgog's castle.

The days passed, one after another, as Macal trod on with sore and blistering feet. He eventually came across a rough roadway; despite the opportunity for easier travel, to avoid any unwanted encounters he purposefully stayed off and followed along near the edge of the road. Fortunately on the second day he came across another relatively clear flowing river and was able to refill his waterskin. Setting his course each morning by the rising sun, he continued his trek southwest toward the castle.

Tired, aching, and hungry, Macal trudged onward. The terrain changed little as he went deeper into Marglamesh. The land was blighted. He remembered his father describing this place as a land of demons and drakes; now after seeing it, he felt that his father had been much too kind.

Already he'd been attacked by innumerable pests. Small yellow bulbous flying insects with multiple stingers. Tiny eight-legged two-tailed translucent lizards. Hand-sized, lithe, copper-colored biting flies. Purple-shelled beetles which, after they tried in vain to bite him through his leather clothing, spoke to him in a tongue he couldn't understand. In frustrated anger the beetles gathered together and swarmed at him, hoping to overwhelm him with their numbers. He ran. They chased after him, snapping their mandibles, chittering and cursing him in their strange language. He was faster though and was eventually able to escape.

Wary from these attacks, Macal now walked with his dagger loose in his scabbard—in case anything else came at him.

Travel in the pitch-dark of night was impossible. By the time the sun sank away each evening, after dragging his feet over the dark soiled earth for several hours, Macal was surprised to find each opportunity to rest was almost pleasant. Each night he'd crawl under some of the thick bramble that grew by the road and lay his head down. Within moments he'd be asleep. In the twilight one night, another memory-dream of Uncle Melkes bubbled up in his mind. He didn't know why, but he was reminded of a story his uncle had told him. Maybe it was the fact that the rock creature had mentioned a time when the world had two suns. He couldn't remember all the details, or even recall where he was or when Uncle Melkes had told the story to him.

Uncle Melkes had looked down and gave Macal his ever-reassuring smile. "There were legends from the Age of Heroes that, when the world was young, it was very different. Many of the old stories spoke of this. They said that the world was much hotter. Zarn had loved the heat, so deserts were the most prevalent terrain across the surface of Aerinth. Eventually, for whatever reason one of the suns either left or burnt out and died. To allow the young races to grow and therefore give the gods more followers, the gods converted the deserts into forests, swamps, plains, mountains, and rivers."

Macal remembered asking a question. "Wouldn't Aerinth be too cold now, if it used to have two suns?"

"How perceptive of you to think of that. Perhaps. But who are we to judge what the gods can overcome or the merit of the legends?"

Macal's last thought before he was overcome by sleep was how, more than anything, he loved to hear Uncle Melkes' stories. The following morning he struggled to his feet and began his march anew.

At the end of the fifth or sixth day, as Macal pushed through miles of bog next to the road—stabbed with the maroon thorns of some black, decayed bushes—he won over his revulsion at the thought of eating a squishy, slimy creature that he had seen aplenty across the surface of the bog water.

The Cloak of Brinizarn had told him they were called wilps, a small indigo creature half the size of his hand, with a bulging belly and many spindly legs. After trying some rotted, fungus-infected fruit from a tree they had come across two days before—at the cloak's urging—and almost immediately becoming violently ill, he had been apprehensive about trying anything new. But the cloak had recognized the insect, and after an unnecessarily sarcastic exchange had finally informed Macal that he knew first-hand that humans could eat it if they were that desperate for food. During the exchange Macal also learned that the cloak thought this "need to eat" was just another of his many "failings."

The wilps were as disgusting to eat as he expected. They burst apart as he bit into them, spraying their juices through his mouth and down his chin. But at this point he didn't care—didn't care that the insects were raw, and that their legs still wriggled in his hand after he had bitten off their torsos. His only thought was to end the pangs of hunger.

The next day he finally escaped the bog, and hoped that tomorrow would be a better day—but he knew it wouldn't be.

Wherever he was the earth was always damp, wet, and putrid. He stopped caring how uncomfortable it was. With the cloak's help each night he found a place that offered at least marginal protection and comfort. He was always physically exhausted and he always fell quickly asleep—but this night he felt like now was the time he should be staying awake preparing and planning for the final battle to come.

For a weapon he only had the dagger, and the blade was far from sharp enough. From a pouch at his belt he pulled out a small sharpening stone. Forcing himself to stay awake until this task was done, he sharpened his blade in the quiet of the hazy purple gloom. He wasn't sure what tomorrow would bring, but he was going to be ready for it.

After the blade was sharp he spent some time pouring out the slime and goo that had accumulated in his boots from the long trek.

Despite being hungry, tired, and wet, covered in slime, scratches, insect bites, and bruises, Macal recalled how much he had hated being in Hormul. And now that he was here in this horrible place he just wanted to be back there more than anything else.

He took a deep breath. A big part of him wanted to cry. Breathing deeply he steeled himself and held it back. *I have to be strong*, he thought.

"You are going to need more than strength," said the cloak.

"This once can you leave me alone?"

For once the cloak seemed to understand and fell silent. Macal really did want a moment alone. To make sure, he unclasped the brooch and lay the cloak on the ground next to him.

It may have taken the entire journey, but in that moment he convinced himself that he might be able to be a hero.

Night had fallen heavily on the moors. The green fog took on a purplish tint at night. He hadn't noticed this glow before—perhaps it was just in this area. He had long ago stopped worrying about the insects that plagued him. If the glow was from some kind of new insect he didn't have the energy to fend them off.

He had never been so tired; so exhausted, so utterly and completely empty. The pain from his stomach was far worse than any other pain from his body. But his resolve did not waver.

If only Shelga were here. He hoped she was okay. If she had been with him he would be eating rations, sitting by a warm fire, and changing into a dry set of clothes. But instead he was alone here, cold, wet, and starving.

He had never been good at much. He had never been brave. He had never been strong. Nobody had ever relied on him. And now he needed to be all these things. For his father, for Aeria, for Elronia. For himself.

This was the moment, he thought. *This is the moment before we find out if I am worthy of the faith Princess Aeria placed in me.* Could he save his father? Save Elronia? He didn't know.

I'm going to find out. I've come this far. I'm not going to fail. Nothing that happened before really matters. All my cowardice, all my failings no longer matter. He had to succeed here to save all that mattered to him.

And besides, he thought, *what better way to avenge Uncle Melkes than to strike a savage blow against the trolls by recovering the war plans.*

When the darkest hours of the night had passed Macal picked up the cloak, wrapped it about himself as a blanket, and on the driest mound he could—a bed of moss under a rotting tree—he collapsed. As he curled up he mustered the energy to look west—up at the eerie castle, sitting high on its dark mass of mountain, looking impossibly far away and insurmountable.

He fingered the gold ring on his finger and thought of Aeria. Just barely visible in the moonlight was the dragon's head, surrounded by a ring of roses. One day he would finally make it to Castle Darkmoor. It was his final thought as he fell asleep.

CHAPTER 31

In the light of a new day Macal looked over his armor. It was battered, torn, and beyond grimy though he'd only had it a few weeks. He no longer wondered why veteran soldiers always looked so worn and gruff.

He knew he was fortunate that nobody expected there to be a boy wandering alone within this realm. After getting away from the first group of trolls he had dodged many more. The Princess may have been right; an army would be noticed, but a lone boy was much more unlikely. Still, recent days had been more eventful than he would have liked.

He also guessed that maybe the trolls were so overconfident that they would never expect their enemies would ever again walk their soil. Not today, not during this war. He lost count of how many armies he had snuck past. He guessed by their volume and size that King Orgog had thousands of trolls on the march toward Elronia.

The previous night's rest had not refreshed him at all. Dragging his feet he strode ever onward. The land got stranger and stranger as he went.

In the early part of the morning he came to a dark wood that he dared not enter. The trees seemed alive, their branches eternally burned with yellow flame and writhed like flailing snakes. He decided to skirt the wood by following its edge south.

At mid-day, as he waded through ponds of dark orange water coated with a film of brown and black slime, he passed a cave from which a magenta-colored, noxious, luminous pale gas endlessly escaped. As the gas billowed out it didn't dissipate into the open air, but instead formed into nightmarish spectral beasts. The conjurations looked like ghostly slithering intestines, with numerous eyeless heads and mouths filled with thousands of teeth. Macal retreated, back-tracked and went northward around the burning woods by the north side.

Just as evening threw its darkened cloak over the world again, he happened upon a group of curious scorpions, with three tails and an almost entirely transparent appearance. After watching them cautiously from a safe distance—and seeing what one of the creatures did to a wandering lebrish, a troll livestock animal generally poisonous to humans and used for its tough, bitter meat—Macal went to great lengths to avoid them.

While the eight-legged lebrish swung its elephantine spiked trunk in search of food, it accidentally struck the scorpion. The scorpion retaliated in a malicious rage, repeatedly stinging the beast with its three poisoned tails.

Every part of the lebrish that the venom was injected into shriveled up, as if it had been dehydrated. Its once meaty, stumpy legs drew in upon themselves to become withered, bone-dry husks. Its trunk dwindled and disintegrated to ash, blown away by an errant wind.

The livestock's dying legs also finally collapsed into dust. As the creature fell it was stung many more times on its body. Macal turned away and wished he hadn't witnessed any of this.

Giving the scorpions wide birth, the boy passed through a brief area of pits. The ground was obsidian, jagged in places and smooth and shining in others. Between the gigantic holes he found a narrow path twisting its way through. Exhaustion, his constant companion, nearly overtook him as he stumbled close to the edge of one of the pits. His boot kicked several black rocks accidentally over the edge, down into the abyss. He listened but was never able to hear them hit the bottom. It was then he saw what the pits held.

The ground shook as an enormous amber armor-scaled worm rose from one of the distant pits. From it emanated a stench more vile even than that of the trolls. It rose high out of the pit, more than a hundred feet, where it swayed this way and that as if stretching its muscles, before it descended back into the comfort of its hole.

They weren't pits, he realized. They were homes.

The Cloak of Brinizarn recognized these too. *"To be exact, they are home to krolo worms."*

"What are they?" Macal responded with his inner voice.

"I just told you. Krolo worms."

"I mean what are they doing here?"

"Oh. That's a good question. I'm a bit out of date on my lore, and you don't seem to have a whole lot of information in this head of yours."

"I'm only twelve!"

"By the time I was your age I'd traveled the world. Helped end three wars. Walked among the stars and was, for a whole week, named King of Vlance."

"Well, I've never heard of these things."

"Maybe it's something new the trolls are trying. Maybe they want to use them in battle."

"What? We have nothing like this. We would need dragons to fight these!"

"Wait! What? You don't have dragons?!"

"Of course we don't."

"I think I prefer the times of old."

"Let me guess, you had dragons?"

"Who didn't?"

"Forget it. Come on. If we can stop this war we will never need to worry about these things."

"I'm starting to doubt you can stop this. Look at what they have. Giant! Attack! Worms!"

"You're not helping."

"I even had a chromatic dragon. And just so you know, I'm referring to the strongest dragon type of legend. I wonder if he's still alive...."

Macal didn't reply and instead crept through the pits as quietly as he could. Shortly he came to a sudden stop. He saw something up in the sky. He hid near the base of a boulder and stared at it.

Against the black sky he saw what looked like an angel of fire streaking eastward. Its wings were flame. Its body lithe and dark. Macal, his breath still in his lungs, watched as the thing diminished into the distance— wondering what it could be while also hoping never to find out.

The days blurred into each other. Each morning Macal got up before the sun broke across the horizon and forced himself onward toward Castle Darkmoor, filling his waterskin whenever he was able.

Staggering through this morning, he noticed a small deep blue glow flickering ahead. As he got closer he saw that it came from a crudely constructed rise of earth. It reminded him of a barrow his uncle had taken him to once, where a lord was entombed; but the barrow had been carpeted with lush green grass, while this one only had broken logs and sticks protruding from its muddy surface.

He brushed aside the lank hair that had now grown to cover his eyes and paused for a moment to examine it. Circling the mound he could see that the blue flicker seeped out of a rough hole in its side.

"I know what you're thinking. This is not a good idea," warned the cloak.

"I know that," Macal replied in his head.

"So, you are not only a dumb thief, by you lack wisdom too."

"I'm very close to throwing you down into the next krolo pit we find, leaving you there for the creatures to eat."

"You'd never do it. You're too afraid of being alone."

"For as much help as you are it's already like I'm alone. So I wouldn't really be losing anything."

"I saved you from the trolls!"

"Weeks ago. And only after you almost let them catch me. Twice."

"Exactly. Almost. There is a very important difference between letting them and almost letting them."

"Just be quiet. I need food. If there is anything to eat nearby I need to get some. Otherwise the trolls might as well have caught me, 'cause I'll be dead of starvation anyway."

"I think you have a good two days left in you. And you can always eat more of those worm thingys."

The thought made Macal's stomach churn in disgust. He didn't respond and instead crept forward.

"You are definitely going to get us killed. Well, you at least. I'm not sure I can die."

Macal continued to ignore him. His hunger had won out over his apprehension of investigating the mound. He snuck up to the hole and peered in.

He quickly guessed the hole served as a window. He had never seen how trolls housed themselves. He had never thought about it, so had no idea what to expect, but this definitely seemed like a troll hovel.

The small round room had a cooking pit on one side where a blue flame was heating an earthenware pot. From the ceiling hung rough pottery bowls, cups, a kettle, and innumerable exotic plants drying. On the other side of the room was a dingy pile of reeds. A recess in the dried mud wall served as a shelf, on which were many pots of varying sizes overflowing with even more unfamiliar herbs. Other than that there were no other furnishings Macal would expect to find in a residence. No table, chairs, rug, or cabinets.

The hovel's austerity reminded Macal of his own cottage. Admittedly they had more furniture. He wondered if he was ever going see that cottage again. As always happened whenever he thought of home, the thought was quickly eclipsed by the fact that he would never see his uncle again.

There was also a troll inside. To his surprise, this troll was like no other troll he had ever seen—mainly because he had never seen a troll wearing a dress, grimy or otherwise. It took a second, but he realized he was looking at a female troll.

He wasn't sure why he was so surprised to see one here in Marglamesh. He knew they must live somewhere. He was aware that they couldn't travel outside the Marg, bound to the troll land by some ancient rite of magic.

She was tall and thin. She was craned forward, so as to not hit her head on the low ceiling. She moved about the hovel retrieving and adding ingredients to the boiling pot. Her scales were a pale green, spotted with the occasional growth of dark blue rocky protrusions.

Macal remembered his father telling him that the female trolls could transform themselves into fairy maidens. He wondered if that was true or if his father had only told him an entertaining story.

He could smell the food she was cooking. It smelled unseemly, but his hunger was so profound that his mouth salivated anyway. Instead of putting him off it lured him in. He hadn't had a good warm meal since he left the Princess.

As he stared at the boiling pot longingly, she turned and with yellow eyes stared at him.

Startled, Macal jumped back, turned, and ran. Behind him the make-shift wooden door of the hut slapped opened as the troll rushed outside.

"Wait!" Her voice was calm and clear, the opposite of the guttural bellows of all the troll soldiers he had ever come across. "Are you hungry?"

Macal slowed his steps. His hunger fought for control of his body.

"Oh, this is a really bad idea," said the cloak.

"I have more than enough food," she said. Macal stopped and turned back toward the female troll. "Come in if you wish. It's almost ready. I'm happy to share."

The boy was surprised by how well-spoken she was. It was like she was from a different race entirely. She turned and went back inside, leaving the door open. Macal hesitated. He didn't know what to do. He knew he shouldn't go in. She was a troll! But he was so hungry.

"Don't do it," said the cloak.

Macal made up his mind and walked back to the hovel and into the door.

"It was nice knowing you," said the cloak.

Cautiously Macal stepped through the threshold. The troll was taking her kettle off its hook. She added some water and herbs to it. "Are you thirsty?"

This seemed so surreal to Macal. He was about to have a meal with a troll. A very real, alive, troll. "Yes," he muttered at last.

The kettle heated up fast over the blue flame. She poured some of the concoction into two clay cups that were wrapped in old sleeves of leather. Macal watched as she took a sip of hers before he tried his own. The ochre colored liquid tasted like a weird mossy tea.

Macal stayed near the door, ready to run at the first hint of trouble. As he silently drank his tea the troll noticed how on edge he was. "I'm not going to hurt you."

The boy remained quiet and continued to drink his tea.

She went to stir her pot with a bark covered stick. "What's your name?"

"Macal."

"I've never heard that name before. But that is easily explained. You are the first human I have ever seen and we don't give ourselves human names.

I'm called Glorrittia. Would you like some bread?"

Macal nodded his head and he was soon handed a moldy gray-colored chunk of bread. He ignored its foul aspect and bit into it hungrily. It tasted like chalk, but he wasn't going to complain.

As he devoured the bread he mused that Glorrittia seemed quite a bit smarter than the troll men he had met. He wondered if all troll women were?

She attended to her cooking pot. "Can I ask why you are here in Marglamesh? You are a boy, right?"

Macal swallowed the last of the crusty bread. "I'm looking for my father." He was not sure why he told her the truth. He felt like he should lie to her.

She gave him a puzzled look. "Father?" The word seemed unfamiliar to her.

"Father," Macal reiterated. "The man who gave me life and takes care of me."

Glorrittia was still perplexed. "Is he a human?"

"Yes. Of course."

"Are you referring to—what is it called? Oh yes, *family*?"

"Yes, exactly."

"Oh, I think I understand. It's a strange idea. Trolls don't have *families*. To us the idea of a family relationship is meaningless. You must take care of yourself. There is nobody to care for you. To rely on another is a sign of weakness."

Macal couldn't help but think that trolls were everything he never wanted to be.

She went to a far shelf and took an ingredient from a jar and added it to the soup. Macal recognized the plant, after all working on a farm had some benefits. He knew it was poison. He made a quick decision, and tried his best to act like he wasn't aware of anything.

The cloak also recognized what the plant was. *"Oh, guess what kind of meat is going to be in her next soup? I'm guessing human boy meat."*

Macal spoke internally to the cloak directly with his mind. *"I know what I'm doing."*

"When do you ever know what you are doing?"

A few moments later she ladled soup into two bowls and handed him one. "I think you call them spoons and I'm sorry I don't have any. They slow down the eating process; we've found that it is far more efficient just to drink from the bowl."

Macal knocked the bowl from her hand. It splashed across the floor. He pulled out his dagger and held it toward Glorrittia "You're trying to poison me!"

"I would if I could," said the cloak.

"Shut up." Macal said aloud. The troll looked at him curiously. She hadn't said anything. "Not you, him. Just...never mind. Why are you poisoning me?"

Her voice was blunt and factual. "You are the enemy."

"So, then I should kill you?" Macal jabbed his dagger in her direction.

She looked confused again. "I'm sorry. Sorry."

"No, she isn't," said the cloak.

"I'm sorry," she continued. "You mean you weren't planning to kill me?"

"No!" Macal was appalled. "But now I might."

"But you're a human and I'm a troll. We are forever enemies."

"We don't have to be."

"Yes, we do."

"If I don't kill you, will you help me? Take me to the castle? I know you can transform into some kind of wind fairy."

"I could never help you."

"You must."

She paused to think. "Maybe there is a way. Maybe I help you and you help me."

Macal looked at her, unsure if he wanted to know what she had in mind.

Inside Glorrittia's hovel, Macal watched as she mixed a salve for the rash he had. He hadn't even known he had a rash until she pointed it out to him. He hadn't seen a mirror in a long while. The rash covered his neck and back; the troll had explained that if left unchecked the infection would grow and probably kill him.

She made them another non-poisoned meal which Macal hastily devoured. She hadn't said anything more about how they could help each other. Macal's curiosity got the best of him. "I won't endanger you more than I need. I just need you to get me to the castle."

Glorrittia smiled. He hadn't known trolls could do that. He told her a brief version of his story. "I'm impressed you made it this far. You're very brave to come here alone. You must have great courage."

Macal beamed at the compliment. "I just couldn't leave my father here. He's the only family I have left. What do I have to do to get you to help me?"

The smile remained on her face. "Something very simple."

"Nothing's ever simple," commented the cloak.

With a rough-skinned hand she applied the salve to his rash. It was warm on his skin.

"What's this simple task?"

She was done applying the salve. "You will have to kiss me."

Macal was more shocked than he had ever been. Never in a thousand years would he have guessed that was what she wanted. For some reason he was scared and nervous at the same time. "Why?"

"Because it will set me free so that I can leave this land. It will break the spell that binds me here to Marglamesh."

"Why me?"

"It doesn't have to be exactly you. Any male from another race kissing a female of my race breaks the spell. Rarely do we get visitors. Not many seek to come to Marglamesh of their own choosing. So the spell is nearly impossible to break."

"Then why did you try to kill me? If I was dead I wouldn't have been able to help you."

"Like I said, I thought you were going to try to kill *me*. I know better now."

"You're not going to do it, are you?" asked the cloak, disgusted at the thought. *"I mean touching your lips to that thing? Especially when you know where it's been. Here! In Marglamesh. Who knows what kind of germs and disease you will catch."*

Macal didn't respond.

"Oh my! You are going to do it." The cloak made some vomiting noises inside Macal's skull.

The boy looked at Glorrittia with reluctance. "Okay, I'll do it." Macal's mind reeled with the realization that the first kiss he was ever going to give was to a troll!

He didn't want to be tricked. "If I do this, how will I know you will still help me?"

"I give you my word. The gift you are going to give is worth a thousand such favors."

Macal felt reassured by the conviction in her voice. He walked over to her and she stooped down. He stood on his toes, craned his neck up, puckered his lips and kissed her on the cheek. In his mind he pretended that he was kissing the Princess.

He was also reminded that he had never got to do this to his mother. Macal's earliest memory was of his mother—since she had died when he was born he knew that what he had in his head could not be a real memory at all. But he liked the idea of having a memory of her. It made him feel close to the mother he had never actually got to meet.

His father and uncle talked about her every now and then, but only briefly. It was after she died that his father had signed on for full campaigns in the army. Uncle Melkes explained that Bertran had needed time away— time to think and heal, and time to forget. His father had loved his mother deeply and when she died his father's heart went with her.

As his lips ceased contact with Glorrittia's scales he expected a magical transformation to occur as the spell was broken, but there was nothing. She just withdrew across the room with a peaceful look on her face.

"In the morning I will fulfill my part of the bargain," she declared. "Let us rest first before we both leave this place forever."

"Where will you go?"

She became thoughtful for a moment. "I don't know. I never thought that I would have the chance to leave so I never entertained the idea. I didn't want to tease myself with possibilities. Do you have any suggestions?"

"No."

"Well, we should sleep." She indicated the pile of reeds for a bed. She separated them into two even piles, one for him and one for her. This didn't make sense to Macal. He was half as tall as her, so he took half of his pile and pushed it back to hers.

As he laid down on the coarse bedding he wasn't sure, but he was confident that he saw several unfamiliar insects skitter away from the reeds. He was so tired that he didn't care. Having a safe place to rest after a meal was far more comfort than he expected to find in Marglamesh.

So here was a troll. An enemy of his kingdom, and he an enemy of hers, and here they were getting along. This experience struck him deeply. Not every person or creature had all the traits, malevolent or benevolent, of their race. Viscount Razz came to mind as another example. Macal marveled that he had made an ally here in this forsaken land. This made him realize that even trolls were not all the same. He guessed that he must have known this, the same way he knew not all humans were kind, like Captain Jengus, but he had never really thought about it. The same could be true for other races as well. It was nice to know he didn't always have to use a weapon to get what he needed.

He couldn't believe she was going to help him. He couldn't believe she *had* helped him. He should have died from hunger. Or from the rash. He was fortunate that not all trolls liked trolls. And with that thought he fell fast asleep.

In the morning they woke and Glorrittia prepared to fly Macal to Castle Darkmoor and his father.

CHAPTER 32

Bertran Teel cried out in pain again. He didn't know how much time had passed. He never did. His torture had amplified. The witches had now conjured a black mist that burned like acid to envelope his hands, but it did no lasting damage—allowing them to torture him endlessly.

He was in a daze now. He felt his mind starting to slow, starting to dim. He was coherent enough to know the Troll King had returned.

"Your son is dead," Orgog lied, trying to force information out of him. Around him the witches laughed gleefully.

"No," he replied weakly, barely able to talk.

One of the witches floated around him. "I like it when he cries."

"I prefer it when he screams," added the second.

"I like to watch his tormented dreams. Men are so filled with hope," chimed the third.

"I assure you he is!" interjected the Troll King. "Your son is dead!"

"I meant no, I won't tell you."

"Your son's life means nothing to you?"

"It means now that he's dead, I don't care what happens to me."

"Do you care what happens to the rest of the people of your kingdom? Where are the plans?" snarled the king.

Macal's father remained silent.

"Your son is dead," explained Orgog. "But there is still much more we can do to him."

A fierceness overtook the soldier. His eyes cleared as he glared at the Troll King.

"The realm of the dead is not beyond the reach of my witches. The pain he is given there can be eternal. Lasting."

"I can't," said Bertran for the hundredth time.

298

"I don't think you realize what happens in Narekisis, the plane of the dead."

"I won't betray my kingdom."

"But you betray your son."

An impossible conflict between two allegiances warred within Bertran. He couldn't give up the whole kingdom just for his son. But he couldn't give up his son for the kingdom either. His heart wailed in turmoil.

Then suddenly with a jolt it all became clear to him. He had no choice. He would never tell where the plans were, even if he had to sacrifice Macal.

The Troll King saw this. He saw the look that came over the man—the resolute and resigned look of honor and loyalty to his people. Nothing was going to break that bond.

In anger King Orgog reached up and grabbed Bertran's right hand with his own massive clawed one. "How many trolls did this hand kill? The hand that wielded Alrang-Dal. How many?! How about we make sure that never happens again!" With a great yank he tore the hand from Bertran's arm.

The king threw the useless appendage to the floor, where it dissolved away to blackened ash. Macal's father screamed in unspeakable pain as the Troll King stormed out. He would have to come up with a new plan, some new strategy that the magical map would not foretell.

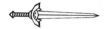

Glorrittia summoned her innate magic and transformed her body into a cloudy whirlwind. She picked Macal up and cradled him in her arms. Then she crouched and jumped up, launching them into the air.

Up they rose, until the details of the land below were lost. With the speed of a furious gusting wind they passed over the land of Marglamesh. Macal looked down and took in the dreadful land of shadows. Past black cliffs they went. Past swamps of vile brown water. Over forests of ancient diseased trees. Over fog-laden bogs and monster-ridden moors.

He wasn't sure how many more days it would have taken him to get to the castle had he continued on foot over this landscape of obsidian soil. Or where he would have gotten the food and water to survive the journey.

For the first time he saw King Orgog's home, Castle Darkmoor, up close. The place he'd thought about every moment of every day since the Princess had told him it was the prison where his father was trapped. He had never seen something so hideous and bleak; and yet, he couldn't help feeling there was a magnificence to it. It was larger than he could have fathomed. It wasn't just mountainous, it was an actual mountain, held aloft by wicked magics. The structure, the gates, the doors, the windows were all larger than the castles in Elronia, the entirety of the castle built to house trolls and not humans. Anywhere else it would have been a blight on the landscape, an eyesore. In this region, in this kingdom, its stark and bleak grandeur was at home.

As he breathed in the air close to the castle he found the source of the horrid stink of the Marg. The castle emanated a retched stench that was nearly tangible.

Glorrittia flew upward. Macal wasn't sure how he would have gotten all the way up here without her help. As they got to the castle she set him down in the camouflage of amber fog at the base of an outer wall.

"I can't take you any farther. If I'm seen here they won't hesitate to come out and put an end to me. Not many females are allowed here."

Macal pulled his eyes from the castle and looked at her. "I understand."

"And I don't know how to get you inside."

Macal glanced back up at the dizzyingly high black wall. He didn't know how he was going to get in either. "It's okay. Just getting me this far is more than enough help. Thank you."

"And thank you, Macal. I hope you succeed in your quest to find your *family.*" The word still seemed foreign to her. "Good bye."

Without a look back she launched herself into the air again and flew off into the clouds. The boy watched her go, wondering where she would end up. With her ability to fly that could be anywhere. He hoped that wherever it was she found happiness. He watched her go until he could no longer see her.

He turned back to the fortress. He had no idea how to get in. Now that he was here he could feel in the essence of his spirit that he was certainly going to die. There was no way that a lone boy was going to succeed in freeing his father from this place.

Macal closed his eyes and prayed to any god who may be listening. He prayed that he would will find a path to his father and be free from here. *I know I can't do it alone. I'm so scared.*

He remembered his uncle once said, "Nothing is more valuable than family."

He shook off the moment of weakness. He reminded himself that he wasn't a wimp anymore. He had to go forward no matter what the danger. No matter how scared he was. He had to go on for his father. Nothing was more important than family.

He asked for one last prayer. He prayed that the Princess was going to send help quickly.

As Macal searched the wall for a way in he hoped the cloak was recharged. He had a feeling he was going to need it.

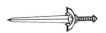

The base of the wall was shrouded in the same emerald fog that coated much of the land, which hindered Macal's vision and made his search difficult. He had been investigating for over an hour and so far he hadn't found any passage, crevice or even a grate-covered opening. He wasn't sure what he should have expected. This was a castle. A fortress. It was designed to keep people out, not allow them to sneak in.

Macal had asked the Cloak of Brinizarn if it had enough of a magical charge left to be able to fly him up over the wall but it had said that it hadn't. From its tone the boy wasn't sure he believed the cloak, but there was nothing he could do about it if the cloak didn't want to help.

"Stop Moving! Did you hear that?" asked the cloak.

Macal hands stopped searching the slimy black stones of the wall. He hadn't heard anything.

"There it is again."

The boy still couldn't hear anything besides the muffled sounds of the general goings-on of a typical castle. He stood still and held his breath.

"It's trolls...well of course it's trolls, what else would be at a troll castle—but anyway, they're out here. Outside the wall. They must be checking the perimeter. Maybe now is a good time to call an end to this little adventure and head on home. Come on, what do you say? I could fly you off this floating rock."

Macal still couldn't hear any approaching trolls. He wondered if the cloak was just trying to trick him into leaving. "I thought you said you weren't recharged enough yet to do anything," he mumbled quietly under his breath.

"Oh yeah, right. You are so correct. I'm useless. Sorry I brought it up."

"You smell dat?" Macal heard a vulgar voice say a short distance away. He looked, but the fog obscured his sight.

"Ya. It smells like men," replied a second voice.

Macal backed away along the wall, hoping to put some distance between him and the patrol of trolls.

"Dats what I was finkin. Whys the smell of mens here?"

"Hows do I know? Maybe it's the stink of the one below."

As Macal continued to back away his boot slipped on a rock slick with the dampness of the fog. He crashed down onto his back.

As he hit the ground the words the troll had spoken went through his head again. *The one below.* They had a human here. It had to be his father. His father really was here and he was possibly still alive!

Lost in that thought, he didn't recover himself in time before the patrol charged over to investigate the disturbance.

The two trolls stood over the boy, leering at him. "I guesses we do have another men here."

"You know we're gonna eat him, right?"

"Oh yeah. We can do that right here and we won't have to share."

"You'se gotta beautiful mind."

Macal scrambled backwards. The trolls lunged forward and grabbed him. They hoisted him off the ground and held him splayed between them, each holding an arm and a leg.

"Let's pull him apart. See who gets the bigger piece."

"Alright, but you'se know I always win dat."

"Well, it was nice knowing you," said the cloak.

The trolls pulled. Macal fought against them but their meaty hands held him with mighty grips. He felt his joints starting to pop.

In spite of the pain Macal glanced up at the looming castle and wondered how he could have come so close only to fail in his quest.

Outside Castle Darkmoor the trolls that held Macal were pulling him apart. Macal cried in pain as they yanked on him again.

"Ya see how thin dis one is? I bet the meat's gonna be all stringy."

"Better dan no meat at all."

The first troll nodded. "His arm won't come free. They always pop off first. Let me get a better hold."

The troll released Macal's wrist to reset his grip, and the boy didn't waste the opportunity—he quickly pulled his dagger from his belt. He was happy he had spent time sharpening it each evening as he stabbed it into the troll's empty hand. The blade sliced deep. The monster howled in pain and released its grip on his leg.

The other troll still holding his other side was surprised by this sudden turn of events. Macal took advantage again. Still in the troll's grip he thrust the dagger twice at the creature, striking him once in the forearm that held him and again in its thigh. Adding to the bellows of his companion, this troll also let go.

Macal fell to the ground. His entire body ached from what the trolls had just done to him. He got to his feet at the same time the trolls recovered themselves and pulled out their axes. No longer did they have looks of amusement on their faces. They glared at the boy with hatred and rage.

"Perhaps, I may be of assistance," said the cloak.

Macal kept the dialogue with the cloak internal. *"Oh, now you want to help?"*

"Better late than never, they say."

The trolls stepped forward and readied their weapons above their heads.

"Well, what do you got? Should I turn into a bear?"

"No, better. Say, 'For the Crown I shall hide the secrets of the kingdom.'"

The trolls swung their axes.

Macal jumped out of the way. "For The Crown I Shall Hide The Secrets

Of The Kingdom."

Unlike the other two times he had invoked the powers of the cloak, this time the cloak didn't burst with light. Instead it did nothing. Macal watched as the trolls frantically looked around.

"Where did he go?" asked the first.

"I don't know. Did you eat him?"

The trolls spun around and around and swatted the fog away. "He must be here somewheres."

It took Macal a moment to figure out what the Cloak of Brinizarn had done. *"You turned me invisible?"*

"Maybe you aren't such a dolt after all."

Macal shook his head in frustration at the cloak. He had never been invisible before. As the trolls looked for him, he felt empowered. He had never been the sneaky type, but he thought he might be able to get used to this. He took a step toward the nearest troll.

"What are you doing?" asked the cloak anxiously.

"They know I'm here. I can't let them set off the alarm."

"No. Let's just keep moving. I can get you inside the castle now."

Macal ignored the cloak. He closed in on the troll, dagger in hand. He had planned it out in his head. Invisible, he knew he had surprise on his side now. He plunged the dagger into the troll's foot through its leather boot. As the beast screamed in pain it bent over to grab its foot, just like Macal thought it would. Macal was now able to reach its chest, and he drove the dagger's entire blade into its heart.

Silenced, the troll toppled over and lay still. The remaining troll's eyes went wide in alarm. It decided it no longer wanted to eat the boy. It also didn't want to be out here alone with an invisible human, it preferred having allies nearby to hopefully absorb attacks that should have been meant for him. So it turned and ran. It would get inside the castle, assemble a large patrol, then they would deal with the intruder together.

Macal also expected this. He ran forward and jabbed his dagger into the guard's calf, jerking the blade sideways as he pulled it out, hoping to cut as much muscle as he could. The troll growled in anguish.

Its leg unable to support him any longer the troll tumbled over. Macal jumped unto its back and with both hands on the hilt drove the dagger deep down into his enemy. After several strikes the troll stopped struggling.

"Well, well, well," began the cloak. *"Guess who's impressed? Me. I so didn't think you had it in you."*

Macal wiped the troll blood off his blade onto the fallen creature's tunic. *"Being invisible helped. After another ten years of training I might actually know what I'm doing."*

"Yeah, you are not very good at this on your own."

"I've only had a couple days' training."

"I thought your father was supposed to be some kind of soldier. A hero. How could he have never taught you how to fight?"

"Because he was never home!" Macal yelled. "He was always somewhere helping the King. Helping the kingdom. Helping somebody else—"

"I'm sure that's what they told you."

"What does that mean?"

"All I know is that being a hero is in your blood. If he is a hero then you should be too."

"I don't think that's true."

"Well, you are proving that every step of the way."

Macal fumed and changed the subject. *"Can you fly me over the wall now?"* he asked, reverting back to his inner voice.

The Cloak of Brinizarn was reluctant to answer. *"Yes. But you can't be invisible and fly at the same time."*

Macal understood. *"Why didn't you fly me up before?"*

"What fun would that be? I'm not a slave. I don't serve you."

The boy spoke the words of flight. As he lifted off the ground he became visible. Up flew Macal Teel over the walls of Castle Darkmoor.

Landing inside the castle, Macal smiled. Besides the troll patrol, getting in was easier than he thought it would be. It made sense though—who would come deep into Marglamesh to sneak into this castle? The Troll King was unlikely to expect such an intrusion, especially from a single human boy.

He was up on one of the lower wall walks. He stealthily followed it until he found a stairway down, which then led to a doorway to the castle's interior.

Just like the differences from Elronia to Xanga-Mor and Xanga-Mor to Marglamesh, Macal felt that entering the castle was like entering a new world. It felt foreign, alien, to Macal. It was huge. He guessed the hallway he had entered was more than forty feet wide and hundreds of feet high. The thresholds were large enough to allow five to six trolls to walk abreast. He felt minuscule here, like a mouse would feel in his cottage. The entire mountain had been hollowed and carved into this enormous castle. The walls, floors, and everything he could see were all roughly hewn from the stone. It was a place of stark grandeur.

As he looked around he guessed he had entered the entry hall. Not far away were the castle's fortified doors, a portal that had never been breached by enemy forces.

While the daylight shone bright outside, the interior was as dim as night.

He stuck to the darkness of the shadows as he stole along. Opposite the fortified doors was a vast archway. Macal peered through the opening. Beyond he could see a long gallery that mirrored the size and shape of the entry hall, lined with a vast display of armor and weapons that spanned all ages of the troll kingdom. He guessed there must had been hundreds of statues decorated with armament.

Macal moved past the coarse archway and continued on. He knew what he was looking for and that wasn't it.

As he crept along, he was again assailed by doubt. He wasn't made for this, for adventure. He was the boy everybody made fun of. He could barely even swim. He wondered how Menk would be doing if their roles were reversed. *He'd probably be great at all this and not just stumbling his way through. Would Aeria have liked Menk more than him?* He didn't want to think about that. The truth would probably only make him feel worse.

But we are doing it, aren't we? another part of him said. *We survived the skirmish with the trolls.*

We weren't much help though, replied the first part of him.

You got through the Tomb of the Lost King and found the cloak, said the second part.

"I was wondering when you would talk about me," chimed in the Cloak of Brinizarn. *"And do you ever stop whining to yourself? Seriously. Accept that you are pretty much a failure and move on already. We have things to do here."*

"You're not helping. Can't you see I don't like being like this?"

"Then stop being like that."

"I am who I am!"

"Then maybe you should accept the things you are not good at. Or maybe just stop being you. I know I would if I was you."

"I think I'm doing pretty good compared to where I started."

"Then stop moping and keep getting better and maybe you'll get through this."

"What about you, you don't want to get through this?"

"I'm a very magical cloak, that is very good at what it does."

"Are you?"

"I am. And I'll get through this because everybody wants me. So I'll find a good home no matter what."

"Good. I'll be sure to leave you with the trolls."

"Okay—Hey, wait!"

Macal's heart suddenly began to beat faster as he found what he was looking for.

He had come to a spiral staircase that wound both up and down from where he stood. Cautiously he waited and listened for any guards nearby. Hearing nothing he crept forward and descended the stairs. The patrol outside had mentioned a man down below, so all Macal wanted was to find a staircase down and now he had. His father must be in a dungeon, or whatever the trolls called it, he thought.

The rank smell of the place got worse every step he went down, causing him to gag. The stairs soon opened to a new floor, but also continued downward. Macal stepped off the stairs to investigate what was on this floor. The only hall led off at an angle to the northeast.

Without consulting with the cloak, he took a moment to turn himself invisible and then followed the passage.

The boy wandered along searching for his father. He had expected filth and disgusting piles of bones and decaying bodies in every corner, the walls crumbling, the place in disarray, but it wasn't. It was well kept, clean, and barren of nearly any furnishings.

The passage soon forked. Macal chose the right side and proceeded. He was surprised he hadn't come across any trolls yet. Perhaps the king kept the forces light here, or more likely, maybe they had all been sent to Elronia.

Next he came to a set of archways, each on the opposite side of the hall from each other. The north side had a closed door. Macal spied into the other open one.

The room was an odd, half-hexagonal shape. Inside were three guards. It was some sort of trophy room; the heads of a wide variety of monstrous creatures hung from the walls. There were shelves of different sized sharp teeth. Pelts, skins, and scales were displayed in honor. He also saw a display of beastly claws.

On a central display table was something that caught his eye, and once it did he was riveted to it. Standing upright, part of the blade inserted into a block of dark wood, was Alrang-Dal, his father's silver sword. Even in the gloom it sparkled like a star.

Several thoughts occurred to him at once. His father no longer had it! But why would he if he was a prisoner? But the sword being here also must mean his father really was here! The Princess was right! He had doubted. Of course he did, but now he was sure!

"You're going to try to steal it back, aren't you?" asked the cloak.

"Of course I am," replied Macal as he snuck invisibly into the room.

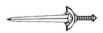

Since he was invisible Macal decided to reclaim his father's sword. He knew he couldn't leave it here, and he also needed a better weapon. All he had was his dagger. If he was going to get a new sword, he couldn't think of a better one than Alrang-Dal.

The boy moved silently over to the display. The three trolls were busy talking. He didn't pay attention to what they were saying, he was too entranced with the idea of holding that sword in his hand.

As quietly as he could he got to the table. The trolls still hadn't noticed him. He climbed up onto the display and with an eager hand he reached to pull the sword free.

"Something is here," said an airy voice from the doorway. The occupants turned to see one of the king's witch brides floating in, cradling in her arms a skeleton cat. Macal thought he could hear it purring as she stroked it.

One of the trolls sniffed the air. "I can smells something. Something human." The others agreed, but looking around they couldn't see anything.

The witch waved her hand in a gesture of sorcery. Once she finished her spell Macal was rendered visible.

"Well, that's not nice!" shouted the Cloak of Brinizarn in Macal's head. *"How dare she!"*

"She can undo your magic?"

"No, of course not. I'm far, far, far too powerful for that. But she can grant herself and those around her the ability to see invisible creatures."

The witch drifted over to the display. Macal froze. She brought her ashen gray face close to his and sneered at him. "I know the smell of your blood. I've tasted it before." She licked her dry cracked lips. Her breath was horrid and evil. He finally understood what evil smelled like—it smelled like a rotting body. "I know who you are, Teel."

Macal's body wasn't reacting, but his brain was churning. He had an idea. He would let himself get captured. As prisoner he'd be taken to the cells in the dungeon where his father was. Then he could use the cloak, turn into a bear and break them free.

"You've caught me." Macal raised his hands in surrender. The trolls came forward and grabbed him.

The witch gave him a malicious smile. "Take him to the kitchen. He will make a perfect feast for the Master this evening."

"You never cease to amaze me with you stupid ideas," complained the cloak. *"Why not just take me off and hand me to them."*

"I thought I would be taken captive. I didn't think they would make me dinner!"

"I know what you thought. You're an idiot."

The guards dragged Macal to a different staircase than the one he had come down and hauled him back upstairs. Soon they were in the long gallery of armor and weapons he had seen from the entry hall when he first entered the castle.

At the midpoint of the room they passed the doorway back to the entry hall, opposite of which were a pair of massive open doors he hadn't noticed before.

As they marched past he looked through the opening and immediately wished he hadn't. It was the most terrifying image he had ever seen. In the distance, languid on his throne sat the Troll King. He was huge. Enormous. Macal could feel the power within the monster.

Even though he overcame the odds to make it here, he still needed to get out with his father. He would have to get past all the guards, past the witches, past that king! And unlike him, his father wouldn't be able to turn invisible or fly! It seemed impossible.

"Be ready for it," said the cloak.

"Ready for what?"

"It."

Macal couldn't help thinking that at least if they ate him he wouldn't have to deal with the cloak anymore. *"Sure. Whatever."*

"Okay! Now! Turn invisible and run! Her spell to see you has ended. I can sense it. Run!"

Now Macal understood. "For The Crown I Shall Hide The Secrets Of The Kingdom."

Surprised by the boy's sudden disappearance the trolls slackened their grip. As they did, Macal pulled free and ran back the way they had come before the witch could cast another spell to reveal him again.

As he fled he could hear the trolls and the witch searching for him. He went back to the stairway and instead of stopping at the first floor he descended to, he continued down another level. *They knew he was here now. He needed to find his father and get out of here as fast as possible.*

Macal arrived at the bottom of the staircase. A single large hallway lead to the north. Having no other choice he followed it. There were no doors or furnishings other than the occasional flickering torch. He thought he could hear wails of pain in the distance.

The passage eventually came to a corner and turned left. Macal continued down it. He saw several doors on the north wall and one on the south side. The noises he was hearing came from up ahead, from a door in a corner. He crept close to listen.

It sounded like somebody being tortured. He could hear voices that reminded him of the witch he had just met. His heart paused several beats. He instinctively knew his father was in this room, and they were hurting him. They were trying to get the location of the war plans out of him. They were hurting him! *They were hurting him.*

All other thoughts fled his mind. All Macal wanted to do in that moment was save his father. He reached for the handle. It was locked. His breathing came hard as he heard his father scream in pain again.

Frantically he looked for a way in, but to no avail. He needed the key. He ran south down the hall, trying each door he came to. The doors on the right wall were all locked, but there was an open door on the left. He peered in.

A slovenly sleeping troll sat slumped on a sturdy stool. Macal guessed he was the gaoler. On the table off to the side of the brute lay a large ring of keys.

"Good security," jibed the cloak.

Macal crept up to the table.

"You know the last time you tried to steal something it didn't go very well. Maybe you should just stab him while he's sleeping."

"No!" replied Macal horrified. He may not be brave, but he had some honor. He reached for the keys. One of them was near the edge of the table and he was able to reach up and grasp it. He pulled it toward him. The keys slid across the rough wood, some of them dangling over the edge.

Macal gave a strong tug to pull the heavy keys down. He hoped he was strong enough to catch them. The gaoler continued to snore.

"Now is probably a good time to tell you that I've run out magic and can't keep you invisible anymore. I need to recharge."

As the cloak finished speaking the boy popped back into visibility as the keys came crashing down on him. He tried to catch them, to stop them from hitting the floor, but they were too heavy and he failed. With a loud clatter they struck the floor.

Macal's attention snapped to the gaoler. The troll opened its eyes and saw the boy. Anger and alarm clouded its face, and with a roar it reached for its club.

Macal pulled out his dagger and jabbed the monster in the leg. In spite of the injury it got to its feet and swung its weapon. Macal tried to dodge, but the gaoler clipped him in the shoulder and sent him spinning into the wall. As the troll approached to finish him off, Macal scrambled to his feet and ducked under the table that had held the keys. The goaler grabbed the table and hurled it aside. As he did so Macal thrust his dagger up and into its belly. Grasping its abdomen the troll fell over. As it did so it hit its head on a corner of the stone wall and knocked itself out.

"Maybe you are a tough boy," said the cloak.

Macal didn't think so. *"I'm just doing what I need to do to get my father."* The dagger still felt awkward in his hand. He wasn't sure he would ever get used to holding a weapon.

"And that's what makes you tough even if you don't realize it."

He could hear his father call out in torment again. As much as he hated to think it, he hoped that his father's cries drowned out the commotion he had just caused in here. He waited a minute, but nobody came to investigate.

He picked up the heavy key ring, hoisted it over his shoulder and carried it down the hall to his father's cell.

Macal got the keys to the door of his father's prison, but he was just too short to reach the lock. He was about to try to use the cloak to fly up and unlock the door when he heard the door unlock from the other side.

He dropped the keys, ran, and hid in the recess of the first door to the south.

The door to the cell opened. Macal prayed he wouldn't be seen. Maybe his small size would finally be of use. Peeking out he saw two witch brides exit the room, lock the door, and go east down the passage. He watched apprehensively as they floated right over the keys, but passed by them unnoticed.

After he was sure they were gone he rushed back to the door; using what little energy the cloak had regained, he flew up, unlocked the door, and opened it.

Macal Teel then stepped into the room and found his father.

CHAPTER 33

A strange system of restraints and clamps held Bertran Teel in the center of the octagonal chamber. His father was a ghastly visage. He was nearly naked, his body bruised, battered, and covered in blood. His head lolled to the side, his eyes closed. Aghast, the boy stared at the stump of his father's missing hand.

Macal had an overwhelming need to set his father free. As if that would somehow be a way to remove the memory of seeing him like this.

He began to cry. "Daddy!" He ran forward and threw his arms around his father.

Bertran mustered the strength to open his eyes. He saw and felt Macal hugging him. At first he thought it must be another trick of the witches, but it was too real. The witches didn't know enough about love to add the boy's tears to the illusion.

His voice was hoarse and dry. "What? How?"

"I came to save you. I had to." Macal's face was buried in his chest. "I've missed you so much. I never thought I'd see you again."

Bertran was overwhelmed by the fact that his son was here, had come so deep into the territory of the enemy to get him. Upon realizing it was really his son he was revitalized. "Me either. I love you so much. I'm so sorry about all of this. About everything. All I've wanted is one more day with you."

"I want to get you out of here and have endless days with you."

"I know. If I could do it all again I would never have stayed in the army. I should have walked away long ago. I should have left to be with you. But there was always another battle, another war. I was wrong. I've been fighting for the wrong thing. It's you I should have been fighting for."

"You have. And for everybody else. You're trying to save people. Keep us safe."

"At what cost? It cost me you. And now you're here. In danger."

"I can take care of myself. I'm going to get you out of here," Macal released his embrace so he could find a way to set his father free, but he paused. "Are you proud of me?"

His father smiled at him. "Since the day you were born. Before you came into my life I don't think I really knew what love was. You gave my life meaning. You gave the battles meaning. Every foe I slayed, I slayed to save you. To stop them from hurting you. I know I haven't shown it, but you're my life. My heart."

Macal hugged him again. "I love you."

"I love you too. Now you've got to leave before they catch you."

Macal searched desperately for a way to open the restraints. "I came all this way. I'm not leaving you."

"You have to. I won't let them take you from me. Go back and live a life that makes you proud. I'm ordering you."

"I'm not one of your soldiers! You can't order me!"

Bertran was surprised by the boy's forcefulness; it didn't seem like the son he had left. "No. You're more important than they are. You're my son. You don't know what it would do to me if something happened to you."

"And I won't let them take you from me. I'm not going without you!" Macal finally found the releases and unlatched them. Bertran fell to the floor, free.

Weakly the soldier rose to his knees. "Flee from here, Macal. It's not safe."

"Not without you." Macal was adamant.

"Well at least close the door, so that we aren't seen. I need a minute to regain some strength."

Macal closed the door after confirming the hallways were empty. "How did you get here?"

"No, you tell me how you got here first."

Macal gave him a brief version of all that had happened. The troll attack on Hormul, the Princess, the tomb, the cloak, and the trip through Marglamesh. Out of guilt he avoided mentioning Uncle Melkes. "Your turn."

"I was captured. They hired mercenaries to find me. Somehow they knew I had the plans. I was brought here and the king claimed Alrang-Dal and had it sent to the vaults."

"I know, I saw it."

"Macal, you have to use that cloak to turn invisible, then get out of this castle. Out of Marglamesh. You have to leave and get the plans. I can tell you where they're hidden. The war can still be won. More than that you have to go home. Forget all this stuff about trolls and war. This is about your life. You have to leave."

"But you are my life. This," he said looking around, "I don't even know if Hormul can even be a home anymore. I'm not leaving unless you come with me."

"Then go somewhere new," offered his father.

"By myself?"

"Macal, it's too risky for me to sneak out with you. I'll only get you caught. I can't risk that. I'd rather stay here and know you are safe."

"You're coming with me. You don't know what I had to do to get to you. You're coming with me."

With a long sigh his father finally agreed. "Okay, let's go. I'm ready."

"We have to stop along the way out."

"For what?"

"I want to get Alrang-Dal. We can't leave it here."

Bertran began to wonder if this was really his son. "No. It's not important. I have you, that's what matters."

Macal stared him in the eyes. "No, we are going to need it to escape Marglamesh and to protect ourselves on the way back home. We are going to need more than one dagger for that. It's not far from the stairway were are going up anyway. I can sneak over invisibly and take it. I don't want to be away from you ever again, but in this place its safest if you wait outside and I'll meet you up on the wall walk in a few moments."

"It's too dangerous."

"I agree. For you, it is. I'll be invisible. I'll be fine"

"You're leaving me, and this time going into even more danger. I don't want you doing this, Macal."

"*Danger?* Dad, I came all the way here."

"I would have never asked that of you. I would never have let you come. I can't believe Melkes did."

The thought of his uncle gave Macal pause. He didn't want to talk to his father about his uncle. It was because of his mistakes that his uncle had died. He didn't want to have to admit that. Not yet. *His choices had led to his uncle's death. Maybe he should listen to his father.*

He shook the thought away. They needed the sword. Macal gave his father a resolute look. "I'm doing this whether you want me to or not. Please, wait outside. I'll find you in a few moments."

Bertran still couldn't believe the change in his son. "Okay, I'll see you outside."

"Good. Watch for me."

They left the cell and headed for the staircase. Bertran limped along as best he could. Macal turned invisible and held his father's hand as he led him. At the spiral staircase they alighted a flight of steps then Macal stopped.

"The sword is just over here," he whispered. "Continue up one flight and go out the door at the top. It will bring you to the top of the lower wall. I'll be right behind you."

Macal became visible for a moment. His father knelt down next to him and looked him in the eyes. "In case something happens, I left the plans in the loft of an abandoned barn on the south side of a village called Maylen. If something happens to me you have to get the plans to the army."

"I will," Macal promised.

"I still don't like this, Macal."

"Don't worry. I can get the sword. I'll be fine. See you in a minute."

In a moment Bertran Teel was left alone on the staircase. "I love you," he whispered.

Macal had an internal irresistible need to get Alrang-Dal back. He wasn't sure what it was, but some part of him knew that he couldn't let the king have the satisfaction of possessing it. If it had been on the other side of the castle behind a legion of soldiers, he wouldn't have entertained the idea of retrieving it, but the sword was so close. Just down the hall. How could he not go get it?

As he crept down the hall he had another idea. He had noticed how hard it was for his father to walk. He was terribly injured. Would he be able to survive the journey home? Maybe they could just find a place to hide in here and wait for the reinforcements the Princess was sending. He'd have to ask his father what he thought of this plan.

He stopped mid-step. What was that he just thought? That he could ask his father his opinion about something? It was a foreign concept to him. A strange new reality that he would be able to ask his father for advice. He couldn't remember the last time that had happened. He couldn't believe he had his father back.

He blinked and brought himself back to the present. *Let's get the sword and get back to him. We've spent enough time away from each other.*

As Macal moved forward toward the trophy room he then wondered if the cloak was strong enough to carry both of them. At least long enough to make it off the castle and down to the ground below.

"Perhaps, and only if you ask me nicely," answered the cloak.

The boy groaned in embarrassment. He was not sure he would ever get used to the way the cloak listened in on every personal thought he had.

A few feet ahead was the entry to the trophy room. Macal smiled in anticipation of holding the sword and of returning it to his father, regardless of how well he could now wield it.

An alarm of horns destroyed the eerie quiet of the castle. Macal thought he could hear the Cloak of Brinizarn chuckle out loud.

"I think they've noticed your missing prisoner. Well, that or they've finally decided to come and look for you. Either way things are about to get complicated."

Bertran hoped that Macal hadn't run into any resistance getting the sword. He didn't understand the boy's desperate need to retrieve it. They should have left the castle already—and would have had they not had this delay.

He had to remind himself that his son was different now. Had come across kingdoms for him. On his own. He survived all that on his own. Macal had proven himself capable of making decisions and taking care of himself, so he had to let him make more decisions, even if he didn't agree with them.

He admitted the sword was going to come in handy. He knew it wasn't going to be easy to get out of Marglamesh alive, especially missing his hand. He wondered how good Macal was at swordplay. He wished he had been able to teach the boy himself.

He added that to the list of things he felt guilty about. He shouldn't have left. That revelation had occurred to him so many times in the past weeks. He had run from the house that was empty of his wife, Larabell. He couldn't bear to see that cottage without her in it.

Of all his regrets that was his biggest. Saying that he was leaving in service to the kingdom, when in truth he was just trying to hide away from the pain. In doing so he had left Macal behind.

Twelve years of running is long enough, he thought. Now I'll spend the rest of my days making it up to him.

He was so proud of Macal. To come all this way. For him! He smiled.

Then he heard the alarms go off.

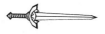

The horns blared so loudly that the noise hurt Macal's ears. He couldn't decide what to do. The trophy room was just a few feet away. Should he run away or grab the sword first? If he wasted time getting the sword that would increase their chances of getting caught.

He couldn't resist the urge. He decided to retrieve the sword and ran into the trophy room.

It was empty of trolls. He let out a sigh of relief. He rushed to the table and prepared to climb up on it.

"*Uh oh,*" said the cloak.

"Wha—" started Macal. Then he understood. He could now see his arms, legs, and body. He was visible once more. The spell was cancelled.

An ancient voice from behind him spoke. "Look who's back here. If the Teels were free of course they would come for the sword. Such an alluring prize it is. The Master covets it as much."

Macal spun around on the witch. "For The Crown I Shall Bear The Strength Of The Kingdom!" he shouted.

Nothing happened.

"*I can't do that yet! You just used all the energy being a useless invisible thief, Thief.*"

The witch flew forward, grabbed his shoulder, and hoisted him painfully into the air. "Let's go see my Master," she cackled.

Macal screamed for his father as he was carried to the throne room.

The horns of alarm had diminished in volume now that the castle was on alert. They continued their song to indicate that not all intruders and prisoners had been recaptured.

The witch no longer held Macal aloft. He had been dragged upstairs, and eventually they made their way into the throne room. As they entered King Orgog rose, and stared down while the witch bride pulled the boy all the way up the dais to his feet. King Orgog reach down and grabbed Macal while the boy called desperately for his father. Macal was so small compared to the troll that he seemed like a doll in his arms.

"Hold him tight, Master," said the witch with the cat. "He has powers of magic about him."

"From that cloak, Master," said the witch with the skull.

"Yes, he can disappear from sight, Master," said the witch with the staff.

King Orgog raised an interested eyebrow. His gripped tightened, bruising Macal's arm.

"He is a Teel, Master!" called the witches together, their voices louder than the boy's screams for help.

"I see," King Orgog lifted Macal up before him. He growled at the boy. "Please keep screaming. Draw him to us. That is what we want."

In an instant Macal went silent. He tore his eyes away from the king's and looked around the room. From the throne he could see that all about the room trolls hid craftily in the shadows, so that it would appear to someone entering the chamber that only the witches and the king were there.

It was a trap. They were using him as bait. He felt sick. If ever the Princess's reinforcements were coming he prayed that they showed up now.

He couldn't believe he had come all this way and now he was just going to get his father caught again and killed. He should have listened to him and just left without getting the sword. They would already be out of the castle and on their way home.

"What? No more cries for help? Scream boy! Scream for your father!"

Macal remained silent. His jaw clenched. He prayed his father wouldn't come. He didn't want to get his father caught. There were to many enemies in the room. There was no chance his father could free him.

Bertran Teel ran toward his son's cries for help. Macal must have been caught. He had to save his son.

The boy's cries the were barely audible over the droning horns. As he followed them down the long hall, they slowly became louder. He knew this floor—the throne room was nearby. He had been taken there several times to be questioned by the king, when Orgog had been too lazy to go down to him. *That must be where they've taken him.*

He scrambled as best he could to the throne room. Hiding outside the entryway he peered in; on the dais he saw all three witches and King Orgog. He had hoped the cries for help were some kind of sorcery, but his heart sank when he saw that his son really was there. He couldn't think of a way out of this. *I have to try. But I can't go in there empty-handed.*

He crept back down the hall to where it turned north and followed it. The stench of foul cooking filled his nostrils, so he guessed this must be the way to the kitchen. The hallway here was lined with doors. Up ahead one of them opened and a troll came out into the hallway and walked away in the opposite direction. *Perfect.*

With his bare feet it was easy for Bertran to sneak up on the monster. For a few strides he matched the troll's gait to get his timing right. Then he leapt up onto its back and grappled it in a choke hold. It flailed and tried to grab him. Bertran held on, his son's life depended on it. He squeezed harder on the monster's neck. His lack of a hand made it difficult.

The troll started to get weak from lack of breath. It threw itself backward into the wall, crushing Bertran. The impact made the soldier loose his grip. The troll stumbled forward, trying to catch its breath. Bertran didn't give up. He couldn't. He had to get to Macal.

He ran and jumped forward back onto the troll's back. He grabbed it around the neck again and pulled with all his might, unleashing all the rage that had grown in him since his captivity. He didn't let go until he felt its neck snap. The troll toppled to the floor. The soldier took the creature's dagger and short sword. He left its large axe, since he couldn't carry it with one hand.

Now armed, Bertran Teel went to save his son.

Now that Macal knew his father would be walking into a trap room he changed tactics. "Don't come! It's a trap! Don't come!" he shouted.

King Orgog shook the boy roughly. "That is enough. Silence the boy!"

The witches tapped into their reservoir of dark magic and cast a spell at Macal. As they finished, something happened to his tongue. It no longer worked. Apprehensively he reached up to feel it, and his hand recoiled in horror. His tongue had turned into a bundle of worms! They wriggled and writhed in his mouth, pushing forward trying to escape his lips. The witches looked at him with malicious satisfaction.

King Orgog surveyed the three entrances to the room. "His father will come. We have his son, and that will give us the leverage we've needed to force the location of the plans out of him. He won't let his son die. Men are weak like that. And then we can end our frustrating acquaintance with him."

"Please, Princess. Get those reinforcements here now," prayed Macal. He couldn't believe because of him his father was going to have to tell them where the plans were. Because of him they were going to make Elronia lose the war!

All the trolls in the chamber must have come to protect the king when the alarm went off. Even as good a swordfighter as he was, there was no way his father could survive, assuming he even found a weapon. Especially without his sword hand—there were just too many of them.

CHAPTER 34

Bertran heard Macal calling, but couldn't understand the words. He knew it had to be his son, no troll sounded like a human boy. He wished he could hear what he was saying, but as he got closer the voice cut off.

He had to hurry. He couldn't imagine what they were doing to his son. With Macal's sudden silence a sense of dread filled him. *Had they killed him?*

The soldier stalked down the hall. He headed in the direction that the guard he had just killed was going, remembering that there was a side entrance to the throne room up ahead.

A door near the end of the hallway opened. Light from the room spilled out and lit part of the hall. Bertran could see that it was indeed the kitchen. Several armed trolls came out and the door closed behind them.

To hide, Bertran hurried to the nearest side door and went in. Inside the dark room he couldn't see anything. He put his ear to the door to listen for the trolls. He didn't think they had seen him, but he could be wrong. In his hand he held the small sword at the ready.

In the hall the trolls passed by, their footsteps faded into the distance. He exhaled in relief.

Bertran left the room, went down the hall, and entered the throne room.

Macal kept praying that his father wouldn't come, but he knew he would. Wouldn't Macal have come? Didn't he come all the way to Marglamesh for his father? Of course his father would come. He would come and he would get caught trying to save his son.

The door on the left side of the chamber opened, and they all turned to see Bertran Teel enter. Macal's heart pounded painfully in his chest; he had never felt so helpless. Macal wanted to shout out and warn his father, but with his wormed tongue he couldn't. He wanted to activate the cloak, but that too was impossible, because of the witch's curse on his tongue. He wished they'd taken away his sight as well. He didn't want to see what was about to happen. He tried to close his eyes, to ignore it all, but found that he couldn't—there was a part of him that felt he had to witness the results of his mistake. Again, he wished he had listened to his father and just left the castle.

Bertran walked and stood in front of the dais, looking up to see his son held tight in the king's hand. The witches fluttered here and there about the raised platform, their unblinking eyes never leaving him. King Orgog made a gesture with his free hand and the troll guards stepped out of the shadows to surround the man.

Bertran had seen them as he entered. There were about thirty of them, he hadn't missed any. He knew there wasn't a lot of hope in this. All he could do was try to get the king to spare his son's life.

The witches cackled merrily. They could sense they were about to finally learn the location of the plans. Then their master would be pleased, and that was all they desired. King Orgog also knew what this moment meant—all the trouble the war plans had generated was about to come to an end. Clutching the squirming worm-tongued key to the location of the plans, he grinned down at Bertran.

All around the Elronian soldier the trolls hefted their weapons, waiting for the king's command to strike down the man. Macal tried to yell, to tell his father to run, but because of the worms it came out only as gurgles. Bertran looked over at his son and worried at what they had done to him.

The Troll King glared at the soldier as he spoke, and his voice boomed through the vast room. "This is where it all comes to an end! All your stalling. All your self-sacrifice. Tell me where the plans are! You know what happens if you don't." Orgog grabbed Macal by the throat and lifted him aloft.

Bertran held King Orgog's gaze. He knew as soon as he revealed where the plans were he was a dead man, but what choice did he have? He had to save his son. He was torn. Could he really betray his kingdom, give up their best chance of surviving the war to save his son? "And he will live?"

King Orgog gave him a mischievous smile. "Of course."

The soldier made up his mind. With a loose grip the man raised his sword out before him and let it fall from his grasp. He pulled a dagger from his loin cloth and dropped it. The weapons clattered to the floor with an echoing din of finality.

Macal tried to choke out a scream for his father to stop, to not give up, to fight, but it came out as gibberish.

"You're doing the right thing," taunted the king in near victory. "What good is your life if you can't sacrifice it to protect your family. Now tell me where the plans are before I change my mind and rip his head off!"

"They have already been delivered to King Stormlion," lied Bertran. He could feel it in his soul that no matter what he told the king, the truth or not, that he and Macal were not leaving here alive.

"Falsehoods!" wailed and screeched the witches. "Lies! Tricks! Demon tongue!"

The king never took his eyes off the soldier's. He had expected nothing less as a first response. He choked the boy in his hand harder. Macal tried to gasp for breath but couldn't. His face turned red and his legs flailed helplessly in the air.

His son so close to death, Bertran could only hold the king's gaze a second longer before he blurted out words that were almost too painful to say. Each one like a dagger strike. Each one part of his betrayal to his homeland. "They are in the loft of an abandoned barn near the village of Maylen. It's just north of where I was captured."

The witches nodded.

"Good," said the king triumphantly. "I really wish you hadn't wasted so much of my time postponing the inevitable." To his guards he commanded, "Now, kill him."

The guards were anxious to please their king. They let their bloodlust take over and stepped forward to kill the human.

The guards cut into Bertran Teel with their swords and axes. He fell to the ground after the first mighty blows, and once on the ground they continued to hack and chop until he stopped moving. Their task complete, the trolls backed away and stood in formation in the center of the room.

Macal watched in horror as his father was cut down. Elated, the king relaxed his grip and Macal broke free from and ran to his father. The curse on him had ended and his tongue had reverted to normal.

He rolled his father over and put his father's head in his lap. "I love you! I love you! I love you!" Tears poured down his face. He could see his father was still alive, if only barely.

Bertran coughed up a little blood. "Brave—Boy…."

Then Bertran Teel went limp in his arms.

"NOOOOOO!" wailed Macal. It was the kind of painful scream that changes a person. Something so painful that there can be no recovery. Something in him broke. Some human part of him in that moment ceased to exist. It was unbearable. It was like losing Uncle Melkes all over again. Everything. EVERYTHING he had done to get here had been for nothing. His heart wrenched. He couldn't breathe. He was in a daze of disbelief. Of hopelessness and nightmare.

Nothing had ever been so painful. So ungodly painful.

He had lost them all. He was alone in the world.

He screamed in rage. In pain. In angst. In endless anguish.

"NOOOOOO!"

Holding his dead father, familiar feelings came to the surface. He didn't want to be alone, but now he was, he was really alone, forever.

Now he had nobody.

Macal knelt there in a daze like a zombie, with his father's head on his lap. In the distance he could hear the Troll King speaking. He was gloating that now he was certain to win the war. They would have the plans again and victory would be theirs. This was his triumphant moment.

"He's right," said the cloak in Macal's mind. The boy didn't respond. *"Hey, are you there? Hello, anybody home?"* The boy was unresponsive. The cloak gave up.

King Orgog was still speaking. "Even now my armies prepare to march on Keratost! Nothing will stop us from claiming victory now." He turned to the witches. "Send your most powerful minions. Get me those plans with haste. Fail me and die!"

"Yes, Master." The witches floated from the room to begin their errand.

The king pointed at Macal and spoke to the guards. "And I will eat the boy tonight as celebration of my upcoming coronation as ruler of the human land, Elronia. Have him ready for dinner. Take his cloak from him as well, before he is prepared. Let's try to keep any more blood from getting on it. It's dirty enough as it is. Have it hung in the trophy room. I might have a use for it in the future."

"No!" shouted the cloak. *"Don't let the filth touch me!"* Macal still didn't respond.

The guards grabbed Macal with rough hands and hauled him to his feet. They pulled him toward the door from which his father had entered. He was docile, in shock, broken, beat, his heart crushed. He couldn't believe that he had gotten his father killed. He had nothing at all left.

It was the longest walk of his life, but he didn't even notice it.

He was dragged into the kitchen. The guards threw him to the floor in front of the cook, a massive slimy troll of great girth. "The king wants to eat him tonight," said one of the guards.

The cook gave Macal an appraising eye. "Not a lot of meat on him." The guards grunted, that wasn't their problem. They turned and left.

"Haha!" the cloak laughed with relief. *"The dolts! They forgot me."*

A moment later the guards returned. "We forgot the cloak. We are adding it to the collection." The cook kicked Macal across the floor toward the guards, who tore the cloak free from his neck.

As the cloak was yanked away its voice faded from Macal's mind. *"Oh, by the gods! They're touching me! They're really touching me! Help! Heelllp…"* Now in possession of the Cloak of Brinizarn the soldiers left again.

The troll cook lumbered over, grabbed Macal and tossed him up on the table. "Not a very lively one," it commented out loud. "But don't you worry, I'll make you real tasty."

Numb, Macal lay on the table. A thousand thoughts spun through his head at the same time. He couldn't help thinking about how the Princess had failed him. Lied to him. Had she been on time with reinforcements, his father would have lived! Now he had nothing. Was nothing. His father's words came back to him, "Brave—Boy…."

Uncle Melkes' words also echoed in his mind, "The most important thing is family."

Well, he had no family left now, did he? They all died because of him. Three of them, including his mother! There was nothing left. In this castle are the monsters that made him alone. These are the creatures who took his family away. He was alone because of them!

Then something else in Macal broke.

Macal blinked. His vision suddenly became clear. He looked around the room confused at where he was. He was in a kitchen.

Only one thing mattered to him now. Only one purpose. Revenge. Now alone in the world, nothing mattered to him anymore. Nothing had any value. Not even his life.

This castle would shake from his pain. All within it would feel his anguish.

The cook was nearby, readying a large pot of water over the fire of the hearth. He added some wood to the fire to increase its heat, then he came back to the table. "I think we are gonna boil you. The extra water may plump up your meat a little. We can add to that a bit of snake entrails for flavor too. Where did I put those? I had them already—"

Macal wasn't going to be eaten. He would fight like his father would have, should have. Like a man would, not as a weakling boy. He didn't need to be scared anymore. What more could he loose? All those years of being afraid of everything, being pushed around. He had felt less afraid as he had travelled here. He knew he had become stronger. He realized he had caused his own problems by letting fear control him. Now he knew all he had to do was stand up to it. And that is exactly what he intended to do.

As the cook searched around the cluttered table for the entrails, Macal rolled over, grabbed a cleaver, and with all his strength he brought it down on the cook's grotesque wrist. The blade of the cleaver went all the way down and into the wooden table. The monster howled in pain.

With a great effort Macal pulled the cleaver free and swung it again at the cook's chest. In panic the creature retreated to avoid the attack. He went too far back and stepped into the blazing hearth, erupting in flame.

Macal didn't give the writhing monster a second glance as he rolled off the table and got to the floor. Before he could get revenge, there was one thing he needed first.

Ignoring the cook's thrashing and cries of pain Macal raced down the hall. He needed Alrang-Dal and then he would get his revenge. Had he only listened to his father, this wouldn't have happened.

He knew he couldn't let King Orgog get the plans. He couldn't let him win. Not after killing his father. All those people needed to be saved. He couldn't imagine Elronia ruled by trolls who didn't even know what family was! He would find the plans and get them back to the army. Then they would win the war, victory would be *theirs*, not the trolls!

What better revenge could there be?

He made it to the stairs and hurried down. A new way of looking at his life was blossoming in his head. He thought of how his love for his uncle and his father had driven him across the world. Even though his father had died, he knew that meant something. There was nothing more important than family.

Once down the flight of stairs he ran along the hall toward the trophy room as he had done before.

Boy or not, he thought, *I'm about to kill the Troll King.*

CHAPTER 35

Again the trophy room was empty. Macal looked up and down the hall but saw nobody coming—now that the alarms had stopped he didn't expect anyone would be. The trolls thought both prisoners had been dealt with.

He was sure the cook, or somebody who found his body, would set off the alarm again soon, but he only needed another minute.

The sword was still in its place, with the Cloak of Brinizarn hanging on a hook to the side. He grabbed the cloak and threw it around his shoulders.

"Wait! No! Don't put me on you filthy disgusti—Oh, it's you." cried the cloak. *"Well, the same holds true for you as well."*

"Be quiet!" ordered Macal. The cloak noted that there was an unfamiliar tone in the boy's voice. Cold. Emotionless. "Are you going to help me? Or do I leave you here?"

Strangely, the cloak felt scared of the boy. *"Um, happy to help."*

Macal strode over to the table that held the Alrang-Dal and climbed up. He took a moment to look over the sword. A magnificent ruby sparkled in its pommel. The shiny silver blade was like a mirror; only the ancient, unreadable runes obstructed its perfect surface.

Bent on revenge, he reached forward to grasp the hilt of the brand—and paused. He was about to lift the blade of his father. The blade his father would never lift again. The blade that was now his.

His fingers finally closed around the hilt. The leather on it felt rough, and yet warm, in his hand. Unblinking, jaw firm, heart pounding, he lifted it free.

As he pulled the sword up he felt a change come over him. He felt the weight of the sword, like the weight of his ancestors' world. Like he was inheriting all the responsibilities his father had left unfinished.

The silver blade glinted.

In veneration he felt the perfection of the blade, felt the power within the eldritch weapon. Nobody knew who had hammered, folded, hardened, sharpened, and crafted it, but they had done so with divine skill.

Words his father once spoke to him came back to him like a whisper. *"You are not better than this life. Life owes you nothing, and it is up to to you to make your life worth something. The same is true for everybody. Your life is what you make it."*

Macal held Alrang-Dal up before him. *I know what I want to do with my life now.*

He willed the sword alight. The silver blade erupted in azure flame, causing the Cloak of Brinizarn to billow about him.

Then, turning himself invisible, he stepped with vengeance out into the hall.

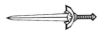

Macal Teel ran down the hallway to the staircase. Anger and pain fueled and urged on his every stride as he rushed up the stairs. Up ahead he heard several troll guardians descending toward him. He didn't pause. He didn't think. The rage in him was in control, making all his decisions.

A few steps later they met. Without ever seeing their invisible foe the trolls died. They only saw brief flashes of silver and blue flame as they fell and tumbled down the stairs.

A moment later Macal arrived upstairs and headed back to the throne room. Two more guards stood watch outside the main entry to the room. Macal strode forward and let himself become visible.

The cloak was shocked by this course of action. *"That's not a good idea! They'll kill you!"*

Macal didn't respond. This was not the time for words. In this moment, in this place, words were now nothing to him. The only thing this place understood was pain, and that was what he intended to deliver.

The guards, startled by his sudden appearance, turned and gave him amused smiles. They were not afraid of a little human boy. They readied their weapons.

Holding Alrang-Dal in both hands, Macal let the brief training the dragonmere had given him take over. Ablaze, the fiery blade sliced through the air. The sword almost moved on its own, knowing its purpose and doing it well.

The monsters were surprised by the sudden ferocity in the boy, who only just before in the throne room had been so docile and meek. Now he was a force of death and power so strong that trolls fell almost effortlessly before him as he reaped a harvest of vengeance. The sword hewed through the guards before they even had time to react. As the trolls fell, Macal, for the first time in his life, felt as if he was in control of his destiny. No longer did fear control him.

The guards now dead, Macal strode into the throne room to face the king.

With the Cloak of Brinizarn trailing behind him Macal entered the throne room of King Orgog, ruler of trolls. The boy's face was grim and stern. His heart as cold as ice.

The king sat leisurely upon his throne, a look of satisfaction about him, enjoying the recent events and greatly pleased with himself. Macal noticed his father's body was gone, though the stain of his blood on the flagstones was still there. The king's three witch brides were up on the dais hovering near their master. They were talking to a troll kneeling down on one knee at the base of the platform.

Macal never faltered as he strode forward to avenge his father. He didn't care if it was him against the king, the three witches, and the entire Marglasmesh force—he was going to get revenge for his father.

The king stared at him in surprise. He hadn't expected the boy back, not unless he was on a plate. He saw the look in the boy's eyes, something he never saw before, a raging fire and strength that seemed to want to take on the gods themselves.

King Orgog's eyes went to the burning blade in the boy's hand next—and he stood and muttered in an annoyed growl, "You are nothing."

Macal continued forward across the long room. "I was nothing for a long time. I'm not nothing anymore."

"You're only a boy!"

"I'm more than a boy!"

"I don't fear you!"

"And I, at last, don't fear you! I'm Macal Teel, son of Bertran Teel, and you have no idea what you're in for."

King Orgog chuckled. "You're just a boy."

Macal's rage burst out of him as he charged forward. "I AM MORE THAN A BOY! I AM MACAL TEEL!"

The king looked down on the troll before him. "Grengrell, before you go and retrieve the war plans for us, please end this nuisance for me."

"My pleasure." The troll soldier at the bottom of the stairs rose up. The creature was enormous, even for a troll, as large as the king himself. It turned to face the boy, blocking his way. In its hand it held a massive spiked mace.

As the boy came near the troll hefted its weapon and swung. Macal dove forward under the slow swing. The mace finished its arc by smashing into one of the pillars, leaving a small fracture.

The brute readied its weapon again, this time over its head for a powerful downward strike on the boy. Macal was now inside its guard. Alrang-Dal tingled in his hand. He let the magic of the sword take over and it danced through the air. The blade sliced deeply across the troll's abdomen and then pierced its chest and heart with swift, precision strokes. The monster collapsed to the floor and lay still.

The king let out a frustrated howl—he was going to have to solve this problem himself. With his witches in tow, King Orgog descended the stairs to kill the boy.

King Orgog and his three witch brides closed in on Macal. Some part of boy's subconscious still knew he couldn't win this. All seemed lost—but he didn't care. He had lost all of his family. He had nothing left and if he was going to die, it would be with a fight.

As they came down the stairs one of the witches twitched her fingers, empowering some sorcery. Into the king's hands appeared a great sword. Immediately Macal rushed forward and swung at Orgog. The Troll King, no stranger to combat (unlike other king's he knew) was prepared for the attack and easily deflected it.

The king took a half-hearted swing of his own at the boy. "You really think you can challenge me, the ruler of Marglamesh? Even with that sword you will never survive this."

"As long as you don't either, I'm okay with that."

The two circled each other, while the witches formed a circle around them, invoking their powers, and calling on their dark magic.

The witch with the skull finished first. Her spell blinded Macal. The witch with the staff finished next. Her spell made his legs feel as heavy as stone, so that he could barely move them. The witch with the skeletal cat finished last. Her spell caused Alrang-Dal to heat up until it burnt his hands and he dropped it. King Orgog laughed as he stepped forward and harshly kicked the boy over.

"I can still see!" said the cloak. *"But I'm not sure I want to. The king is still coming nearer!"*

Macal tried to scramble backward on all fours, but the king put a heavy foot on him and held him in place.

"This is where it ends, I think," continued the Cloak of Brinizarn. *"I guess I can be honest now then and say you really weren't absolutely totally terrible as an*

adventurer. Not totally."

Macal couldn't breathe, the king's foot pressed down further and further upon him. He wanted to cry out in frustration at not avenging his father. At not saving Elronia. At failing at everything.

"He's raising his sword now—" informed the cloak. Macal wished he wasn't getting this commentary, that the cloak wasn't speaking. He'd rather not know.

Just then a large explosion from the outer halls echoed around them and shook the floating mountain. It came from the front gate. The horrid sound of trolls screaming and dying followed.

Uncertainly the king removed his foot from Macal and took a step back up the stairs of the dais. He turned to the witches. "What's that?"

The witches avoided his gaze. None of them knew the source. With the witches' concentration broken, the spells on Macal faded away to nothingness.

Horns of alarm split the air, summoning more troll soldiers. They poured into the chamber from the flanking entryways to protect the king. The front gate of the castle boomed again, shook as if struck by a giant. Dust burst from the seams of the massive timber planks. The bolts of the hinges bent. The security bar began to crack.

The king pointed out of the main archway and toward the gate. "Go and find out what is happening! Put an end to it. Now!" The guards obeyed without comment and charged from the room.

Another mighty blow struck the great gate. It further loosened in its bindings and bowed inwards, and cracks appeared in the castle walls. The guards all rushed to the gate to reinforce it, reaching it just as a third explosion sounded. The power of the blast was so great that the barrier and the trolls were blown apart by its fiery force. More cracks appeared throughout the castle; dust and rock fell from the growing fissures in the mountainous structure.

They all watched as a thin shadowed silhouette came through the wreckage, speaking in a harsh voice. "I hope I didn't miss any of the fun."

Macal couldn't believe it. He couldn't have even dreamed it was possible. He knew that voice, just like he recognized the gait of the man's awkward walk. How could anybody who had ever met him forget it?

In utter amazement Macal watched as through the smoke, dust, and debris of the fallen doors stepped Lalliard.

And he looked angry.

Macal had to blink several times. He couldn't believe it. Lalliard! Here in Marglamesh! *Why was he here?* Macal had no idea, but he couldn't have been happier to see the wizard.

With the aid of his staff Lalliard limped into the throne room, and with a look of determination set on his face he headed straight toward the witches. "You take stinky over there and I'll deal with his playmates," he said as magical energy crackled about his fingers.

The witch brides understood the threat Lalliard was to them. In unison they combined their magic, chanted, summoned dark power, and shaped it to their will. From their outstretched hands shot six bolts of lightning that joined together and fired at the wizard in one mammoth bolt of energy.

Lalliard uttered his own incantation and a violet dome-shaped shield appeared on his arm. The bolt struck the mystical barrier and was deflected up into the ceiling behind him, blowing a large section of rock apart. A rain of rock, rubble, and dust crashed down into the chamber as a large section of the ceiling collapsed.

The wizard casually looked behind him at the destruction. "Glad I don't have to pay the repair bill."

The Cloak of Brinizarn was as surprised by Lalliard's arrival as Macal was. *"He's a friend of yours? Wait. I didn't even know you had friends? That you could find anybody that would actually like you, for ya know, being you. Especially somebody powerful. And how did he find you? Do you have a Ring of Luck I don't know about? Cause I'll be a bit jealous, if you do. I'm territorial like that."*

Macal was still dumbfounded. Many questions flew through his mind. If it had been a god who had stepped forth through the gate he would not had been more surprised. Macal finally got to his feet and picked up his sword. "Can you quiet down? We have something to do."

"As you wish, Mister Lucky Pants."

King Orgog had retreated to the top of the dais. A hatred seethed inside the boy that he couldn't control—that he didn't want to control. He needed his revenge. He needed to hurt the creature who had hurt him. To hurt the monster that had killed his father. Macal charged, screaming "For The Crown I Shall Bear The Strength Of The Kingdom!"

"Oh, let the fun begin!" shouted the cloak inside Macal's head as it transformed him into a large brown furious bear.

Macal met the king at the top of the platform. He held Alrang-Dal in both his paws. The king charged at him and their swords clashed together, the clanging of the blades rang sharply around the chamber.

Lalliard hated defensive spells. They took up space in his mind that could be used for additional offensive spells. Reluctantly he admitted they did have their uses, but he much preferred attacking than being attacked. He grinned as he closed in on the witches. Not much made him happy anymore, but a battle would always be one of those things, and now it was his turn to attack.

He mouthed the words of one of his favorite spells. It had been made by Xay the One, an ancient wizard, one of the first, and very few wizards made as many spells as he did. What Lalliard liked most about Xay the One was that he also didn't like defensive spells. All his creations produced violent effects, and that was exactly what Lalliard needed right now.

The witches had no idea what they were in for.

Up on the dais Macal and King Orgog growled at each other over locked swords.

"You think whatever enchantments you wield will stop me from killing you! You're nothing! I'm a king! An *EMPEROR!* You can't kill me!"

Macal bared his grisly teeth, his green bear eyes glared into the troll king's eerie blue orbs. "Tell me that in a few minutes!"

With a roar King Orgog used his great bulk and strength to hurl Macal backwards. The bear stayed upright and skidded to a halt, its back claws cutting into the stone of the platform. Before Macal could recover the king charged forward, slammed into him and knocked him off the dais and down the stairs.

Macal toppled down to crash into the floor below. He rolled over just in time to see King Orgog launch himself into the air down at him, his sword raised, ready to strike the final blow.

Macal had barely enough time to bring Alrang-Dal up and block King Orgog's attack. Even so, the troll's blade, prevented from cutting through his neck, bounced off his sword and cut a long gash into Macal's arm. Alrang-Dal fell from his paw, its flame instantly extinguished.

The bear roared in pain and lashed out with his other forepaw. The king was too slow to recover from his aggressive attack; the claw struck his grotesque flesh and rended a huge tear across the Troll King's leg. Orgog howled in anguish and stumbled back.

In spite of his injury Macal scrambled to all fours. Physically he was numb. Emotionally he was dead. Only one thing mattered—destroying the king.

He pounced forward onto the falling king and let the bear take over. Let its instincts and combat prowess control him. Holding Orgog down with his front paws, his hind legs scrapped and tore at the king, shredding his abdomen.

Not far away Lalliard finished his spell. A swirling black disc of misty acid appeared, centered on the middle witch, who shrieked in torment as the acid burned and dissolved her leathery skin. The other two witches attempted to move away, but an emerald vortex appeared in the center of the disc and drew them toward it. The pull was so strong that none of them could fight it. None could resist. In a moment all three of them were crushed together at the center of the spell. They wailed and screamed as the acid ate at them.

The spell's short duration lapsed and the witches fell to the floor. They all glared at the wizard. It had been centuries since they had felt such pain. It had been centuries since anybody dared hurt them so. Weakly, all three rose off the ground and spread out, so as not to be caught like that again.

Lalliard let them rise up and gave them time to disperse. After travelling all the way here, he wasn't ready to let the fun end yet. *And, at least spread out like that you can't channel each other anymore,* he thought.

The witch bride with the staff cast a spell, and as she finished Lalliard heard a deafening roar behind him. He spun about to see what sort of beast the witch had summoned.

When he saw it, he went pale.

The king was battling for his life. The bear on top of him kept raking his body with its claws, tearing him apart. But Orgog wouldn't give up. Couldn't give up. He wouldn't stop fighting until he stopped moving. He was the king! Soon to be emperor!

He rallied enough strength in spite of the pain of his injuries to hurl Macal off of him. The bear rolled across the floor. King Orgog scrambled to pick his sword back up and jumped onto the bear.

"For Glory!" he shouted as he slid his blade into Macal's side.

Macal's eyes went wide as the blade pierced into him. He felt the uncontrollable urge to cough and when he did a gout of blood spilled out of his mouth. Seeing the light fading from the bear's green eyes, the king stood up and smiled triumphantly down on him.

Orgog clutched his stomach in pain, and yet he laughed. "Oh, you think that hurts? Trust me, it's only going to get worse."

CHAPTER 36

L alliard turned around to find out what beast the witch had summoned to destroy him—and looked into the face of a prismatically scaled dragon. Its enormous bulk filled the remainder of the throne room. Its wings flapped, buffeting him, so that he could barely stay standing. He kept on his feet only with the aid of his staff. Gouts of fire streamed up out of its flaring nostrils, and black acid dripped from its toothy maw.

The witch who had summoned it laughed. She enjoyed the wizard's shock and alarm. Lalliard looked fearfully upon the mighty creature as it took in a lungful of air as it prepared to incinerate the man before it in a blast of volcanic fire.

As the dragon snapped its head forward and released its breath, a great fire burst forth from its mouth and shot toward Lalliard.

The wizard blinked and shook his head. This didn't make sense. He could feel it in his bones, this wasn't right. The flame enveloped him.

He blinked again and when he did the dragon and the flames were gone. He stood there unhurt by its fire, unaffected by its presence. *Illusions. I hate illusions!* He turned back to the witches with a scowl. These creatures weren't powerful enough to summon such a creature. Even he wasn't that powerful. *They would have to do better than that to trick him.*

The witch with the skull had moved to his right. She finished her own sorcery. Her gray hand lit up with a weird brown radiance that she hurled at Lalliard. He wasn't able to stop it and it struck his staff. The impact caused the staff to explode, its splinters tearing through his hand and boring into the whole right side of his body. He fell to his knees in distress. He looked at his hand, which was now a bleeding mess.

The last witch had been biding her time, waiting for the optimal moment to strike. She saw her chance, unleashed her summoned power, and directed it at the wizard.

She was sure he wouldn't survive this.

Macal the Bear lay on the floor before the Troll King. Orgog just stood there watching as Macal's blood, his life, seeped out of his body. Through bloody lips Macal forced out in a weak whisper, "For The Crown I Shall Hide The Secrets Of The Kingdom."

The king looked around, at first angry that his foe had disappeared. Then as he understood what it meant, he looked around in fear. Frantically he searched for some sign of the invisible boy.

He noticed that Alrang-Dal had disappeared off the floor.

The final witch finished the spell she was casting at Lalliard. As he knelt on the floor a cage appeared around him. The front and back side were lined with spikes and at the witches mental command those two sides started to close upon the wizard.

He forced himself to get back to his feet, buying the maximum amount of time before the spikes would get to him.

As the tips of the spikes began to poke him, the wizard thought that perhaps he shouldn't have toyed with the witches so much. He should have ended it as quickly as he could, but he knew he didn't often make the best decisions. The cage continued to collapse, and numerous spikes bit into him. He knew he had to act quickly, before being both crushed and pierced to death.

He didn't have an incantation to dispel the cage. He only had one choice then—he had to end the witches.

"Gronusiha Hela Sporinmar!" he shouted through the pain. Titanic stone hands grew out of the floor and rose up about the witch who cast the cage spell. They closed together around her and crushed her like a child would an ant. As she died the cage instantly disintegrated and dispersed.

Lalliard didn't relent. "Palwez Unin!"

He used the magic to warp the base of several pillars near one of the remaining witches. The stone softened to clay, and the tops of the large columns toppled over and crashed down upon the second witch. She died screaming under the avalanche of stone.

With the supporting pillars gone, the ceiling, which had already been damaged, now began to collapse, raining down huge chunks of stone.

The last witch couldn't believe her sisters were gone. It seemed impossible. How could the mortal have done such a thing? She was in real danger—she was alone, the castle was falling apart, the king was wounded and needed help. She couldn't decide—should she risk trying to stop the wizard or should she try to save the king?

She abandoned both those ideas and chose a third option, and turned to flee from the collapsing chamber.

Lalliard saw her move to escape. She was flying towards one of the side exits. Lalliard had no honor, and he knew it. He didn't care if her back was turned and she was running away. He pointed his finger at her and sent forth from its tip a ball of icy death. It sped across the room and struck her square in the back. It exploded, unleashing an artic storm of whirling ice shards about her.

When the spell ended, there was nothing left of the final witch.

Feeling true fear for the first time in years, King Orgog looked around in panic. *Where was the boy?* He stumbled back up to the top of the dais as best he could. One hand still clasped the injuries of his stomach and the other held his sword out weakly before him.

As he dodged chunks of the collapsing ceiling, Macal hadn't reappeared. He thought maybe the boy had left. That he escaped to tend to his wounds. He hoped that were true. He needed time himself to heal.

Then he heard a strained battle cry behind him. A cry of unending rage and pain. He spun, but it was too late. The last thing King Orgog saw was a flash of silver and azure as Macal Teel, son of Bertran Teel, swept Alrang-Dal through his neck.

The king's head rolled down the stairs of the dais with sick sounding thumps.

Turning visible, Macal fell to his knees and cried.

The castle continued to collapse around Lalliard. He looked up at the dais just in time to see Macal slay the Troll King. He hurried to the boy and dragged him to his feet. "Come on," he said. "Of all the places we can die, we don't want to die here."

The two of them fled the throne room. Lalliard took a few more steps, then stopped. "Stay here."

Macal watched as the wizard ran back and picked up something off the floor. When he returned Macal saw it was the skeletal cat.

Lalliard half-carried the boy forward. "Let's go."

Macal stumbled along numbly, the last moment of the king's life repeating in his mind. In that last instant he had seen true fear in Troll King's eyes. It was a human kind of look, a fear of death and the beyond. He had stood there and watched the life fade from the troll's eyes. He found that he relished this moment as much as he hated it.

He had been pushed to fight, pushed to slay. It was something he never wanted to do; he wanted to stay and watch the long-term effects of what he had done, so that he would never forget what the taking of a life really meant. Troll or human, the one thing Macal now understood after all that had happened was that life was sacred and also very brief. The boy stopped, oblivious to the crumbling mountain about him.

Lalliard grabbed him under the shoulders and dragged him the rest of the way out of the castle as it collapsed in on itself. The wizard glanced back; he doubted anything still inside would survive. Through the glowing green fog he could see that some trolls had made it out of the castle before it fell to ruin. They noticed him and Macal, and in a fury they charged at the humans.

Still dragging Macal, Lalliard ran and leapt off the edge of the floating mountain.

The cat, the wizard, and the boy fell to the world below.

"*Umm,*" said the cloak to Macal as they hurtled toward the earth. "*I'm out of magic. You kind of used it all up back there. I can't make you fly.*"

Macal felt the wind against his face, felt the cloak trailing behind him, felt the warmth of Alrang-Dal in his hand—but none of it truly registered in his mind. He was lost in a haze of thought and misery. At that moment the world outside his heart and mind didn't exist.

Lalliard—having no clue about the cloak's powers anyway—had his own idea. He could hold only so many spells at a time and could only cast so many a day, but to get up to this castle he had needed a particular one. The same one he needed now.

He pulled the boy and the cat close in a hug and uttered the incantation of Nermalise's Wondrous Wings. Gorgeous golden angelic wings sprouted from his back. He knew the duration of the spell was limited, so turning toward Xanga-Mor, he used it to glide as far from the castle as he could.

Down below, scattered across the landscape he could see more troll forces taking notice of them. It was the only thing he didn't like about this spell. The wings radiated with such brilliant light that it was hard to be inconspicuous.

Lalliard flapped the wings, trying to make as much distance as he could, but with extra weight of the boy they continually drifted downward.

The trolls swarmed across the land below in chase, hoping to catch the invaders when they landed.

Nermalise's Wondrous Wings carried them as far as they could. They came down on the far side of a pungent brown bubbling lake into a large copse of gnarled, moldy, and moss covered trees. The wizard's wings dissolved away like a cloud torn apart by a harsh wind.

Lalliard looked to the northeast. In the distance he could see a range of white quartz formations covering a small rise like spikes. He didn't think the trolls would be very far behind, since these humans had just slain their king and destroyed their castle. He assumed they were not going to give up easily—they had a great motivation for revenge.

He looked over at the boy. Macal stood there like a zombie. His eyes were dull, lifeless. He was staring back up at the floating mountain.

Lalliard spun him around and slapped him. The shock of the blow awoke the boy. Clarity returned to his eyes. The wizard looked him up and down.

"Good. Though I was hoping I would get to do that again." He took note of the boy's injuries. He was pale, bruised all over, caked in dried blood and he had his hand clamped to his side. "Stop looking back. Once you start you can never stop," he paused a moment as he continued to study the boy. "You are so many levels of stupid I don't even know where to begin. Leaving me and running off. Running to here! By yourself!"

Macal's face was emotionless, but he looked at the ground, not knowing how to respond.

Lalliard filled the silence. "Fortunately, the trolls are even dumber than you. How do you feel?"

"Not well."

"I wouldn't imagine so. Swords being on the inside of your body, instead of on the outside tend to have that effect."

He pulled Macal's hand away to see the wound. Surprised by what he saw he took in a quick breath. The wound had nearly closed, nearly healed.

"How?" he asked.

"When I changed back to myself from being a bear it hurt less. Like part of it healed."

"Good," was all that Lalliard said, though part of him had many questions about this magical cloak the boy had acquired. That would have to wait until later.

"You're welcome," said the cloak. *"I am that awesome, aren't I?"*

Lalliard picked up the skeletal cat that was rubbing itself against the hem of his robes. "We need to keep ahead of them. That means we need to be running and not be standing here."

Macal stared at the skeletal cat as if seeing it for the first time. "What's that?"

"See? You really are stupid. It's a cat."

"I know it's a cat. Why's it here?"

The wizard gave Macal an annoyed look. He hated to think that the boy might get the idea that he was kind and caring, or one of those other foul emotions. "I couldn't leave it there to be crushed. And at least this one won't eat much."

Macal's eyes were drawn back to the floating citadel as if by a malign magic. He stared at it again and felt sick. He couldn't figure out what exactly he was feeling. He wasn't sure he wanted to. Was it pain from losing his father? The wound in his side? Regret? Remorse? Shame? Guilt? All of them?

"I...I killed him—" he muttered, his voice grave and distant. "My father's dead...."

Lalliard turned and walked away toward the rise he had seen. "No time for that now. Later. Unless you want to be the next thing that's dead."

Forcing his eyes from the castle Macal turned and followed the wizard.

As they fled from the trolls the evening soon turned to night. On the far side of the rise of quartz formations they came to a murky bog of thick brown liquid. With the trolls not far behind Lalliard decided that they had no choice but to go directly through it.

Macal, feeling much better thanks to the cloak, chased after the wizard who was surprisingly fast for somebody with a limp and without his walking staff. "How did you get here?" he asked.

Lalliard didn't slow his uneven stride. "By climbing over the dead bodies of trolls I slew."

"But there were so many."

"There are less now. And you seemed to have pruned the castle forces nicely before I got here."

"I didn't want to—"

"That took a lot of courage," the wizard cut him off. He did not want to allow time for reflection which, knowing the boy, would only lead to grief. But he could see Macal needed some kind of support, otherwise he would collapse beneath his self-doubt and wouldn't be able to go on. "Standing up to the king by yourself. I doubt there are many soldiers in the Elronian army who would dare do such a thing. I actually don't think there are many people besides myself who would dare take on the Troll King, his witches, and his guards all at once. You are either crazy or you have all the courage of Elronia in your breast."

Macal ducked under some thick purple-veined vines that covered the area in a thick canopy. He didn't know what to say.

"You were always a fantastic boy, it just took a little time for you to have the chance to show the world."

As the wizard spoke Macal was surprised to realize that he was actually proud of what he had done, defeating the Troll King. But he couldn't forget the reason that he had the motivation to do it was because of the consequences of his own actions, his own mistakes. Had he listened to his father this wouldn't have happened. All he had to do was leave the castle and his father would still be alive. All he had to do was listen to his father.

His father had been right. There were things he couldn't and didn't see. His father, more experienced, did see the danger and understood it. *And still he came to save me, even when I didn't deserve it.*

"You could have died coming to save me," said Macal.

The wizard grunted. "If only I was that lucky."

Macal didn't respond and continued to follow the wizard through the disgusting bog toward Elronia...and home.

CHAPTER 37

The trolls had still not caught up to the wizard and the boy. Lalliard guessed that it was past midnight when they escaped the mosquito-infested bog and now he was getting too tired to continue on.

"The wings may have flown us farther than we thought," said Lalliard. "Or given us a better lead than I thought we had." His feet slowed and he came to a stop. "I need to sleep. I need to regain some of my magic. I used too much, too quickly."

"You want to sleep now?" asked Macal. "There are trolls after us."

"I like sleeping, and I get grumpy when I don't get my sleep."

"Miss a lot of sleep then, do ya?" muttered Macal before he could stop himself.

Lalliard was about to deliver a scathing retort, but somehow he was able to hold his tongue. He thought about what the boy had just gone through. He knew he needed to be gentle with the boy, for now. Otherwise he might not recover from it all.

Consideration of another person's feelings was new territory for the wizard and he definitely wasn't liking it. "If they caught up to us now I'm not sure how much good I would be. You should get some rest, too. You have a lot of healing to do, and I'm guessing not just physically."

Macal was too drained to respond.

Lalliard found the driest patch he could among the muddy earth and lay down with his back against the stump of a fallen tree. Within a moment he was asleep.

Macal sat down next to him and leaned against the stump. Seeing the wizard drift off he tried to sleep as well, but found that as much as he wanted to, he couldn't. Even as exhausted as he was, he mind wouldn't shut off. Wouldn't stop going over everything that had happened.

His stomach growled and he felt a pang of hunger. *When was the last time I ate?* He had no idea.

The night moved on with a painful slowness. His head drooped and a few times he almost drifted off, but always he snapped painfully back to consciousness.

This time he thought he heard something. A movement in the swamp's murky waters. He stood up and looked around. Did he just see a pair of yellow eyes out in the darkness? Or was it the fog playing a trick on him? Then he heard it again—the sound of something moving through the water. Something big.

He pulled Alrang-Dal from its sheath. He felt comforted having it in his hand. He took a step toward the sound.

"*Um. What are you doing?*" asked the Cloak of Brinizarn.

"You know how since we left the castle you've been pretty quiet?" whispered Macal.

"*Yes,*" said the cloak. "*I just thought you needed some time—*"

"—Well I preferred you that way."

Macal walked to the edge of the dry ground. He was sure now there was something out here, and not just one thing. Many things.

The trolls had found them. He was sure of it. He knew they shouldn't have stopped.

"For The Crown I Shall Lift The Glory Of The Kingdom," he whispered. The cloak glittered for a moment and then Macal launched himself into the air.

He flew out over the swamp slowly. It took a little time to find them, but under the light of the gibbous moon he could see the reflection of many sets of yellow eyes in the darkness and fog. They were headed toward where Lalliard slept. They were about a hundred yards away from the wizard.

He could see at least eight. The beasts were trying to sneak up on them, to be quiet, but they were trolls. Macal had learned quiet wasn't in their nature.

The thought of going back and waking Lalliard for help never crossed his mind. Lalliard never crossed his mind. He saw the trolls and anger took control of him.

He willed Alrang-Dal to light up. The azure flame illuminated the sky about him. Down below he could now see the trolls in a crescent-shaped line wading through the water toward their camp. He had been wrong. There were ten of them, not eight.

With the aid of the cloak he hurled himself toward the swamp and splashed down in front of them like an avenging angel.

Startled, the brutes came to a halt.

"Do you know who I am?" shouted Macal at them. His voice full of venom. "Do you?"

The trolls looked at one another in confusion. They had no idea what the human was talking about.

"I'm the boy that killed your king! Do you think you have the power to kill me? Do you? *He* couldn't. Come on! Attack me! And I'll show you what I did to Orgog! ATTACK ME!"

Fear and uncertainty crept over the trolls faces. Macal stared at them. "For The Crown I Shall Bear The Strength Of The Kingdom." As a bear he let out a roar and held out his magic sword, ready to strike.

Everything the boy said went through their small troll brains, and they concluded that since the king was dead, nobody was forcing them to get revenge on the human invaders. So why should they risk their lives doing so?

A new look passed over the trolls' faces as they took a slow step backward. Macal wasn't sure what it was, but he thought it might have been respect.

Cautiously, eyes never leaving the bear, they took a few more steps backward, until at last they turned and retreated into the night at a run.

That was the other thing Macal had learned about trolls—they had no courage. He watched them recede and splash away into the darkness. "If ever I see you again, any of you, you shall be food for worms!"

There was a part of him that still wanted to chase them down, to defeat them and rid them from the world forever, but he fought down the urge. Slaying the king had been necessary, he knew, but there was still part of the old Macal somewhere in him that was uncomfortable with that level of violence. That part of him remembered some things could be solved without fighting. He didn't want to lose that part of himself.

He returned to find Lalliard just as he had left him. He was happy to see that the wizard was a heavy sleeper. He sat down beside him again and waited for him to wake up.

Several hours later Lalliard finally awoke. Macal hadn't moved since he had returned. The sun was just cresting the horizon, beginning to bathe the world in its warm light.

Lalliard groaned as he got to his feet. He ached all over. He looked over at Macal and saw that the boy's eyes were again on the fallen castle in the sky. He shook his head, annoyed.

"Did you get any sleep?"

Macal didn't acknowledge him. He found that he had no desire to tell the wizard what had happened last night.

The wizard studied him for a moment. "So tell me, where did you get that cloak? I can guess where you got the sword."

Macal finally spoke. "A lot has happened since I last saw you."

"So it would seem."

Macal got to his feet and walked toward Xanga-Mor. "Come on, let's keep moving."

The wizard followed after him. They walked for several hours in silence, which the wizard was perfectly happy with.

The two Elronians were now nearing Xanga-Mor. They could see it a short way off in the distance. It was Macal who finally spoke as the sun hung high above them.

"I'm hungry."

"Well, if you recall, you really didn't give me a heads-up on the plan to come here. I didn't know I'd be travelling across three kingdoms, so I didn't really come prepared for this. But I agree, we need food. It's been days since I've eaten."

"We also need to get the plans back. My father told me where they are."

Lalliard had no idea what the boy was talking about. "What plans?"

Through everything that had happened Macal had forgotten that he had learned all the details about the plans only after he had left the wizard, so Lalliard had no idea how important they were or what his father really had to do with them. As they passed over a rough plain of obsidian rock Macal explained all that had happened to him and what the plans were.

Lalliard didn't need time to think through the boy's story. He had let Macal talk without interruption as he told his tale of adventure, but once he had finished the wizard spoke right away. "You are right, we do need to get the plans. Even with the Troll King gone, some of his forces still roam about in Elronia. The plans can be used to find them and run them all down."

The wizard stopped. He had noticed something odd all morning. For some reason he couldn't hear the trolls behind them anymore. "Why aren't they following us anymore?"

Macal paused for a moment, looked back at the wizard, shrugged, and started walking again. His brow creased in thought, the wizard followed after him.

Up ahead they could see that the shadowy land of Marglamesh was finally coming to an end. There was a small forest that, even though it had been abused by the trolls, still had a bit of life to it—implying to both of them that it must be in Xanga-Mor. Macal hadn't expected to feel anything anymore, but he was relieved to be leaving this place.

Lalliard increased his stride and came up beside the boy. He placed his bony hand on Macal's shoulder. "You are going to be okay. You know that, right? I have been where you are now, alone and frightened. But as evil as life is, it's not too hard to kick it in the teeth and take what you want from it."

Macal looked up at him and saw a rare gentleness in the wizard's blue-gray eyes. He couldn't think of anything to say so he gave the wizard a nod.

Then from the growth of trees up ahead they heard something. Both of them could easily tell that a large force was approaching.

Lalliard walked toward the forest and stood boldly in the path of where the approaching force would emerge. In his mind he prepared some spells. Their words were ready to escape his lips. After being chased for over a day he had some frustrations he wanted to take out on whoever stood in his way.

Behind him, Macal turned into a bear and lit up Alrang-Dal with flame. Then he came to stand beside the wizard. Lalliard cast him a glance, somewhat impressed by the transformation.

A small company of soldiers spilled out of from the trees. Macal hadn't thought he could be surprised anymore, and was shocked to find his mouth hanging open. Before him were heavily armed soldiers and cavalry. Human soldiers. Some were mounted on strange creatures Macal had never seen before, others were on jotuns. Winged elves appeared, flying over the treetops. Soldiers of massive stature walked out of the tree line carrying ancient magical weapons, while powerful sorcerers hovered about them.

He also saw weird wisp-like creatures and great armor-scaled beasts with poisoned tails that he had also never seen before. Lalliard recognized them as zygysts and grurts.

In front of all of them on a white jotun rode a proud-looking man in golden plate armor. A vicious looking well-used mace hung from his side. On his chest was emblazoned a black and white coat of arms of a female angel over an upturned crescent moon. The rest of the company bore this same crest on their armor, shields, and banners.

The man urged his mount a few steps closer to them, leaving the others behind. "Hail from Elronia. I'm the company commander, Lord Wreyghul. I assume you, the bear there, are Macal Teel. We were sent to help you."

Dumbfounded by this unbelievable turn of events, Lalliard turned to look at Macal. He could sense the force in front of him wielded an incredible amount of power. Why would they be coming to help a boy from Hormul?

Macal stared at the lord. The lord's words kept repeating in his head. Without willing it to happen he shrunk back into a boy. His heart pounded in his chest. He just stood there staring at the man. One thought traveled through his brain. *The Princess had kept her promise.*

Lord Wreyghul looked around and saw only the boy and the wizard, so he filled the boy's silence with a question. "I never met your father, but I heard he was a good man, a great soldier and loyal to the kingdom. Under his command, the Amber Dragoons did some of their best work. Where is he?"

Macal didn't respond, so Lalliard did. "He won't be coming back to Elronia."

Lord Wreyghul understood and nodded.

Macal hadn't looked at it in the past day, but now he looked down at the ring the Princess had given him. He had given up on her, but she had kept her promise—however late she was in doing so.

"Princess Aeria, the Rose and Jewel of the Kingdom, sent us to help you. She told us of the plans and your mission here. I swore that once my lands were safe we would come and offer any aid that we could. I came with the remnants of my army. There is only a quarter of us left now. A lot of us were lost just cutting a path through the troll forces to get here."

Macal finally managed to speak. "Is the Princess okay? I saw a force heading toward them when I left. I had no way to go back and warn them."

Over the next several moments Lord Wreyghul recounted the story of the Princess being attacked and blockaded in the keep.

Lord Wreyghul dismounted and came closer to them, his armor jangling as he walked. "I do have to ask, and I'm sorry if this is a crass time, but did you retrieve the plans?"

Macal turned back to him and with a flat and hollow voice explained everything he knew about the plans, just like he had done to Lalliard.

"That is good news," said Lord Wreyghul. "My force has greatly diminished of late, but it is more than enough to get us home and get back the plans."

"Yes, we should all go and retrieve them," began Lalliard as he spun Macal toward him. "Except you. You should go home. You've done enough."

Macal looked at him incredulous. "What? No!"

"Yes," said the wizard. "You are just a boy. Go home. After all that I've seen of you recently I am sure, once we get back to Elronia, you can handle the rest of the journey yourself now."

"Why don't you come with me?"

"Because with something like this, something this important I want to make sure nothing goes wrong." The wizard turned to Lord Wreyghul. "No offense."

"None taken," replied the Lord. "He is right, Macal. You've done your part. Once we are back in Elronia you should have fairly safe passage back to your village. It's a similar route to that from which we have just come and cleared the way. We can get the plans and make sure they make it to Keratost and the King."

Lalliard could see that Macal was still uncertain. He knelt down in front of the boy. "You have done what you set out to do. You found your father. You proved he wasn't a traitor."

Macal stared at him, his eyes unmoving. He now wished he had failed at everything, perhaps then his father might still be alive. Out loud he said, "Fine."

"And besides," snapped the wizard. "You would probably just run off on me again anyway."

Lord Wreyghul returned to his forces and mounted his steed. He called out some commands and the army turned. With Macal and Lalliard they returned to Elronia.

Not long after reaching their homeland Lalliard and Lord Wreyghul's army went their own way toward the east to recover the plans while Macal, who had been supplied with a backpack of food and gear, was left alone to head northeast toward Hormul and his empty house.

CHAPTER 38

As Macal marched back to Hormul, he couldn't help but wonder if anybody would really believe his story when he got home. He knew he wouldn't if he had heard it from anyone else in town. He decided that he wouldn't care if they believed him or not. What would their opinions matter to him? He would always know the truth, however much he might not want to.

He traveled for several weeks through Elronia. A few times he had come across large troll brigades that he had to either sneak around or go far out of his way to avoid. He didn't mind the slow going, he was in no rush to get back to Hormul. *Why would he be? There was nothing left there for him.*

As time went by, Macal lost count of how many times he had thrown up after thinking about what he had done. How he had gotten his uncle killed. His father killed. And if he thought about it, his mother killed too.

He had caused the death of his entire family. And now he was alone. It was the worst punishment he could think of. Yet, he felt like he deserved so much more.

He did entertain the idea of not even going back to Hormul. But where else would he go? He thought of Keratost, but he was too ashamed to see the Princess. If he saw her he'd have to admit to what he had done to his father.

Knowing her, she would probably think him brave and a hero for killing the Troll King and helping end the war, but he wouldn't be able to stomach that kind of praise from her now. It would all be a lie. He wasn't brave. He didn't kill King Orgog to save Elronia. No, he killed him out of revenge. Out of hate. Out of pain. The worst reasons of all.

He didn't deserve to see her. He didn't deserve that kind of joy and happiness. So, dragging his feet, he continued onward toward Hormul.

347

Eventually he came to a tablet at a crossroads that pointed to Hormul just off to the east, and numbly he went on. The trees of the surrounding hills had begun the transformation to their glorious autumn colors. Soon he saw the familiar structure of Lalliard's house, and the rest of Hormul beyond it.

Then, on the horizon he saw a figure. It stood on the roadway looking toward him. Macal blinked—the person looked like a mirage. Like a dream. It had to be one of those things, because he knew that man and that man couldn't be standing there. Couldn't be. Couldn't be....

Before Macal knew what he was doing he was already running toward the figure. He couldn't have run faster if he tried. He ran and he ran until at last he threw his arms about Uncle Melkes. They hugged each other as if the world mattered once again.

Uncle Melkes and Macal walked through Hormul toward their cottage. They had to go slowly because Uncle Melkes still hadn't recovered from all his injuries. Macal could see much of the destruction wrought by the trolls was being fixed. Many of the houses had been repaired or were being rebuilt. Many people who he had never thought to see again waved at him, just as surprised to see him.

He hadn't let go of Uncle Melkes' hand. He couldn't—he was still afraid this was a dream and if he let go it would all disappear. His uncle seemed to feel the same way and held onto him just as tightly.

He couldn't believe that his uncle was alive. He wasn't sure he was allowed to feel joy, not after everything he had done, but he did. He couldn't hold back a smile each time he looked up to see his uncle alive and walking with him. He couldn't remember the last time he felt this happy. That didn't matter, whatever it was, whenever it was, nothing could compare to how he felt right now.

They hadn't really talked yet. They hadn't needed to. For both of them this moment was more than words could express.

Macal realized something about the little village as they passed through. Even though it was being rebuilt, somehow it just didn't feel the same to him anymore. With all that happened here he wasn't sure it would ever feel like home again. He wasn't sure what he expected when he got here, but he now knew it was never going to be the same place he left when he fled into the night those many moons ago.

They went up the final hill and arrived at their cottage. On the porch Macal finally spoke. He undid the belt that held the sheath of Alrang-Dal and held up the sword to his uncle.

"Take this," he said.

Uncle Melkes looked down at the sword. He had seen it the moment the boy ran up to him and knew what his having it meant. With gentle hands and a long sorrowful look, he took it. He then sat down on one of the battered crates that littered the porch, his gaze never leaving the sword. "You will have this again someday. Along with the farm."

Macal sat down next to him. His uncle could see that the boy before him had changed. That something irreversible had happened to him. That he had somehow broken and been remade. The old man did the only thing he could think of and pulled the boy close into a hug. For a long while they just sat like that in silence.

"I thinks it's my turn to tell you a story," said Macal eventually. "Can I tell you now and never have to tell you again what happened?"

"My boy, we can do whatever you want." Uncle Melkes' voice was as gentle as Macal remembered. Macal couldn't believe how much he missed that. Couldn't believe that he hadn't lost it forever.

Macal took his time and told his uncle everything he could remember about his adventure. About how he had left Hormul, about the morgog, about the Princess and the Viscount, about the cloak, about going into Marglamesh, about Lalliard saving him, of his battle with the Troll King, and of his father.

"Tell me he'd be proud of me," said Macal crying as he finished the story.

Uncle Melkes gave him a warm sympathetic smile. "He is, and so am I."

Macal wanted to stop crying, but he couldn't control it. All the emotion of his journey was finally escaping. "Even after all these weeks, I don't feel any better."

"No, and you probably won't for a long time." Uncle Melkes stroked the boy's hair with a comforting hand. "That's one of the things about life, it's short, but it takes a long time to get used to it. You can't be afraid of it. You just have to enjoy all its blessings and the dark times won't seem so bad."

"I should have listened to him...."

"Perhaps you should have, your father was a wise man."

"I know. He was right. I was wrong. And that's all I can think about."

"That too shall pass. Just never forget what he did and why he did it. And remember he did it because he loved you more than anything else in the world. Just like I do. Remember what you have learned and gain some wisdom from it. It will take a while to get back to normal, but the color will return to your world, and so will laughter and music. The nightmares will fade and blissful dreams will come again."

"I'll always miss him."

"Yes, you will. And that will make you strong. That will make you remember. And that will help you to be as great as he was."

"I love you."

"I love you, too."

Macal put his arms around his uncle, buried his head into his uncle's side, and wept.

As the months went by, Macal started to forget what life was like outside of Hormul. When he first got back he would have thought that impossible, but as the days passed and the year faded away life had returned to its simple mundane, melancholy routine. He helped his uncle bring in what little they had of the fall harvest. So much of the village had been destroyed by the troll attack that they were both uncertain how they were going to survive the winter—but both had decided that was a problem that would have to be dealt with when the time came.

No matter how much time passed, and how much was rebuilt, one feeling did not diminish for Macal—how much he missed his father. He had traveled across kingdoms to find and save his father. Instead he had only gotten him killed. Knowing that it was all his fault still constantly weighed on him.

While the rituals of day-to-day life had gone back to normal, his uncle was concerned that Macal was no longer the same boy that he once was. He had become withdrawn, and didn't talk as much. It seemed the spark of curiosity and wonder within the boy had gone out. He didn't seem to take enjoyment in anything anymore, except the stories his uncle told to him. So Uncle Melkes did his best to tell him a story or two every day, but now, after so long, he was starting to run out of new stories and had begun to repeat himself. Macal of course noticed this, but he was so sullen that he didn't comment on it.

To help make some extra money to buy food for the approaching winter, Macal occasionally worked as a stable hand down at the Waywitch Tavern. He did have to admit to himself, even if his uncle didn't see it, that he found some satisfaction in it. He found that helping the animals gave him a sense of peace. Therefore he spent as much time there as Grunc would allow.

One late autumn afternoon he was down at the stable, using a pitchfork to toss some fresh hay into the stalls, when Menk and his goons, Gornod and Nesty, arrived. As the three of them shambled in they made a point of blocking the exit behind them.

"I told ya he was here," said Nesty excitedly. "I told ya!"

Menk ignored his friend. He gave Macal a malicious smile. "Hey twerp! I missed picking on you."

"Yeah, look, it's the sissy who ran away," mocked Nesty.

Gornod closed the doors behind them and then came to stand near Menk. "We heard the stories they've been telling about you. Ya know, I don't believe any of it."

"Yeah, none of it," said Nesty.

Macal wished his uncle hadn't told everybody all that had happened during his adventure. He knew something like this was going to happen. Nobody was going to believe it. He wouldn't have believed it himself if he hadn't been the one who had done it.

Menk took a step closer to Macal. "It's all stupid lies from a small and stupid boy."

Macal didn't move. He looked at them impassively.

"They say he met the Princess," said Gornod.

"Yeah, I bet it was a troll princess and he fell in love with her!" Nesty laughed at his own joke. The other two boys didn't.

Menk clenched his hands into fists. "Let's show him what we do to liars!"

"Yeah, liars!" cheered Nesty.

Macal still didn't respond. His face was placid, but inside he was getting angry. The three bullies approached. They moved to surround him, all grinning in anticipation of what was to come.

"Did the trolls eat your tongue, loser?" asked Menk.

"They probably spit it out, cause he probably tastes like feet," added Gornod.

"Yeah," said Menk. "Even a troll couldn't stomach him."

The three bullies closed in on him. Gornod was the first to attack. From behind he swung his fist at Macal's head. Macal ducked under it and as he came up he brought his knee up into Nesty's stomach. The boy doubled over, the wind knocked out of him. He fell to the ground and wheezed into the dirt.

Menk jumped onto Macal's back. "Oh, you wanna play tough? Fine by me!"

Macal nearly collapsed under the boy's weight. He spun out of the grapple and shook Menk off, but he had to drop the pitchfork to do so. Menk looked at Macal strangely; the bully wasn't used to people fighting back, especially Macal.

"Good idea." Gornod pulled out a knife. "Let's play rough!"

Macal saw the knife and for the moment forgot about Menk. He snatched his pitchfork up off the floor. He put the fork side down on the dirt and kicked through the handle. It broke with a snap. He lifted up the wooden pole and held it like a sword in front of him.

The bullies paused, amazed at what they were seeing. This was Macal Teel. The wimpy kid who lived in the rundown cottage up on the hill. The boy who was scared of everything and who, in their opinion, couldn't defeat a five year old girl who had a fever.

Macal took advantage of their hesitation and capitalized on the moment, just like Viscount Razz had taught him. He lunged forward and whacked Gornod on the legs with the wooden rod. As the boy bent over to grab at his injured shins Macal struck him hard again on the back. The boy, and his knife, fell to the ground wailing.

Menk, angry that his friends had failed him, jumped at his foe a second time, but Macal retreated to make sure he still had distance enough to swing his weapon efficiently. Menk didn't care and charged forward. Macal snapped the rod down on one of the bully's outstretched hands, and heard a satisfying crack as the boy screamed in pain. Relentlessly he swung again and bludgeoned the boy's ankle, toppling him over into the dirt among his friends.

With all three of them now on the ground and writhing in pain Macal backed away and lowered his weapon. "And that was pretty much how I beat the Troll King!" he proclaimed. All three bullies, groaning in pain, got to their feet and ran out of the stables.

"Next time I can show you what I did to his guards!" he called after them.

It was a long while before Lalliard returned to Hormul. Macal heard the news one evening from his uncle, and at once he ran across town through the night to the wizard's house.

Uncle Melkes called after him from the doorway of the cottage that he had other news, but Macal didn't care. The only thing he wanted right now was to find out what had happened since they had sent him home and continued on to get the war plans.

As he passed through the center of town he was surprised to see that the plaza was much more alive with people than usual. He paid it no attention and let it slip from his mind. Right now he only cared about seeing Lalliard.

As he got close to the wizard's house he could see smoke rising from its chimney. *It was true! He was back!*

While he had no reason to doubt his uncle, he just couldn't believe it until he saw it himself. He had waited for this moment since he and Lalliard had parted ways. He wondered if the plans that had caused so much trouble really did have any value.

Out of breath, he arrived at the door of the wizard's cottage and was about to knock when he looked down and saw the skeletal cat emerge from an ill-maintained bush. The bony cat came up to him and rubbed against his legs. He wasn't sure what to do, it was a new experience to play with an animated cat skeleton. Instinctively he reached down and petted it. The cat, now satisfied, turned and sauntered off back into the bushes.

He watched the cat go, and then knocked on the door. From inside he heard a grumpy voice call out, "Go away!"

"It's Macal."

"As I said, go away!"

Macal looked at the door hoping that it would open. It didn't. "I need to know what happened."

"How can you possibly travel across the world and yet not understand what 'go away' means?"

"Did you get the plans?" he called through the door. Macal thought he could hear the wizard sigh in frustration.

"Yes. We got them. We delivered them. The tide was greatly swung against the trolls. The war should be over in a few months when the cleanup is done. Isn't it a wonderful world? Are you satisfied? Do you feel all sunny inside? Now go away!"

"You're not going to open the door?"

"Of course not. Why would I? Oh, if you are going to bother me, I guess this is for you." The wizard slid a grimy envelope under the door to Macal.

The boy picked it up and stared at it. He couldn't read what was written on the outside of it, but the wax seal on it was embossed with a dragon's head surrounded by a ring of delicate roses. He recognized it immediately. His heart raced—he couldn't believe what he was seeing. It was the Princess's crest, and she had written him a letter.

"Um..." said Macal back through the door.

"You're still here?"

"I can't read," admitted the boy, embarrassed.

Inside the wizard grunted in frustration again. "First I have to travel to Marglamesh to save you, now I have to read your correspondence, too?" The door swung open in a rough fashion. Macal looked up from the letter, and there stood Lalliard. The boy thought he looked the same—the trip to retrieve the plans and his time in the capital hadn't changed him at all.

The wizard stuck out his hand. "Give it back. I should really spend some time teaching you how to do this yourself."

Macal handed him the letter. The wizard tore it open gruffly. "I'd like that," said Macal. "Before, I never thought that I would need to read."

"That's because you are a fool." Lalliard unfolded the letter and stepped back from the door. "Come in. Sit at the table and don't eat any of my cats."

"Eat your cats?"

"I can tell by your scrawny physique that you haven't been eating much. I'm sure you're starving. Don't eat the cats."

Macal sat down as instructed. "Okay."

Lalliard sat down next to him. He looked at the boy over the top of the page. "Are you ready?"

"Yes."

"It says:

Dearest Macal,

I can't explain how happy I was to hear that you are alive and well. Lalliard told us about what you did in Marglamesh. That you succeeded in defeating the King of Trolls. From the moment I met you, I always thought you were special and then you proved it true many times over.

I'm sorry that it took me so long to send you help. I tried as hard as I could. It would have been easier if we hadn't run into another war brigade. I'm told that Lord Wreyghul informed you of what happened. I'm sure I've cried about that every day since.

I'm sorry about what happened to your father. I doubt my words will help you at all, but you have my condolences and you are in my thoughts. Often.

I know that your part in this story is over, but always remember this—whether you believe it or not, you saved many lives. And you, Macal, are a hero.

Fondly,

Princess Aeria Stormlion'"

Finished, the wizard folded up the letter and handed it back to the boy. "I'm sure it would have sounded better coming from her, but she is correct. Regardless of all the bad stuff that happened a lot of good came from it. You should be somewhat proud of yourself. I guess, even as annoying as you are, I'm a little proud of you to."

"You do have feelings!" said Macal.

The wizard scowled at him. "No, I don't! Stop saying things like that."

"Yes, you do. You care about me."

"Hmmp!" grunted the wizard. "See? You are annoying."

Macal reached over and put his hand on Lalliard's. He knew there was nothing more to be said. He knew his life had forever changed. He knew he was no longer like most of the people in Hormul. He had seen more of the world than most of them ever would. He had seen things and had experiences he never thought possible. What all this had taught him was that life was brief, but it was also very big, if you let it be.

Lalliard got up to pet a cat who had made its home on top of a haphazard pile of books on a shelf. "You should go back to the town plaza, because of the news I brought they are going to celebrate the impending victory over the trolls."

"There's a party?" As he spoke Macal now realized what else his uncle wanted to tell him and why so many people were milling about in the center of town.

"Didn't I just say there was?"

"Are you going?"

"Me? No! Why would I want to do that? There will be people there. And I have to stay to feed my cats."

"Come with me. For me?"

The wizard scowled. "Fine. But only for you. And I promise you I won't enjoy a minute of it."

As they walked toward the plaza Macal couldn't help but smile for the first time in a while.

EPILOGUE

Macal hadn't put the Cloak of Brinizarn back on since he returned from his adventure. He had placed it in a chest at the end of his bed, along with Alrang-Dal, and he hadn't touched it. He couldn't. It reminded him too much of what had happened. It reminded him of his father.

Months later, as snow covered the hills and trees, sparkles of magic began to rise off the cloak and leak out between the seams of the chest.

"Uh oh," said the cloak to itself. *"The Thief is going to need me soon...."*

The End

ABOUT THE AUTHOR

K R. Bourgoine lives in New York City with his wife, two sons, two cats, a parakeet, and a dog named Nugget. He is an avid gamer, both of tabletop and video games. Some might say that he spends far too much time playing Minecraft with his boys, but he would actually say he doesn't play enough.

He has written and published many short stories and novellas, some of them including Macal or Lalliard.

Mr. Bourgoine has also written several stories about Gord the Rogue with Gary Gygax, which is one of his proudest accomplishments. Additionally he wrote four other very short stories for Gygax's fantasy magazine, *Lejends*.

Also in his portfolio is a non-fiction computer title *Build the Ultimate Gaming PC* published in 2005 with John Wiley & Sons, Inc. in 2005.

Besides playing games he enjoys making them. He has released Adventurer the Card Game with two expansions and several add-ons. The game features an adult Macal, Aeria, Izgar and Lalliard, who all appear in *The First Fable*. You can find at Adventurergame.com.

One day when he finds a programmer he can partner with, he will release his app game, Immortal Forge.

Made in the USA
San Bernardino, CA
27 June 2017